PRAISE FOR MARIE KIRALY
and her masterpiece of dark sensuality and forbidden passion . . .

MINA
The Dracula Story Continues

"A stunning reading experience . . . This is a most excitingly written adventure story, filled with sensuality, a raw intensity of emotion and a suspense that will match and surpass Bram Stoker's original story." —*Affaire de Coeur*

"Strong . . . sensual . . . surprisingly tender . . . *Mina* displays a resonance unlike its source material, humanizing people Stoker merely used as pawns." —*BookLovers*

"Kiraly takes the Dracula legend beyond its original ending . . . a nicely twisting sequel."
—*Milwaukee Journal*

"Throbbing with the rich sexuality which marked Bram Stoker's *Dracula*, *Mina* is an erotic ride through the life of a liberated Victorian woman who no longer desires to repress her dark passions." —*Shadowdance*

"*Mina* is a tremendous novel that Stoker would have been very proud to have authored. Marie Kiraly successfully incorporates the events of the original novel [and] splendidly goes beyond . . ." —*The Talisman*

"Destined to be considered a literary classic . . . a wonderful read."
—*Eclipse*

Now Marie Kiraly takes us into the darkest shadows of New Orleans — where beauty hides a terrible secret and passion never dies . . .

LEANNA
Possession of a Woman

LEANNA: POSSESSION OF A WOMAN

BY MARIE KIRALY

THE BERKLEY PUBLISHING GROUP
200 Madison Avenue
New York, New York 10016

If you purchased this book without a cover, you should be aware that this book is stolen property. It was reported as "unsold and destroyed" to the publisher, and neither the author nor the publisher has received any payment for this "stripped book."

Reviewers are reminded that changes may be made in this proof copy before books are printed. If any material from the book is to be quoted in the review, the quotation should be checked against the final bound book.

LEANNA

A Berkley Book / published by arrangement with
the author

PRINTING HISTORY
Berkley edition / March 1996

All rights reserved.
Copyright © 1996 by Elaine Bergstrom.
This book may not be reproduced in whole or in part,
by mimeograph or any other means, without permission.
For information address: The Berkley Publishing Group,
200 Madison Avenue, New York, New York 10016.

ISBN: 0-425-15224-3

BERKLEY®
Berkley Books are published by The Berkley Publishing Group,
200 Madison Avenue, New York, New York 10016.
BERKLEY and the "B" design
are trademarks belonging to Berkley Publishing Corporation.

PRINTED IN THE UNITED STATES OF AMERICA

10 9 8 7 6 5 4 3 2 1

Dedicated to
Vlad and Lynda,
what sweet music they make!

This book would not have been possible without the imput of so many different sources. I would like to thank all the researchers whose meticulous efforts have preserved the Vodun, Voodoo and Yoruba oral traditions particularly "Ita, Mythology of the Yoruba Religion" by Oba Ecun, "The Magic Island" by William Seabrook, and "Voodoo" by Ron Bodin. I would also like to thank Louis Martinie of Maison de la Lune Noir for a chance to hear and feel and participate in a Voodoo rite. And last, to the only foreign country in the United States, the City of New Orleans where a part of my soul always rests.

PROLOGUE

The child lies in her bed, the white lace canopy and drapings making it seem less like a mattress than a fluffy white cloud.

"Fit for my angel," Mama told her every night, just after she tucked her into bed and kissed her. And Mama's perfume always lingered in the room, comforting as the pink ballerina night-light beside the bed, the little crystal music box that played "Lara's Theme." Each night, after Mama read to her, she would wind the box, and the sound of it, the beautiful tinkle of its tiny parts, would carry her off to sleep. She had not heard its sound for three weeks, indeed had refused to let Jacqueline turn it on, or to open a book, though she was otherwise an obedient child. Now she refused even to sleep. Jacqueline had told her that Mama was finally coming home.

Headlights flash through the lace curtains of her window as a car pulls into the side drive. A second pair of lights follows. Men talk outside her window.

Though she isn't supposed to get out of bed, she runs to the window, unlatches the screen and looks down at the station wagon parked behind Papa's sleek black coupe. She wonders why he isn't driving the little green car he and Mama used the night she went away.

As she watches curiously, two men in uniforms open the back doors of the wagon and lift out a long, narrow bed. Mama lies on it, a dark colored blanket wrapped tightly around her body, straps crossed above it to keep her secure. One of her hands is uncovered, delicate and trembling

1

against the dark blanket as the men carry her onto the porch and through the downstairs doors. She peeks into the hallway and, seeing it is clear, sneaks to the top of the stairs, peeking through the open railing at the people below.

"This way," Papa calls to them from midway up the stairs. "We've prepared space in the bedroom."

The men look at the stairs. One of them swears. "We can't carry her up there."

"Her room is up here. Of course you must," Papa says, his voice hoarse.

With Mama separating them, they consult.

"I'll help," Papa insists. "But you must bring her up here."

"You won't be a help," the older man tells him.

"Do what he asks, please." Mama's request seems so soft, as pitiful as Louis sounded on the nights when he was ill and in pain.

Boots stomp on the stairs. Mama cries out.

"Careful!" Papa calls. "For pity's sake be careful!"

Safely out of sight in the shadows of the long hallway, the girl stands and listens until, hearing the last, she forgets all about the spanking she might receive. She runs to the stairs to see what happened to Mama.

And looks at her mother's face—at eyes open but filled with tears, at beautiful features twisted with agony.

The nurse walking in front of the men sees her standing near the rail, goes up and crouches beside her, studying her. "A darling child," the woman says. "And she so resembles her mother. Such a consolation."

The girl looks from the woman to her papa, who acts as if he has not heard, to her mama, who stares so sadly in her direction but does not seem to see her face.

And she knows with terrible certainty that her family will never be the same again. Her tiny hand brushes her mother's cheek then she turns and flees down the hallway and into her brother's room to tell him everything she has seen.

ONE

Hailey Martin sat at her computer and flexed her fingers before spreading them over the keys. It was only a habit, though one that signified that she was, indeed, ready for work. But as in all the days before, her mind seemed drained of all thoughts, all words.

She looked at the screen and thought of the plot that had begun to form. Starting was always the hardest part—placing those first words on the empty screen held a kind of terror, a terror that the next four hundred pages would be less than perfect, less than her reputation deserved.

Since the publication of her first best-seller, she had moved beyond the realm of demanding editors. She could write exactly what she pleased. Usually the freedom exhilarated her but now the responsibility in it froze her thoughts as never before.

Last night's dream had been vivid and troubling but dreams had never affected her before. It must be the date, she admitted reluctantly. Did she really think that five years could dull the memory?

She and Bill had been so hopeful when, after three miscarriages, after three shattered dreams, her pregnancy had finally lasted beyond the first tenuous weeks. At night, she would lie in bed, her hand over her womb willing the life inside her to thrive and grow and be born whole and strong, as if the habit itself could assure it.

At the beginning of the third month, her doctor suggested a few tests be run. After all, he told her, there had been no diagnosis of what had caused her difficulties. Bill, more

3

painfully aware than she of what these difficulties might mean, urged the test then stayed with her throughout it, and in the hours after the amniocentesis when she refused to move until she was certain that no harm had come to the child within her. Bill had been her strength, her rock through the tragedies of the past three losses—no wonder that, when the genetic tests were complete, the doctor had called him first.

Hailey was adamant. She would not end this child's life. Then the bleeding started as it had three times before and the choice became heroic means or none.

At four months, you no longer abort a tiny mass of unformed cells, you deliver a baby. She had argued that to Bill, only to be countered with the brutal truth. "Can you really watch our child die? Day by day, you'll watch him die, Hailey. I've seen it. I know. Let it end, Hailey. Let it end now as God intends it to end, for all our sakes, the baby's most of all."

Bill was right, she admitted, and so sensitive to her pain. At the end, when the doctor mercifully sedated her, the last thing she felt was Bill's hand gripping hers.

She stayed sedated for days afterward, first at the hospital then at home. Bill would leave in the morning and return at night and she would still be in bed, lying with her knees pulled tight against her chest, her eyes dry but red-rimmed. She hid the worst of her days from him. When he asked, she would say she had been writing, but she never showed him the chapters as she had before.

The doctor prescribed pills for the depression, mental exercises to improve her outlook—as if the mourning were somehow wrong, or unnatural. The pills gave her a curious undirected energy, better suited to housecleaning than the introspective work of a writer. And though they helped her to sleep, she had terrible dreams. Tiny hands moved across her body, tiny hands with claws ripping at her skin.

She stopped taking the pills, and stopped seeing the

therapist who did not approve of what he called Hailey's
"setback."

But, even without them, she did no creative work.

Finally, desperate, Bill brought home a stack of books on
Tay-Sachs.

Before, she had only heard of the symptoms. Now she
could read about them—painful accounts of living with a
child doomed to death from the moment of conception. She
cursed herself for being so despondent over a decision that
was the only decision she could make. Then she sat at her
word processor and channeled all her pain into her work—a
story of a child like hers, born but soon dead.

Watching Aaron Die became her first best-seller, followed by a second equally successful novel ten months
later. The day she and Bill went on national TV to tell their
story, she thought she had put the past behind her.

It returned viciously to haunt her.

She wrote under her maiden name but the talk show host
had used her husband's last name. Anyone with access to a
Milwaukee phone book could find their number and did.
There were calls from mothers, often in the middle of the
night, their voices so apologetic for disturbing her. She
would lie and say it was no trouble, listening to them weep
as they offered sympathy or told their own sad story. And
there were others as well, vicious whispers suggesting that
her son's disease had been deserved, God's punishment for
what they were.

A huge red swastika appeared like an angry scar on the
riverside door of their boathouse. They had no idea it
existed until a neighbor from across the river hunted down
their house one morning to tell Hailey.

Though she hated recorded messages, she bought an
answering machine that same morning and spent the rest of
the day painting over the damage while the river, gravid in
the spring rain, flowed behind her. When she was finished
and there was nothing more she could do, she sat at the
window overlooking the river and thought of the man—to

Hailey such hate could have only come from a man—who
had painted the obscenity.

That evening, Bill found her still sitting in that same
chair, guarding her work, her house, her life. He brought her
a glass of wine, made dinner and forced her to talk to him.
Later, in bed, he fingered her white-blond hair and repeated
something he'd said in the interview. "My wandering Jew,"
he called her. "Maybe that's what attracted me to you in the
first place."

"Do you think so?" She stared at him, demanding a reply,
and for the first time since the ordeal had begun, he could
not meet her gaze.

No, he'd been attracted because she was fair-haired and
blue-eyed, because he believed she was as far removed from
the flawed genetics of his Hasidic ancestors as any woman
could be. His parents had been raised strictly and had
rebelled against their past together. Reformed and liberal,
they accepted Hailey just as avidly as their son. They did not
even suggest that she convert to Judaism, though she had
gone through the motions of doing so, as she had gone to
Catholic church when she was young, believing more in
form than substance.

"I don't know," he replied honestly, then added, "I love
you."

They spoke of other children. Alone, her child might
carry the Tay-Sachs gene but would certainly show no
symptoms. Like her. Like Bill. Only the product of their
coupling was doomed. They discussed adoption. Insemina-
tion. But they both wanted children of their own, if not
together then apart. She sold the house—their house—in
the spring following the third anniversary of their child's
death.

Hailey bought a house in the Wisconsin woods with its
back to a tiny spring-fed lake and a national forest. Summer
passed easily, then a quick fall gave way to an early snowy
winter. With it came thoughts of what she had done. The
whiteness of the landscape mirrored the whiteness of the

doctor's office, the snow on the ground when they'd left the hospital that last time, the white walls of her bedroom where she'd spent so many days in the blank cloud of her despair.

The depression closed around her again, like a dark, terrible wave, sucking her into its undertow, draining all sparks of life.

Each day she stayed in bed until well into the morning, rising only to eat before napping again. Her answering machine collected calls from Bill, from her mother, and finally from her therapist, while she slept, oblivious to her work or her life.

Finally, in the middle of the dead season, she began to dream of sun and warmth and life, dreams that stayed with her through her days, dreams that called to her, demanding a response. In mid-November, she closed the house. Taking only her computer and one small suitcase full of lightweight clothes, she drove south, stopping only to sleep until she reached New Orleans.

She stayed in the French Quarter Holiday Inn for the first few days, judging the atmosphere of the town as she might the tone of a social gathering or a relationship, deciding finally that the Quarter filled the need in her for light, energy, laughter. Decision made, she contacted a rental agent and began her search for a place she could call her own.

Most of the better apartments were too large and expensive for a writer making mortgage payments on a house in the Wisconsin woods. Others were so run-down or in neighborhoods so seedy that she would not feel relaxed enough to work in them.

She was about to consider a permanent move when, seemingly by fate, she found exactly what she was seeking around the corner from her hotel. After looking at six places with a rental agent, she parked her car in the hotel lot and decided to look for someplace different for dinner. Sonya's Kitchen, at the next corner, was usually packed with customers. That day, only a few people waited for tables.

She joined them, and while she stood there, she read a For Rent ad posted beside the cash register and asked about it.

The stairway to the second-floor apartment was on the side street behind the restaurant kitchen. It had a private balcony with a lacy iron rail above the main restaurant entrance. The room faced southwest, and in the afternoon, it was drenched with sun. Though it had no kitchen, it did include a built-in buffet with a counter, a pair of hotplates and a large sink in the bathroom where she could wash her few dishes. Best of all, it came with a parking space in the rear.

She walked through the room thinking of life within its walls. She stood on the balcony, noting happily that it was wide enough accommodate a desk and computer. And its atmosphere, one of faded secrets not her own, seemed ideal for creativity. The room had been separated from the main second-floor house and, with its tiny rosebud wallpaper, had probably belonged last to a little girl. Now it was furnished with dilapidated near-antiques that the building's owner suggested could be placed in storage if Hailey wished.

Hailey did not wish. The huge room suited her in a way she could not quite understand. She moved in that same day and went shopping. By nightfall the bed was covered in a bright African cloth, her worktable with a second that clashed perfectly with the first. Later in the week, she found a fake oriental rug to cover the worn spots in center of the room's spotted wine-colored carpet, then placed the room's only good piece of furniture—a red mohair divan with a carved wood frame—near the French doors that led onto the balcony. Beside it she hung a brass incense holder.

When everything around her was perfect, she thought, then she could begin her work.

Her wardrobe changed from dowdy Northern tweeds to brightly colored caftans. She wore a gris-gris bag around her neck that had been prepared by a Yoruba priestess to bring her creativity and luck. Her middle-aged Corolla, though hardly a car in demand, had a fetish on its dashboard to scare away thieves. She shopped in the same markets every day, ate breakfast out in the same two restaurants. Clerks and waitresses called her by name. Alone, though for the first time in months far from lonely, she belonged here.

On unseasonably warm days such as this one, she kept the balcony doors open and the room filled with the damp river air, air so thick she seemed to inhale the life of the city itself. In the distance she could hear the crowd on Rue Dumaine, the beating of the drums of a street band, the clanking of pans in the kitchen of the restaurant below her—familiar, happy sounds.

Now, in spite of a new location, a different kind of life, the words still would not flow from her mind to her fingers to the keyboard and her machine. The mystery she had so carefully plotted on the hours of her drive seemed overdone and her approach trivial. Knowing it was useless to force the beginning of a book, Hailey turned off her computer, pocketed a small notebook and went for a walk.

The day stayed bright as she wove her way through the streets, past the cathedral and to the Café du Monde, where she sat sipping coffee and watching the thin winter trickle of tourists flow by. A mother with a toddler in a stroller sat at the next table, sharing a plate of beignets, the child laughing as the powdered sugar fell down the front of his jumper.

Hailey's expression caught the mother's attention. "How old is he?" Hailey asked.

"Nearly three. It's a good time to travel with him. We're from Chicago. And you?"

Three. "Wisconsin," Hailey replied.

"I never would have guessed if it weren't for your accent. Milwaukee?"

Had her own child been born, he would likely be dead by now. "Yes, but I lived in Eagle until recently. I moved here four weeks ago."

"Here? You're so lucky. It was snowing when we left Chicago. Isn't this spring weather wonderful?"

Dead . . . and her grief only sharper from the loss.

Hailey nodded. Though her expression had not changed from that of casual interest, she did not want to risk speech.

The woman was holding out her camera. "Would you take a picture of us before we go?" she asked.

Hailey did, then ordered a second cup of coffee. The setting of her novel was wrong, she decided. She had always written about the Midwest but now she lived here and should write about here. She jotted down notes through two more cups of coffee and would have ordered another but the sun abruptly disappeared behind a line of dark storm clouds.

On her walk back, the temperature fell and the wind rose with the first drops of rain. By the time Hailey got home, the balcony doors she had left cracked open had blown inward and the room reeked of the ozone smell that always reminded her of bloated worms on the sidewalk after a spring downpour.

Papers were scattered across the floor, and the rug and wall next to the door were as soaked as she was. The computer keyboard was damp and the monitor screen danced when she turned it on.

"Very stupid, Hailey," she said out loud as she turned on the electric space heater. She would get no work done today.

It took four bath towels to sop up the water on the floor, and as she wiped down the wall, bits of the wallpaper flaked off, sticking to the towel. She looked at the mess, then at the rest of the walls around her. The yellowing rosebud paper was ugly, utterly at odds with the brightness of the room. Now an entire section of it had begun to peel.

Well, if she couldn't write, there was always other work to do.

Hailey took the soaked towels downstairs and put them in the washer behind the restaurant kitchen, then went through the narrow courtyard passage to the restaurant's front door. "Is Frank here today?" she asked Norman, the only waiter on duty during the slow afternoon hours.

Norman stared at Hailey, his expression too haughty to be considered insolent. She found herself wanting to apologize but wasn't certain what terrible deed she had done. "I'll get him," he finally said.

Soon after, Frank Berlin maneuvered his heavy body through the closely spaced tables in the front dining room. The house and restaurant had been inherited, but he'd built the business on his own. His skill as a self-trained chef was undeniable and in the last few years Sonya's Kitchen, named after his grandmother, had become one of the Quarter's best restaurants.

"Do you want some coffee?" he asked.

"No. I want to ask you if I can strip the wallpaper in my room."

"You hate it too, huh? Sure, go ahead. I warn you, though, you start and you finish. The stuff may look like it's falling off the wall but some of it is probably married to the plaster by now. I stripped this room," he waved at the walls around them, pale mauve made all the brighter by its contrast to the dark original woodwork. "A week for this, two more for the back room. I own a steamer. I think you'll need it."

"And the paint?"

"Keep the receipt. I'll pay for it."

"I didn't mean that, I only wanted to know what colors I could use."

"Lord, you tightass Yankees. Make it any color you want but lay down an anti-mildew primer first or the walls will be gray in six months. And you should get something for all the work. Five lunches a week for a month, OK?"

"A month?" It seemed too much.

"You don't know the job you're facing. Come on. I might as well get you that steamer now."

TWO

Hailey started cautiously on the soaked wall behind the balcony doors. If the work really did prove to be too time-consuming, this section could be painted white to match the built-in cupboards. The sheets pulled off easily, though the wall behind them was gray with mildew. The first sheet on the opposite wall came off just as easily, especially since Hailey used the steamer before she began. The next two had been overlapping and they fell off together almost as soon as the steamer mist touched them. Hailey caught them as they fell and laid them with the other scraps on the balcony. When she turned back, she saw the graffiti that had been hidden beneath them, large and bold and colorful.

A snake with a coiled body and raised head covered nearly all the space from ceiling to floor. Its eyes were wise, its forked tongue long, flanked on either side by lethal-looking fangs. Resting with their backs against its coils were a pair of chubby naked boys, their penises raised parallel with the snake's head. Facing away from each other, their features seemed deliberately the same, their expressions malicious. Beneath the drawing someone had scrawled the words *Protect the innocent!*

Protect them from what? Hailey wondered. From this wallpaper pattern, most likely. She laughed nervously to herself, and went on.

Now the work went much slower, the steamer and scraper together hardly enough to strip the walls. It almost seemed that she had been intended to find the drawing and that once

13

the purpose had been completed, the force that had compelled her to begin had vanished.

A thought befitting a suspense writer, Hailey decided and laughed again more calmly. Nonetheless, the wallpaper that remained looked no different from the earlier sheets, and those had fallen off. She wondered what would have happened if she had started in the opposite corner of the room.

Hailey ran out of energy by early evening. By then the computer's blower had dried out the machine and she could have worked if she'd had something to write. She tried reading instead but the drawing, huge and insistent on the one stripped wall, was more compelling than anything else. There was an urgency to it, a determination to the strokes of the brush. The final exclamation point had been made with such force that the period on the bottom had leaked in a thin line beneath it like a black tear flowing down the wall.

At ten Sonya's Kitchen closed. Hailey waited until she heard Frank's heavy footsteps in the hall then opened her door just as he was unlocking his apartment. "Frank," she called. "Can you come in here for a minute?"

"I warned you about the job. How bad is it?" he asked, a teasing I-told-you-so grin on his pudgy face as he pushed past her.

And stopped, staring at the wall. "Holy God!" he whispered, one of his hands moving out in a gesture before Hailey could move beside him.

Hailey's curiosity deepened into something far more serious. "The drawing was under the paper. Do you know what it means?" she asked.

Berlin didn't respond for a moment, waiting to speak until he managed to pull his attention from the wall to Hailey. "The room was protected. The snake is a symbol of good luck. The twins are a symbol of luck as well."

"Voodoo?"

Berlin nodded. "She drew it. It could only have been her but I don't know how. That paper's been on these walls for over twenty years. Morgan only rented the room eight years ago."

"The wallpaper over it came off easily. The paper could have been stripped then repasted."

"And no one would know, that would be like her." Berlin sounded no more relieved, as if the woman, whoever she was, had somehow bested him.

"Who was Morgan?" Hailey asked.

"Her lover. He killed himself."

"In here?"

"Yeah." Berlin pointed at the ceiling. Hailey followed the direction and noted that a section of plaster around the ceiling fan had been replaced. "There used to be a heavy glass chandelier there. Years ago it started working its way loose and my aunt had an extra hooks mounted in the main beam to support it. Morgan looped the rope through the hook and hung himself."

"Do you know why?" He only looked at her, his eyes dull with shock. "It's my room. If something tragic happened here, I think I have a right to know." Hailey gripped the gris-gris bag around her neck, implying that she believed that spirits existed and that if he didn't tell her, she could find someone who would.

Berlin laughed. Though Hailey knew he was trying to break the tension, he didn't succeed. They were both too nervous. "Lord, Yankee, there's not a house in the Quarter that doesn't have at least one great tragedy. You've got a right to know all of it but I don't want to talk about it in here. Come down the hall to my place and I'll tell you what I know."

Berlin paused at his door. "Go inside and put on some music," he told her. "I'll be right back."

Though they had shared the second-floor space for two weeks, this was the first time Hailey had been inside Frank Berlin's apartment. She had formed ideas of how the chef lived but none of them came close to matching this.

Unlike the turn-of-the-century decor of his restaurant, the

interior here was modern. The apartment walls were white, the old woodwork painted to resemble marble with random streaks of rose and aqua that matched the countertop of the open Kitchen on the far end of the room. One wall held a collection of Ivory Coast masks and fetishes, another a series of vivid color photographs of Indian street scenes, including portraits of street vendors, beggers and a pair of bald young monks.

His taste, she decided, was exquisite, though hardly her own.

Hailey scanned the selection of classical and new age CDs neatly stacked in the oak entertainment center. As she did, she noticed a photograph of Berlin, his thick legs in a pair of yellow bermuda shorts, one pale arm draped across the well-tanned shoulders of Norman, the snooty head waiter. Well, now she understood Norman's dislike of her, she thought, as she chose a piece by Sibelius, something light to contrast with the story Berlin would most likely tell. As the music started, she scanned the room. That single photo was the only personal memento in the space.

Berlin returned with a pitcher of mint ice tea and a pair of frosted pilsner glasses. On her first sip, Hailey discovered it was heavily laced with rum. She detected a scent on Berlin's clothes as well—spicy sweet and familiar. Marijuana. Apparently Norman wasn't her landlord's only vice.

In the last few minutes, he had exposed so much of himself to her. Was his memory of his neighbor so terrible that he had to take one more risk? She took a few deep swallows from her drink, wishing she could find her calm as easily.

Berlin lowered himself into one of his sling-back chairs and, playing with the glass in his hand, began.

"Joe Morgan was our tenant for nine months before he died. My aunt had partitioned the upstairs flat and rented the room to him just before she had her stroke. After I moved in to take care of Aunt Sonya, I was the one who collected his rent. Otherwise, I can't say that I knew him. He used to stop downstairs for a drink every now and then, but otherwise he kept to himself until the last few months before he died."

"Then he changed?"

"For the better. In the beginning, he was quite a drunk. I'd hear him yelling to himself through the wall separating his room from my bedroom. He beat on the walls until I threatened to evict him. Once he broke a pane of glass in the French doors with his fist because the lock had jammed. He cut his hand that time and there was blood all over the carpet. He was bleeding so bad I had to mop up the mess. There's probably still a few spots but you can't see them since the carpet's so dark itself.

Blood on her carpet. Was that what she'd smelled when the rain soaked her room? Old blood, she reminded herself. Eight years old and harmless. Hailey poured another glass of tea. "Did Morgan stop drinking?" she asked.

"Not completely. Funny, I'd always took him for an alcoholic but he cut back on his own. He started looking better too, and finally I discovered that he was seeing a woman. In the beginning, they were real discreet. He'd bring her in late at night and I'd sometimes hear them in bed. He dried out a little too late, though. A month before he died, he told me he lost his job. I thought, That's it. He'll hit the bottle again and you'll have to evict him, but he didn't.

"It was the woman, I think. Leanna de Noux . . ." His voice trailed off, as he remembered or perhaps tried to recall her last name. "Dark thick hair, blue eyes and light skin. Georgia Peach, my aunt used to call that complexion and with her hair it was . . . well, striking. He'd bring her into the restaurant sometimes. One of my waiters became infatuated with her, and when she realized it, she'd flirt with him. She was no lady, so she made her advances obvious. The poor kid would hang around after he got off just to watch her and Morgan sitting at the bar drinking together, hoping that she'd say a few words to him. If he started to lose interest, she'd whisper something to him then go back to Morgan and tell him what she'd said and they'd laugh like the kid's lust was some kind of joke. She was that kind of woman."

"You said Morgan cut back."

"*He* did. I don't know if she drank more or less around him but she drank a lot. I don't know what he thought of her drinking but he tolerated it. They'd sit together or with the crowd they sometimes brought in. Then the two of them would disappear upstairs."

Hailey detected less disapproval than envy in his tone and wondered at it. Snooty Norman with his cheekbones and deep-set black eyes had to be more than enough for a middle-aged chef. "How did the woman die?" she asked.

"Morgan killed her two weeks to the day before he killed himself."

"What!"

Berlin shook his head. "I never understood it or maybe I did and didn't want to admit it. He was crazy about her and that kind of love makes people dangerous. Maybe that was enough." He paused to pull a cigarette out of the antique case he always carried. As he lit it, his hands shook, making the lighter's flame dance. He took a deep drag then went on. "She died in his room. She'd been stabbed fourteen times, the police said. I didn't hear any commotion but my aunt must have because I found her unconscious in the hall outside of Morgan's door. She died three days later without ever waking up.

"I think I called for help then pushed open Morgan's door. He was out cold and the woman was lying beside him covered with blood. I couldn't bring myself to go in, so I went back to my flat and called the police."

"Did they charge Morgan with murder?"

"No but I think they would have eventually, even though when they came, Morgan was drunk or drugged, more out of it than I'd ever seen him. And they didn't find the murder weapon either. They said she'd been dead less than an hour when they got there.

"That was the end of Morgan. I never saw him sober after that night. Sometimes, I'd lie in bed listening to him chanting her name. Leanna . . . Leanna . . . Leanna. When he killed himself, I thought his death was a blessing."

"Did he leave a note?" Hailey asked.

"Yeah but not exactly a suicide announcement. *I love her. I will always love her. I'm sorry,* I think it said."

"That doesn't make sense."

"Neither did the murder." Berlin paused and watched the smoke rise as he exhaled. "She told him she was leaving him," Berlin said, nodding as if this must have been the truth. "Killing her would make sense then, wouldn't it? Then he killed himself out of guilt. That makes sense too."

Frank Berlin was right. In a sad, tragic way, it did make sense. "Did your aunt ever say anything at all?" she asked. "Even if she just sounded delirious?"

"No." He lowered his head and it seemed to Hailey that he wanted to bury his face in his hands and sob after so many years. "The poor old girl was lying with her cane out in front of her when I found her. The shock was just too much."

"With her cane out like she had been lunging at someone or maybe trying to protect herself?"

"If there had been a killer, why didn't he kill my aunt too? Morgan must have done it. The knife he'd used was even at his feet when he died, retrieved from wherever he'd hidden it, I suppose."

"And what about the message on the wall?" Hailey's voice had grown louder. She wanted the message to have come from Morgan and Leanna, wanted there to be some hint that another person might have killed Leanna.

"There were a few renters before you. Maybe this is somebody's idea of a sick joke?" He sounded hopeful and she tried to accept the words the same way.

"Frank, was she . . . was Leanna killed in my bed?" she asked.

"Yeah. But the police took the mattress."

Hailey frowned. She didn't understand.

"When they shook Morgan awake and he saw what he'd done to her, he wet it. They wanted to test the urine, I suppose. I don't know what they turned up, if anything."

"So she died in my bed but not on my mattress? Does that mean I can rest easy?"

Berlin giggled. Hailey had never heard a man so large giggle before and the sound was infectuous, the laughter breaking the horror of his story. "I would have bought a new one anyway," he said. She laughed with him and felt better afterward.

"You want some more tea?" he asked.

Hailey accepted, thinking that even with the rum she would not rest easy tonight.

That night Hailey sat on the bed—the bed with the new mattress, she reminded herself—and stared at the drawing and words on the wall. Huge. Insistent.

She had known what it meant even before she asked Frank about it. On the day she had purchased her gris-gris bag, she had talked for some time to the Vodun priestess. If Leanna had been a practitioner, she would have believed that her spirit would remain to protect her loved one or to seek vengeance for her death.

"Was he guilty, Leanna?" she whispered. "Or did he need protection from someone else?"

With her eyes closed, she pictured the night the drawing had been made, the pair of them carefully ungluing the loose sheets of paper, Leanna's hand moving with long, firm strokes, the drawing taking shape. Afterward, they replaced the paper, hiding their protection. Leanna. What a beautiful name, so soft, so feminine, so unlike her own, picked because her father wanted her to be just like him—hard-nosed, practical, masculine. When she was young, she had longed for a name like Leanna.

"Leanna. Hailey imagined her in peach lace, a cameo on a ribbon around her neck, her hair a black cloud over her pale shoulders.

And for the first time in her life, Hailey slept and dreamed as a man. . . .

THREE

. . . One day always seems to flow into the next, his work detestable. From his years in police work, he developed a knack for prying into people's lives, but there is no justice to be found in publicizing their sordid secrets. People should be allowed their vices, he long ago decided. Now he knows it all too well. His own addiction is just as inexorable as the other, forbidden ones.

He reached the right level of intoxication with his last drink and now he sits in the tiny rear courtyard of the tavern, listening to the band playing inside, their tinny zydeco beat softened by distance and the sultry night air.

It rained earlier. Now there are drops of water on the chairs and tables around him. It falls from the trees above him, landing on his hair and in his mug of beer. His pants are damp from the chair. In the summer heat, the feeling is pleasant.

He has ordered another, and is drinking the remainder of the first more quickly—it is best to keep the pace just right to maintain a workable oblivion—when over the sound of the accordian, the beating of metal-tipped fingers on the washboard, he hears laughter, sees a flash of brilliant fuchsia under the pale globe lights—a woman standing near the open courtyard doors.

There are others with her. Five are men, the sixth a mousy woman gripping tightly onto her escort's hand. They say very little. The woman talks for them, breaking finally into peals of wild, savage laughter.

Hailey sensed herself, an entity separate from Morgan,

23

yet trapped in him, feeling what he felt as the sound carried through the open doors, pulling him from the empty dullness of his thoughts. "How can this be . . . ," Hailey whispers in his voice, and the sound of his whisper draws her back to him, to the core of his being.

". . . happening?" Morgan finishes for her.

The woman laughs again and it astonishes him that the band has not fallen silent, the dancers have not stopped their motions to turn toward her.

She steps into the courtyard to survey the damp tables and chairs. Her hair is long, falling in unruly ringlets over her shoulders. Her face is not conventionally beautiful—the almond-shaped eyes are too far apart, the lips too wide and full. Perhaps there is a trace of Negro blood in her. It would hardly be surprising in a town such as this. He waits for her to come closer to his table but she turns, motioning the others to retreat.

Morgan, infatuated, smooths back his unruly hair and follows her into the smoke and noise of the music hall.

The band is setting a wild pace. The washboard rhythm grates on his ears as he walks past the woman, now seated near the bar. He pauses just behind her and inhales the scent of her hair.

Musk and spice. Not an innocent scent. Not a common scent.

She stands and turns to face him as if she has sensed him watching. Perhaps one of her friends noticed him, but if so they gave no indication.

"Your perfume is lovely," he says. It isn't what he wants to ask but the other questions seem too forward.

What is the color of your eyes in the sunlight?

Is there someone else in your life? No, the question would be wrong. It would make no difference in how he feels.

Does he know where to touch you?

She raises her arm slowly with her hand palm out until her wrist is even with his face. He understands and inhales again while the mousy woman titters nervously.

"Norell," she whispers, her lips close to his cheek. If he dared, he would kiss her. Consequences be damned.

"I'm Joe Morgan. May I buy you a drink?" he asks.

She frowns. "Of course." She does not ask him to join her party but instead walks with him to the bar to claim a Sazerac, then returns to her group. She does not look at him again.

Morgan chooses his drinks with greater car. Hours pass before the woman leaves, alone. He follows her outside and watches her walking away from him, her keys already in her hand. Her car is small, black, foreign. He writes the license plate number on the back of his hand then goes to his own old Ford and drives in the direction she went, hoping to catch up with her.

He thinks he sees her car on Girod Street. He pulls behind it, following it toward the river and onto St. Charles. She glimpses him in her rearview mirror and increases her speed, past Audubon Park then left onto a narrow street in the Garden District. He follows her to one of the rare old houses that maintain the integrity of their original grounds and watches her pull inside the black iron gates and into the garage. He drives past and parks and stands beside his car hoping to glimpse her. There has to be a door to the house, however, for she does not appear again.

The rain starts up again as he walks across the street. Inside the lit window, he sees a cadaverous young man with tiny round glasses and the same dark hair as the woman embrace her. Their kiss is fleeting, yet passionate. The man hands her a glass of wine then goes to the window, looking out before closing the heavy blue drapes.

Has she told the man that she was followed? Is that why Morgan is being denied another glimpse of her?

He continues to stand there as the rain increases, soaking his dark hair, running down his face like tears.

He knows nothing, nothing at all about her. But he will. He vows that he will.

He has never felt such passion for a woman before—not

even Denise, whom he loved more than anyone, had married, had stayed married to for eight years. Since then there has been only swift, easily forgotten affairs. And now this woman, scarcely more than a girl, has roused his passion with her laughter, her perfume, her eyes.

A beagle, old and arthritic, hobbles down the street with its equally old master. The man looks at Morgan and shakes his head. "We fools in the rain," he says and laughs and goes on.

A flash of lightning. A roll of thunder. Hailey woke, dream and reality merging for a moment as, disoriented, she looked out her bare window at the growing power of the storm.

Like the dreams, she'd had when she'd been taking the drugs for her depression, this one refused to dissipate with the coming of morning. Hailey sat on her balcony, writing down what she recalled of it. By noon, she'd reached a decision. She pulled on jeans and a bulky cotton sweater and left to catch the St. Charles trolley. It seemed to her that if she found the street, and the house, she would be certain.

Of what? That she wasn't having some strange flashback from pills she'd stopped taking months ago? That she hadn't lost her mind? That somehow the spirits of the dead were calling out to her?

At least she was in New Orleans, where the dead and the living always seemed on the verge of some enlightening communication. The thought stayed with her on the trip, enhanced by the scent of the trolley's power contact, a smell oddly holy, like incense at a high mass.

She could not recall what street Joe Morgan had turned down in her dream but it had been just past Audobon Park. She got off the trolley one stop early and walked through the corner of the park under the ancient trees, so full of their own silent memories.

Rhododendrons lined the front yards of the houses bordering the park, their leaves dark and wilted from the winter chill. Nothing bloomed and the streets, like the gardens, were empty of life.

Hailey walked slowly two blocks down, then down the crossroad, looking like a new tourist as she examined each house.

In truth, she felt as if she had entered some alien country, a country she'd heard of only in whispers.

And then she saw the house, bathed in sunlight, the high Doric pillars and portico floor washed clean of past sins by last night's rain. In her dream the fence had been black iron. In the years that had passed someone had painted it white, giving it the look of the delicate lace balconies of Quarter. She saw the corner drive leading to the garage, the same dark blue drapes hanging in the tall side windows.

If she went up to the door, would the same thin man with the round glasses answer her knock? Had he been Leanna's lover? Her friend?

The postman was coming down the street, a stack of mail in his hand. She stopped him just as he was going up the walk to the house. "Can you tell me how to get to Monroe Street?" she asked.

"Ah, that isn't easy from here." He began supplying directions. As he did, she nodded and took a long look at the name and address on the top of the mail pile. Louis de Noux.

"Are you all right?" the postman asked.

His voice gave her something to focus on, an island in this murky unreality. "Yes, of course," she said.

Hailey wanted time to think so she walked back to the Quarter, past the houses that grew older and less ornate with every block.

She knew exactly why she had been so shocked to see the de Noux name. Until she saw the name, she could have justified the dream. She had walked the streets of the Garden District before. She might have seen the house, might have transferred it to her dream.

Now there was no denying the truth of last night's

somnabulant adventure. Her room—perhaps even she herself—had been possessed.

She paused at Lafayette Square. There were a number of choices open to her. She could accept the dream as that one strange thing that had happened to her, as such things happen to everyone in the course of a lifetime. If she did, she could wait and see if another dream followed the first.

Or, she could take the initiative. It was, after all, her nature to do precisely that.

And it occurred to her there in the winter sunshine, occurred with such clarity that she wondered why she had never thought of it before—what a novel their affair would make!

If so, there were things she ought to know. She crossed the square, went inside the *Time-Picayune* building and asked for admittance to the newspaper's archives.

Berlin hadn't told her the date of the murder but she could make a good guess the year had to have been '85 or '86. Since a story like that should have made the headlines, she only needed to glance at every day's paper, and she had time.

When she found the story of Leanna's murder, the pictures of Frank Morgan and Leanna de Noux were displayed just under the two-inch headlines. They looked much as they had in her dream—Morgan better groomed, somewhat stern in the formal Lake Charles Police Department ID photo; Leanna younger, more subdued, but no less sensuous. Morgan's picture had been provided by a local TV station for which he'd worked. Leanna's had been taken from the paper's archives, the photo submitted with her wedding announcement five years before her death.

Hailey read all afternoon, then, not certain that she'd caught everything of importance, went to the old clerk at the desk and asked for copies of every article.

He noted her subject and looked at her with greater interest. "I'm surprised more people aren't curious. If this were a recent crime, that pair'd be the movie of the week for sure," the clerk commented as he began copying the pages, handing the oversized sheets to her one at a time. "People didn't pay so much attention to personal tragedies then." He spoke as if the crime had occurred half a century ago. "What are you making copies for?" he added.

Hailey hesitated, then decided there was no harm in the truth. "I'm considering writing a book about them," she said.

He nodded as if that explained everything. "It's high time, I'd say. You know, before he met the woman, Morgan would come in every once in a while, looking up background on stories for the news station. I took an interest in the case because I'd met him. If you need to know anything . . ."

"Do you think Morgan killed the woman?"

The clerk laughed softly. "That's a direct one. He might've; he was strung a little high, if you know what I mean. Then again, she was divorced no more than six months before her murder. Nobody thinks about the husband."

From the news accounts, Hailey had gathered that the marriage had ended much earlier. It seemed odd that the paper hadn't discussed a recent divorce. She'd have to read the articles again to find some mention of the husband's name.

"And they were living apart for a year before that," the man went on. Then he leaned across the service counter, lowering his voice as if someone who might care about his remark would overhear. "Nobody thinks about her lovers, either, the ones before Frank, that is."

"How would you know?"

He pointed to her picture, not that he had to. Hailey had seen her alive only last night. "What do you think?" he asked.

That it was a terrible judgment to make from an old, though admittedly provocative, news photo, Hailey thought. Yet if Leanna were like the creature in Hailey's dream, she'd had lovers, maybe more than Hailey could imagine. Hailey shook her head. "I don't know," she replied.

The clerk gave her a manila envelope for the stories. The thin parcel seemed oddly precious to her and she held it tightly on her walk back to the flat, filled with memories too terrible to fade like the roses on the wallpaper, memories unwilling to do the decent thing and quietly die.

Her room seemed so still when she opened the door, as if the dampness somehow muted the sounds of the street. The sun slanted through the French doors, the shafts of light from each pane taking form in the hazy air.

Hailey piled the news stories on her desk then turned on her computer. Reading each account, she began carefully noting names of friends and witnesses, places Leanna had frequented, details of the case.

As she had hoped, the story of Leanna and her obsessed lover grabbed hold of her. This was her next book.

There had always been a tradition in their home—hers and Bill's. Once the decision on a book was made, she would call him at his office and tell him that the hardest part was done. He'd usually manage to come home as early as he could, carrying a bouquet of flowers. He'd pop the bottle of champagne she'd chilled. They'd make love before going out to dinner, her pleasure heightened by the ecstasy of her own creation, and the anticipation of the wonderful days that stretched before her, when the lives of her characters would slowly take on form and substance, unfolding on the pages.

Now she surveyed her tiny room with only a hint of depression, barely any sadness. If she was alone, so be it. She could celebrate on her own.

The florist shop on the corner provided the roses. After she arranged them in a glass jar and placed them on her bedside table, she went downstairs. Sonya's Kitchen had only a few late afternoon patrons. Hailey took a seat by the window and ordered a bottle of champagne.

Frank brought it to her table. "Celebrating something?" he asked as he displayed the label.

"Beginnings. I've just begun to record the tragic saga of Leanna and Joe."

"What!" his ruddy face grew white. "You're going to write about it?"

Hailey fought the urge to smile. Was Frank really that conservative, or merely possessive of the building's tragedy? "Don't worry. It's going to be fiction so the names will be changed. Nobody will know that any of my story took place upstairs."

"Then I suppose it will be all right." He still looked doubtful.

"Frank, writers find their plots everywhere. Usually a novel doesn't bear a lot of resemblance to the actual event that inspired it."

His worried expression relaxed somewhat.

"Would you have some with me?" she asked him, and pointed to the bottle.

He had a glass, then another, while Hailey told him stories of the real-life inspirations for some famous novels. At five the restaurant's early dinner trade began trickling in. "I have guests to seat," he said. He thanked her and left.

She had a bowl of shrimp bisque, bread and salad but passed on dessert. The champagne was definitely affecting her—not with giddiness but with a sudden desire to be alone. She took the rest of the bottle upstairs and sat on her balcony with her feet on the railing, taking swigs from the bottle. She felt young, and somewhat wicked, as if she were back in college and this the spring vacation she'd never taken.

Yes, she thought, holding up the bottle to toast the city around her. Yes, this is where I belong.

An old man standing by an open window in the building across the street from hers held up one arm, mimicked her gesture, then smiled and waved. She waved back, thinking he would turn from the window. Instead, he stayed where he was, watching her with an expression of vague longing on his face.

He made her uneasy. She went inside and closed her drapes.

FOUR

Fuck it! She's had too much to drink.

Again, she reminds herself. Too much to drink . . . again.

Dangerous, Louis would say. Especially when she came here alone.

Music flows from the tavern she left just moments ago, the heavy dance beat. Ideal background music for the fight threatening to break out inside.

Rage. She's seen enough of it to last the rest of her life.

The record playing on the jukebox skips, recovers then stops altogether. She hears the bartender yelling, and someone yelling back with words slurred together. "What-the-hell-do-you-care-long-as-I-pay?"

"Yeah, you'll pay, you son of a bitch! Then you'll get your ass out of here!"

"I go only if he goes! I'm gonna bust his head."

A patrol car pulls up outside. Not the police, she notices, but a private firm. The driver and his partner pull out their nightsticks.

Some poor little shit is about to get more of a hangover than he bargained for.

Blows. Blood. Damage. The outcome makes her shake, not out of concern for the poor victim, but from the too vivid memories of her own past.

If she dared, she would start the car and go but she knows that moving from this spot is impossible.

When did a bad habit get out of hand? she wonders. Why couldn't she control it as she once did, using the alcohol or

33

the drugs just enough to suit the need of a spell, to make her free enough to let the spirits come? She knows the answers, and contemplates them only at times like this. Memories scratch at the inside of her brain, trying to escape and reveal things best forgotten. Drink pulls her power, but it dulls theirs too.

She lowers her head until it's resting on the padded steering wheel of her Porsche—such a convenient driver's pillow—and waits for the dizziness to pass.

Sparse drops of rain fall on the car windshield, the leather seats, her bare arms, and bare thighs below her short flared skirt. She could put the top up—you are able to do that, she reminds herself—but perhaps the rain will sober her enough that she can drive.

She raises her head and looks at the gray sky. A drop of water hits her open eye. She blinks.

"Leanna?"

Her eyes try to focus on the man.

"Leanna, it isn't safe for you to be here," he tells her.

"Safe?" She manages a smile. Manages a laugh that almost seems charming. The street might be narrow, ill lit and empty. There might be bars on the windows of the beauty shop across the way but at least no one is threatening to break chairs over her head. "It's safer out here than it was in there."

"Let me take you home."

"Home?" That is funny and she laughs again. This time the laughter sounds pathetic—strained, desperate.

"For coffee? Something to eat?"

He sounds so earnest that she takes a better look at him. He's probably thirty-five or so, tall and thin except for the shoulders. Rumpled check shirt. Faded jeans. Dark hair. Lean features—like Carlo!—and intense dark eyes. "I know you," she says, not quite certain.

"We met last week. I saw you here yesterday and now today. You told me you were coming."

"You know my name."

"We met. Remember?"

She drops the keys on the dashboard and slides around the shift into the passenger seat. She is aware how high her skirt has slid, of the damp leather seat slippery and cool against her bare skin, but she does not try to adjust her clothes. The seat is tilted back so she is facing the sky, the soothing drops of rain. She closes her eyes. "Then drive," she says.

(And in the darkness, Hailey—the observer and recorder of others' lives—is flung from her body into . . .).

Morgan gets in. He cannot hide the trembling of his hands. When he first saw her inside, alone, he even flattered himself and thought she'd come looking for him. Now he feels guilty for taking advantage of her, yet unwilling not to try. "How do I put the top up?" he asks, amazed that he can speak at all.

"Leave it down."

He does as she asks. As they move, a fine mist covers both of them, slicking down her wild dark hair, pressing the thin red cotton blouse against her breasts. Her nipples are hard, sharply outlined. All he has to do is touch. Considering the way she sits, she might even be expecting it. "Where would you like to go?" he asks instead.

"Home."

"Home?"

She gives an address he already knows and he drives slowly toward it, unwilling to finish the trip, unwilling to relinquish her to her own separate life, unwilling to do anything but whatever she asks.

But when they reach the house, she pulls a remote from the glove box. The gate swings open. The garage door follows, and as it rises, a fluorescent light inside clicks on.

As soon as the car rolls in, the doors close automatically behind it.

She exits the car too fast for him to help. "How do I get out of here?" he asks.

"Leave? I expected you to come inside," she tells him.

She's through the side door and into the house before he manages to pull the recessed door latch.

He finds her standing barefoot in the center of the entrance hall, her head cocked, as if she is a young girl sneaking in past curfew, frightened that a parent will hear, listening for some sign that her parents are asleep. "My father is gone for a month and my brother . . . is . . . not . . . in . . . tonight," she tells him, the words clipped and spaced and quite clear. Until now, he thought her drunk but if she were, her recuperative powers are incredible.

"Your brother?"

"I always dreamed of being alone in this house and now when I occasionally am allowed—no, that isn't true—I am requested to be here to guard the family treasures, it seems unbearable. The walls remind me of the past, and their voices are too . . . eloquent."

She pauses; he has nothing to say.

He has been in houses like this one—stately old mansions with wainscotted rooms. The vastness of their spaces and the darkness of their walls made him feel both small and closed in, as if he had just experienced conception and, only a few cells into life, was already given a glimpse of his coffin.

"Fix us a drink," she says, motioning toward a pair of wooden doors mounted to slide into the wall. He pushes them apart. The bar is on the opposite side of the flock-papered room, bottles and glasses haphazardly arranged behind a glass-doored armoire. A pair of twisted brass chandeliers dangle like spiders from the high ceiling. The rug beneath his feet is thick, an intricate Aubusson design on a teal ground. How many hours and how many hands labored to create it, all of this?

"Anything," she adds.

He pours them brandy. As she takes a glass from him, she starts toward the stairs. "Follow me," she tells him.

He touches her shoulder. "Wait!" he says.

"Wait?" She turns, one foot on the bottom stairs, her expression troubled.

Why couldn't he simply take what was being offered? Morgan dreamed of it often enough in the last week and now some prudery seems important enough to interfere with his desire. "Do you know my name?" he asks.

"And if I don't?" Her smile makes him wish he'd said nothing; he wants so desperately to ignore his pride and kiss her. "Unkempt hair. Fierce dark eyes. Strong arms. A pirate if ever there was one. And his name is Morgan."

"How did you know?" he asks incredulously.

"You told me last night. As to remembering, I am cursed with memory." She looks past him, focusing on nothing as she asks, "Would it have really made a difference if I hadn't known?"

"I'm not sure," he answers.

"Dignity is so rare, and so pleasant," she replies, her voice honey sweet. He wants to slap her, to kiss her, to rip off the clothing separating his body from hers and take her on the stairs. Instead, he follows her upstairs to a large front bedroom in which a single light is burning on the bedside table, waiting in its rose-tinted glass case.

She starts the gas log in the white marble fireplace that dominates most of the inside wall, turns out the light. The room is patterned with the flickering of the fire, the dancing shadows thrown by her body and his as he moves beside her, close to the warmth of her presence and the flames. "Is this what you wanted?" she asks.

"This is better," he responds and kisses her. Her clothes are still damp and he fumbles with the tiny fabric-covered buttons of her shirt. She takes his hands, pushes them away. Her eyes are fixed on his with an intensity that makes him wonder why she fears to see anything else.

"Sit," she tells him, and he does as she asks. The heat of the fire dries his hair and back as he watches her slip the blouse from her shoulders, unfasten the skirt and let it fall to the floor. Panties—no more than a thin strip of black lace—follow.

So what if she knows my name. I could be anyone, he thinks, and it would make no difference to her.

Six drinks tonight. Even after he saw her come into the place, he ordered another. Six drinks—at least two too many for a full erection. He could try to please her as she wanted to be pleased, take her as quickly as she seemed to be demanding, and he would fail.

And that, as a country singer might croon, would be the end of Leanna and Joe.

He won't allow it. Instead, he kisses the top of her foot, and moves his hands slowly up her smooth calves, her thighs, pressing his face against the downy nest of hair dark as the curls falling down her back, breathing in her scents of perfume and musk.

It works some magic on him.

His penis swells, pressing against the zipper of his jeans as he begins to arouse her. Her fingers first brush the back of his neck, sending delicious shivers down his back, then catch in his hair trying to pull him up, away from her.

At the end, he can hear her panted breaths, her sobs, her begging him to stop, and still he stays, until, unable to bear the touch of his mouth any longer, she falls backward onto the carpet, her hair a dark pillow around her head, and shoulders.

"Please," she whispers, pleading now as he intended to make her plead. He does as she asks, and takes her savagely, amazed at how hard he has become, how long he lasts. . . .

Hailey didn't have the same queasy feeling when she woke from the second dream. Perhaps it was because she was growing used to the journey through time, perhaps because she was allowed to wake naturally.

But the memory of the dream—if it had been a dream—was no less vivid than before. And the result was an excitement she found unbearable—as if she, not Leanna, had experienced Morgan's skill; as if she, not Morgan, had become obsessed. Her sex felt swollen and used, her thighs wet.

As before, she recorded the dream immediately; then, not certain how to deal with what had happened—again!—she dressed and went outside.

It had rained the night before, and a cold wind swept through the damp streets, cutting her to the bone, even through the thick wool of the coat she'd been cautious enough to bring on her long drive south.

Still, it was hard to think of this chill as belonging to December, or that it was less than a month to Christmas. She had no obligations this year. Her parents were, as usual, spending the winter in Florida. She could fly down and be with them if she chose but she doubted they would miss her all that much if she did not.

No, she decided. She would not leave this city now.

On the edge of the Quarter, she turned and headed down Bienville Street toward the river, skirted the pair of huge hotels, behemoths that shaded the old buildings around them. On a street so narrow that sun never touched its dirty pavement, she went into a tiny storefront whose windows were painted bright red, not to attract attention but to give privacy to customers venturing inside.

The store was L-shaped, the long front stacked from floor to ceiling with used books and old photos of New Orleans life. In the back, separated from the store proper by a beaded curtain, was a room full of old magic and myths, as dark as the continent from which they had come. There, surrounded by herbs and rough painted masks, by bits of bone and straw-stuffed dolls, the voodooienne Celeste Brasseaux met her customers.

Hailey had discovered the store during her first week in the city. It had been a slow day for Celeste and they'd sat together at the front counter drinking coffee and discussing the city's life. Since then, they'd met from time to time, and

Hailey often made a point of stopping in the store in midweek when Celeste would have time to talk. She found the woman's natural empathy more soothing than the advice of any detached therapist she'd seen.

"Come in!" Celeste called when she saw Hailey standing behind the beaded curtain. "Come and tell me, has the new book begun well? Are the others doing splendidly?"

There was a customer with Celeste, an old woman with coal-black skin who looked curiously at Hailey as she pocketed the wrapped package Celeste had prepared for her, and left without a word.

"Something has happened, not wonderful but . . . you are intrigued. Sit, tell me," Celeste said, motioning toward a chair. Her hands were a shade of coffee and cream that seemed almost white against the wine-colored paint on her long nails. Though Celeste had to be nearing fifty, she could easily have passed for a woman of thirty, not because of her features but because of her exquisite grace.

"I need you to come with me, Celeste. There are marks painted on my walls, old marks. I need to know what they mean."

"I cannot leave the shop now but I can come tonight. It will cost you, though."

"It's all right."

Celeste smiled. "You are terrible at bargaining, dear. But I only request that you buy me dinner downstairs. Frank is such a genius."

"Is dinner at five too early?" Hailey asked, thinking of the lines Sonya's Kitchen always seemed to acquire after dark.

"Seven. Reserve. I'll come at six. Try to get one of the back tables so we can talk while we eat."

"Then I'd better go and try to get some work done this afternoon."

"Try? You shouldn't have to try." Celeste laughed and pointed to the rawhide strap of the gris-gris bag she had made for Hailey, hidden as Celeste had suggested, under

Hailey's shirt. "Cup it in your hands, breathe in the scent of it, concentrate. The inspiration will come."

Inspiration already had, Hailey knew. She'd fought with the inevitability of it for the last two days. Even after standing in front of that magnificent white house, she had fought with the truth: Leanna de Noux had some claim on her soul. Until the woman's story was told, Hailey would be able to write nothing else.

Before she began her writing, she turned her worktable so that it faced the drawings on the wall, then filed away the pages of the manuscript she'd abandoned. As always, she methodically backed up her work files onto a disc and placed it with the others in a separate box in the bottom of her closet.

If the story had been compelling, rather than useless wandering in search of a plot, she would have made a second copy to mail to a friend in Wisconsin, guaranteeing that even a disaster such as fire or flood would not destroy her work. Later, she thought, this story of Leanna and Joe Morgan would probably deserve that special treatment.

Before she sat down, she performed the exercise Celeste had taught her. The scent of the bag, spice and musk, brought the dreams vividly to her mind. For the hour that passed, she managed the delicate writer's trick of merging with her characters. The words came quickly, and as she walked through Joe Morgan's mind, she wasn't surprised to find herself becoming once more aroused.

"Leanna," Hailey whispered aloud and, in a manner entirely out of character, she did not edit the words she'd written. Instead, she spent the next hour before Celeste was due to arrive reading over the news accounts of the murder, looking for details she might have missed in her first quick pass.

Hailey was sitting on her balcony enjoying the final warm rays of sun when Celeste turned the corner of her block, a half hour past the time they'd agreed on. As usual Celeste dressed to be noticed, in a flowing yellow silk caftan and matching turban. During her walk, she'd attracted a faithful follower who spoke excitedly while she strolled, serene in her power, down the street.

"I must go," Hailey heard her say, then watched as Celeste gripped one of the man's hands in both of hers. "Do as I advise and all will be as it was," she told him in a tone that would make him want to believe. Then she disappeared inside.

As Celeste stepped into Hailey's room, she wrinkled her nose. "Something smells musty. No, it's something more than the damp. I don't like it."

The smell of old blood, Hailey thought. "This is the wall," she said and pointed at the drawing.

Celeste studied it with her usual quiet interest, then explained in words almost insulting in their simplicity. "The snake is Zombi, of course, the symbol of God and a force of good. The twins are a sign of power. You don't see them so often here but in Haiti they are quite common. The phalusses on the boys are huge, a sign of added strength. Everyone wants strong boys, yes?" Celeste raised one eyebrow, punctuating the double meaning of her words.

"And the writing?" Hailey asked.

"I'm not certain." Celeste stared at the drawing, taking in the whole of it rather than the individual pieces. "It's a petition, I think, but the demanding tone of it would be strange from anyone but a priestess." She turned toward Hailey. As she did, she noticed the news accounts spread across the worktable and paused to stare a moment at Leanna's picture. "I was going to ask who did the drawing. Now I think I understand."

"I don't know if Leanna de Noux wrote it."

"She died here. This was his room. I remember now. Odd how the mind blocks out something so unpleasant," Celeste said.

Hailey was prepared to tell Berlin's story but Celeste did not ask. Instead, she went to the French doors and peeled back a loose section of carpet, examining the floor beneath it, shaking her head when she saw that it was soaked. "Storms come on so suddenly here," Hailey commented, knowing the excuse of the damage was not a good one.

Celeste nodded impatiently, went to the door and lifted back the hall carpet. After licking her finger, she dipped it in the dust on the floor, tasted it then rinsed her mouth at Hailey's sink. "Salt. I expected it. It was probably under the outside doors as well until the rain washed it away."

"What does salt mean?"

"You might read some of the books you buy from our store," Celeste commented. "Salt at doors and windows protects against evil. If I'd searched this room before you moved in, I might have found more, not that it is really important now. After all, the spell wasn't strong enough. And so Leanna died, as did her lover." She rinsed her hands in Hailey's sink, and dried them with a dish towel. "That is all I can tell you about this room. Now, shall we eat and you can tell me why a few pictures and an old murder fascinate you so?"

Hailey grabbed everything she had written and followed Celeste down the stairs.

As he did with any local celebrity, Frank Berlin fawned over Celeste, addressing her by name a number of times as they wove through the crowded dining room to the secluded rear table. Celeste waited until they had chosen their meal and agreed on a bottle of wine to share, then, with her attention fixed entirely on Hailey once more, she asked the question Hailey had been expecting. "If the police had seen those symbols, they would have understood that Leanna's murder had been more than a crime of passion and consulted me, or someone like me. How were they hidden?"

Hailey explained about the wallpaper, telling Celeste about it in a matter-of-fact way she could have used with no one else she knew.

Near the end of her story Frank Berlin appeared carrying a plate of steamed soft-shell crabs and garlic butter. He heard the last few words as he set down the plates. "She showed you her wall, did she not?" Celeste asked him.

"She did."

Celeste's piercing stare made him nervously go on, "It doesn't do any good to place charms on walls to keep out snakes when there's one lying in bed beside you."

Celeste nodded at his comment, picked up a knife and halved the crab with one quick slice.

"If you need any help from me, you come and ask," Frank said to Hailey then turned his attention to another table, where an older woman was gushing about the texture of his corn chowder.

Trying to ignore the good-natured hum of his voice, Hailey described her dreams, the terrible vividness of them.

The meal came and they paused to dine on channel catfish steamed with fresh herbs and roasted spice, yellow rice and smoky red beans. When the main course had ended and Hailey gave the pages she had written to Celeste, her hands shook.

"I don't like to share things that are in such a rough stage but I didn't want to edit. I was afraid . . ." Hailey's voice trailed off uneasily. What she felt compelled to believe ran counter to everything she accepted about life and death and the absence of any heaven for even the holiest.

"You were afraid that your skill would alter your vision. I understand. It's quite wise," Celeste commented and began to read. Hailey tried to explain a part of the account but was silenced by an imperious wave of Celeste's beautiful hand.

"I knew Leanna de Noux," Celeste said when she'd finished. "She came into my shop often to buy herbs or just to browse through the books. She had a great deal of knowledge and I know she was involved in some ceremonies here in the city. The de Noux family was originally from Haiti, which explains her interest, I suppose." She handed the papers back to Hailey. "I remember how she looked and moved and what you have written here captures my impression of her."

"How can this be happening?"

"How?" Celeste laughed, a deep throaty sound. A young woman at a nearby table followed her escort's eyes and looked over her shoulder with a longer and more hostile glance than politeness demanded. Like Leanna, Celeste attracted attention. Unlike Hailey, she seemed to revel in it. "Any religion will have its own rationale," she continued. "What you really want to know is *why* this is happening to you."

"All right. Tell me why."

"*Loas* are able to possess men and women because they are spirits with incredible powers. The spirits of human dead are not so powerful. But when your guard is lowered as it is in sleep, they are able to move inside of you, and to share their past. This is the source of prophetic dreams, of the feeling people call déjà vu, of nightmares that tragically come true. I will come tomorrow and bless your room as she did. It will give you a new shell of protection."

"No!" Realizing she might have insulted Celeste, Hailey quickly added, "If it is only spirits who come, I want them to."

"I was not thinking of the spirits of Leanna and her lover. I was concerned about the evil Leanna de Noux wanted to keep out."

"If there is any sign at all that I need such protection, I will not hesitate to send for you. But for now I . . ." Hailey hesitated. Words failed her. "I don't want to upset the balance."

"Excellent!" Celeste said, clapping her hands silently together. "You have great understanding for one who does not believe. And great empathy. But promise me one thing—if you ever begin to suspect that Leanna rather than you is making your decisions on how to act or think, don't assume you are strong enough to control her. Come to me and I will help you."

Frank brought them desert—pound cake and strawberries with crème fraîche. "Are you going to paint over the drawings?" he asked Hailey.

Hailey hadn't considered the matter.

"Yes," Celeste answered for her. "The woman who made them is dead. They have no use any longer."

"Did you mean that?" Hailey asked after Frank left.

"Don't trust him. Don't trust anyone who knew either of them. And don't tell anyone else about your dreams. This is a town that will take them seriously. And if Joseph Morgan did not kill Leanna de Noux . . ."

She left the thought unfinished but Hailey understood it far too well. "Frank will be expecting me to paint the wall now," she commented.

"The protection surrounding the room has already been broken. The drawings have served their purpose. Go ahead, paint."

A hot shower, a long walk and two more glasses of wine did not make Hailey sleepy. Nonetheless, she lay on her bed. The sheets felt so cool and smooth against her skin that she pulled off her nightshirt and lay naked between them, staring up at the ceiling fan, letting the motion of its blades lull her to sleep.

FIVE

The child wakes to the soft cries of her twin brother, caught in another of his terrible nightmares. She climbs out of bed and pads across the hall to wake him. The handle of his bedroom door is difficult for adults to turn, impossible for a three-year-old and she has no luck.

The cries continue, horrible sounds of terror and loss, muffled by the solid wood door. She runs down the long hall, past the guest room and bathroom to the huge corner room her father and mother share. The door is cracked open. Flickering candles light the room.

She is not supposed to be out of bed. The housekeeper, Jacqueline, has warned her of this and so she pauses in the doorway, shivering in her white cotton nightdress, one finger in her mouth, not certain if she wishes to be noticed, for if she is, she will never understand what she sees.

There are two large beds in the room, arranged close together along the inside wall. One is her father's. Often Leanna and her brother sleep in it when he is out of town. The one closer to her is her mother's and Leanna has never seen her leave it before.

Her mother is out of bed, sitting in her wheelchair, facing the mirror of her dressing table. Candles cover the table. Candles burn on the nightstand as well. Her mother wears a red satin gown with only thin gauze covering her still full breasts, a blanket over her wasted legs. Jacqueline stands behind her, brushing her mother's long dark hair. As she works, she chants in a low voice, in a language Leanna does not know an' Hailey does not recognize. There is a scent in

47

the air, cinnamon and sage. It comes from the candles perhaps, or the pot of oil one of the candles is heating.

"Are you in pain, madam?" Jacqueline pauses in her chanting to ask.

"A little. The oil makes it go away."

"Then more, madam," Jacqueline says and reaches into the pot, massaging the warm oil into mother's hands and feet.

Leanna hears footsteps on the stairs, takes a chance and slips into the room, hiding in the shadows between the huge armoire and the wall, carefully sliding the hamper toward her.

When she is found, she will be punished, but it is worth it to see.

Henri de Noux is a huge man who seems to fill the doorway. He wears a brown dressing gown. His legs and feet are bare. "Joanna," he calls softly.

Jacqueline turns the chair so mother faces him. He goes to her, ignoring the dark-skinned housekeeper standing silently behind her.

"My love," he whispers. "You are as beautiful as ever." He kisses her, the lightness of his touch so at odds with the passion in his voice, as if he dares not press against her skin and hurt her.

Leanna never touches her mother, not since the accident the year before.

Her mother winces. "I'm sorry," he whispers. "I want you so much."

As if on cue, Jacqueline wheels the chair to the side of Leanna's father's bed. The covers are thrown back. From her hiding place, Leanna watches her father standing beside it, one hand clutching a single lock of his wife's hair. Jacqueline unties the belt of his gown and sits on the edge of the bed. Her hands are moving across Henri's stomach. He penis grows hard and Jacqueline bends forward to kiss it before wrapping her lips around it.

Henri de Noux does not look at Jacqueline. His attention

is fixed entirely on his wife and her eyes are dry and calm. "My love," he whispers as Jacqueline continues to arouse him.

Finally, unable to hold back any longer, he thrusts the woman away and swings her around, taking her roughly from behind, his head turned toward his wife all the while.

The act is over as quickly as it began. "Forgive me," Leanna's father whispers to his wife, repeating the words while Jacqueline arranges her robe over her body.

Leanna takes advantage of the moment to crawl down the length of her father's bed toward the open door.

"Leave us," her father says.

"My mistress needs me," Jacqueline counters.

"I'll tend to her," he replies.

Jacqueline reaches the door just as Leanna does. She gives no indication that she sees the girl, but once they are in the privacy of the hall, she grips Leanna's wrist and leads her back toward her room.

"Why did you get up?" Jacqueline asks as they walk down the hall.

"Louis." As if on cue, her brother begins to cry again.

Jacqueline opens his door. Leanna follows her into the room and watches her lay a hand on the boy's forehead. "*Merde!* He is so warm." Jacqueline whispers softly into the boy's ear. He quiets. "Go back to bed, Leanna. I'll tend to him."

Leanna shakes her head, her dark heavy curls brushing her shoulders. "I help," she demands.

Jacqueline smiles, her teeth glistening against her painted lips. "Very well, little nurse. Come, we need water."

Jacqueline carries the basin and washcloth. Leanna, so pleased to be allowed to help, follows with a bottle of baby aspirin and a thermometer.

Louis cries out as Jacqueline wakes him, then grips her tightly until the terror of the dream subsides. "Mama," he whispers, clutching the woman.

Leanna wants to slap him. She wants to cry. She does neither.

Leanna is certain that her brother is very ill, for Jacqueline frowns when she reads the thermometer and makes Louis take four of the orange-flavored aspirin rather than two. She angles the floor fan upward so the draft won't blow directly on Louis, then strips off his shirt and begins to rub him down with cool water and camphor. When she is finished and he rests beneath a light blanket, she leaves his door cracked open and takes Leanna to her room. After she tucks the girl into bed, she sits beside her.

"Mama was up," Leanna says, not certain if that meant some sudden improvement in her illness.

"And in pain. When someone hurts all the time, the pain becomes unbearable. Do you understand, child?"

Leanna nods. "You helped?" she asks.

"I do everything I can for all of you, child," Jacqueline answers.

Leanna pulls the covers back. "Stay with me until I sleep."

Jacqueline's breath purrs in and out when Leanna slips from her bed and pads across the hall to her brother's room. He has thrown off his covers and lies, damp and shivering. His eyes are fever bright, looking not at her but deliriously somewhere near the place where she stands. Leanna retreats, closing the door behind her.

Jacqueline does not wake when Leanna returns to bed and presses her body against the woman's back.

Jacqueline's warmth is so comforting. The dream blurs with the child's closing eyes.

Someone screams outside. . . .

Hailey, trembling with a child's fear, sat up in bed, her back and shoulders tense.

"Louis!" she cried. The room seemed to reek of camphor and incense, sweat and semen. Hailey clutched the blanket to her chest and lay back down until the dream vanished completely and her trembling stopped.

Hailey got out of bed, and not bothering to find a caftan, sat naked in front of her screen, hurriedly recording the dream. After, shivering, she carried the cordless phone with her to the warmth of her bed. It was just after midnight, hardly late for Celeste.

There were so many questions Hailey had wanted to ask her that afternoon. She had not done so because she wanted to test the truth of each dream, to discover if they were Leanna's memories, or if her preoccupation with Leanna changed the dreams.

Hailey phoned Celeste. The voodooienne did not seem surprised to hear her voice. "There was a housekeeper—a mulatto, I believe—named Jacqueline, who raised Leanna. Jacqueline was also the father's mistress. She practiced voodoo. Is this right?" Hailey asked.

"I think so. Later I heard that the woman—"

"No! No more, Celeste. Just tell me if my facts are correct."

"You don't want to know the rest?"

"I'm afraid that my dreams and Leanna's are going to merge, and fact and fantasy get all jumbled together. I'll never know the truth then."

"Is the truth so important?"

"It is to me."

Celeste sighed. "I'll find someone who knew Leanna well and make certain."

"Thank you, Celeste." Hailey hung up and closed her eyes, eager now to dream. But if Leanna came to her again, she did not remember.

Hailey avoided her computer the following morning. Indeed, she drank a cup of iced coffee then dressed and walked to the Café du Monde. On the way, she bought a paper and spent the better part of an hour poring over the news. The paper discussed the possibility of a cholera epidemic if sanitation and immunizations did not improve in the poorer delta parishes.

Poor Louis. For a moment the past she had dreamed seemed so ancient that she forgot that the events in her dream must have taken place no earlier than 1960. For a moment she actually thought the boy's illness might have been something as exotic and lethal as cholera.

Yet thirty years ago, Louisiana had been a different state, Jacqueline a much different woman from a liberated creature like Celeste. Hailey could no more imagine her life than she could the ritually ordered existence of her husband's Hasidic grandparents in Kraków.

Ex-husband, she reminded herself with some annoyance, amazed that the divorce could still hold so much pain.

Did Jacqueline love Leanna's father? Tolerate him for the security he gave? Did she take pleasure in his body or only in his wealth? Or was she trapped by the demands of a powerful family?

Did she train the girl in her art out of love or revenge?

Hailey had no desire to wait for whatever guidance the spirit that had once been Leanna could offer through her dreams. Far better, she thought, to initiate the contact.

Instead of going home, she visited Celeste. The shop was more crowded this morning. Two women stood behind the beaded curtain discussing their problems with Celeste in French. Hailey waited her turn behind an arthritic, and overweight, Creole woman with a cane, and a little dark man in a business suit with a nervous tic on one side of his face. "Had it for months," the man said, pointing to his twitching cheek. "Mama Celeste gives me something to relax it."

"Have you ever seen a doctor?" Hailey asked, aware of how the arthritic woman's attention suddenly focused on her when she asked the question, as if Haley's doubt constituted a sacrilege.

"Yeah. Can't do nothing but give me something that makes me too sleepy to work. Maman Celeste, she knows why."

The woman nodded emphatically.

Celeste certainly does know how, Hailey thought, as she watched the money change hands behind the beaded curtain. Nonetheless, the clients looked satisfied when they left. And who was she to question them anyway? She was here for advice as well.

Though the three new arrivals waiting after her were browsing contentedly through the books in the main store, Hailey came straight to the point. "If Leanna is trying to contact me, might I be able to somehow help her?" she asked.

Celeste smiled knowingly. "Of course. If you'd been less uneasy when I came to your little room, I would have suggested it." Celeste began discussing options in a precise, almost scientific tone.

Hailey left the store with incense; *damiana* and *gotu kola* teas, oils, candles, fetishes; chants meticulously handwritten in red ink; a tape of sacred drums and a slim volume on contacting the dead. None of it came cheaply but, Hailey reminded herself, she never gave her novels away either.

"Start with the methods which make you feel most at ease," Celeste said as she carefully wrapped and bagged the purchases. "And don't be afraid to innovate. The gods reward creative petitioners."

Creativity would have to be utilized, Hailey decided, after the musky incense gave her a headache while the drums and chants seemed only distracting.

Considering what Joe Morgan's room was most likely used for, she tied the fetish to the headboard of the bed. While she heated water for her tea, she placed the candles on either side of her computer monitor and the envelope containing the news stories on Leanna's death in front of one of the candles.

As Celeste had instructed, she lifted one of her kitchen bowls with plums, poured a few drops of rum on top of them and placed that in front of the window as an offering to Legba, the master of the barrier between the living and the dead.

By then the teakettle had begun to whistle. Hailey brewed Celeste's tea deliberately strong, adding honey to mask its bitter taste. It seemed to take effect almost immediately, heightening her senses. She lit the candles and it seemed that her worktable suddenly became a veritible voodoo altar to creativity. She giggled, not because the actions struck her as silly but because they seemed so right. These were the conditions Leanna herself might have wanted had she chosen writing as a profession.

Had Joe Morgan worked like this?

Before she sat down, Hailey fixed a second cup of tea. She dabbed the oil onto her forehead, the backs of her hands, the tips of her fingers, then lit the bright red candles.

"Leanna," she whispered as beads of melted wax rolled down the candles like slowly falling tears.

Hailey was always astonished at how quickly time seemed to pass when she entered the world of her books. Yet she was always aware of the passing of time, the words falling into place on her screen, the all too real effort of creation.

This time, the candles had been fresh when she began. When she noticed them again, they were burned down to their holders, their wax puddling on the wood table beneath them.

Her head pounded; the pain so intense that it seemed to radiate through her body. Migranes must feel like this, she thought. She'd begun to dig the bottle of aspirin out of her desk drawer when her stomach did an abrupt twist, forcing her to rush to the toilet. Though she'd had a large breakfast, all she vomited was bile. Her legs felt too weak to hold her and so she sat beside the toilet until she felt steady enough to move.

The experiment had hardly been worth it, she thought, then she noticed that the file that had been twelve pages long when she started was listed as having seventeen pages now. With no idea of what she would find, Hailey brought it up on the screen.

*   *   *

. . . Better. Not as easy as entering your dream yet now I think. I feel. In this body which makes me a welcome guest, I move. I remember. Still, using your hands like this requires so much effort and I have always hated these damned machines.

Don't fear my presence, Hailey Martin. I respect what you do, your search for my truth, your trust. Do what you will with the account when you are done with it. I give permission as my payment for your help,.

I do not know when I first realized what Jacqueline meant to my father. Once I did, I made certain that she loved me as much as he did. It was an easy task. My father, Henri de Noux, practiced law throughout the state and kept a demanding schedule. During the day, and often at night as well, Jacqueline, Louis and I were alone in the big house near Audubon Park.

Five years following Louis's illness, Mama took advantage of a rare night when Jacqueline was ill in bed to call me to her room and asked me to go down to the kitchen and bring her bottle of pain pills from the cabinet where Jacqueline kept them. I saw her expression. I thought she must hurt terribly. Though I was never to go near the medicine cabinet, I did what Mama asked and brought some juice as well. My mother thanked me but did not take the pills until after I went to bed.

She may have tried to save herself at the end, at least the doctor thought so, for Papa found her half out of bed, her arms stretched out, reaching. . . .

I had killed my mother. I was eight years old.

Papa told Jacqueline that Mama must have saved up her pain pills, hiding them away until she had a lethal dose. He said this in my presence so I would understand exactly what I'd done, and feel some guilt.

He seemed more angered than grief-stricken by Mama's death. He forbade us to ever mention her name in his presence though I could see her memory all too often in the shifts of emotion in his eyes. He was always a cruel, demanding man but he loved her as he did no one else.

After, Jacqueline took care of us as she always had. Louis grew from a fretful toddler into a sickly child. The measles had left him with weak eyes. Bright light gave him terrible headaches. Like my mother, he did not bear pain well and his complaints were as grating on my father as my own manners were ingratiating.

Louis would be sent to bed to rest or to cure the headaches or the colds or the weariness he always seemed to feel. Jacqueline would go to him, doing what she could with her herbs and camphor before sending, as she inevitably did, for a more acceptable physician. I would help her in the work, pouring the hot water into the metal basins, stirring it to dissolve the salt, chanting with her the words of healing and protection.

In time, Jacqueline came to love me. And I found that, surprisingly, I cared almost as much for her as I did for what she could teach me.

As soon as our life settled into a regular pattern, Jacqueline began hiring a mulatto girl to sit with Louis and me on the nights my father was gone so that she could leave the house herself.

When it became clear to me that she was not mentioning these excursions to my father, I decided to sleep in her bed one night to see when she returned.

It was nearly dawn when she stole into the room. She wore one of her older dresses, now mud-caked, the hem ripped. She carried her shoes. They were clean, but her feet, like her clothes, were coated with mud. My head was covered by the blankets. I saw all this, and her expression of alarm when she realized I was in the room. I peeked at her through nearly closed eyes as she backed slowly from the room. A moment later I heard the door to my father's room close, the shower running in his private bath., When she returned wrapped in one of the huge bath sheets, carrying her dirty clothes in a tight bundle under her arm, I was sitting up in bed, ready to talk to her.

"Where have you been?" I asked.

"Visiting," she replied.

"There's mud on your clothes."

"The car broke down."

"Papa will have it fixed." As I said the words, I knew she would never mention the event to him. Nor would I. Unless I had to. It would have pained me to do so, but I would have my way. "Or maybe he'll buy you a new one."

"I made it run."

Jacqueline could not change a tire. "It hasn't rained in days. There's only one place you could have gotten so muddy. You were in the bayou, weren't you?" I asked. I already knew something of what went on there and the mystery of it fascinated me.

I could not have been more than ten but I was right. When she replied, I knew she lied. I ignored the denial. "I won't say a word to Papa if you take me."

"You're too young."

"How old were you?"

"It's different," she said.

Years later, she explained how she felt in that moment. I had the power. She sensed it in me. She longed to have me trained. Yet, I was also white and wealthy—Henri de Noux's daughter. I had just made my First Communion. I went to the best Catholic school in the city. The nuns had sharp eyes, and if they sensed what she'd done and told my father, her comfortable life would be ruined. Yet she also knew that I would make good my threat. It is to my credit that she agreed to my demands as quickly as she did.

Hailey began to understand exactly what sort of a child Leanna de Noux must have been. She would have worn the drab parochial check skirts and round-collared white blouses with a flair Hailey had never demonstrated. Her hair would have been perfectly combed, her grades undoubtedly excel-

lent, her demeanor so perfect that none of her teachers would
have realized how much she despised them.

Hailey had hated girls like her. To her, some essential part
of their souls was missing. It was clear even now in Leanna,
clear even though she had moved beyond material concerns.
Leanna de Noux cared about little but herself. Hailey read
on.

*We did not have another chance to go until All Hallow's
Eve. Earlier that night, Louis and I had gone out with our
friends. He had painted-on whiskers and plastic teeth and a
brown fuzzy blanket for his werewolf's pelt. All of it looked
utterly ridiculous when combined with his thick black-
framed glasses. I wore some of Jacqueline's gaudiest
jewelry, a long, flowing skirt and a knit shawl that had
belonged to Mama. I remember the costume well because
Papa took our picture and put in the scrapbook.*

*Soon after we returned with our full bags of candy and
coins, he left for a conference in Memphis. The colored girl
came within the hour. Whatever Jacqueline gave Louis to
make him sleep knocked him out so quickly that she became
concerned and did not want to go. I made her. That night
was my night. I would not be denied by his weakness.*

*Jacqueline dressed me in a simple gingham jumper that
any colored child might have worn. She tied up my hair and
wrapped a red cotton scarf around my head.*

*Some great adventure was about to begin. I felt it as I
stood there, letting myself be ordered about, then even more
potently as I tiptoed behind her into the dark garage.*

*Jacqueline made me lie down in the back of the car and
covered me with a blanket. I remained there until we
crossed the river on the Canal Street ferry and moved south
beyond the lights and the streets full of people who might
recognize the car or me.*

*She didn't always travel so far, she told me. It was on my
account that she did so.*

*I didn't contradict her; it was hardly worth the trouble it
would cause.*

*We crossed the river again at Braithwaite and drove a
few more miles before turning onto a gravel road. Eventually, I saw the flickering of bonfires, heard the steady beat
of some huge drum. Jacqueline pulled up on some high
ground between a pair of old trucks. We both took off our
shoes before we got out. The ground was so muddy I would
have lost mine easily.*

*"You are SueAnn," Jacqueline whispered. "My sister's
child."*

*"SueAnn," I repeated. So that was to be my name for the
night.*

*"Keep in the shadows. If you're recognized, you can
never come back," she reminded me.*

*I looked at the dozens of cars parked around us, at the
figures moving around the bonfires. I thought of Jacqueline
and the little colored girl that took care of us without asking
for a fee. Who could have stopped my training when the
rituals went on every day throughout the city?*

*No, Papa would not be able to forbid it. And Jacqueline
would not dare.*

*I pulled my hand out of hers and walked confidently
toward the soft firelight.*

Leanna might have written more, Hailey thought. After
all, she'd had hours. Perhaps Leanna couldn't type. Even
without the sickness, Hailey far preferred the dreams. She
read the opening sentences again. No, she did not fear
Leanna. She had opened her mind and the invitation had
been accepted. As long as it took an act of will on her part,
Hailey could always refuse to cooperate.

The afternoon was almost over. Now that the headache
was fading, and the nausea with it, Haley felt energized, as
if those hours had been spent napping rather than in a trance.
It occurred to her that, while Leanna felt compelled to relive
her childhood, Hailey could easily visit the places Leanna
had frequented as an adult.

She closed her eyes and recalled the bar where Joe
Morgan first saw Leanna. As she expected, it came to her

with all the clarity of the dream. She might have been standing there, staring at the name written above the long wood bar: Twilight Time.

She checked the phone book. The place was still in business.

She didn't dress in her usual clothes. Instead, she pulled on a pair of tight black jeans and a black scoop-neck top that clung to her breasts. Her earrings dangled against her bare shoulders. For the first time in months, she decided to paint her nails. When she opened the bureau drawer where she kept her cosmetics, she noticed a bag from the perfume shop down the block. Inside was a tiny spray bottle of Norell cologne and a tube of red lipstick.

"You bitch!" Hailey whispered. "You used the hours I gave you to go shopping!" Eighty dollars was missing from her wallet. It couldn't have been just for the cosmetics. Leanna must have purchased something else.

Hailey pulled open the drawers, checked the closet again. Nothing.

As she returned her wallet to her purse, she saw a bag in the bottom of it. Inside, wrapped in dark blue felt, was a thin knife in a black suede sheath. The handle was flat, the guard curved. It fit as beautifully in her hand as it would in a boot or strapped to her thigh.

A gift like this was hardly something she needed. She checked the bag to see if there was a receipt and found a note instead.

I know you are as capable of using this as I once was, it read. *If you pry too deeply into my affairs, you may very well need it. Please heed this warning. I would not wish my tragic end on another. Leanna.*

The writing was not in Hailey's upright, precise hand. Instead it slanted far to the right. The loops were long and pointed at the tips. The *t*s were crossed with a flourish. In spite of the beauty of it, there was hesitation to the writing. It alternately seemed that the pen had pressed too hard and barely at all against the paper. In other places the letters were shaky. Nonetheless, the signature flowed across the bottom of the page with every flourish the live Leanna must have used.

None of this surprised her. The contents of the note did.

The first week she lived in her house in the Wisconsin woods, Hailey had been unable to sleep. Every small sound made her wake and think how she was too far away from her neighbors, even farther from the police. The phone at her bedside didn't calm her. The gun and knife she purchased on her next trip to town helped just a little. It was the lessons in self-defense that allowed her gradually to relax. After a while the fear went away but the training remained. She clenched her fist, remembering how meticulously she'd been taught to make it. She tested the balance of the knife.

How perfectly Leanna had controlled Hailey's body, and her memories. Oddly, that perfection gave Hailey no fear. And Leanna's warning only made her more determined to continue with this strange affair. Through dreams only, she reminded herself. The other way was uncontrollable—and painful. She'd never attempt any sort of merging again.

She placed the note into the envelope where she kept the news stories of the murder. Someday, it might prove useful. Afterward, with Leanna's cologne scenting her hair and the knife in the rear pocket of her oversized purse, she left in search of Leanna's past.

The night was useless. All Hailey learned from it was how long five years could be.

Hailey spoke to the tavern's new owner. From him, she learned that all but one of the employees were new hires. The veteran would be starting her shift in an hour.

Hailey waited for the woman in the same place in the rear courtyard where Joe Morgan had sat. The courtyard was as deserted now in the chilly December wind as it had been after the storm. The doors were open to dissipate the cigarette smoke and she heard the voices and laughter inside.

How lonely Morgan must have felt as he sat here, and how well she understood that feeling. She ordered a second beer, drowning in a misery she created from her natural empathy.

A thin girl in a pair of stretch jeans came outside and walked over to her. "You the writer?" she asked.

"Yes. Are you the one who worked here at the time of the murder?"

"That's me. Give me a minute and I can sit down." She returned with another beer for Hailey and one for herself. "On the house," she said as she settled stiffly into the seat across from Hailey. In the dim light, Hailey could see the fine lines in her face, the age her lithe body had not yet revealed.

"Lots of people came by at first," she said. "Mostly reporters trying to get a fix on the sort of man Morgan was."

"What did you tell them?"

"Nothing. I really didn't know him well enough. I'm sorry."

He must have had acquaintances, at least one close friend. Hadn't the news articles mentioned a friend? "Did anyone else come by? Someone who might have known him?"

The woman frowned, concentrating on the past. "There was just one, a cop a little younger than Morgan. He wasn't working on the case, though, because he'd been partners with Morgan on the force in Lake Charles. He said he came to ask some personal questions."

"He didn't leave a card, did he?"

"No. But he didn't have to. His name was Eddie O'Brien."

"How can you remember?" Hailey asked.

"One of the other girls here had dated a guy by the same name. She'd been a real user—pot and coke and LSD—and her Eddie was the supplier and a real badass sort. So of course we ribbed her after the cop showed up. His name was no great coincidence, though. There's a lot of O'Brien's in this town. At least this one's on the force. Cops don't move around much."

"What was he like?" Hailey wasn't sure what she hoped for from the answer. Some clue, maybe, that the man would take her situation seriously.

"We joked a little about his name. I remember that I was sorry I couldn't help him, because he seemed so concerned."

Concerned. That was good. Hailey definitely wanted to find someone who was concerned. "Did he come here more than once?" she asked.

"He might of, but then Morgan killed himself. Case closed, I suppose."

The kind of ending a novelist might dream up on a particular tight deadline. Too pat to ring true. After the woman had gone, Hailey laid a five under the beer bottle and left.

Once home, she lit some of the incense Celeste had given her then went to bed. The smoke made her sneeze. She cracked open the balcony door and lay in bed, shivering until she finally slept.

. . . The girl moves on the edge of the sparse crowd, beating her bare feet against the spongy ground. Once this had been a courtyard garden, the houses around it fashionable and ornate. The old iron railings that had not been salvaged for other houses have rusted, the beams of the balconies have rotted from the damp.

Leanna had stolen through the sentinels, mingling with the crowd. The white cotton dress she wears is soft against her breasts, the loose skirt beats against her bare legs, the fabric cool in the heat of the summer evening. Smoke rises from the torches around the center ring. The drums set a soft, pulsing rhythm, the chants of the devoted are barely a murmur. This is a city gathering, best not to make themselves too obvious.

Cowards! Fools to think the gods were not insulted by their timidity! Leanna moves into the center of the circle, her long hair brushing against her back, the gown slipping off one shoulder as she dances, merging with the music. Later, she falls to her hands and knees, beating her palms against the earth, howling ever louder.

Someone hands her a glass of rum. She drinks it eagerly. Another. Another.

(How could the child not be drunk? Hailey wondered.) Yet the brew seems to have no effect save to make her movements more frantic. Finally, she drags herself forward until she lies at the feet of the night's king. As he looks down at her, she rolls on her back, ripping at her clothes, inviting him to take her.

"*Yemaya*," she cries, rubbing her hands against the side of the man's legs. "*Yemaya*," she whispers, begging now.

The king, a lean, dark man with a beaded tattoo running down one cheek, claps his hands once then follows with a series of gestures. A pair of men step forward. One carries a huge staff that was perhaps once twisted branches. Now its form is obscured by carved and painted grimacing faces and curving multicolored snakes. The king takes it and, with a quick downward thrust, buries its point in the earth between Leanna's spread legs. She quivers but does not cry out.

The second man brings a rooster, which he waves in one hand. It flaps frantically, trying to escape until the moment the king pulls a knife from the blue cord around his waist and deftly cuts its throat.

The blood flows around Leanna's white dress, across her bare breasts, her dark, tangled hair. And the king dances as the bird gives up its lifeblood in dark drops that sprinkle welcome as holy water over the eager crowd.

"*Yemaya*," Leanna cries again, and sitting up, she begins to stroke the carvings on the staff in a seductive motion that gave hints of the woman she will become.

The king turns to her, his jaw clenched in passion and fury. He pulls the staff from the ground. The crowd makes way for him as he disappears into the shadows of the building. The ritual ends for the night.

Later, Leanna finds him alone in his little house on St. Claude. Her dress and face are still covered with blood. Her eyes are still bright from the ritual. As she faces the man, now drained of all power and energy, she knows she is the stronger one. Her will shall prevail. "How can you refuse one possessed by the gods?" she asks.

"Go and wash," he tells her, refusing to look at her.

Does he feel her power? Could he really fear a child? "I offered myself. I was possessed and you refused me," she says again, incredulously.

"You've read the history of our beliefs. You knew the right names to say, the right motions to go through but you lie about the rest. Go back to your father, and the nuns who teach you. You will not pervert the names of our gods any longer. You will learn nothing more from me, spoiled child. Never again."

"You said I have talent, that I have power."

"There are many kinds of power and I am no fool."

"You'll be sorry." It is the threat of an adult, not a child.

"Leanna de Noux, I already am."

And she goes, running barefoot through the dark streets reeking of damp earth and ancient trees and full blooming roses. She runs heedless of the soiled white dress or the tears rolling down her face, past the ever grander houses until she reaches home.

Once her house is in sight, she stops to discard her gown in a neighbor's trash can then throws a pebble against an upstairs window in her own home. A moment later, Louis lets her in the side door.

She walks proudly past him, a native queen with no need of clothing to hide her shame. She washes in his bathroom then slips on one of his shirts and sits cross-legged on the bed.

He does not seem to notice her exposed sex beneath the open white shirt. Or if he does, he does not care. His face is much the same as hers but some differences in their personalities makes him look less attractive. Perhaps it is the glasses that make his eyes rounder and far too prominent, or the worried look that pinches his lips together so fiercely. "What did you see?" he asks.

"Everything. And the feeling, like nothing I have felt before. For a time, Louis, the *loa* possessed me. I was not myself."

"You listened too much to Jacqueline," he complains. His voice is unlike hers, still a childish whine. He does not believe, indeed he seems to view her adventure with distaste.

(Hailey noted his use of past tense, as if Jacqueline had also died or left the house.)

"Did anyone notice I was gone?" Leanna asks.

"No one went into your room. Belly came by with a my homework. He wanted to talk to you but I told you were sick."

"Perfect." She kisses him lightly on the lips.

"I've been reading one of Papa's old books on religion in Haiti. Some of the practices are quite unusual. You might want to borrow it."

"If it's anything like this one on African myths and legends, it will only put me to sleep. You're the scholar, Louis. I'm like Laveau or Dr. John. I learn by doing." She kisses him again and leaves. Her room is a child's room, a canopy bed draped with cream-colored lace, blue wicker dressers, vanity and mirror. The space is spotless. She keeps it that way so no one else will have an excuse to enter and find the secrets she hides beneath her hair ribbons and lace-trimmed lingerie.

Before she retires, she carefully removes a tiny fetish she has hidden on the frame above the door, reciting a prayer to St. Cristopher as she places it in a drawer.

SIX

"I'd like to get in contact with one of your men, Officer Edward O'Brien," Hailey said to the uniformed clerk at the front desk of the police administration building.

The young woman, absorbed in what sounded like a personal telephone conversation, sighed and smoothed back her short dark hair. "Just a second," she said to the person on the other end of the line, then she checked the roster. "Detective O'Brien is at second dictrict this morning. Would you like to leave a message?"

Hailey had hoped for that response. A written introduction, however brief and vague, was preferable to a surprise phone call. She took a sealed envelope out of her handbag and handed it to the woman. "Would you please see that he gets this?" she asked.

"Shall we send the envelope interoffice or would you like us to fax the contents?"

"Send it sealed," Hailey said, and watched the clerk write *Personal* beneath the name.

Hailey returned to her apartment. She had correspondence to handle, details to work out on a spring signing tour for a book to be published in April. It should have been mundane work, easily finished, but she couldn't concentrate on it. The room had a will of its own. What went on here must concern Leanna de Noux and nothing else.

Hailey called her agent. As she expected, Charlie Mullen was intrigued by the story she told of the drawing on the wall—just the drawing, no need to let him think she was headed for another breakdown. He became excited as always by her excitement. All that faded when she told him that she intended to use the actual murder as the base for her novel.

"It's not like I don't have experience in that field," Hailey countered. *Watching Aaron Die* was similar enough, she reasoned.

"But these are real people. Your characters have relatives. Relatives have lawyers. And I don't have to remind you that publishers and some writers have a lot of money to lose."

"Do you mean I can't do this? The story is public domain, after all. Besides, the murderer seems to have had no close family and the victim's parents are both dead."

Hailey knew her voice had risen. She hoped he understood from that how much she wanted to write this. A long pause followed and she knew Charlie was thinking of some way to make the story work. When he finally spoke, his tone was soothing. Charlie liked his writers to be happy, wanted them to be successful as much for their sake as his own. It was this personal attention to her needs as well as her career that had kept Hailey with him for so long. "Is there anyone in the victim's family that can give permission for the story?" he asked.

Hailey thought of the handwritten note. Would that constitute permission? Perhaps in New Orleans. "There's a brother," she said.

"Talk to him."

"Does the decision rest on that?"

"If you want a hardcover book, if you want publicity, if you want any advance at all for the story, it does."

They discussed a few other matters. As soon as they were done, Hailey called the station where O'Brien was working. The letter was on his desk. Now her phone message would be with it, both waiting for him when he returned from lunch.

She had written a short note to him to emphasize her interest in the case. Whatever else she told him would definitely have to wait until they met face-to-face and she could see what sort of a man he was and how much he would allow himself to believe.

She went over her account of last night's dreams, filling in details she'd overlooked earlier. Leanna had been such a tiny, beautiful child. Yet, Hailey had sensed the undercurrent to her perfect manners all too well. The child was what Bill would have called a "hedonist" even at that early age. And as the beat of the drums touched her body, Leanna had responded in a way that seemed far too adult.

But if she had believed, truly believed, wouldn't her response have been natural?

Hailey, no more than agnostic in her most fervent moments, considered this.

Leanna had believed.

The beating seemed to return to fill her little room. Hailey found herself sinking easily into the trance she'd accomplished with difficulty yesterday. She saw the bayou, the fire, the flapping white dresses of the dancers. The adult Leanna is at their center, her arms raised, her head thrown back. And on the edge of the crowd she sees a tall man she recognizes from somewhere. As she focuses on him, a harsh ringing flung Hailey back into her body; this time, so suddenly that much of the vision was lost to her.

"Hello," she said, gripping the receiver as if it were anchored to the wall and she about to float away.

"Mrs. Martin? This is Detective O'Brien. You sent a puzzling note. Can you explain it to me?"

"Yes, but I need to meet you first. It's important that we talk about Joe Morgan."

"What are you, a witness? An old friend of his?"

"Neither. A writer."

"I see." His voice sounded suddenly remote.

"But it's more than that." How could she explain with anything but the truth? "You see, I live in his room above Sonya's Kitchen and I . . . well, I found something. I really can't speak about it on the phone."

He took the bait, wrote down her address and promised to be there soon.

She spent the time she had going over her notes and organizing her data, pausing only long enough to comb her hair and freshen her lipstick. She'd learned when she was very young that professional first impressions always improved the odds, even in the most difficult situations.

Ed O'Brien didn't look like a person willing to believe in ghosts, but then he didn't look like her idea of a policeman either. He was tall and lanky, with red hair, a pale face dotted with freckles, ruddy cheeks and eyes bright like those of a kid rather than a man of thirty-something years. The round Irish nose made her think of Peter Rabbit, not Popeye Doyle. Maybe he could be an officer in a TV town like Mayberry. Not New Orleans. Not even Lake Charles, from what she knew of it. And he was a detective, as well.

But what astonished her more was her instinctive response to him.

All her life, Hailey had the gift for recognizing extreme people—those truly dangerous, as well as those she could always trust. Those instincts were still alive. She had intended to be guarded in what she told this man. Not anymore.

Hailey showed O'Brien the wall, repeated Frank Berlin's story and what Celeste had discovered concerning the room. He listened quietly, his interest as much in her as in her words. Then, ignoring Celeste's warning, she described her dreams with an urgency that astonished her. She wanted someone else, someone other than a believer like Celeste, to understand what she was going through. Since O'Brien had known Joe Morgan, she was careful to describe Morgan as precisely as she was able.

Her skill with the last had the desired effect. He stared at her incredulously, not willing to believe yet unable to dismiss her account as merely imagination.

He read the accounts, including Leanna's handwritten

note. Through it all, he said about a dozen words. His expression never changed.

"I know this is hard to believe but if there was a way to touch someone from beyond the grave then Leanna de Noux . . ."

"Would be the one to do it? Yes, I understand that well enough. I also know that a little imagination, spurred on by a healthy dose of gris-gris on the wall can cause one hell of a strange dream, particularly in tourists who aren't used to all the mumbo jumbo going on in this town."

"I described Joe Morgan perfectly, didn't I?"

He nodded. "The case made national news. Maybe you read about it and saw his picture. When you heard his name, your mind pulled his face from your unconscious. As for the rest of the description, yeah, you're accurate but most alkies pretty much fit Joe's pattern."

"You sound like . . . a therapist." She had almost admitted something—her best kept secret—to a man she wanted so hard to impress with her sanity.

"That just one facet of my job."

"All right." Hailey tried to think of some way to convince him but none came to her. "I'm not asking you to believe. I know I wouldn't believe it myself if I hadn't experienced her . . . presence, I suppose you could call it . . . inside me. But could you at least help me? There are things I need to know."

For the first time since he'd arrived, O'Brien smiled and his little boy face looked even younger. "All right. I'll take you up on the coffee you offered. I don't see how it would hurt to talk to you about a few things, especially since Joe's dead."

Now that he'd agreed to help, Hailey felt less anxious. She poured him the last of the pot, then began brewing a second. Hopefully, he'd stay long enough to share it. Though her attention was centered on Leanna's story, it occurred to her that O'Brien was the first person besides Celeste and her landlord that she had invited into her room.

With that came a rush of pleasure at having him here, along with the realization that, in spite of her deliberate isolation, she had been lonely.

"You were Joe's partner?" she began when they were settled across the table from each other.

"For three years in Lake Charles, until he got the ax. Afterwards, he moved here. He worked for a security company for a while and was let go from there too. Then he did a little bit of writing, crime reporting mostly. I moved here a year after he did. We saw one another from time to time, sometimes socially, more often when he wanted information."

"You say that he drank. Why did he drink?"

O'Brien settled into his chair. "It's like this. Some cops go home and pound the walls. The worst go home and pound their wives and kids. The rest of us find some other way to cope with the pressures of our job. Joe coped through booze. No one thing drove him to drink, it was just a bunch of little things, the stresses that add up day after day. I guess he started with a taste for rye. Over the years, I watched him develop an intimate relationship with it."

"Did you see him after he met Leanna de Noux?"

"A couple of times. He loved her like he'd never loved his wife or his family or anyone. I didn't like Leanna much but I liked seeing Joe so passionate about someone, especially since he was drinking less."

"For her?"

"For himself. You see, one of them had to be on their toes. Her father didn't approve of him. Neither did her ex."

"Carlo Bucci." Hailey had managed to find a brief mention of him in a feature on the case.

"Big Booch. Yeah, he tried to keep a grip on her even after the divorce."

"Did he file first or did she?"

"She did. He didn't want any part of it but the de Noux . . . Well, they're all alike. Once they make up their minds about something, it's impossible to change them. The kids both took after old Henri. Other lawyers used to call Henri the Pit Bull because he'd hang onto a case long after anyone else would have given up."

"And Leanna was like her father?"

"No matter how hard the Booch threatened her, she wouldn't back down and abandon the divorce. Losing her was a blow to his business and his pride, especially the last since she took her first lovers even before she walked out of his house."

"Joe Morgan told you this?"

O'Brien laughed. "You must be just starting out on this novel of yours or you'd know. In this town there's petty crime and major larceny and at the top of both lists there's Big Booch. Cops take a lot of interest in what goes on in his life."

"Crime boss?" Hailey asked, wondering if she were revealing her ignorance with her choice of words.

"Crime law. First counsel to the cons. Hijack a truck and get caught in the act? See Booch. RICO and IRS problems? Booch can help. Slit the throat of some poor colored guy whose only mistake was seeing a pack of money change hands outside the box he'd crawled into to sleep off a drunk? Booch can get you acquitted." From the bitter way he spoke at the end, Hailey knew he'd worked on the last case.

"Do you think Carlo Bucci killed his wife?"

She detected no mirth in O'Brien's laughter. "Hell, no, Joe Morgan did it. Everybody knows."

"I don't believe it. Do you?"

"You've got the line to the expert. Ask Leanna."

"She seems to be on a schedule of her own," Hailey replied. Her tone was as flippant as his remark. She hadn't meant it that way and he appeared to understand that.

"Look, Mrs. Martin . . ."

"Miss, please."

"All right, *Miss* Martin. I've worked with psychics on a couple of occasions, so I do have a little bit of respect for the so-called forces beyond our control. I'm not sure that what you tell me is the truth, though I think you believe it, but I have to warn you. If, and I stress if, Joe didn't kill Leanna, then it could have been an arranged hit. In that case Leanna might not have known the guys who did it."

"So she's solving the crime through me. It makes sense."

"In a way, I suppose it does. And I suppose you also know that if Joe didn't commit the crime, then the ones who did will have a lot of interest in what you're up to."

"I intend to be careful."

"I'd say you already made a mistake—you're talking to me."

"I am because I . . ." She fumbled for the right words and went on. "I'm not naive. My telling you the truth has nothing to do with your being a police officer. I just trust you, partly because Morgan trusted you, mostly because it feels right. I don't know how to explain my reason any other way."

"I'd say you did a pretty good job. Now, what kind of experience do you have for detective work?"

She smiled ruefully. "None."

He placed a hand over his coffee cup when she reached for the pot. "I do have to go," he said. "No, I won't mention this meeting to anyone."

"One more thing, please. Did you ever meet Leanna's brother?"

"Louis? Yeah. I went out a couple of times with him and Joe and Leanna. He was a hell of a lawyer then, better than his father some people said, until the murder. Afterward, I hear that his eyes gave out and he passed a lot of his clients onto other lawyers in his firm. About five years ago, his partners bought him out and he moved his office back to the one his father used on Royal Street. Of course, he doesn't have to work. Henri was loaded. Now Louis is the sole heir."

"A mystery writer would say that makes him a prime suspect."

O'Brien only shrugged.

Hailey thought of the Garden District house, the magnificent grounds, all speaking so eloquently of old money and genteel Creole manners. "Did the brother approve of Joe Morgan?" she asked.

"They got along. How well, I couldn't say. In the last couple years of his life, Joe was a guy most people just tolerated. Maybe Joe seemed a little less tarnished after the Booch, or maybe Louis was happy to have someone else keeping an eye on his sister for a change."

"How did Joe pay his rent?"

"Criminal investigations, then crime reporting. He ended working for one of the local TV stations. He'd interview witnesses before the film crews got there. It saved time and they never had to worry about whether he was fit to go on the air."

"Would he have been?" Hailey asked. Both Berlin and O'Brien had said Morgan cut back on his drinking at the end.

"Maybe. That didn't solve the problem, though. They had to be sure."

"Did he like his work?"

"He never talked about it, or anything else that would have a bearing on this case." O'Brien stood and grabbed his suit coat off the back of the chair. "I really don't think I can be much help to you."

"Is there a way I could see the investigators' file?"

"It's buried somewhere, rather deep considering the Booch. I might be able to do some fast talking and get my hands on it. But you? I doubt it."

"Talk to the investigating officers?"

"To put it politely, the detective who handled this likes his cases to stay closed," he said with disgust.

"Call you if I need something checked out?"

"You can. What I can do depends on what you ask." He slipped his coat on as he walked the few steps to her door.

Was he anxious to leave, or only guilty because he could do so little to help her? Could she be opening some old wound? "Mr. O'Brien, one last question. You went to the Twilight Time and asked about Joe. Why did you still care?"

He responded with a blank look followed by a wry smile. "You don't have much experience in police work, do you? Joe and I were partners. We put our lives in one another's hands. Of course I cared. Even if I thought he was guilty."

"I'm sorry, I should have understood."

"Most people don't actually. But I would like you to ask Leanna one thing—whatever made her choose you?"

There was no insult in his tone, only curiosity. "I'm not the first person who's rented this room since the murder, so that can't be the reason," Hailey replied carefully. "But I am . . . open to people. Empathy is the mark of a good writer, or so we writers say."

After she walked him to the door, they shook hands. "Empathy," he said, winking as he looked down at her. "Say hello to Joe for me when he shows up again."

After O'Brien left, Hailey stood with her back to the door, looking at her little room the way she might some particularly interesting character she met on the street. The room itself knew everything, but the souls inside—one living and two dead—were in the dark.

"Come to me tonight, Joe Morgan," she whispered. She spoke with the same breathless passion she might use to a lover, then laughed.

Her ghosts would not be mocked. She spent a terrible sleepless night until at dawn they forgave her.

SEVEN

The gallery was crowded earlier, but after the jazz trio stopped their playing and the coffee and cookies had been devoured, the crowd thinned. Eventually, the outside doors were locked and the window drapes closed, so the invitation-only party could begin.

The sleeveless black crepe dress she wears is tight over the bodice, flaring slowly to a long loose skirt with an uneven hem. The tips of it brush her ankles and the ankle straps of her backless, high-shoes. Hailey, observing the room through Leanna's eyes, catches a glimpse of her in a carved wood-framed mirror, sees her dark hair hanging loose from a cloisonne barette at the crown, violet highlights accentuated by the darkness of the dress. Leanna picks up a glass of wine from the table. The server eyes her, his interest sexual rather than legal. He does not ask her age.

A man moves confidently through the group. He is about her height, his slim build made masculine by his broad shoulders. When he takes off his tailored suitcoat she sees powerful arms, pale olive skin covered with dark hair.

She's noticed him at other places, glimpsing him occasionally in the back rooms of the taverns she frequents. And once, at one of the few voodoo gatherings she's attended since her return to the city, she saw someone who looked much like him, a rare pale face in the dark-skinned crowd.

"Michael, who is that?" she asks her escort for the night, a tall young man with an earnest expression and fleshy, shiny lips.

He follows her gesture, stares a moment. "I think it's Carlo Bucci," he replies.

"Ahhh." A breathy sound that expands in her throat. A sound filled with all the possibilities of her thoughts.

Her papa has mentioned the man's name often enough on the nights he and his children were home to dine with one another. An unscrupulous man, even a dangerous one, and old Henri despises him.

Ah, how pleasant that he was also so beautiful.

The young man with her is a friend of her brother's. Michael worships her, so passionately that he rarely looks at her, and speaks only to answer a direct question. He stops to speak to someone while she moves on, circling closer to Carlo until they stand side by side in front of an outrageous vase, a single Gaudi shaped pillar of fused glass. Its price is far beyond that of the lovelier and more delicate pieces in the show.

"Would you call this rococo, bad taste or merely outrageously overpriced, Carlo Bucci?" she asks without looking at him.

"Actually, I was about to purchase it, Leanna de Noux," he replies.

"You know my name?"

"I know of you. I asked after the night I saw you dance."

"What did you think of that?"

"That you're a heretic. You danced for yourself and no one else." As he speaks those last few words, his hand closes around her wrist. Slowly, giving her plenty of time to say something or to pull away, he leads her through the crowd and out the side door. A passage leads to a courtyard. The glow from second-story windows and from the street-lights shining through the passage and reflecting off the low clouds above them gives the only light to the space.

She laughs, delightfully and without a hint of uneasiness. She might be a child sneaking off without permission to meet a friend.

"Do you know who I am or only my name?" he asks.

"I know both."

"What else?"

"Other people's opinions. Do you really want to hear them? It isn't a night for insults, after all."

He shakes his head. "No," he says after a moment, though she can see him well enough.

He offers her a cigarette. As he lights the match, she notices his hands first, the well-manicured nails and long fingers; then his eyes, dark and large, passionate as they look at her.

He lights his own cigarette. They say nothing as they lean against the outside wall. A woman stands in front of one of the upstairs windows, gesturing to someone in the room with her. Music flows through the open windows of a ground-floor apartment. A pair of women are arguing in another, one of them sounding close to tears. Through it all Leanna's more primitive senses are focused on the man beside her, the heat of his body, the sound of his breath, the scent of his cologne.

The ash grows brighter as Leanna inhales. "Would you like to go somewhere?" he asks.

"Back inside," she answers and begins walking down the passage, toward the lights and distant voices.

He moves behind her, grabs her shoulder and spins her around.

"What do you want?" she asks, not surprised by what he has done.

"For you to dance for me the way you did for those savages," he replies and kisses her, his mouth grinding so hard against hers that she cuts her lip on her teeth.

He lets her go. She continues walking, her gait in the high heels a bit unsteady for a moment. She does not look back, ignores him when he calls her name.

Carlo Bucci, she thinks and smiles, not pleasantly.

(Hailey senses a deep and potent hate, the source of it unknown.)

The lights of the gallery have been turned up. They are

blinding after the darkness outside. Leanna pauses just inside the door. Her escort joins her, the happiness in his expression barely hiding the grief he must have felt when he discovered her gone.

"They're closing. Where would you like to go?" he asks.

She glances at the doors. Bucci has not returned. "Out for a few drinks then home," she responds.

He frowns. She laughs. "It doesn't make any difference if you take me home drunk or sober or at all, Michael. Louis will be spending the summer working for the firm. Papa only has work enough for one intern." She rests her hands on his shoulders, forcing him to look at her. "Was it so difficult to go out with me for my own sake?" she asks.

He blushes, stammers some denial.

"Then let's go."

When they reach her car, she pauses to take down the top then pulls away, down the gaudy streets of bright lights and clashing music from open tavern doors, of tourist crowds and street performers, of junkies and drunks who stare dully at her as she passes.

They pull into the Sheraton parking lot, leave the car with a valet and find seats near the bar. A jazz trio is playing, softly so that guests can converse. Leanna says nothing, merely sips her bourbon and water.

A dozen red roses arrive with the second drink. A dozen white with the third. There are no notes. There is no need for them. Michael furiously scans the room while Leanna sits—a serene ice queen accepting homage as her due.

"What in the hell's going on?" Michael asks.

"Someone playing a joke. Wait here," she replies and walks to the bar. "Where is he?" she asks the waitress who served her.

"The man who gave me the flowers for you is over there." She points toward the elevators beside the registration desk.

A black suit, patent loafers. The man could have been any guest except for the roses he carries. She stops in front of him, holds out her hand. He hands her Bucci's card with a room number written on the back.

The elevator door slides open. She steps inside.

(Alone with Leanna, Hailey struggles to grasp her thoughts but they are dull and unfocused, beyond the reach of her new and unexpected talent.

The darkness threatens to engulf them both, but Hailey fights it and with effort remains within the dream.)

Doors open. The room is huge, plush. A vase of roses sits on the Queen Anne table in front of the window. Beside it are two glasses, a bottle of wine, iced, the cork partially pulled.

Carlo has removed his suitcoat, unbuttoned the front of his short-sleeve shirt. The hair on his chest is black and fine. As Leanna studies him, she recalls his kiss, appraising it as one might the skill of an adversary rather than a potential lover.

Michael, sitting downstairs with the drinks and the scented bouquets, has been forgotten and abandoned. (Hailey feels a pang of pity for him as she pictures him growing ever more anxious, waiting for Leanna to return.

And Leanna. How can she not feel the danger of this man? How can she not sense the insult behind his passionate display? Yet there is something incredibly arousing in his audacious pursuit, his intensity well matched by Leanna's reckless response. Hailey, who had never dared to be so bold, cannot condemn Leanna de Noux for her boldness. In a way she envies it.

But where had that boldness led?

A bitter thought, not at all suited to the way Leanna kisses the man, to the way she lets a strap of the low-cut dress fall from one shoulder, exposing one breast to his hands and his lips.)

"Carlo," Leanna whispers and tilts her head back, inviting his touch.

(They are beautiful people, experienced, skilled. Had Hailey merely watched them, she would have been aroused.

But this is more, she is a part of it, feeling the passion build in Leanna, understanding her need to pull Carlo inside of her, her hips to rise to meet his downward thrust.

Leanna had never been possessed like this. As for Hailey, she had never imagined that such pleasure from another could be possible.)

"Carlo!" Leanna screams, and the voice seems to be Hailey's own, coming from the past, from now.

Hailey woke, her skin moist with sweat, her heart pounding from the passion that she had shared with her long-dead possessor. She absorbed the darkness of her little room, the emptiness of her bed, and experienced the most terrible loneliness she had felt since the loss of her child.

Alone by choice, she reminded herself.

Nonetheless, she buried her face in her pillow—as if anyone would hear, as if anyone who might hear would care—and cried.

After talking to Hailey, Ed O'Brien cruised the city for a while. Driving helped him relax, and with his conscious attention on the road, the rest of his mind was free to wander.

Back to Lake Charles and the years he'd spent as Joe Morgan's partner.

Morgan had joined the force five years before Ed. By the time Ed joined, Joe had been decorated twice. The first time, a burglary had gone bad, hostages had been taken. A hostage was already dead when Joe shot and killed one of their captors and wounded the second. The decoration hadn't been for bravery but for marksmanship, Joe had carefully explained to Ed.

The other had been for what was usually called "Service Beyond." Joe had been on his way home when he passed a house where the door hung open. He heard a woman yelling. It could have been at the kid Joe heard crying or her husband, but something in her tone sounded wrong. Joe pulled over and went inside and discovered a man pounding on a boy no more than eight. The kid was already missing one of his front teeth, and there was blood all over the floor.

Joe stepped in, got the worst of the fight until his own adrenaline caught up with the situation. Then, as he explained to Ed. He started swinging, not stopping until backups came to take the guy away.

The wife pressed charges then asked the judge for leniency at the sentencing.

One of the last times Ed talked to Joe before he died, Ed had been suspended pending an investigation into a situation with remarkable parallels to Joe's. He and Joe had carried a six-pack down to the piers behind the Expo Center and watched the car ferry come and go between the Quarter and Algiers.

"I got a medal in Lake Charles. You're in hot water in New Orleans. That's where decency takes you in this town," Joe said bitterly.

Ed had never thought of Joe as decent, but he was. In spite of the stubble on his chin, the stains from the cigarettes on his index finger and thumb, the worn clothes, the booze, and the scruffy hair hanging over his forehead and collar, Joe was decent and dependable.

A man someone could count on, even when drunk, to do the right thing.

After Leanna's death, O'Brien wanted to be there for Joe. He waited through the long questioning, then asked to talk to him.

He went into the windowless room where Joe had been grilled from the time he'd been able to talk. He'd expected Joe to be emotional, insane with grief and horror and furious that he would be a suspect.

What he saw was far worse.

Joe looked at him with eyes so expressionless that he might have already been dead. When they released him, O'Brien took Joe home and kept him there until the authorities had finished their meticulous work on Joe's apartment. He made Joe eat, tried to keep him from drinking, then—because it was all he could think to do—tried to get him drunk.

Joe's eyes never lost their vagueness. Eyes like that looked strange when filled with tears.

When he got the news that Joe had killed himself, Ed hadn't been surprised. But he had to know for himself whether Joe could have killed Leanna. So he'd asked questions. All he managed to do with that was get on the wrong side of Ethan Collings, the detective in charge of the case. Collings never forgave imagined insults. To this day, they were barely on civil terms, and Ed suspected that Collings was the reason it had taken him so long to make detective.

When he got tired of cruising, Ed went home, poured a beer and sat in the kitchen thinking of how sometimes when the stress of the job got to him, he'd find himself talking to the empty passenger seat in his unmarked car as if Joe were still riding shotgun for him.

Now this woman had brought back the past. He hated the thought of her digging around, bringing back all that sad history—hell, bringing it back for *him*—but maybe it was time someone did.

He'd mentioned to her that he'd worked with a psychic. Actually, he'd done so more than once. At first he'd been skeptical that a stranger could lay hands on an object and see the face of its owner, or could touch the sleeve of a little girls' sweater and say that she'd been killed. Both perceptions had been dead accurate, as accurate as Hailey Martin's description of a man she'd never met.

And Ed realized with some surprise that he wanted her to be telling the truth, wanted some answers to all the doubts this case had given him. Tomorrow, he would definitely try to find out what he could to help her.

EIGHT

Though Hailey's appointment with Louis de Noux was for two the following afternoon, she decided to arrive at his office a half hour early. She wanted to spend the time sitting in his waiting room, talking with his receptionist, gauging what kind of man he might be before deciding how much to tell him.

She had expected a small office building, not the elegant storefront with the tall carved mahogany door and antique brass lamps on either side of it. Nor had she expected the office to be closed. Well, there was nothing to do but wait.

A few minutes before their meeting time, Louis de Noux turned the corner. Hailey recognized him not from the child Louis of her dreams but because of the resemblances he bore to the adult Leanna.

They were both tall, both with the same dark hair. Hers fell in waves. His was a mass of short, dark curls that framed his face. He still wore the same style of round glasses she'd seen in her dreams. Their style, along with the dark formal suit and cane, made him look like a turn-of-the-century dandy.

She waited until he reached the office and pulled out his key, then introduced herself.

He frowned. "We did agree to meet at two, did we not?" His voice was smooth, melodic and precise. She could picture him mesmerizing a jury or client with it.

"I was prepared to wait," she replied.

"I see." He unlocked the door and followed him inside.

The waiting room was sumptuous. The carved wainscotting, an old copper ceiling in an intricate grape-and-vine pattern and wood floors had all been beautifully maintained. In one corner of the room, a pair of oxblood leather sofas faced each other. The glass-topped table between them rested on a magnificent bokhara rug. In another corner a secretary's desk held a neat pile of mail, nothing else.

Hailey took it all in quickly and followed de Noux into his private office.

It was an extension of the first room but in its smaller space the dark wainscotting made the walls seem too close. The picture of Henri de Noux that hung above the gas fireplace was stern rather than comforting. The room had not been designed to put clients at ease, Hailey decided, but since Henri de Noux had specialized in criminal law, ease was hardly the point.

De Noux offered her coffee, which she declined, then poured himself a cup from a carafe on the corner of his desk. Its steam clouded his glasses and he paused to clean them. Without them, his face was much like Leanna's, though his eyes were out of focus and curiously blank. They made Hailey uneasy and she looked away until he put the glasses back on.

"You mentioned to my secretary that you are a writer and listed some of your books. The titles are very impressive, Miss Martin, particularly the one on your son, which touched my secretary a great deal when she read it. However, if this is a legal matter regarding your profession, I must tell you up front that copyright law is hardly my specialty."

"I'm here to discuss your sister," she replied.

"Leanna?" He seemed astonished. "Whatever for?"

"Through some rather compelling coincidences, I've become aware of her story. I'd like to use it as the basis for a novel. I would like your permission to do so."

"I see." If he had cared for Leanna, if her memory caused him pain, he gave no indication of it. "And what coincidences are these?"

She explained about her room, and the drawings, and some of what Frank Berlin had told her. She did not describe the dreams.

"Will you be using the family name?" he asked.

"No, though to be honest there will be enough similarities that people who read the book and know of the case will assume that the book was based on her."

"Do you need my permission?" Again, the question was asked in the same cold tone. They might have been discussing any murder, any family, instead of his own.

"No, but I would like to have it."

"That's honest, and far more charitable than the reporters were when the murder dominated the news. Now, how do you intend to deal with her death?"

"As a tragic romance. From all accounts, Morgan loved your sister. Whatever motive he might have had for killing her will be fiction and come from me."

"Have you spoken to her husband?" For the first time, de Noux's voice held some emotion, most likely disgust.

"Ex-husband. She wasn't married when she died."

"That makes no difference. Carlo won't take your proposal well, not at all. That's a warning, Miss Martin, one you should keep in mind."

Hailey chose her words carefully, to be certain that the impression she was about to make was the right one. "Mr. Bucci's opinion of my novel is irrelevant. I am only concerned about your feelings. I would like your permission to do this book."

"May I think about it for the night and give you an answer tomorrow? Better yet, may I offer you dinner tonight? If you are going to pry into my sister's . . . 'affairs' shall we call them, I'd like to know a bit more about the woman doing the prying."

"That's fair enough. I'm free."

He jotted his home address on the back of a business card and handed it to her. She recognized the address, but didn't comment on it. Though she did not perceive him as

dangerous, something about Louis de Noux's cold detach-
ment seemed distasteful and oddly out of place. Then again,
lawyers were trained to hide emotions. He and Leanna had
been twins; they were close. Even if they had grown apart,
feelings would have remained.

Reality seemed to shift as she walked through the iron
gates of the de Noux house, onto the wide white porch,
through the doors and into her dream. Once inside, however,
she discovered that all semblance to the past had vanished.
The walls that had seemed so drab in their gray-and-blue
fleur de lis patterned paper had been stripped and painted
flat white. The stone face of the gas fireplace in the parlor
had been removed and replaced with colorful Dutch-style
blue-and-white tiles. The floors that had been dark and
polished had been stripped and lightly tinted with a pale
blue stain. And all the magnificent woodwork of the wide
archways had been marbleized, the gray base streaked with
mauve and teal and silver. The change seemed so radical
that it could easily have served a single purpose—to make
the rooms utterly different from what they had been before.
Only the staircase remained unchanged, its black lacquer
spindles and pale oak banister curving magnificently to the
darkened second floor. She had only a moment to glance up
at the hallway before de Noux led her through the dining
room and the oversized kitchen with its oak-and-tile work
island and into the spacious sunroom at the rear of the
house.
Though it must have been added later, it maintained the
charm of the house's design. Its outer walls were dominated
by a trio of tall, arched windows in carved wood frames.
Between each of them were narrower windows in geometric
patterned colored glass. The room was lit by gaslight, the
soft glow undoubtedly intended to be restful to Louis de
Noux's eyes. Hailey walked across the red tile floor, to the
display of orchids just setting their buds, and azaleas in full
bloom. As she looked between the plants to the yard outside,

she saw lights there too, and a high stone wall to keep out intruders.

Near the rear doors, a pair of bamboo loveseats faced each other over a glass-topped table. On it was a copy of *Watching Aaron Die*. She wondered what Louis thought of it, but did not ask. A square white iron bistro table and chairs sat near the doors leading to the kitchen. Wine sat in a chilling bucket beside it.

"Such a beautiful room," Hailey said.

"Thank you. I finished it last year," de Noux replied in the same expressionless voice he'd used when discussing his sister's death.

"You're the designer?"

"I also did most of the work. I like to be an exception to the rule that intellectuals can't work with their hands."

Witty words, coldly delivered. "I'm amazed that you'd have the time," Hailey said.

"I have limited practice. I see no reason to add to wealth when I have no use for it, nor any children to inherit. As for fame, my father had that, enough to last the family a few more generations." He punctuated the remark with the quick removal of a wine cork and poured them each a glass, then picked up his plate and requested she do the same. She followed him into the kitchen, where poached salmon and dill waited with a variety of side dishes. "And you cook as well?" she commented.

"On some nights. On others I dine out. I love my city's food, don't you? We Creoles have a primitive oneness with our food, found only I think in places where people rip small crustaceans in half to suck out their meat." He smiled, again with the same languor he'd revealed earlier. It made her wonder how ill he might be. "A barbaric habit, don't you think?"

He dished out their meals then led her back to the solarium. After placing his plate on the table, he pushed in her chair. His hand brushed against her bare shoulder and she stifled a shudder.

Louis de Noux, for all his charm, was not a man Hailey wanted to touch her.

Throughout the meal, she laughed at his witty remarks, keeping her attention entirely on him not out of any attraction but out of wariness. He did not seem to mind her questions about Leanna, answering them with a candor that surprised her.

"I was trapped in darkness for years, Miss Martin. . . ."

"Hailey, please. I was raised in the Midwest. We tend to be less formal, particularly over dinner."

"Very well, Hailey. I was housebound for years so my eyes could rest and perhaps heal. While I lay there all alone, Leanna lived for both of us." He spoke with more animation now, his voice husky with grief. "We were close," he went on. "Because of my infirmity and her . . . shall we be kind and call it her 'adventurous nature' . . . we became halves of some perfect whole. In our own way, we balanced one another."

"You balanced one another?" Hailey asked.

"I could not tolerate the harsh lights of the schoolrooms, so Leanna took notes for me. I doubt she would have gone to school otherwise and I doubt that even Papa could have made her attend. But, out of love for me, she brought me the assignments along with notes meticulously taken, and words recorded, I suppose you could say, with no thought to the meaning behind them. We were both fond of adventure stories, and she would read them to me. We shared Dumas and Stevenson and Melville.

"She also brought me gossip from school, and most precious of all, shared her life with me. I heard every detail of her trips into the swamps and bayous with Jacqueline, of the spells and incantations the woman taught her. I know when she lost her virginity, where, to what man, and how well she enjoyed it. I knew of all her affairs, the casual lovers as well as those she took on for the knowledge and power her partners could prove."

"You talk about her affairs so . . . openly."

"Do you find that odd? We were twins, Hailey, whole only when together. I suppose things would have been different if we had not both been so damaged. Because of Leanna's practices, she was respected but not liked by her schoolmates. Because my eyes limited my activities so much, I had few close friends. She was the best one.

"As to her life, I did not approve of much of what she did but I cannot bear, even now, to condemn it. Because of this, she told me every secret she had and I kept them safe in my heart."

"Your eyes seem better now," Hailey commented.

"They often are for a time. When the headaches begin and the light glares so painfully, I shut myself up in this house and remind myself how fortunate I am to be able to see at all."

"When did Leanna leave here?"

"After high school she went to Georgetown because Papa wanted her there and had pulled some strings in spite of her grades. She hated it and, rather than wait to fail, returned home by the middle of the semester. By then, I was in college as well, here at LSU. My grades were everything hers were not so for the first time I could recall, Papa ignored her and focused all his attention on me, a mixed blessing to be sure. Leanna met Carlo Bucci a few months later. They were married when she turned twenty-one.

"It was a lavish affair. Carlo paid for it all. My father did not attend."

"Did you?"

De Noux nodded. "Papa never forgave me for that. Leanna already knew he wasn't coming. He'd made that clear enough, so she took her revenge. My father's mulatto mistress gave her away. Any chance of reconciliation ended when Leanna walked down the aisle on Jacqueline's arm. Though Papa never spoke to Leanna again, she and I kept in close contact. Her marriage was a disaster. Love ended within months of the wedding. Carlo had to control her, you see, as he controlled everyone else. Stronger wills have tried and failed."

He poured them each more wine, her second glass, his third or was it fourth? The bottle looked nearly empty and de Noux seemed a little drunk, a state not at all surprising considering how thin he was. "I think she would have come home within months of the wedding had Papa not been so opposed to the match. So she stayed with Carlo rather than admit her mistake.

"In the four years which followed, Carlo abused her physically as well as mentally. She gave as good as she got, belittling him in public as well as in private. For the last year of their marriage, she wasn't faithful to him and I cannot blame her for finding what affection she could in others since as far as I know Carlo had never intended to be faithful himself. Be certain to give Carlo Bucci a strong role in your story. He deserves it."

Hailey changed the subject, asking him about his work, and they spoke of legal matters throughout the rest of the meal.

In the end, after schaum torte any German restaurant in Milwaukee would have been proud to serve, she made a request that could not be avoided, no matter how personal or prying it might seem.

"May I see Leanna's room?"

If de Noux noticed the emotion in her voice, he gave no indication. Instead, he took off his glasses and casually polished them with the corner of the tablecloth. "The second room to the left at the top of the stairs," he said. "Forgive me if I don't come with you. I rarely go upstairs any longer. Memories, you know."

What did she expect to find? she wondered, as she slowly climbed the stairs. A stronger link to the past than her dreams? Some clue that Leanna herself might have over-looked?

"Who killed you?" she spoke the words so softly they might have been thought. No answer came from the hall.

She moved slowly down it, giving her eyes a chance to become accustomed to the dim light. At the door, she hesitated, then pushed it open. Darkness and the scent of fresh rose sachet met her. Her hand moved frantically down the wall until she found the switch.

The white four-poster was draped with rose-colored lace. It rustled against the pale wood floor, most likely moved by the draft from the open door.

"Leanna," Hailey whispered, and stepped inside a space with walls of lilac paper and altar candles before a statue of the Virgin Mary.

White candles for purity. Rose lace for a girl almost a woman.

And what of the child's darker side? Was that here as well, hidden beneath the satin throw pillows in their heart and diamond designs, inside the carefully painted porcelain head of the Pierrot sitting insolently against the vanity mirror?

She walked to the dresser, where bright silk scarves lay in a green crystal bowl. Beautiful shades, she thought. As she fingered them, she felt something hard hidden beneath them.

Candles—six of them—pairs of red, green and black. Passion. Money. Power. Hailey tried to rationalize their presence. What other things mattered to an adolescent?

When Hailey was eighteen, all she had cared about was peace and some fifties notion of true love.

How innocent Hailey's beliefs seemed now. How innocent those nights when one lover erased the pain caused by the last.

Music flowed up from the main floor, a haunting atonal piece by a composer she didn't know. Certain she would not be discovered, Hailey opened the top dresser drawer.

Lace and satin panties of various colors lay neatly arranged beside slips and stockings. The scent of rose sachet was stronger now. She lifted the mesh packet and sniffed. The sachet inside was new.

The strangeness of the place hit her fully. This was a shrine to Leanna, nothing out of place, everything carefully preserved. If Leanna returned from the dead, she would find everything as it had been when she left this room.

Hailey closed the drawer carefully and stole into the hall. Across the way, another door waited. She had to look.

The hinges creaked as she pushed open the door. Cobwebs hung from the corners and from the glass candleholders on the black lacquer dresser.

If she went inside, she would leave footprints in the dust on the wood floor but she did not need to do so. The drawers would be empty, the faded green bedspread would have no covers beneath it.

Louis de Noux had gone on with his life while Leanna's past was frozen in the perfectly maintained room behind her.

Hailey retreated as silently as she could and joined her host downstairs.

He'd poured them each a coffee and brandy. Hailey drank hers, grateful for the numbing heat of the alcohol.

"Did you see what you expected?" he asked.

"I don't know. You miss her very much, don't you?"

"Miss here? Do you have a brother? Are you close?"

She nodded. "He's ten years younger, the baby of the family. No, we aren't close."

"Suppose you were the same age, shared the same crib, the same breasts. We looked alike. We thought alike. We came to believe that we even shared past lives—that we were once siblings, parent and child, husband and wife. And now she's gone and I'm left here without her. Missing is hardly a strong enough word to explain the loss of her."

"Mr. de Noux . . . Louis, I'm sorry if I've caused you pain. It wasn't intentional."

"I know. Come on, I'll escort you down to St. Charles."

They walked in silence past the huge trees, the great white houses—ghosts of a more genteel past. As the trolley approached, he kissed her hand and whispered, "I'll send a letter in the morning. I'm sure your publisher would like my permission in writing. As for your book, I will do what I can to help."

"What made you decide?" she asked.

"I read the book on your son this afternoon. I admit that I cried. Someone should cry for Leanna, don't you think?"

As the trolley pulled away, Hailey watched him leave, tall and thin and elegant in his black suit, swinging his carved walking cane. He had been so kind, so polite, so flattering. Yet her heart was racing, and as she became aware of this, she also noticed that she was compulsively rubbing the back of her hand against her skirt as if she could wipe away the memory of his lips against her skin.

NINE

Hailey did not dream that night and for once she was thankful. Before she returned to Leanna's world, she wanted to sort out what she had learned of it.

The letter of permission from Louis de Noux arrived by messenger the following morning. The tiny gray-haired man who brought it handed her a form, pointing to where he wanted her to sign for the letter, smiled as she tipped him and departed, all without a word.

As Hailey expected, the letter was both complimentary and legally correct. She spent the remainder of the morning putting together a brief outline for the book. Plotting a story whose ending seemed completely beyond her control exhausted her, so much so that she called Federal Express rather than walking the few blocks to the post office. After the courier left with her package, she stretched out on the bed to rest her eyes for just a little while.

. . . The dresses are so beautiful, hanging slightly apart in the scented closet. Leanna pulls one after another from the closet and holds it up to herself, examining the color in front of the dusty mirror in the little guest room where her mother's things have been moved. She chooses a princess style with spaghetti-strap sleeves in powder-blue satin. The color is so popular this year that perhaps none of the other girls will realize that her dress is old.

It smells faintly of the mother's perfume and she holds it close to her face as she carries it to her room, remembering the times she saw her mother wear it.

She hangs it on the back of her door and begins to prepare for the night, watching the clock all the while.

An hour later, she steals downstairs, and waits by the door, praying that Steve will come for her soon, as they agreed—soon, before anyone catches her going out.

Why does Papa always punish her for every little thing just before some important event? She sniffs back the tears and examines her makeup in the hall mirror. It would do no good to feel sorry for himself, start to cry and have her mascara run.

She hears the knock, pulls open the door. Steve is standing there, a red rose in his hand. His car, as they agreed, is parked down the street. Only after they reach it and speed away does she let him stop and pin the rose above her breast. As she looks down at it, his lips brush her cheek.

"Will you get in trouble for sneaking out?" he asks.

She nods. "It's OK. It's worth it." She lay's a hand on his thigh, resting it there as they drive on. . . .

The girls and their dates stand in well-defined groups: the smart ones; the rich ones; the ugly ones who came with each other; the dark-skinned ones with their nervous escorts, admitted on scholarship by the liberal teaching order; the beautiful ones standing with their handsome escorts, their eyes fixed on their own images in the cloudy mirror along the back of the gym wall. On school days, girls in navy bloomers do their stretching exercises in front of it. Now it is framed with pink-and-white crepe. More crepe is draped around the swinging doors, dove ornaments made of real feathers hung by thin nylon strands from the exposed beams in the ceiling.

The band begins playing. Only a few of the couples are on the dance floor for the first slow waltz. Leanna take's her date's hand and joins them, pressing against him as they slowly turn.

"The witch came," one of the beautiful girls comments as she moved past. "And she conjured a date, how skillful."

She tosses her honey-colored curls as she and her partner circle on.

"What does she mean?" Steve asks.

"Nothing."

"As if you had to search for a date," he responds, kissing her forehead. "You're the prettiest one here."

Throughout the next hour, Leanna stays close to her escort, never leaving him alone with anyone. Tonight, in spite of who she is and what she knows, she wants to be just another girl at her junior prom on a date with someone she cares for instead of some friend of her brother's who knows nothing about her.

At times like these, she wishes she had never been so curious, never let the power of her belief grow in her, never forced the training to begin.

(Forced, Hailey thought. Yes, that was exactly what Jacqueline had told her.)

And now, after all the compromising she has done, she cannot turn from that belief, at least not in this town where there is always someone in a crowd who has heard rumors of her practices. At least there is no need for whispers.

Everyone knows what she is.

If she reveals the reason for her power to them, will they respect her? Pity her?

She pulls back to arm's length and smiles at her date. Far better to be feared, she thinks, to be despised.

"I have to be home at eleven," she says.

Papa is due home at twelve. Plenty of time for a good-night.

Because it's early, her escort drives through Audubon Park, stopping on the dark road that circles the golf course. "Where else can you see the stars like this?" he asks.

In the bayous where the trees are sparse and the stars hung low above her. In the courtyards of deserted city squares. In the boats that cruise up and down the river carrying the worthy to their nocturnal ceremonies.

No, I am not just any girl, but kiss me—chastely, the kiss

of a date, a friend who can be something more. She leans against him, waiting.

In that moment he is on her, his body pressed against one of her arms, one hand fumbling with her panties beneath the dress.

"Don't," she demands but says nothing more. His lips taste of fruit punch and the chocolate cookies they've been eating. She bites down hard.

"Bitch!" he swears as he pulls away. There is blood on his lip. She looks down at her chest and sees dark patches. Blood, she thinks, wondering for a moment how she will clean the dress. Then she notices that the patches move when she sits up, and fall to the ground when she runs from the car. The rose he had given her had broken in the struggle. She unpins it as she runs and holds the pearl-tipped hatpin in her hands.

"Bitch!" he screams after her. "Bitch! Do you think I don't know who you are?"

Any girl. How could she have thought she could pass as any girl?

By the time she reaches the house, the porch lights are on. The living room curtains are open. Too late. She leans against the front door and sobs.

The doors opens slowly. Her father motions her inside, and closes and locks the door behind her. His expression is hard, his eyes flat, implacable.

She fights back the tears, wanting so much to be comforted. Instead, her father's expression grows more intense.

"Where were you?" he asks, his voice deadly calm.

"At the junior prom."

"With?"

"A boy. No one I knew. Someone fixed me up." She does not implicate her brother.

For a moment, she thinks her father isn't angry, but it is only a sham. The moment she begins to walk past him, he grabs her hair, slamming her back against the door. His arms are on her shoulders. "Your mother's dress," he bellows. "Some boy touched it. Some fucking boy touched *you*."

His arm rises, his hand flat as he strikes the side of her face. The force of it knocks her sideways. A shoulder strap breaks, the bodice falls. "In public, dressed like that!" he rages, striking the side of her exposed breast. It's something she's used to, has come to accept.

Not anymore.

The hatpin, so thin, slides an inch into her father's shoulder. He howls with pain and pulls it out while Leanna retreats from his grasp toward the stairs.

"Touch me again and by God and all the saints, I will make you pay for what you've done."

She watches him, looking for some sign of fear. Instead there is only rage, an emotion she knows too well. "Do you think anyone will believe you?" he asks.

"You fool," she says and smiles, serene in the power she has never used against him. "There are other ways."

The scene shifts to Carlo with the older Leanna in his hotel room bed. She moans as his hands squeeze her breasts, as his lips press against the side of her neck, as his hips rise and fall, possessing her. And Carlo becomes another and another and another, ending with the face of Joe Morgan, looking down at her as if he were her first and he owed her ecstasy.

Through the dreams, Hailey hears the steady beat of footsteps on bare wood, a door opening and closing, a child's wrenching cry.

Henri de Noux must have his blood. If not Leanna's, then anyone's will do. . . .

Hailey woke with tears in her eyes, her heart pounding. Though the windows were closed, the drawn curtains swayed back and forth as if there were a faint breeze in the room, or some presence brushing against them.

Everything Hailey needed to know had been contained in that brief vision. She wrote through the rest of the day and much of the night, breaking only to walk to the Sheraton Hotel and eat lunch in the lobby at a table just below the place where Leanna had sat and collected Carlo's bouquets. Even then, she had her pad and paper with her, recording her victim's life. By the time she went to bed, exhausted by the work, Leanna—the young and tragic Leanna—had begun to take form. If Hailey were wrong in her assumptions, or in any of the facts, Leanna did not feel a need to correct her.

. . . The dress she wears to dinner the following night is the same one from the dance, the ripped shoulder hastily pinned together, the torn seam hidden by one of her mother's scarves. She wears her mother's earrings as well, and her perfume. She washed off the heavy makeup she'd worn through the day to hide the bruises. Her hair is piled high on the back of her head, falling in loose ringlets as her mother's once did. Even the shoes with the high heels and silver buckles belonged to her mother, bought many years before and worn so briefly.

She takes her mother's place at one side of the table while Louis stares at her, his eyes round, his expression filled with pain as he notes the bruise now clear on her cheek. Jacqueline comes in from the kitchen, sees where Leanna is sitting and shakes her head furiously, but like Louis, she remains silent.

Henri de Noux had stayed home that day, drinking in his den, mumbling—at times to himself, at times to his wife or Leanna. Now he enters the room, his steps uneven, his eyes glazed. He looks from the table with its gold-edged china and white brocade cloth to Leanna, snorts derisively and takes his place. The roast is in front of him with the carving set ready. He slices off a piece of rare beef and throws it onto his daughter's plate, then his son's.

"A sissy and a slut in league against me. Don't think I don't know what you're doing," he warns.

Leanna, knowing exactly what she is doing, and the emotions she arouses, feels nothing. She looks directly at her father and smiles sweetly. Her mother's mouth. Her mother's expression.

They eat in silence. Only Henri takes seconds. "Rage expends so much energy, doesn't it, Papa?" Leanna asks.

Without asking permission, she pushes her chair away from the table. "Good night, Louis." She kisses her brother and father lightly on the lips and goes, swaying her hips as she leaves the room and climbs the stirs.

She has left Louis to Papa's mercy, but there is nothing she can do for him anymore.

Upstairs, she lights the double-wicked black candle she had formed herself, and recites the last words of a novena to St. Jude, the patron saint of lost causes. And when she began, her cause did indeed seem lost. Not anymore. She has made Papa believe in her power; now she must make him believe in the power of her wrath.

"Yembo, protector of women, raped also by one you love, give me the strength I need," she quickly adds as she strips off the dress. A rosewood box is filled with oil which she smears on her body, the subtle scent of it mixing with her mother's perfume.

She stands in the center of the room, her oiled body shining in the candlelight, and waits.

Not long, she prays. Please Jesus and all the saints, not long, or my courage will fail me.

Henri storms in, his face dark with fury, his fists clenched. A brown cashmere robe is loosely belted around his thick body. His legs are bare and there are worn blue slippers on his feet, a gift from his wife so many years before. "How dare you laugh at me?" he bellows.

As he sees that she is naked his body reacts. Arousal comes suddenly, flaccid to hard, the tip parting the folds of his bathrobe as he once parted the folds of her mother's sex, of hers, of Jacqueline's.

And Louis? Louis does not speak of it, but she knows that he is not immune from his father's lust.

Never again! She begins the incantation—gibberish mixed

with an occasional known word. No matter. If the chanter believes, and the recipient believes, nothing can stand in the way of success.

"Never Yembo . . . never Yembo . . . Nada . . ."

And on, and on. Unknown words spoken by the *loas* who gave her power, flowing into her as she stands nearly motionless, watching intently as her father's passion fades.

"Never again. Never while I am a prisoner in this house, will you lie with another. Not with me; nor with Josephine; not even with your son. That is your curse, and our blessing. Yembo wills it."

"Harlot!" he screams and lunges for her. The oil makes her slippery. He loses his grip and falls at her feet, landing on his side, breathing heavily.

"Your curse, Papa," she repeats. Crouching beside him, she kisses him long and passionately. His body, always too ready, gives no response. He believes, as strongly as she does, in the spell she has cast.

She leaves him, lying on the carpet, goes into the bathroom and showers. She does not bother to lock the door. He will not touch her again.

As she expects, Louis heard the argument and struggle, and waits to learn the outcome. For all his intelligence, he is such a fool, concerned rather than pleased when she goes to his room and tells him what she's done.

He finally blurts the real reason for his concern: "He'll send you away. He'll send you away and I'll be alone with him."

She holds him, comforts him. They sleep together in his bed, lying close like children, though neither is innocent any longer.

What would it have been like for the twins? Hailey wondered as she recorded the dream the following morning. She thought of the adversaries: Henri de Noux, powerful and respected; his ill son; his terrified daughter, her reputation already ruined by her beliefs. If the children had gone to the police, who would have been believed?

Hailey had no doubt of the answer.

Yet Leanna had fought back, the only way she knew. And she had won, for eventually Henri did send her away, as far away as he could.

But what of Louis?

She wished he did not repell her so terribly, wished that she had some liking for him, enough to get to know him and to share what she had learned.

She considered doing so in spite of her aversion to him.

All her instincts told her to stay far away.

She was just about to break for a walk and lunch when Celeste called her. "I tracked down Josephine!" Celeste exclaimed. "She's one of my customers. Until I inquired from some older friends, I never knew it was her."

"Did you tell her I'd like to meet her?"

"She asks that you come this afternoon. I know it's short notice but do it now before she loses her nerve."

Jacqueline Menieur had lost the beauty of her youth. The long, thin face that had once seemed so exotic was criss-crossed with lines. Her mouth seemed set in a permanent frown, her gray hair pulled back in a severe bun. Whisps of it had escaped the clasp and hung untidily from the crown. The shade did not harmonize with her complexion.

But what she had lost in beauty seemed to be balanced by incredible energy. She moved through the living room of her private quarters attached to her nephew's house, dusting the delicate blue-and-white china cups of her tea service, setting them on a silver tray which she placed on the table between matching high-back velvet chairs. With the setting ready, she went into the kitchen to fill the pot with chicory coffee and cream. All of this was accomplished with a great deal of unnecessary motion. If there had been nothing to do, Hailey suspected the woman would have paced to dissipate her nervousness.

In the few moments that Hailey was alone, she studied the room. Outside of the crucifix above the outside door and a tiny statue of the Virgin Mary among the curios crowded inside a glass-doored cabinet between the lace-curtained windows, there was nothing to indicate that Jacqueline Menieur was anything more than a devout Catholic. Could there be some other room in this house where she kept the cluttered altar, the pictures of gods and saints, the fetishes? Or had she outgrown that belief? Hailey doubted it. In her experience, age always seemed to make devotion stronger.

When Jacqueline returned, she poured their coffee and sat on the edge of her chair, as if ready to bolt should the conversation grow too unpleasant. "I would not speak of Henri de Noux had Celeste not asked," Jacqueline said bluntly.

"I am more interested in his family, and in you," Hailey responded.

"His family?"

"Leanna and Louis."

"I see." Jacqueline's expression became guarded. "What did you wish to know?"

Hailey told the same story she had told Louis de Noux, noting Jacqueline's veiled interest in the drawings. She added that Louis had given her permission to write a novel based on the murder.

"Whatever for?" The woman's eyes, the color of milk chocolate, fixed on hers, making Hailey feel oddly vulnerable as well as ill at ease.

"Maybe because I would do it anyway," Hailey responded. "On the other hand, he seemed almost anxious that I would write it. That's one of the things I can't understand."

"I see. And what else?"

"Why Leanna made that drawing on my wall. And why she married Carlo Bucci, a man who by all accounts was a bigot."

Her last remark hit a raw spot in Jacqueline. The woman abruptly looked away, hiding whatever emotion Bucci's name had evoked by pouring a second cup of coffee for them both. "Did you know her husband?" Hailey asked.

Jacqueline shook her head, responding with a question of her own, "Do you really think Leanna was so liberal?"

"I don't know. I assumed that because you raised her and . . ." There was no way to go on without revealing more than she was supposed to know, but Hailey took the chance. ". . . and because you instructed her in your religion, that she was not one to notice race."

Jacqueline laughed dryly. "Not one to notice race? Perhaps. But she noticed station well enough and made certain that I was always reminded of mine. When she was younger, I lived in that house constantly in fear that I would say or do something wrong and she would tell her father about the places I took her, or the people that she met through me, as if I had some control over her."

"But you were Henri de Noux's mistress, weren't you? Didn't he care about you?"

"Oh, he cared for me the way any good master does for his slave. No, in spite of my devotion, the only creatures he ever loved were his wife, and Leanna because she looked so much like her mother. By the time the girl was fourteen the resemblance had become uncanny. She knew it. She cultivated it. She wore her mother's clothes, her mother's perfume. She even sat at her mother's place at the table, a place that had always been left vacant out of respect to Madam's memory. It was no wonder that—" She stopped abruptly.

"That what?"

"Nothing. . . . It isn't right to speak so of the dead."

Hailey, who already knew about Leanna's life in the de Noux house, did not push the matter. Instead, she asked, "When did you leave Henri de Noux?"

"After Leanna went off to school. I don't know how she talked him into letting her go but she did. He grieved as if he had lost his wife again. I suppose I should have been more understanding, but after years of raising the children and giving myself to him, I felt useless, as abandoned as he did. We fought. He ordered me to go. Later, he provided for me, well enough that I own this house. Because of his generosity, I always hoped that he would ask me back. Then Leanna came home from school and moved into the house with him."

"And Louis?"

"Louis often stayed away. When he was able, he maintained his own house. When he was home, I felt less like his mother or his maid than his nurse. In spite of all his hardship, he was always the perfect gentleman, you know, a quiet little mouse with never a harsh word to anyone."

"But by then you were gone."

"Monsieur Louis has always been a friend to me. I visit the house often now that it belongs to him. But before, I went when I could. If Henri glimpsed me, he tolerated my presence. I thought he sometimes even welcomed it.

"But what did Henri need with me after Leanna returned? Then Leanna met that thug, that terrible man with blood on his hand. I was as opposed to their wedding as her father must have been. But when Henri refused to attend the service, she came for me."

Jacqueline went to the doorway, striking a dramatic pose, her hands now tight fists. "She stood right where I'm standing now, decked out in seed pearls and white satin like some society bride, and ordered me to put on the dress she had bought for me."

"Why didn't you tell her no?"

"Leanna?" Jacqueline laughed. "How badly you know your victim. No one ever said no to her, least of all me. I did as she ordered. I performed at her wedding as she demanded."

Jacqueline paced the room as she continued. "The description of the wedding was in all the papers. If there had ever been a chance for Henri and me to reconcile, she ended it out of spite. I suppose it made no difference. Henri passed on two months after Leanna divorced her husband."

"Did you ever meet Carlo Bucci?"

"Just at the wedding. He was barely polite. I suppose he tolerated me for her sake."

"Why did she marry him?"

"She was a powerful woman. Carlo had his own kind of power and I suppose it attracted her. I like to think she loved him in the beginning. But every time I saw her, the happiness had faded a little bit more, like the color in a dying rose."

Hailey had been considering the dream she'd had about Carlo and what it meant since she'd experienced it two nights before. "She married him because she hated her father, didn't she?"

Jacqueline looked as if Hailey had slapped her. "No! I cannot believe that. It would be monstrous for her to feel that way about her own papa!"

"Would it?" Hailey asked gently.

The woman's eyes filled with tears. She rubbed them away with the back of her hand. "Go," she said. "I won't say any more. To speak so of the dead invites revenge."

Hailey took her coat from the rack by the door. "Do you still have my number?" she asked.

"I do. But I'll tear it up before I use it."

For the first time since Hailey had arrived, Jacqueline was sitting in her chair, her back stiff. Her hands which had been constantly moving were now folded in her lap. Decision made, she'd become abruptly calm. Hailey doubted that anything she said now could change the woman's mind.

Nonetheless, she tried. "Does Leanna ever come to you?" she asked.

Jacqueline shut her eyes and gave no sign that she had heard the words.

She sat there, still, as Hailey let herself out.

TEN

The package Hailey sent to her New York agent had included news articles on the murders, photos, as precise a plot outline as Hailey could manage and Louis de Noux's permission. She also included the opening pages describing Joe Morgan's meeting Leanna de Noux. Afterward, believing she might as well go through the motions of practicing the religion about which she'd be writing, she began keeping a green candle lit to ensure success. As always, she found it difficult to work for the next few days so, instead of trying to force what would not come, she labored on her walls.

When they'd all been stripped and washed, she laid down primer and teal-colored paint the gloss finish of which seemed to glow on the walls. Ignoring Celeste's advice, she kept Leanna's drawing intact, framing it with thin strips of walnut board.

The work took the better part of four days. Later, as she sat in front of the computer screen, staring at the words she had already written, wondering how she could find the state of mind necessary to continue with them, Charlie Mullen, her agent, called. She had expected a quick response, but nothing like the enthusiasm with which the proposal had been greeted by her publisher.

"Fifty thousand," Charlie said. "And, there'll be a full publicity campaign before and after next June's release to assure summer sales. Of course, the first draft will have to be done by tax day but you can manage four months, can't you?"

111

Hailey stared at the steady candle flame, thinking of her good fortune, the house payments she could finally afford to make.

"Because of the book, they'll be more publicity for *Fragile Memories* too. The publishers will try to book you on some radio and TV talk shows in March. Are you up to doing that while you're finishing the new book?"

Up to it? Hailey could finally afford the laptop computer that would allow her to write on planes and in hotel rooms. Her creative world had suddenly exploded beyond the confines of these four walls, or the terrible slow motion of ink on paper. "Of course," she replied.

They discussed a few more items, future proposals that would have to wait. Through it all Hailey felt the temptation to tell Charlie how the story was being written but she knew what he'd think—that she'd finally lost her mind completely.

After the conversation ended, she fixed her eyes on the candle flame and thought of Leanna and Joe. "We've got work to do, so no more games, please," she said aloud.

But she could not tolerate the thought of letting Leanna take control of her body again. Though she was hardly sleepy, she drank some of the tea Celeste had given her and lay down on her bed. "Share your pain with me, Leanna. Help me to understand who you were."

. . . She always hates waking in Carlo's room. The dark flock paper in gold and green is too oppressive, the old double bed too rickety to hold two active lovers. But it belonged to Carlo's mother and he reveres her.

All the more reason to banish the damned thing to a guest room, but Carlo will not hear of it.

As to waking beside Carlo, the romance of that died soon after their marriage.

What had seemed like passion when combined with drink felt more like abuse in the cold and far too sober light of morning. He claimed her freedom, had hired men to watch her every move. She sits up slowly and stares down at him, at the hair on his chest and arms slick with perspiration, the stubble on his chin. He hasn't shaved last night and the side of her face burns.

Last night the roughness, fueled as usual by an argument, had felt wonderful. Now. . . . ?

She moves carefully, knowing his appetite in the morning, and tiptoes from the room and up the stairs to her own.

Leanna chose a small rear bedroom whose main charm was the sloped ceiling and the little balcony overlooking the yard with its pond and raised deck.

She stands there, thinking how the yard will be decorated tomorrow with garlands and potted flowers for the spring party Carlo has planned.

As always, she will have nothing to do with his family and friends and their dowdy wives. She hates having her home invaded by caterers and hired servers. She hates the hours she spends at Carlo's side, her demure manner, her forced smile.

And yes—it does not good to avoid the truth—she hates her cowardice most of all.

If she dared, she would have taken an interest in this social, enough of an interest to have addressed and mailed the invitations herself. She'd have doubled the guest list and introduced the dowdy Metairie matrons-in-training and their so-careful thug husbands to a side of New Orleans they'd rather ignore.

Carlo would have killed her.

The thought makes her smile. She strips off her green satin nightgown and walks into an adjoining bathroom. Nearly as large as her bedroom, the room is decorated in shades of delft blue and white, and is dominated by a huge tub the underside and claw feet of which are covered in gilt paint.

She fills it, adds gardenia-scented oil and steps into it, watching the oil bead on the bruise Carlo had made on her breast, on her tiny, dark nipples hard with memory of last night's passion. Her hand slips between her legs. She is sore there as well.

Ah, such an impatient man.

His voice sounds in the hall, calling her name.

"In the tub," she responds. When he appears in the door, his robe loose around his compact body, the morning erection waving from beneath its folds, she holds out her arms. "Join me," she says.

"I thought you were furious," he reminds her.

"That was last night. Now . . ." She pauses, tilts her head, motions him forward. "A compromise?"

He does as she asks, sitting behind her with his legs wrapped around her hips, his penis hard against her back. "What do you have in mind?" he asks.

"Your party Saturday. Mine two weeks later. Agree and I'll promise to be as polite as I possibly can to even your most boring guest."

"Just a party?"

"Dearest, I mean what I say."

His lips brush the side of her neck. "Face me," he says.

"Agree first," she replies and laughs, a husky sound she hopes will convince him that she is sincere. . . .

Blindfolded children swinging at a piñata on the lawn beside the pond. . . . Adults drinking champagne and mimosas, the women's hats constantly in danger of blowing away in the stiff April breeze.

Leanna, a smile glued to her carefully made-up face, stands alone as she has been for most of the afternoon. No longer minding her isolation, she observes, lost in a fantasy.

. . . Piñatas break. Candy falls, the black wrapped taffy forming bats' wings. Tiny clawed feet lift the ladies' hats and circle low over the screaming children. Tiny mouths open, gibbering, screeching with a sound no bat has ever made.

The wind rises, shredding the lace-edged canopy over the patio.

The guests drop their glasses and, clutching their children, run screaming for the house.

Carlo falls onto the stones, the broken glass. Spilled champagne and orange juice mingle with his blood. "Witch!" he bellows at her. "Witch!" . . .

Ah, to possess such power! But then, she reminds herself, the temptation to use it would be too great. Marcus Sullivan, a portly lawyer from Baton Rouge, walks over to thank her for the invitation. She smiles with the sultry, inviting look intelligent men find so irresistible. "I feel like a guest myself," she tells him, patting his hand. "Carlo is terrible with introductions."

"Is he? Well, I can help with that."

In a moment, he will walk her through the crowd, introducing her to men who desire her and the wives who despise her for something as inconsequential as her enticing smile.

"Thank you," she tells him and takes his arm.

Before they can leave, Carlo joins them, his arms wrapped around her bare shoulders. "A beautiful day, don't you think?" he asks.

"Lovely," Sullivan responds while Leanna turns her head sideways so Carlo can kiss her cheek. . . .

Darkness rolls like a stage curtain over the scene, and when it parts once more, Hailey is in Carlo's house, noting its design through Leanna's eyes.

When Carlo purchased the house, he hired an architect who gutted the main floor, replacing the walls of tiny rooms with carved oak pillars for support. The space, brilliantly lit through the new picture windows, flows in a circle around the open center stairs, from the white enamel kitchen to the dining room through the foyer to the huge living room with its marble fireplace and white leather sofas. Flowers are arranged in crystal vases on either side of the mantel. A matched vase on the coffee table has been overturned, the water puddled on the table's beveled glass top. A woman sits back on her heels beside it, the tight black dress she wears riding high on her thighs. She leans over, taking the first pair of a half dozen lines of coke arranged on the table, then passes the rolled bill to a man waiting beside her for his turn.

"Join us?" she asks, looking directly at Leanna. Her eyes, Hailey notes, are dark and slanted, her skin more tan than brown.

Leanna shakes her head, sips the liquid in her glass.

Plain seltzer. This is her party. She will stay in control.

Two men have claimed the wing chairs in the corner. A woman sits on the arm of one chair, lighting a pipe, dragging deeply then bending down, kissing the nearest man, blowing smoke into his lungs. She repeats the procedure with the man in the facing chair while the one closest to her slips his hand inside her blouse. She does not appear to notice.

Leanna briefly joins the crowd congregated around the dining room table drinking glasses of wine and rum punch. She exchanges a few words with them then wanders into the kitchen, where the hired cook is filling the drink pitchers and arranging canapés on china plates. The woman is doing her best to ignore guests too hungry, and too rude, to wait until the plate is finished and served.

"They won't leave me alone," she complains.

"Concentrate on the drinks. The cattle can forage for themselves."

"Madame . . . ?"

"It's all right, Susan. Just do the best you can." She is glancing at her guests, wondering if she should order them to keep out of Susan's way, when a voice in the foyer distracts her.

She goes to greet the new guest, a tall black man carrying a large crystal decanter. "For you," he says in an accent Hailey can only place as Haitian or Jamaican, and hands the bottle to her.

Leanna kisses him lightly on the lips and takes his hand, leading him into the crowd.

Hailey had been to parties like these but never in places quite so elegant. Nor has she ever been in a group with such a varied racial backgrounds. Yet the hedonism of so many shocks her. The woman with the pipe is circling the room, blowing smoke into the open mouths of both men and women. A black woman, beautifully dressed in a blue silk shirt and pantaloons, has bared her breasts and is swaying in time to the slow reggae beat from the stereo speakers. Two men circle her waiting for her to fall. Raucous laughter bursts from the dining room, and in the shadows beside the stairs, a woman is complaining to her partner, her voice alternating between whines and sobs.

And through it all, Leanna stands on the stairs, her hand still joined with her dark-skinned companion, her expression regal, a plumed carrion bird feeding off the energy unleashed by this crowd.

Nourished, yet alone—as alone as she was among Carlo's perfect guests.

"Louis is upstairs waiting for you," Leanna tells him.

"Join us," the man whispers in his soft patois. The brush of his hand against her bare shoulder makes her feel weak with desire, but she fears him as well.

"I can't," she says softly and starts down the stairs. One step and she feels a tightening as if some invisible hand has gripped her womb. She pulls in a quick breath, not from pain but from understanding what the pain means. She is still Carlo's mistress, and treated as a mistress. The thing that would have made her his wife has once more eluded her.

"What is it?" her guest asks.

"Nothing," she lies. Tears betray her.

She had been two weeks late. She had hoped almost as much as Carlo. . . .

"No!" Hailey moaned. The sound woke her and she lay shivering, understanding finally the nature of the bond between her and Leanna. As she wrote down the details of the dream, she cried for Leanna and the child that was never born.

Yet, empathy did not make her blind. Leanna would not have been the most ideal of mothers, nor a woman foolish enough to believe a child would not burden her life. She had years in which to conceive a child. Why such a rush with a man like Carlo?

You're too cerebral, Hailey, she told herself. The most unlikely candidates choose to become mothers every day.

But whatever motive pushed Leanna toward motherhood remained a mystery. As Christmas approached with its usual astonishing speed, Hailey slept alone.

For days after, Hailey's dreams were her own, not pleasant. Eventually, she stopped sleeping at all, lying awake as her mind traveled in frantic worried circles, moving nowhere. Desperate for relief, she dug the little bottle of green-and-tan pills out of the bottom of her dresser drawer. There were only ten left and no refills on the antidepressant. She'd ration them to one every other day and call her doctor after the new year to arrange a refill. In the meantime, at least she'd work.

The last few days in New Orleans had been unseasonably cold, so cold that Hailey found frost on her car's window when she left for her breakfast meeting. The icy morning weather did not sit well with the thin-blooded natives, and the streets were almost empty as she drove north.

After her meeting with Jacqueline Menieur, Hailey had gone to the courthouse and looked up the death records for Leanna's parents. The same physician had signed the cause of death for both of them. Though near seventy, the man was still in practice, working in a charity clinic near the fairgrounds.

She met him for breakfast at an all-day café near the doctor's office. Whatever Robert Chase's qualifications as a doctor, he certainly looked the part. Handsome, and just portly enough to be fatherly, Chase had gray hair that had probably been dark when he was younger. He wore a pair of glasses only for reading and the rest of the time fixed his gaze on whoever was talking to him with an intensity any patient would have found reassuring.

As Hailey tried to explain about the novel she was writing, she discovered that Chase also seemed to know a great many people. She was constantly interrupted, first by the waitress that served them, later by a pair of teenage girls, one of whom kissed his cheek, then by an old beggar who saw him through the window, waved and came inside to ask for loose change for coffee and toast.

Chase said he'd pick up the man's tab, then turned his attention to Hailey. "What in the hell do you want to write about that for? Seems to me that family suffered enough."

"Louis de Noux gave me permission to write it. I suppose I could call him and ask about his parents but it seemed kinder to get the information from someone less close to the family."

"Less close? Compared to the kids I guess that's true. I was Joanna's doctor for the last three years of her life and Henri's for all the rest of his."

"What did you think of him?"

"You going to quote me?"

"No, I'm just curious since he was so much in charge of the family."

"In charge? Yeah, he ruled them all with the warmth of Stalin or Hitler. But he was brilliant, and one hell of a speaker. Because of it, clients overlooked his shortcomings, though I doubt he had any friends."

"How did he die?"

"Just the way I marked it down. In layman's terms, his system failed—kidneys, liver, heart, brain. The only things that seemed to survive until the end were his lungs and his lousy disposition. He must have gone through half a dozen nurses in the last month of his life. And it amazed me how dutiful his kids were about running to his bedside every time he looked about to croak. At the end, Louis even sent the nurses out of the room and sat alone with the body for an hour after he passed on. He shook his head. "Devotion is a curious instinct," he said.

"What was Joanna like?"

"A saint, at least compared to Henri. Up until the accident, she'd been the most beautiful woman I'd ever met. Even after, when she was in so much pain, I'd rank her up in the top ten. Poor thing. I don't believe in mercy killing but I might have made an exception for her if she'd asked. She never did."

"Louis mentioned the pain. He didn't explain the cause of it."

"An auto accident. Her spine was crushed but some of the nerves were intact and raw. For the rest of her life, she had peace only when sedated. As for Henri, he had to live with the guilt."

"He'd been driving?"

"No." He considered his words, decided to go on. "On the night of the accident, we'd had one of those winter cold snaps like we're into now. Henri'd been drinking so Joanna had to drive. She spun out on an icy bridge north of Mandeville.

"He worshipped her, as well he should have since she married him. He never forgave himself."

"How did he take it when she killed herself?"

"She didn't."

"She took pills, didn't she?"

Chase looked astonished. "How in the hell did you find out about that?"

Hailey conjured a quick lie. "I interviewed a friend of Leanna's. He told me that she'd mentioned the pills to him."

"Well, somebody's got the facts wrong, missy. You see, Joanna always took a lot of morphine so she built up a tolerance for it. The pills that were left in her prescription bottle wouldn't have been enough to kill her. They only made her pass out. When I saw her, she was hanging over the side of the bed. In that position, she couldn't swallow right. In lay terms, she choked on her spit."

Or maybe she'd come to when she started choking. With no way to summon help, she'd died.

"Was no one there?" Hailey asked.

"The kids were asleep. When Henri found the body, he had the good sense to leave her as she was and call me. The signs of what had killed her were clear. I found the bottle under the covers when I examined her. I put it in my pocket and never mentioned it to Henri. That family had already been through enough."

But Henri had seen it, Hailey thought.

And he'd used the information, as he might have used it against a hostile witness, wearing down his daughter's defenses until all she could do was submit.

"Your check," Chase said, handing it over to her. The beggar's meal was on it as well but the food had been a bargain. Hailey paid it all.

Back in her room, she added the doctor's information to her notes. Midway through the work, she paused and stared at the drawing on the wall.

"Do you understand what I've learned, Leanna? If you can hear me, take comfort now. You didn't kill your mother. You never had to live with all that guilt."

ELEVEN

Ed O'Brien spent six days thinking about his meeting with Hailey before he called her. However, he could not delude himself. His call had nothing to do with Joe Morgan. Tonight he wanted her understanding, the empathy she hadn't had to mention because he'd noticed it in her expression when he spoke about Joe.

Of course, she made an assumption and asked about the murder as soon as she heard his voice.

"No, I haven't seen Leanna's file," he said. "But you had asked about the city itself. I thought that maybe you'd like to go out to some of the places where she went, get some notion of the local color."

"For research?" she asked.

"If that's the way you want it." He didn't try to hide the disappointment in his voice.

She caught the tone right away. "Yes, I'd like to see you," she said.

"If you don't mind a weekday evening and the short notice, tonight would be good since I'm off tomorrow."

She laughed. "I set my own hours. Tonight will be fine."

They decided on eight.

She worked until nearly seven, then showered and stood in the center of her room, staring at herself in the full-length mirror she'd hung on her closet door. Her sedentary job had deposited an extra layer of fat around her hips but she was still slim. A bit too flat chested, her mother used to say. That problem had gone away, briefly, in her pregnancy but she did not miss the sight of those breasts now. No, what

123

troubled her most was the tight set of her lips, the severe expression in her eyes, as if, having experienced pain, she was determined never to open herself to it again.

And she hadn't. Not one date since the divorce two years ago. She'd considered going out with a few men, but always she had shut down the feeling, uneasy at the attraction she felt, uneasy too about the occasional advances. Eventually her loneliness became habitual.

She chose her clothing with care, black lace panties and bra beneath the red silk shirt and jeans. She applied her makeup using more color than usual then played with her blunt-cut hair until it hung softly around her face. Lastly, with a touch of daring, she opened the bottle of Norell that Leanna had purchased and dabbed a bit of it behind each ear and between her breasts. "Share with me, Leanna," she said aloud, knowing that she meant more than just the perfume.

Ah, the temptation to be just a fraction as wild as her ghost!

O'Brien arrived a few minutes late. When she'd seen him before, he'd appeared slim beneath his loose-fitting suit coat. Now, in a cable knit sweater and jeans, she could see the muscles in his arms and the width of his shoulders.

How odd that she should notice his body so quickly. Was she really prepared to behave like a romantic fool on her first date?

But Leanna would have noticed the man's physique. And Leanna could hardly have been accused of being either romantic or a fool. Hailey stifled a smile and offered her date some wine.

While she was pouring it, he complimented her on the changes she'd made in the room, then stepped onto her balcony. When she joined him, she found him leaning over the railing, watching the crowd coming and going in the restaurant below.

"I used to eat downstairs when I first came to town," he commented. "Back then Frank's restaurant was just a greasy

spoon. He had a knack with spices even then. It's good to
see real talent get its due."

"Have you eaten there since?"

"Once. I was hoping it would be a special occasion."

"And it wasn't?"

"Things didn't work out." He seemed about to add
something more, but instead veered in a slightly different
direction. "Have you ever been married?" he asked, stress-
ing the pronoun slightly.

"Once. It ended. . . . politely."

"Kids?"

"No." She wanted to talk. Wanted it desperately. Someday maybe, if not with Ed than with someone else. "And
you?" she asked.

"A girl, Willie. She turned thirteen today. I've never
missed her birthday before but my wife . . . ex-wife . . .
moved up to St. Louis to be close to her mother and took
Willie with her. I just heard she's getting married again
soon."

So he needed someone to pass the time. The thought
didn't hurt. Undoubtedly there had been other choices. "Did
you split up recently?" she asked.

"Seven years ago." He gave few details, noting simply
that his work made his wife too anxious; that she'd wanted
him to quit but he'd loved the job. "What about you? How
long have you been divorced?" he asked.

"Almost two years." Would she feel the same cutting
anguish she detected in Ed O'Brien when the number
reached seven? Most likely not. The circumstances differed.
Nothing held her and Bill together. "I'd rather not discuss
this," she said.

He shook his head and broke into a sheepish grin.
"You've been patient," he said and looked beyond her at the
red haze over the city, the oncoming night. "Shall we go?"
he asked and finished the last of his glass.

She slipped on her leather jacket. In Wisconsin she had

used it in the fall. Here, it was carrying her comfortably through the winter.

They started at the farthest place, a little tavern and dance hall on Robertson just west of Napoleon Street. Though there was a stage and dance floor, it was too early for music and only a few stragglers, many in work clothes, congregated in the bar, their hands wrapped around glasses and bottles of local beer.

Hailey walked along the edge of the dance floor, studying the pictures of bands that performed there, while O'Brien got them each a beer. "Leanna liked the bands with a heavy beat," he said. "Joe told me they always came when this one was playing." He pointed to a picture of what could only be a rock band, the woman in the center probably naked from the waist up, her breasts obscured by her long back-combed hair. The autographs on the picture were illegible.

"Just a second," O'Brien said and returned to the bar. As he rejoined her, a heavy bass band started on the bar's sound system.

"Yeah, them," he said before she could ask.

Hailey closed her eyes and let the music fill her, thinking of Leanna and how she would have moved in time to it, her long, thin arms above her head, her hips swaying. The deep rhythm beating against her chest moved naturally down, until she felt it in her womb. Her arms were empty—and waiting. Her sex was warm—and waiting. And for a moment only, Leanna became real, became. . . .

"What is it?" O'Brien asked as she opened her eyes, suddenly as if she'd begun to doze off and he's shaken her awake.

"Nothing. . . . Well, I guess that writer's empathy I mentioned got the better of me for a minute."

"If your hair starts changing color, I promise to let you know right before I run." When her expression made it obvious that she wasn't quite sure he was joking, he broke into a boyish grin. "I didn't like the woman. I especially didn't like how she was all Joe could talk about every time we saw one another."

"He adored her," Hailey replied, recalling the dream.

"Everyone adored her, so why did she take up with a guy like Joe?"

Hailey had wondered the same thing. The answer lay in last night's dream. In time, she thought she'd sort it out or, more likely, Leanna would help her find it.

They found a quiet table near the back of the dance floor, just inside the closed doors to the courtyard, courtyards being, Hailey decided, as necessary in New Orleans taverns as tappers and washrooms. The courtyard reminded her of the beer gardens at home and she began describing Wisconsin, the cool summers, the long, snowy winters. She discussed her work and last, because once she mentioned her most important book the topic was unavoidable, she told him about her child.

She noticed that for a little while his eyes were as bright as hers. In spite of the horrors he must see every day in a town such as this, he could still find a source of tears.

She took his hand and described why she had come here. For a long time, she didn't think of Leanna at all.

They moved east to another tavern and then another, both too crowded for anything but a quick beer. "I don't know anywhere else she might have gone," he said as they left there.

"Then take me somewhere you'd like to go," she replied. "Someplace quiet where we can talk."

He chose the second floor bar in the Sheraton, and as she sat across from him, sipping her wine and listening to the modern jazz band, the breathy contralto singer, she thought of white roses and all the lovers meeting and parting in the rooms above her—the thought so filled with passion, the passion so real.

Ed O'Brien saw the change in her expression. He lifted her hand and kissed the back of it.

"Did you go to Leanna's funeral?" Hailey asked as they walked down the narrow street to his car.

"I went with Joe. He wanted the support."

"Who came?"

"Her brother, of course. The old housekeeper. Celeste, a voodooienne who—"

"I know Celeste."

"And about a hundred of Leanna's crowd of hangers-on. Quite a few of them were drunk."

"Her husband?"

"Ex. He sent flowers, white roses as I recall. He came late for the service, sat in the back and left before it was over."

Roses again. Would a man who killed his wife send a reminder of the night they'd met? "Was he a suspect?" Hailey asked.

"Just being Carlo Bucci made him that. I figure that he didn't want to face the brother."

"They don't get along?" Hailey asked, recalling Louis de Noux's barbed remarks about his sister's husband.

"If duels were still legal, one or the other of them would have been shot by now. Probably Louis."

"How did Louis act when he saw Joe there?"

"Polite. I was able to see his expression when someone pointed out Carlo, though. That was definitely hotter."

"So he'd passed judgment?"

"I'd say so. I did look into finding you the police report, by the way."

"And?"

"Not available. I figure that Bucci or maybe Louis had it buried."

"Could you talk to the detective who did the investigation?"

"One left the force. The other one . . . well, he's no buddy of mine. He'd want to know why I'm asking."

"You were Joe's friend, isn't that reason enough?"

"And it's an old case."

"All right. I won't ask you to stick your neck out for me. Let's forget about all of it for a while."

They tried. But in spite of their conversation about music, and foods, and favorite restaurants, neither of them could quite forget what had brought them together. The third time their conversation returned to Joe and Leanna, Hailey admitted defeat and asked, "Where is Leanna buried?"

"St. Vincent's. It's not far from here. I could drive you past, maybe even get you in since the sexton lives next door."

"You're not getting him up this late. I can go some other time. Now, if you wouldn't mind a visit to Sonya's Kitchen, I'd like to treat you to one of Frank's outrageous creations."

As she expected, he talked of his marriage while they ate. Later, over snifters of Benedictine carried up to her room, he discussed his work. She listened carefully to his details on how police analyze a crime scene, from the position of the body to the shape of the blood spatters to all the minute pieces of hair and fiber. Was that done for Leanna's murder or had they just assumed Joe Morgan was guilty? And if so. . . .

No, Hailey, she admonished herself, don't bring up your case now.

She looked past him at the drawing on the wall. Just for a moment, she concentrated on Leanna. The result was a tingling in her body, the presence she had come to know so well.

O'Brien didn't know whom he saw, but he did recognize the intensity of the passion in her eyes, the open-lipped smile that belonged to the ghost of another woman.

He'd been intending to go. Not anymore. He pulled Hailey to her feet and kissed her. There, in his arms, Leanna released her hold.

And Hailey, amazed at how right his kiss felt, stayed.

Her hands shook as she undid the row of tiny silk-covered buttons on her blouse, even more as she unbuttoned his shirt. Weren't there things she was supposed to ask?

Protection she should demand? And if he had brought
something, how should she feel?

He reached into his back pocket and took a condom from
his wallet.

Safe, she decided, as he laid his shirt over her blouse on
the back of her desk chair, as he turned and reached for the
front hook of her bra.

For a time she forgot that this was not entirely her room,
and thought not of Leanna but of the hands and the lips, the
scent of the body of the stranger beside her.

Later, after they'd used her settee in a way the cultured
turn-of-the-century owner would have only imagined, after
they had ended in the bed, after O'Brien had dozed off
beside her, she stared at the ceiling and wondered what she
had done.

Outside, she heard laughter, and it echoed in the silence
of her room.

Hailey woke to the sound of knocking on her door,
O'Brien calling softly. He'd gone to the café on the corner,
returning with coffee and a pair of apple croissants. As she
dug napkins out of the sideboard, she glanced at her
reflection in the cupboard glass. Her hair was rumpled, her
eye makeup smudged. The sight reminded her of a meticulous purebred collie her mother had owned. It had gone into
heat and managed to get out. When it returned the next
morning, it looked pretty much like she did now.

"About last night, I don't, well actually I never . . . ,"
she began.

"You made a first date exception for me?"

"Yes." More than that, actually, but she wasn't about to
admit it.

"I'm glad." His grin had to be returned.

By the time they left her apartment, it was after ten. They
stopped for breakfast at a converted house painted a muted
shade of pink, picked by O'Brien because the Crawfish
Benedict came with genuine béarnaise sauce.

"Why didn't they arrest Morgan right away? Wouldn't it be obvious to them that he would have been the one?" Hailey asked while they ate.

"They might have but Joe was unconscious when the police got there, and from the shape he was in, he'd probably taken or been slipped some drug hours before. At the time, Leanna had been dead less than a half hour."

"So he couldn't have done it?"

"He could have but it was highly unlikely. At that time, the Booch was the most likely suspect."

"Suppose the police had gotten there later, say the next morning, after Morgan woke up and found the body?"

"Joe could have proven that he'd been drugged but the extent of it would have been impossible to gauge. Yeah, he would have looked a lot more guilty in the morning."

"Where had they gone that night?"

"A few clubs. They finished with drinks downstairs then came up here. Somebody stabbed her less than an hour later. By the way, she did run into her ex at one spot. He gave a statement to the police to that effect and there were witnesses that placed him elsewhere all night."

"But he wouldn't have done it himself anyway."

"Exactly." His expression altered, becoming more concerned. "But it did have all the marks of a crime of passion, and hit men are rarely passionate. Listen, as far as the police are concerned, Joe solved the crime with the note he left. Let the matter be. Write your book as fiction. Change the names. Solve the murder however you want. Invent some crazed ex-lover or some superstitious bastard who killed her in retaliation for an imagined hoodoo. But don't fool around with Carlo Bucci, because he knows people who will bury you so deep that no one will ever find you."

The last sentence stuck in her mind on the drive to St. Vincent's. And as she walked along the raised crypts and the occasional stone slab, over those who wanted a more traditional burial, she recalled the tales she'd heard of heavy rains and floods and how bodies refused to stay politely interred. Bury someone too deep and they'd most likely rise in New Orleans. Was it no wonder that the living would question whether a loved one had indeed passed on?

And no wonder that they would placate their ancestors so carefully. Hailey doubted that she had ever seen so many fresh flowers on old graves anywhere else in the country.

"Here it is," O'Brien said, pointing behind her at the de Noux family crypt. Though the pink granite columns holding up a pair of stone arches were clean, there was an air of antiquity about the crypt. The earliest name on it belonged to Leanna's mother. Henri de Noux's name was on the plaque for the space beside her, Leanna's just beneath her mother's. There were spaces for at least a dozen more nameplates, though the crypt could only hold one more body.

"Old Henri believed in planning ahead, didn't he?" O'Brien remarked.

"I don't understand. Where will they put the extra bodies?"

"Ah, you're a tourist. I forgot." He pointed at the crypts around them, showing her that the number of names had nothing to do with the space inside the tombs. "You see, burial aboveground is a custom dating to the time the Spaniards held New Orleans. There are only a handful of cemeteries in the city limits and all of them are small. They accommodate the need, however, because bodies decompose so quickly in the heat and damp. A year and a day after they are interred, another body can be added. Then the sexton opens the grave, removes what is left of the casket and uses a broom to sweep back the remains. They fall down the rear of the tomb to mingle with bones of their ancestors and make room for the fresh corpse."

"So Leanna is resting in the space her mother had occupied?"

"Yes, and if the family dies on schedule, Louis will eventually occupy Henri's space beside her."

Hailey nodded then stooped down to study the crosses

scratched into the door beside Leanna's name plaque, the small pot of violets on the ground in front of her tomb and the pieces of tattered lace and wilted flowers scattered on the stone ledge beneath it. "People believed in her power, didn't they?"

"Some still do. If she were interred at St. Louis Cemetery instead of here, you'd see more signs of her followers/"

"Wouldn't they come anyway?"

"Offerings are discouraged here. They make the grounds too messy. Even so, the sexton will leave these for a while."

Hailey faced the crypt, wondering why she had bothered to come here. There were no answers to be found among these beautiful stones, these lush tiny squares of grass. As for the ghosts of the departed, she doubted they'd be found anywhere in the vicinity of their mouldering bodies. "Let's go," she said.

He pulled up in front of Sonya's Kitchen, kissing her before she left. "Dinner Sunday night?" he asked.

She nodded, thankful that she had four days to sort out her feelings.

TWELVE

For the next three nights, Hailey dreamed only of Leanna.

Leanna the child, slipping into her brother's bed, holding onto him tightly while the screams of their dying mother echoed down the long, bare halls. There are tears in Louis's eyes but Leanna's expression remained as impassive as her emotions. Nothing would touch her soul any longer. . . .

Her mother's casket. The pale blue lining that is meant to complement her coloring instead makes her look thinner, more drawn, as if the agony of her last days has not been erased by death.

Leanna stands beside Louis, her grief so profound that she has no way to express it. Tears leak from beneath her brother's dark glasses; his body shakes with strangled sobs. Henri de Noux comes up behind the pair, standing between them. His hands rest on Leanna's shoulder, squeezing hard enough to cause pain.

She winces. Tears come to her eyes now. Papa must have his correct display of grief.

Later, Leanna and Louis, as always side by side, stand at the crypt in St. Vincent's, watching their mother's body laid to rest on the heavy marble stone.

Leanna returns to the cemetery later that night, a thin, frightened waif clutching Jacqueline's hand, leaving a glass of water and a plate of cookies on the stone slab below her mother's resting place. Before she leaves, she rips a button from her coat and lays it beside the food. . . .

Leanna in a white round-collared blouse and check wool

135

skirt—the latter far too warm for anything but the deepest of the New Orleans winter—walks home from school alone. All around her other children are laughing, talking. One sings a church song in a high, beautiful soprano. Leanna ignores them, her mind fixed on the ceremonies she will attend that night. . . .

Leanna and Louis at the dinner table, their father at the head with his eyes shut, his head bowed in prayer. In the shadow by the kitchen door, Jacqueline waits to serve the meal. Leanna looks up at Jacqueline, winks and smiles. Jacqueline's eyes grow wide. She puts her hand to her lips, reminding Leanna of the penalty for impiety. Leanna straightens her shoulders and winces at the sharp pain across her back from a recent blow.

It seemed to Hailey that she was being made to view the more ordinary aspects of Leanna's youth—perhaps so she would trust Leanna's spirit more, perhaps so she would find pity or even affection for her.

Instead Hailey felt manipulated, impatient. Nonetheless, she jotted down the descriptions of the dreams, including the most minute details she could recall. And, with no spirit to guide her, she began filling in the gaps in the more recent dreams, painting an ever darker picture of Henri de Noux— the rages and brutality behind his intellectual facade. Hours rolled by. Page after page was added to her file. Often, she lost track of time, as if she slept or Leanna had possessed her. But the words were always in her own style, and never unfamiliar to her as they'd been in her brief, still unsettling, experiment.

In her book Leanna and Louis were orphans, and Henri their uncle. A thin disguise but far enough from the truth to pass as fiction.

O'Brien called briefly Friday afternoon to set a time for their Sunday dinner date. In the last four days, with the exception of a few words exchanged with shopkeepers and waiters, he was the only person she'd spoken with. But she had hardly been alone.

*   *   *

Celeste stopped for a visit late Saturday afternoon, sweeping into the room in her powder-blue wool cape and red jersey turban. Against Hailey's dark wall, the color of her clothes, her nails and her lips made her resemble most an exotic painting on velvet. "I wondered if you saw the Sunday news," she asked.

"Sunday?" It never occurred to Hailey to buy her Sunday paper on Saturday.

"Here." Celeste pointed to a feature column on the front page that detailed city events. The first section was devoted to her.

Hailey Martin, author of a series of books for Russ Chitin Press, is spending a few months in New Orleans researching a suspense novel based on the murder of Leanna de Noux.

Ms. Martin states that she became familiar with the murder after she moved into the apartment where the crime had been committed and discovered voodoo drawings on the wall, which she believes were made by de Noux herself.

The story went on to describe the murder and suicide that happened in the one-room apartment above Sonya's Kitchen, then concluded with a summary of Hailey's own background. Henri de Noux and Carlo Bucci were both mentioned, Carlo far more than once. The article concluded with a thought Hailey found especially alarming.

Previous renters of the apartment where the murder and suicide occurred believe the room to be haunted. If so, we can only wonder what muses will be assisting in writing this novel.

As Hailey read the article, a sick feeling grew in her stomach. "I didn't know about this," she said.

"I didn't think you did. Who do you suppose called the press? Your agent perhaps?"

"No. And not my publisher either; at least they've never done anything like this before without discussing it with me."

"So who would have wanted everyone to know?"

"Frank Berlin maybe. The story might be good for his business, though he hardly needs a longer line outside the place. Louis de Noux might have, just to make Carlo Bucci squirm."

"Or the story could have come from any of the waiters downstairs who overheard Frank or you talking about it," Celeste added.

Or Jacqueline, for the same reason as Louis, Hailey thought.

"Call the paper. Ask them where the story came from."

"On Saturday night?"

"News doesn't stop on weekends. Someone will be there."

Hailey did as Celeste suggested and reached a night editor who sounded earnest and helpful. After she explained who she was, he put her on hold and made a call, most likely to the person who had written the story. When he returned to the line, he said, "Ma'am, I don't understand exactly . . . well, why you called. Adam Wolfe said that you called in the story three days ago. He checked it with your publisher and . . . and . . . Was something wrong with it?"

"No . . . no, nothing. Thank you. I'd like to talk to the reporter, though. When can I reach him?"

"Call Monday after eleven."

She lowered the phone slowly to the receiver, staring at it as if it could answer the questions rising in her mind.

Celeste was staring at her as if Leanna's ghost stood between them. "Is something wrong?" she asked.

"A woman called and said she was me."

"Why is that so shocking? Anyone on the list could have had someone else do the calling. Unless you thought . . . Has she taken control of you, Hailey?"

"Only when I've let her. You helped me do that and it was a disaster." Hailey showed her what Leanna had written, then described the migraine in excruciating detail. She left out only the shopping trip; it seemed too private a matter between her and her ghost.

Finally, she told Celeste about the dreams she'd recorded in the last few days. "Would the spell have worked on a man like Henri?" she asked after Celeste had read the file.

"He believed it had. That was the important thing."

"You mean there isn't anything concrete?"

Celeste smiled. "Are prayers concrete? Hardly, yet they give great solace to the one who says them. Everyone, even the wicked, wants God on her side." She stood in front of the painting on the wall, ran her hands over the letters. "I will never admit I said this, Hailey, but voodoo is easily explained. It is the religion of the powerless, nurtured in those years when bits of straw and hair and scraps of cloth and the magic of ancestral spirits gave the only power on which the poor uprooted believers could rely.

"From what she's revealed to you, it seems that Leanna was just as powerless. No wonder she became such an adept."

She stared at the wall a moment longer and turned to Hailey. "I'm sorry but you must let me help you now. This room must be protected."

"It isn't necessary," Hailey replied, amazed at how calm she felt. "I don't fear spirits. Leanna's presence can handle them well enough. Besides, spirits didn't kill Leanna, and the men who did won't know that there's salt around my door or a fetish mounted inside to keep evil from entering my house. And if they do, they'd hardly care."

"Hailey, please. Let me do this."

Hailey circled the room, unwilling to allow the ceremony if she sensed any sign of disapproval from Leanna. She felt nothing. "Do it," she said.

"Tonight," Celeste replied. She sat on the bed, folded her long legs beneath her and shut her eyes. Hailey sat and watched her until she realized that Celeste's trance would last for some time. She tried to work, not at all surprised that she accomplished little until Celeste, apparently satisfied by what she'd learned, left her, promising to return at ten.

A shaft of sunlight moved across Hailey's wall and touched the edge of her computer screen. In the hour it took for that daily event to occur, Hailey sat staring at her last words on the screen, waiting for the inevitable, anxious to have it done with.

Even so, the fierceness of it shocked her. She'd just decided to take a break from the snail's pace of her work when the sudden pounding on the door froze her in the center of her room like a frightened rabbit.

She swallowed her fear. What could anyone possibly do to her on a Saturday evening? A crowd of gourmands had to be loitering in the restaurant lobby with nothing better to do then notice someone going upstairs. She went to the door, worried that she would reveal her fear, and opened it.

"I am Carlo Bucci," he said in a voice that managed to sound seductive in spite of its fury. Without waiting to be asked in, Bucci stalked past her into the room and thrust the section of the paper where the article had appeared into her hands. "Explain this!" he demanded.

Hailey had seen the man in her dreams, had felt him in Leanna's arms, but the experiences hadn't prepared her for his presence. Though he was not a large man, he seemed to fill the room. Perhaps it was his anger; the air seemed to crackle with it. Perhaps it was the fact that she could not look at him directly without being trapped by the intense expression in his eyes.

Under the circumstances, the expression was natural.

Or perhaps it was because she knew, as she always knew when confronted with real evil, that Carlo Bucci was a dangerous man.

"The article means exactly what it says," she replied.

"A book? About her?"

"A novel, about someone *like* her." She pointed toward her glass-topped dining table. "I was just about to brew some tea. Would you like to sit down and have a cup?"

He didn't appear to have heard her. Instead, he stared at the wall. "The article said there was a drawing. I thought it would be some little thing like the scraps of paper she used to leave around the house. These certainly look the same but this . . . is . . ." He turned to her, his expression one of such astonishment that she wondered if the emotion was real or some grandiose overacting. "Why did she do this?"

"I don't know. Do you have any thoughts on it?"

"She was never afraid of me, if that's what you mean. I used to think she wasn't afraid of anybody since she stood up to her tyrant of a father from little on. Later I learned that her entire life was one long defiance of her fear."

"Of whom?" Hailey tried not to make the question sound like a challenge.

"Of her father. Of her mother's ghost. And though she never admitted it to me or anyone, of her brother."

He and Louis despised each other; of course he would say that. "Did Louis share her beliefs?" Hailey asked.

He didn't seem to have heard the question. "But she was never afraid of me. She would go toe-to-toe with me in any argument. Usually she won. If she had been afraid of me, she never gave a sign. I found that—"

He never finished. Celeste stood in the open door, her lips forming a perfectly red oval of surprise. She dropped a large carpetbag just inside the door, recovering her composure as she did so, then glided toward Bucci with both hands extended. "Monsieur Carlo! Such an unexpected pleasure! I haven't seen you since Leanna's funeral. How have you been?"

He kept his hands stiffly at his side. "I'll answer your question about Louis," he said to Hailey. "They shared everything. She dabbled. He excelled." He turned and left as abruptly as he'd arrived.

Hailey leaned against the door and let out a loud sigh. "Whew! I feel as if a panther had been pacing the room. If your protection is anything like your timing, I think I need it!"

"Well, you attitude is better anyway." Celeste slipped off the blue coat. Underneath she wore a black knit jumpsuit that hugged her body, and black boots that rose to above her knees. Hailey hadn't seen a woman look so perfect in such a revealing knit since she'd fallen into an adolescent crush over Diana Rigg, and her character in *The Avengers*. "Now, can you do as I ask and not giggle?" Celeste asked.

"I'll try."

"Then here." Celeste handed her four white pillar candles and instructed her to put them in the four corners of her room, then light them. Meanwhile, Celeste laid a line of salt in front of the inner and balcony doors.

"Shouldn't it go all around?" Hailey asked.

"This is protection against men, not spirits. We will not upset the others who live in your room, *oui*? Now, stand here in the center, with your arms outstretched. I bless you, then this room, and we are done."

Hailey did as Celeste asked. The ceremony was similar to the one she'd participated in when she'd purchased her gris-gris bag, but now Celeste's voice sounded more emphatic. Beads of perspiration rose on the woman's forehead as she chanted first to Hailey then to the door and the window.

". . . to the saints Jude and Joseph, to the Orishas Baba and Yemaya and their children who walk the earth, protect this woman." Celeste scattered salt over Hailey's head.

"Protect these walls." A second scattering of salt in front of the doors.

"Protect this house from all evil." With this last, Celeste opened the inside door and scattered salt in the hall. Someone must have opened the downstairs door at the same moment because a cold draft rolled into Hailey's room. The candles flickered from the force of this unwanted guest but the flames did not die.

"Do we have to start over?" Hailey asked.

"No." Celeste replied. "That was the sign I'd hoped for. It's done." The woman fell into Hailey's desk chair, leaned back as far as the springs would allow and rubbed her temples with both hands.

"Berlin's maid always vacuums the hallway," Hailey commented.

"That salt was not a permanent thing. It was intended to scatter any malignant spirits who might be outside the door seeking some way in."

"They come through closed doors but not through walls?"

"And you once drank the blood of Christ as I still do, but in spite of our belief, it never tastes like anything but cheap wine."

Hailey understood all too well. "I'm sorry," she said. "I just like things to be logical."

"Then I'm surprised you haven't moved." Celeste rubbed her forehead with the back of her hand.

"Is your work always so exhausting?" Hailey asked.

"I took my cue from Leanna's drawing. She expected the worst; so did I. I've been preparing for tonight all afternoon." She accepted the wine that Hailey offered. "I haven't eaten since this morning so this is bound to go right to my head," she commented as she sipped it. "Now that I can break my concentration, tell me what Carlo Bucci said to you."

"Not much. I thought he was trying to scare me into abandoning the book but then he saw the drawing she'd left and he forgot whatever threats he'd planned to make."

"So her spell was strong enough to still work," Celeste said. "Now, I think we had better find me something to eat before I pass out in your bed."

Sonya's was impossible even at ten, the area around the cash register crowded with hungry souls. Celeste led the way to a tavern whose walls and ceiling were covered with photos of tourists who had eaten there. A single performer stood on the narrow stage playing guitar and synthesized rhythm, singing requests from the sparse audience. Though the outside doors were open, the narrow room was hot and steamy, warmed by a butane burner and a cauldron filled with boiling water. Beside the cauldron, live crawfish writhed in their crates, waiting their turn in the pot.

Ten dollars bought them both a feast-to-fill of fresh crawfish with garlic butter and French bread to soak up the grease. They dined—if that civilized word could be used to describe such barbarity—until the garbage plate they shared was piled high with empty shells and both their shirts were spotted with grease. If any of Celeste's followers were in the crowd, they sensed her mood and left her alone.

"Finished?" Celeste asked after they'd devoured their fourth serving.

"Maybe I have room for one more," Hailey replied and grinned. Whatever danger the future might hold had little impact on her mood tonight. She'd not felt this lighthearted in some time.

"Let's go back to your little home and talk some more."

They took the longer route, walking beneath the soft glow of the antique streetlights, through crowds sparse in the penetrating cold.

The door and stairway to the apartments were steamy, the lower hall and stairs filled with the scents of spices and chocolate from the neighboring restaurant kitchen.

Celeste inhaled deeply. "Chocolate sin tomorrow?" she asked.

"Every Sunday." Hailey pushed the murder from her mind and fumbled for the apartment key as they climbed the stairs.

As she glanced at the worn gold-and-green carpet in the hall, Hailey had a sudden vision of Sonya Berlin collapsed outside her door, her stockinged legs sticking out from beneath her long skirt, her cane outstretched.

And she had seen . . . ?

Perhaps she had glimpsed Leanna lying in the bed, or the murderer with his blood-coated clothing. Perhaps she saw the knife the police had never found until it reappeared at Joe Morgan's suicide. Perhaps . . .

Eight years, Hailey. Yes, eight years ago fear killed her. Now let it go.

As she touched the key to the lock, the door swung open.

Hailey backed away from the door, listening for some sound inside. "I locked it," she whispered to Celeste. "I know I did."

Celeste moved beside her, and kicked the door open. "Did you leave the light on?" Celeste asked.

"Maybe."

Celeste moved toward the doorway. "Wait!" Hailey said. "Someone might still be inside."

Celeste shook her head and stepped into the room while Hailey, more cautious, lagged behind.

"Is everything all right?" Celeste asked when Hailey joined her.

The drawers were shut, the closet undisturbed. Her jewelry case—the one with the combination lock that Bill had given her in anticipation of the gems she would one day own—was still in its place on the dresser. Even her desk looked as it had, with the articles on the murder still in their envelope. "Everything is fine, except that I did lock that door."

Celeste examined the outside of it, looking for signs that the lock had been picked, or the bolt somehow slipped. "If someone knew what they were doing, I suppose I wouldn't notice anything," she said.

"Or the protection you gave this room held."

"Often protection is a matter of little more than good luck. We may have returned just after the burglar broke in. He could have heard us coming and gone down the back stairs."

Hailey didn't answer. Had she closed the door all the way? Had she checked it to be certain?

She opened the top dresser drawer. The knife and perfume were exactly where she'd left them. "I could be wrong about someone being here," she admitted. "Let's just forget it."

Celeste stretched out on the divan. "Then tell me more of your recent dreams."

Hailey gave her the printouts on Leanna's two terrible memories of her father. As Celeste read them, her expression became intense, as if she were going into a trance herself. After she'd finished, she held onto the pages as if she were trying to absorb the emotion from them.

"When I was a little girl, my family lived with my grandmother in a town south of here. My best friend was Licinda, a little mouse of a child who lived next door to us. Every night her father beat her for some reason or another and he probably did other things, though in those days people didn't speak so openly about incest. If her mother tried to interfere, he beat her as well.

"Finally Licinda couldn't take it any longer. She packed all her father's things in paper bags and set them on the porch with a note telling him that she didn't want him to be her papa anymore. When he found it, Licinda was home alone. He became enraged and killed her.

"He said it was an accident. His wife said she believed him, but later, when he was released, the woman came to my grandmother to get a spell to determine if he was innocent or guilty.

"My grandmother gave her a tonic to slip into his drink. Then the woman was to wait an hour, tell him what she'd done and ask him if he had murdered Licinda. If he was guilty, the tonic would kill him. If he was innocent, he would live.

"Of course, he died. Everyone knew he would."

"What was in the tonic?"

"Nightshade. The moment the woman said what she had done, the rush of adrenaline mixed with the poison and froze his heart."

"Did your grandmother go to jail?"

Celeste smiled. "For bayou justice? Grandma only did what the courts couldn't do." She paused, went on. "So did Leanna. As I read this, I became sorry that I judged her so badly. She wasn't the bored little rich girl I believed her to be. Like the slaves who practiced their rituals in secret, she had reasons for learning as much as she did. I admit that her knowledge fascinates me. She wasn't just trained here either. She calls on the old gods, the ones whose names were once revered by the Yoruba, remembered only in Africa and Haiti."

Celeste described her own studies in Haiti, and a trip to Nigeria that she'd taken some years before that. At another time, Hailey would have been fascinated by the accounts. Not tonight. Someone had invaded her space. She sensed it in the uneasiness that seemed to emanate from the walls themselves.

After Celeste left, Hailey made certain the locks on the French doors were secure, then, for the first time since she'd some here, she fastened the chain on her door.

It wasn't enough. She slept fitfully that night until the dawn light touched the dark corners of the room and the streets came alive.

THIRTEEN

O'Brien arrived early the following night with a bottle of vintage Merlot and a pair of rosebuds in a milk glass vase. Hailey waited until she'd poured their wine before mentioning the news story. As she'd expected, he'd learned about it at work last night. "Everyone's assuming your publisher leaked it," he commented.

"The paper said I called. I can talk to the reporter tomorrow and clear the matter up."

He didn't remind her to be careful, while she, wanting this evening to belong to them alone, never mentioned her visitors or the open door.

They dined in a family restaurant on the north end of the city. "I thought you'd like to see more of the town than the moldering streets by the river," he told her. As they shared a plate of fried catfish sticks, he described his work, the hunches that paid off, as well as the mistakes.

The conversation at the tables around them grew softer as people began to eavesdrop. Hailey couldn't blame them. Ed's accounts were fascinating, and the last, a description of a woman who'd executed a most intricate plot to kill her husband then gone home and confessed the crime to her baby-sitter, was hilarious.

"Are criminals usually so stupid?" she asked.

"Just the ones we catch. The really intelligent ones can get away with murder for years, usually because no one's even certain a crime has been committed. The bodies never surface, or if they do they're so decomposed that Forensics is lucky to be able to determine the cause of death, much

149

less find clues about the murderer. And if the body turns up, it's usually nowhere near the actual site of the murder."

If Carlo had killed Leanna, wouldn't he have done it that way? "What about hit men?" Hailey asked.

"Professionals. Their weapons aren't traceable and they have no ties to the victim, so all they worry about is being seen. And if they are caught, they never talk. Now if Leanna—"

"No," she said, "don't mention her tonight."

Or what, Hailey—she might steal into your body, control your mind, ravish your man?

He smiled, so warmly she knew it was exactly what he'd wanted to hear.

After dinner, he drove to a beach on Lake Pontchartrain. The cold night air raised a thin mist from the water that curled upward, obscuring the stars near the horizon. The only other people at the beach were an old black woman and a little girl, most likely her granddaughter. They sat together on a bench near the water, the old woman whispering to the girl while the girl nodded and tilted her face toward the stars.

Hailey, the observer of others' lives, wanted to move closer, to listen. Instead, she pulled her coat tightly around her.

"Cold?" Ed asked.

"A little."

"I've seen your place. Can I show you mine?"

Something in Hailey, the part of her she wished wouldn't possess her so strongly, wanted to say no, to order her to go home to her little room and dream of lovers. She ignored it and reached for Ed's hand.

His house was on a narrow street with houses on one side and a park on the other. The design seemed more northern fifties than New Orleans—the huge picture window in the living room, the kitchen with a dining island, the bath with its original pink plastic tiles.

"And three bedrooms down the hall. Perfect for the modern family," Ed said. "Only my aunt's husband died a few months after their marriage, so they never had kids. She didn't remarry; instead she became a second mother to her nephews. About the time of my divorce, I moved to New Orleans and she invited me to live here. She died suddenly last year and left me the place."

The living room was decorated in a blend of provincial and colonial, perfect "aged aunt" right down to the crocheted lace doilies on the back of the green brocade sofa and high-back velvet chairs.

He guessed why she was trying not to smile. "I don't have a lot of free time. When I'm here, I like the little reminders of her. And no, I haven't seen any sign of her since she passed on." He turned off the living room lights and pointed toward the park across the street. "On the other hand, if there is any other place besides your room that is haunted in New Orleans, it's there in Bayou St. John where Marie Laveau and Dr. John held their rituals, and where Leanna most likely learned much of what she knew. They called on the spirits often enough that a lot of natives think the ghosts are still hanging around, like guests that don't know when the party's over."

Hailey moved closer to the window, straining to see the water through the thick shrubs and trees.

"Sometimes late at night, I think I still hear the drums," he said. "There were plenty of rituals there when I was just a kid. Once, I snuck out to watch. No one knew I was hiding in the bushes near the site. I hid for hours and saw it all—the little kids dancing with their parents, all looking possessed, and the poor animal they killed."

He pressed against her back, his arms circling her chest as he went on. "It's a religion, I know that. But it gives no solace, no guidelines for a better life."

"That's probably why so many of its believers also go to church," Hailey said.

"I wish I'd met you some other way," he said.

Then I wouldn't have been ready, Hailey thought. Leanna prepared me for you. Leanna even kissed you that first time. She turned and put her hands on either side of his face, looking at him a moment before pressing her lips against his. After, without a word between them, she followed him down the narrow hall to his room.

Stay away, Leanna. This time the beginning as well as the end belongs to me.

Unlike the rest of the house, the bedroom had Ed's touch—from the Danish modern teak bed with its dark check cover to the scent of Old Spice and bay rum. It was, however, as meticulously neat as the rest of the house.

Good husband material, her mother might say. But then she'd said the same about Bill.

Besides, there was no use in making more of their affair than it was. They hardly knew each other. Such things took time.

So what are you doing there? Her mother's nagging voice again. Go home.

She ran her hand across the top of the teak dresser. "A beautiful design," she said.

"I'd hoped you'd notice."

"That you shopped?"

"Now I am complimented. I made it, and the bed as well. This is how this cop unwinds."

"Creatively," she said, then added. "And safely."

"Safe my ass!" He held up one hand to show her the scar across the palm.

She kissed it, then moved close to him and raised her head.

After their first joining, he turned off the lamp and opened the curtains. The backyard was dominated by a huge willow that threw broken shadows into the room as they made love again, this time by the light of the moon.

Early the following morning, Hailey carried her clothes

into the bathroom, which appeared even more garish in the daylight, and dressed. After dropping a note on the table, she walked across the road and down a footpath to the bayou. Its thick brown waters seemed to have a sluggish rhythm independent of current or wind. The few trees that grew near the bank were thin and sickly and coated with dried moss.

Dead hands, she thought. Rotted shrouds. Rotted flesh reaching for the light, the air—for life.

A fallen log made a handy seat, and with the thin morning sun against her back, Hailey pulled out a small pad and paper and began to record her impressions of the land around her.

Ed found her there. He'd brought coffee, which she welcomed as much for the warmth the cup provided for her hands as for its taste.

"Let's walk," he said. She followed him down a winding footpath, her feet sinking into the spongy ground. He stopped beside a wide circle of rocks and logs and pointed to a fire pit at its center, then at a pile of rocks higher than the others, capped by a flat stone slab. "The king sat there," he said and she knew he was talking of the night he'd come here and watched.

"And the dancers circled the fire, carrying their offerings of bread and meat," she added and circled it herself, trying to feel what they had felt, to see them through the land. There were brown stains on the stones beneath the place where the king would have sat and, outside the circle, bones picked clean and scattered by scavengers that came long after the revels were over.

"Do they still hold rituals here?" she asked.

"Sometimes people come but not often anymore."

More like a pilgrimage to an ancient church, Hailey thought. Out of respect for Ed's dislike of the religion, she did not say the idea aloud.

"One of the women was really caught up in the the dance.

She rolled on the ground, ripping her blouse at the shoulder. When she jumped to her feet the fabric fell away and she was naked from the waist up. She didn't care, and I suppose the people with her were too caught up in the ritual to notice, but hell, I was eleven. I'd never seen a woman's breasts, or witnessed that kind of insanity. They brought a cat to sacrifice instead of a more traditional ritual animal. The poor cat was frantic, hissing and clawing anyone who came near its cage. We always had a cat at home, and I sat in the bushes wishing I had the courage to rush through the crowd, open the cage door and let it go. Instead I watched them pull it out of the cage by its tail and cut its throat so the priest could smear its blood on the lips of the believers.

"I had nightmares for weeks, but I could never tell anybody why."

The words had poured out of him—forced, Hailey thought, from some need to finally confess. "There wasn't anything you could have done," she said.

"I know. But the memory stays. And it's so strange. I've learned to ignore so much I can't help. Damn, if I didn't, I'd never have lasted the first year on the Lake Charles force. But when I have a nightmare, it's always about that cat."

They walked the better part of an hour, holding hands and saying nothing, until the path took them back to the road, and the road to the house.

He fixed her toast then drove her home and walked her to her—locked!—door. "You're working today, I suppose," he said.

"Eventually. We could find someplace for a late breakfast but first I want to solve the mystery of that article. Come on in."

He followed her, sitting on the edge of the bed while she dug through the papers on her desk, looking for Adam Wolfe's number, then realizing that she'd called no one since she'd phoned the paper. The redial on her phone connected her to a recorded message on an answering machine.

"No one is in the office this morning," a businesslike woman's voice droned. "Please leave a message at the tone. If you need to speak to Mr. Bucci . . ."

Hailey stared at the phone in her hand.

"Is something wrong?" Ed asked.

She broke the connection, handed him the phone and pressed redial again. "I didn't call him," she said after he'd listened to the message. Though she didn't want to worry him, she told him about the open door.

"Nothing was moved or taken," she concluded. "We thought the burglar hadn't even made it inside except he must have . . . but to make a phone call?"

"The bastard has an interest in knowing what you're doing," Ed commented. "He'd want your manuscript or your computer files. Maybe the person he sent hadn't expected to see that old five-inch drive so he called his boss to ask if he should just take the machine."

"Isn't that sloppy . . . for a professional, that is?"

"Not if someone was coming up the stairs and he didn't have time to erase the number."

"Or maybe he broke in just to make that call and throw me off."

"Nobody is that subtle. Have you heard from Bucci?"

"He came here."

"Damn!" He ran his fingers through his hair. "Hailey, I don't want to give you a lecture but I have to. You can't stay here. You have to finish this story somewhere else."

"He was furious at first," Hailey went on, ignoring his advice. "Then I told him the book would be fiction. It calmed him down a little. The drawings seemed to astonish him as much as they had me when I first saw them. I think that if a friend hadn't come when she did, we would have reached some kind of understanding."

"Understanding! With him? Hailey, listen to me. Don't be a damn fool, don't risk your life for something that's over and done with when—"

"My novel is in this room, and it's fact as well as fiction. I know you don't believe it, but it's true. I can't leave. Not until I know the outcome."

"Even if the outcome means that you wind up just like Joe and Leanna? Christ, Hailey, nothing's worth that!"

"I have to finish this."

He rested his hands on her shoulders. "If you have to stay in the city, stay somewhere else, where you'll be safe. I have room."

She shook her head and leaned against him. "I can't."

"Hailey, you have to know how much I—"

She took a step backward, then another. She didn't want to hear him tell her what he couldn't possibly know yet, and to have to wonder if he were sincere or only worried about a woman whom he might one day come to love. "I'm sorry, Ed. If I thought there were any way it would be possible for me to write my story anywhere but in this room, I'd agree. I can't."

"There has to be some way. . . ."

"No," she said, as gently as she could. "Now, if we can't just drop this, perhaps you should go."

"All right."

He agreed too quickly. "Ed," she said as he opened the door, "please understand."

"I think I do. I'll call you. I promise. Hell, I'm too damn worried not to."

And she was alone, with all the dangers that seemed to present.

She sifted through the scraps of paper on her desk until she found the reporter's phone number and called him.

"Adam Wolfe here. What can I do you for?"

He sounded informal, and hurried, not at all at pace with the city he covered. "This is Hailey Martin. I wanted to ask you about the article you wrote on my book."

"Yeah, the kid told me. Something wrong?"

"Where did the story come from?"

"You called me, remember?"

"Actually, I don't."

Wolfe paused, then asked, "Were the facts right?"

"Well, yes."

"Then the story was news and whatever it is you're trying to pull—"

"I'm trying to find out who called you."

"The voice sounded pretty much like yours."

"Pretty much?"

"Well, like yours without the northern accent. I said you talked like a native, remember?"

She couldn't ignore the second insult. "Mr. Wolfe. I never called you."

"Have it your way. I don't care."

He hung up before she could ask where he had obtained his information about the previous tenants.

Her voice without the northern accent. "Leanna, you damned bitch!" she whispered, too much the well-trained lady to scream, even now. "Are you so lonely you need to get me killed too?"

She covered her face with her hands, wishing desperately that Ed were here to comfort her, knowing she would never tell him, or anyone, what she had discovered.

A short time later, calmer, she did what had to be done. She called a locksmith and requested dead bolts for her front and balcony doors. While she waited for him to arrive, she copied her work on the novel onto three sets of floppy discs then erased the documents from her computer's hard drive. One set of discs would be mailed to Wisconsin; the second would be hidden in the apartment; the third would stay with her at all times. Let them come, she thought. Let them take the damn machine. The thing was worthless without the data.

She'd just finished the work when the locksmith arrived. She waited until the man had finished the work, before going downstairs to find Frank Berlin.

Sonya's Kitchen always closed early on Monday nights but it was the night the staff stayed latest. Hailey had grown used to the smell of kitchen cleaner and the droning of the industrial vacuum in the restaurant below her. Berlin had confessed to Hailey that he hadn't always been so meticulous, not until his apartment and the rental flat had been invaded by roaches following one of the restaurant's infrequent sprayings.

Berlin was at one of the tables that gave him a view of the kitchen, his huge body wedged into a captain's chair, the week's receipts in piles on the table. A ceiling fan whirring above him did little to dispell the sweat beading on his forehead, or dry the wet circles under his arms. "Is something wrong upstairs?" he asked, not pleased by her interruption.

"Something was." She laid the second set of dead-bolt keys on the table. "I took care of it." She told him what had happened.

"Jesus, I'm sorry," he said when she'd finished. "I saw the story yesterday morning but I didn't figure anybody would care enough about the murder to break in. Did you report it yet?"

"No. I'd rather you didn't, either. Nothing was taken. I just wanted to make sure my luck held."

"I guess it's your choice but if anything else happens, you let me know and I'll change the locks downstairs too. And if you hear anything funny in the middle of the night, you call me."

And Frank would come running in his black silk kimono brandishing a cleaver and fry pan. Sumo chef extraordinaire to the rescue. "I promise," she said.

"Good."

She could sense how busy he was, nonetheless he asked, "Would you like something? Bread pudding? Cheesecake? The last piece of chocolate sin?" He wiggled his thick eyebrows as he said the last.

She laughed. "The devil himself wouldn't sound so tempting. But what I'd really like is a drink."

While he fixed them each a vodka gimlet, she studied the photographs along the back of the bar. "Is that the way Sonya's used to look?" she asked, pointing to a photo of a crowd sitting on stools around the bar. Though the fashions and the setting appeared modern, the black-and-white photo had been developed in sepia tone to give it an antique look.

"Yeah. That hunk in the glasses is me fifty pounds ago." Frank took down the picture and handed it across the bar so she could see. With the amount of bulk he carried, Frank didn't look much different than he did today; a little more hair, a little less girth, but that was all.

"The bar went all along the front of the building and halfway down the side wall. It was so long I had to hire an extra bartender on weekends or risk falling while doing it all myself. There were a half dozen tables in the back but I couldn't afford a waitress so most of the regulars just ate at the bar."

"Was Joe Morgan a regular?"

"Ah, you're working, I should have guessed. He was for a while. Then I wouldn't see him for weeks. He usually sat right there, and when Leanna came in with him, she sat next to him." Berlin pointed to a spot just to the left of the hostess desk.

"And what did he drink?"

"Whatever he hadn't had the night before. He was picky that way."

Hailey moved to the spot, and tried to picture what they had seen.

"The old bar may have been wood but it was really pretty ugly. Not one of those ornate turn-of-the-century things that are worth saving," Berlin said.

"I see."

Those were the last words Hailey really heard. She felt a rushing inside her head, a tingling in her ears.

The bottles behind the chrome-and-tile bar suddenly looked shinier, more inviting.

She drained the remains of her glass and set it on the bar. "I have to go," she said and retreated.

Upstairs in her room, she fell upon the bed. The room spun around her with delightful abandon. "Leanna," she whispered and held out her arms.

FOURTEEN

Sunlight streams through the window, across the floor and the edge of the bed, across her bare foot poking out the end of the red chintz quilt that covers her. It wakes her slowly, and as it does she hears the soft music flowing from Sonya's room in the apartment next door, a glorious soprano singing an aria from *La Traviata*. Though the morning—a glance at the clock tells her that, yes, it is morning but not for much longer—is cool; the inevitable dampness makes her sticky, especially in the places where her body presses against Joe's.

Hard not to when the bed is so narrow.

Still she likes being here. The smallness of the room comforts her; the age of it makes her think that whatever spirits might watch them in this place have gone beyond the concerns of mortal men and women and mean them no harm. And the music Sonya plays is always beautiful, the way the world ought to have been made.

She only feels that way in this room, only feels safe with him. In the month they've known each other, she and Joe Morgan have spent nearly every night together, all but the first of them here. For some unfathomable reason, she never felt as secure in the house she shared with Carlo, or the place she owned in the Quarter, as she does in this room with the peeling rosebud paper.

She stands next to the bed, shaking the tangles from her damp hair, looking down at Joe. She kept him up so late—so delightfully late!—last night. He'd worked most of yesterday as well. No wonder he sleeps so soundly.

She'll go alone, she decides. Spending an afternoon in the old house with Louis and Papa is hardly Joe's sort of entertainment. Besides, she shouldn't lean on him. She's never leaned on anyone before.

Now that Papa is no threat to her, she enjoys torturing him in little ways. After her shower, she dabs perfume between her breasts, then slips a sundress over her naked body. Later, her makeup perfectly applied, the long, ruffled skirt beats against her bare stomach and thighs as she drives the few miles to her father's house.

The gate is unlatched, so she doesn't have to try to use a key that might not fit any longer. The front door hangs open. Even before she steps through it, she hears her father's voice, loud with fury, coming from the study.

She listens to her brother's reply, the reptilian smoothness of his voice. The tone never alters, even in anger or stress. She envies him that calm, that ability to act as if nothing is wrong in even the most terrible of circumstances. She pulls open the study doors and goes to stand beside her brother.

Henri sips his bourbon, the drink of gentlemen he used to say, though Leanna knows gentlemen never drink so early or so often. He began drinking during their mother's illness, out of guilt Jacqueline used to say. Louis told Leanna that now he even drinks before going to court. It's a mark of his genius that no one seems to notice.

But since his stay in the hospital after the stroke, everyone had begun to remark on the change in his appearance. The thick black hair has thinned and grayed. The trim figure has begun to go fat. Today she sees the strange ashen pallor to his complexion.

Drink has finally claimed him. His liver. His brain.

No, drink claimed his brain long ago.

He pours a second glass, holds it out to her. "Look at you," he says to both of them. "Useless, both of you."

She senses, rather than sees, a slight stiffening of Louis's shoulders. He has been carrying the firm for months, and managing it as well as Papa ever did. "Your children, Papa," Leanna says for both of them. "You made us what we are. We owe you for that."

"Owe me? Yes, I suppose you do. Well, remember, what was made can be unmade."

Leanna laughs. "Are you burning black candles to St. Michael, Papa? Are you praying for our deaths? Or have you some spell to alter the past so that we never even existed."

"Only legal spells. I'm no witch like you." His voice is slurred, malicious.

"You cannot fire me, Papa. You have partners," Louis said calmly.

"I can disown you. I can order you out of my house."

They know his moods too well to be frightened by his threats. "Does that mean I am suppose to leave the royal presence?" Louis asks. As always, there is a hint of a smile on his face, as if life is a joke and he the only one who understands the punch line.

"Put miles between us." Henri says. "Leanna and I are dining alone."

Louis looks at her. "Leanna, are you staying?"

She shrugs. "He's probably saving the majority of his wrath for me."

She waits until Louis has gone then sits on the arm of a chair and lights a cigarette, holding it exactly as her mother did. Her smile is her mother's smile, her voice her mother's voice. She knows it as well as he does.

"The house was Mama's. Even in the worst of times, Louis has always lived in it. You can't make him go," she tells him. Logic is wasted on him now, she knows, but perhaps he will remember her words tomorrow.

"He battles in court. Outside of it, you fight his battles for him. But this is one you and he will have to fight individually."

She refuses to be baited. "Let him stay, Papa."

"Well, I may, at least for a while. You, however, are on your own. I'm cutting you off as of today."

What does he think? That she's still a little girl in need of an allowance? "My separation agreement from Carlo takes care of me well enough."

"And how long will it last with the way you spend? Now I understand that you have a new lover to support."

"He supports himself."

"Badly, if the rumors are correct, and I doubt he'll have his job much longer, in which case you'll have to support him." He pauses, waits. She ignored the threat. "Are you happy?" he asks.

"I am."

"Well, that's something, but I have to tell you more. Yesterday, I visited your mother and I remembered a promise I made her before she died. This house was made for a family. That tomb was made for our heirs. Before she died, I told her that I would leave the house, the money—all of it—to whichever of you gives me that heir. It won't be Louis, I can guarantee that. It will be you."

Does he know how much Carlo wanted a child? The rumor probably gave him the idea for his threat. "And if neither of us oblige you?" she asks.

"Everything goes to charity. Breed soon, girl. The doctors tell me that I won't last long."

"And if I do, you'll attach no strings to the money?"

"None. Give it all to Louis if you wish. I don't care so long as there's a child." He pauses to finish his drink then pours another. She holds out her glass as well. "We always shared a taste for good bourbon, didn't we, girl?"

She does not answer. His tone makes her uneasy. It reminds her too much of the past.

The scene shifts away from the dark wainscotting, the bourbon and cigar scents of de Noux's house, to Joe's room—Hailey's room—and to Joe waking alone.

Leanna always sleeps fitfully, and usually rises before him, but Joe is used to seeing her in the room. Sometimes she reads or sits crosslegged in her meditating pose on the carpet.

There are two small mirrors strung on nylon line in front
of the outside doors, reflecting out, turning spells on their
makers. There is a small fetish above the inside door. He
would find the eccentricity of her belief charming did he not
sense the terror at the base of it.

Has she gone somewhere? He shuts his eyes and thinks,
recalling a vague memory of her mentioning something
about seeing her father. The phone at the de Noux house is
busy. He waits, calls again, and once more, then dials the
second line. Also busy.

If one line was busy, an answering machine should have
gotten the second line's call.

Unless the phones are off the hook . . .

Leanna rarely speaks of her father, but the few things
she's said about him are enough to make Joe concerned. He
dresses quickly and goes after her.

The front door of the great house is slightly ajar. He
pushes it open and enters. After the harsh sun, his eyes take
a moment to adjust, and find her crumpled in the corner
like a discarded porcelain doll, her white dress ripped at the
bodice, her cheek bruised, her body shaking with deep, dry
sobs.

He holds her, rocks her, until she seems almost calm.
"Who did this?" he asks.

"Papa," she replies and buries her face in her hands, as if
she were the guilty one for confessing.

He mumbles something and goes into the den, where
Henri de Noux is sitting in a chair with an empty glass in his
hand, his eyes fixed on the far wall. There are two deep
scratches on his face. "Look what the bitch did to me. How
can I go out in public after what she did?" he asks
woodenly.

The rage Joe felt when he saw Leanna's face, grows
stronger. "If you ever hurt her again, I'll kill you."

The old man gives no indication that he's heard.

If Joe touched Henri de Noux, his emotions would carry
him to some terrible conclusion. Instead, he returns to

Leanna—holds her, helps her stand, and walk, and go. She says nothing, not on the drive home or in the hours that follow.

Later, her brother brings Leanna's car to her. Though they have not met, Joe recognizes him immediately. He walks past Joe without a word, and goes to the bed where Leanna rests. She holds up her hand. He clasps it, and sits beside her.

Brother and sister.

Twins.

Joe's envy seems natural—Louis has known her forever—but his jealousy comes from a darker, more troubling place.

"Papa repeated what he told you," Louis said. "It's all right."

She grips her brother's hand so tightly. "He said he'd change the will. What he plans, he usually does."

"So? Morphine and Jack Daniel's is hardly a combination that assures sanity. I can have any new will declared invalid."

"He said he made a vow to Mama."

"Our mother is dead, Leanna. She doesn't care about his vow. Don't give Henri the satisfaction of thinking that he can drive a wedge between us with such drivel, you promise me that, all right?" He looks at her curiously. "You've never wanted children, have you?"

"Carlo did," she says and begins to tremble again, pressing against him. Finally, after hours of silently hiding the pain, the tears begin to fall.

And she is in her brother's arms, not Joe's.

Joe leaves them their privacy, and steps out on the balcony. Down on the corner a street band is pounding out a lively drinking song, the crowd around them singing happily along. He remains there even after Louis comes out to tell him good-bye.

"Joe?" Her voice is soft, broken by emotion.

He turns and sees her standing in the doorway, one hand

on the frame to steady herself. "You shouldn't be out of bed," he says.

"I'm not hurt, not really. Papa is too old to do any real damage."

"Why did he beat you?"

"Because it makes him furious that he can't do anything else. I made sure of that." She takes his hands, draws him inside.

And there, in the stillness of their little room, she tells him what Henri did to her for so many years, and the guilt over her mother's suicide that made her such an easy victim for so long. She describes the defenses she learned to protect herself, the empty months away at school when she longed for her brother and the city. She tells him how since her return she has made it a point never to sleep alone.

He'd heard of her reputation before they met. It hadn't mattered then, and doesn't matter now.

She does not cry, indeed displays no emotion. Neither does he, certain that any sympathy, any pity he would show would silence her.

When she finishes, she takes his hand and kisses it. "You were a policeman once?"

"Years ago," he reminds her. What must she think of him, she with the pot and the home-brewed rum, the spells and fetishes—those at least legal, though frowned on.

"Did you ever kill a man?"

Three actually. He was his force's crack shot, called on twice to end stand-off situations. But there was one special case, the man he killed after Ed was shot. He watched the man's face as he pulled the trigger and brought him down, not because of his job but because he wanted the man to die. "Yes," he says, thinking only of the last.

She begins unbuttoning his shirt. "How did it feel to take a life?"

Relief that the danger was over. The rest came later, after the ambulance had come to lift Ed out of the puddle his blood had made, after he had filed his report and gone home.

He tried to sleep but he saw the shooter, the surprise as he fell, the moment when his muscles went slack and the instant that life—that marvelous, miraculous spark—ended.

"I'd never seen a man die before," he says. "I never thought the memory of it would be so lasting."

"Do you feel guilty?"

"It had to be done. I had no choice. I don't feel guilty but I still see his face sometimes. Someone will remind me of it, or I'll go to a funeral, or cover a news story about someone who was shot."

"I shouldn't have asked."

"I'd think about him anyway. I can't help that. Talking doesn't make any difference."

But it did. "Your father's an old man, Leanna. From what Louis tells me, his health is terrible. Stay away. Don't give him a chance."

"I've only felt safe from him twice in my life—in the years with Carlo, and now with you."

"Not entirely safe." He points to the fetish above the door.

"That protects against magic, not men."

"Has someone been using magic against you?"

She does not look at him. "I don't know. I think so."

"Then let it stay, until you're ready to take it down."

In the days after he heard about the intruder in Hailey's apartment, Ed tried not to worry about her. It was impossible, especially when word got out at work that he'd gone out with her.

"Those suspense writers are all alike," one of the older detectives told him. "She'll drag the information she needs from you, make a big play for publicity then dump you after the book comes out."

"I know fear when I see it," Ed countered.

"Yeah, fear her act wouldn't work. Let it go. If somebody

really wanted to know what she was writing, they would've lifted the machine. If they were trying to stop her, they would've ransacked that apartment and broken everything they could find, and maybe left a dead chicken or something in her bed as a kind of warning. After all, the crowd the Booch hangs out with ain't exactly subtle."

"I told her that. She won't listen," Ed said.

"Yeah, brave girl. You'd know why she's so damn brave if you just started thinking with your brain instead of your dick."

What could he say? How could he explain? Hell with it, if he tried, they'd only think he was insane instead of horny.

Sometimes he agreed with them.

That feeling intensified after he paid a visit to Adam Wolfe. He'd met the reporter a few years before. At first he hadn't liked the barrel-chested little man with the clipped speech and equally precise manner.

Wolfe's fastidious facade hadn't lasted long. Ed found him easy to deal with, and the information he provided was always reported correctly. They'd even met informally for drinks and a few games of pool. Then Wolfe had asked for a transfer from the police beat and he and Ed had lost touch with each other.

"So you're involved with this too," he commented after Ed had asked about the story on Hailey. "I don't know what in the hell is going on but I'm sick and tired of that woman's act. I'm not shielding her from any criminal charges so I don't have to stand on writer's privilege. Hailey Martin called me, OK? I wrote down what she said exactly the way she said it."

"I doubt you talked to her," Ed replied.

"You don't believe me? OK, listen to this."

Wolfe pulled out a tape player, a tape and his notes. "I record all my phone conversations so I can double-check my facts. Like I say, I'm accurate." He advanced the tape to the number noted in his book and pressed Play. Ed had to admit that the voice on the tape sounded like Hailey, if Hailey had been raised in Louisiana.

Only the accent kept him from vowing to never speak to her again. After all, she'd been the first to admit it—her apartment was haunted, and she had been somehow possessed.

All of which would sound absurd to him if it weren't for those psychics with the miraculous hands, and the strange power that made him almost believe in a spirit world beyond his limited comprehension.

So instead he decided to help her as best he could. As he had expected, no one wanted to talk about the de Noux murder except for one of the medical examiners, an older woman who enjoyed flirting with him.

He bought her lunch, and asked about the drugs in Joe Morgan's system.

"I told the officers on the case that I'd have to testify for the defense. Joe Morgan couldn't have killed Leanna de Noux. He had a mix of chemicals in his blood that would have knocked out a man twice his size. Chloryl hydrate was the main drug, a little morphine and some odd things that made no sense unless someone was trying to kill him too."

"Odd?"

"Damiana. And some kind of venom, but the quantity was so minute we couldn't pinpoint the source."

"Could the venom have been intended to make Joe Morgan lose control?"

"After he lost consciousness? Maybe that's what it was intended to do, but if so, someone badly misjudged the dosages. I wish I could be more helpful."

"I'd say you've done a lot. Thanks."

Hailey didn't answer the phone when he called after work, but he reached her the next morning and asked how things were going, trying to sound as nonchalant as possible. Trying—hell, why not admit it!—to find out if he had any reason to be worried about her.

She sounded so glad to hear from him that he was forced

into honesty—he felt the same way. Instead of asking how things were going, he invited her to lunch.

Hailey might have turned him down, but there were only ten days until Christmas—a terrible season for loneliness, a worse one for fear.

He was her Joe Morgan. He made her feel safe.

They met at a diner on the north side of town. No Cajun food on the menu unless crabby corn soup would count. Ed told her they had the best deep-fried catfish in the state. They shared a platter of it. Over coffee, he told her about the examiner's report, then added that he'd visited Adam Wolfe and heard the tape.

"I don't have that unusual a voice," she said. "Someone who'd talked to me could have picked just the right friend to make the call."

Her voice had an edge he hadn't heard before. She was lying, not to him but to herself, and she wouldn't do so if she wasn't afraid.

He decided not to ask her why. "My suggestion about moving still stands," he said, as close as he'd come to warning her again.

"I know."

"I have to get back to work."

"Can I buy you dinner on your next night off?"

"That's tomorrow. Too soon?"

"Tomorrow's fine."

She went home and, with a burst of surprising holiday spirit, spent the next day preparing for the Christmas she'd intended to ignore.

When he arrived, she was waiting for him in a bright red blouse and black suede skirt. A tabletop tree lit the corners. Strings of colored lights adorned the balcony and the ceiling of her room. Her dining table was covered in a lace cloth with red liner, and on it a pair of votive candles flickered in their cut crystal holders. Red wine and one of Frank's uncut chocolate sins shared the table.

"I tried for a Midwest look right down to the chocolate,"

she told him and held out a wrapped box. "Merry Christmas," she said.

"I got you something but I thought we could exchange on Christmas Eve," he said.

"Aren't you going to St. Louis to see Willie?"

"I'd like you to come along."

"Is that right? I mean we haven't been going out very long."

He played with the ribbon on the package she'd given him. "Peg informed me yesterday that she'll be introducing me to her fiancé. They're getting married next month. It came as something of a surprise."

"How long have they known one another?"

"About four months."

"A quick courtship."

"Not for Peg. She and I only knew one another for six weeks before we got married."

"Weeks!"

"I'm good at snap decisions." He put the package on her table. "I know my asking is sudden, but we've had two evening dates ending with two mornings together. If I have my way tonight will make three. That's definitely a record for me for the last five years. How about you?"

"A lifetime record," she admitted. "But I have a deadline."

"Rent a laptop. Type in the car. I promise not to sing."
She laughed.

"We'll be gone four days max. Come with me, please. I want you to meet them both."

Leave her room? Her ghosts? Though she suspected that might be the reason he'd asked her, a vacation from them did have its appeal. "I'd like to give it just a little more thought."

"You mean I have to keep on being this charming all night?" He looked positively devastated, a small boy buttering up his mom for a favor.

"You won't be so charming when you discover what a beast I can be when I'm working."

"Really?"

"Really."

"Well, I ought to find that out early on, don't you think?" She smiled. He didn't press for an answer.

Instead they drove across the causeway into Mandeville then west to an old plantation house renovated and turned into a restaurant. There were white lights on the magnolia trees outside, huge pastel flocked trees and table arrangements in every dining room and the scent of cinnamon and bayberry filling the air.

They spoke of inconsequential things—Christmas customs in their homes, odd gifts they'd received, favorite relatives and events. Neither mentioned the murder, the threats or even his invitation, both of them willing to forget for the moment the most pressing concerns of present and past.

Midway through the meal Hailey reached across the table and took his hand. "I'd love to go north with you," she said.

He grinned. "I'm glad I didn't have to hold out the big carrot," he said.

"Carrot?" She looked hopefully at him, then coaxed, "Come on, what is it?"

"Joe Morgan's ex-wife is a friend of Peg's. I don't know her address and the phone is unlisted but Peg should have it. She and Denise used to be pretty close."

The waitress brought a dessert tray to their table. "Would you like to choose something?" she asked.

"Wine and sin," Hailey said, looking at Ed as she spoke.

The dessert tray wobbled, seductive sweets ready for the tasting.

"Just bring the check," Ed told the waitress. "We'll do our sinning elsewhere."

On the drive home, she sat as close to him as the bucket seats would allow, her fingers tracing patterns on the back of his hand.

Norman was carrying out bags of trash from the restaurant kitchen when Ed pulled his car into one of the private parking spaces in the back. When he saw Ed help her out of the car, Norman paused and—amazing!—smiled.

Had he really thought her a rival for Frank? Hailey wondered. If so, what must he have thought of Leanna, everyone's rival, when she sat beside Joe in the bar?

You're seeing the murderer everywhere now, she complained to herself. Besides, Norman didn't work here when the murder happened. Frank told you he came later.

He came after Sonya's kitchen struck gold. But that was hardly Hailey's problem.

The key to her dead bolt still had its rough edges. Hailey coaxed it past the tumblers and pushed open the door.

A different, more garish, Christmas was waiting inside. And along with the lights and the tiny tree, she detected a distinctive, familiar scent.

Leanna's perfume.

She pulled open the drawer and saw the little box of Norell exactly where she'd left it. "Looking for something?" Ed asked.

"We'll have to make do with paper napkins," she answered.

"Later?" he suggested and kissed her.

For a pair of outwardly civilized people, Hailey thought their courting rituals amazingly sparse.

And their dining habits downright immodest as they sat naked and crosslegged on the bed, eating the dessert directly from the serving plate.

"How many calories are in this thing?"

"How many calories did we burn before we ate it?"

"How many can we burn while we're eating it?"

"While? . . . Hey! Watch it! If you'd missed me, there'd be chocolate all over the blanket."

"I'll worry about that tomorrow. It's my blanket after all." Hailey pressed the mound of chocolate mousse flat against his stomach, her hand leaving a dark streak in its wake as it moved across his skin in a languid spiral.

Much later, sleepless from too much caffeine and chocolate, Hailey lay beside Ed watching him sleep. His expression grew troubled. His hands twitched. She wondered if he were dreaming and if the dreams were like hers.

If she were certain, she'd know whether or not to wake him.

In the morning, he didn't mention them. His job would give him plenty of nightmares, she decided. He hardly needed hers.

Ed didn't mention his dream because he wanted time to decide if it had been caused by merely sleeping in a room his lover thought was haunted or by Joe or Leanna having somehow ordered it.

He dreamed of the night he and the couple and Louis de Noux had dined together. Joe had been nervous, holding onto Leanna's hand, alternating between constant chatter and utter silence, when he realized he was monopolizing the conversation. Louis sat silently, a fixed smile on his face, as if he found Joe's nervousness amusing.

Ed guessed that Leanna's brother despised Joe. Yet after the meal he'd given them both his blessing. In the months before, Louis had arranged his sister's divorce. As a result, Leanna had walked away from the four-year marriage far wealthier than when she'd entered it. Maybe Louis thought she could afford Joe.

Leanna had used the divorce settlement to purchase a condo on Rue Dumaine which she used primarily for the swimming pool and sunny courtyard, warm through most of the winter, and to entertain lavishly. Before she met Joe, she had spent occasional nights in the old house when Henri was away. After, she spent them in Joe's room. Joe once told Ed that Leanna must be ashamed of him, then sheepishly shook his head.

"She just prefers your room," Ed told him. "It has a real den-of-sin look to it."

In time, Joe must have agreed, because Leanna, never known to stick with one lover, stuck with him for nearly a year, until her death.

Ed never understood.

FIFTEEN

Ed was true to his word on the long drive north. He said little as the land grew browner, the trees barer, until, a dozen miles north of Memphis, they crossed the snow line. After that Ed, whose experience with driving in snow was limited to one terrifying three-month period in Buffalo, asked her to drive.

Hailey had taken this trip not just out of curiosity about Ed's family or her need for a vacation from her work, though these were certainly two of her reasons. The most compelling reason—one she admitted now only after she saw the outcome—was her curiosity about how she would react to the sight of snow.

The landscape had been drained of life by the implacable cold. Its barren beauty troubled her, but the winter pain did not have sharp edges, only the dull ache of mourning. She could go home anytime she chose, and if she weren't happy, she would at least be content.

She could even go back for a visit now and take Ed with her. He had the week off. As he had suggested, she'd brought a laptop and all her work discs, though she'd done little work on the drive.

Later, perhaps, she'd suggest it. Not now.

The drive to St. Louis took one full day. The hotel Ed had chosen had a pool and atrium decorated for Christmas with trees trimmed in red ribbon and white lights. Ed had reserved a two-room poolside suite. "It will give me something to do with Willie when we're not at the house," he explained. "And if you want to work, there's an extra room for privacy."

While Hailey settled in, Ed called his ex-wife. He sounded at ease with her, which made Hailey more comfortable about coming. "Peg invited us over for breakfast tomorrow. Afterwards, I'll have Willie for the day," he told her. "I'd like it if you'd come along."

"For breakfast, then you can drop me back here. It's your day with her."

"Yeah, it is. I just wish I'd seen her more than once in the last year. Fourteen. Hell, I don't even know what to talk about."

"You'll do fine," she said and kissed his cheek.

Though Hailey had seen a picture of Willie and knew the girl had thick brown hair, she'd expected Ed's ex-wife to be Irish rather than the tall, dark-skinned Spanish woman who fussed over Hailey as if she were already one of the family.

Peg and Willie O'Brien had the second-floor flat of a brick duplex on a treeless street in a western suburb. The rear entry led past two bedrooms and through a kitchen and breakfast nook to a merged dining and living area dominated now by the Christmas tree wedged as tightly as possible into the corner. The rooms were heated with radiators, which had no apparent means of adjustment, and the air seemed hot and steamy.

Willie was sitting in the living room, dressed in old jeans and a worn oversized T-shirt, absorbed in a Christmas special. She managed a fleeting smile as she and Hailey were introduced, then returned to watching TV. Ed joined her on the sofa while Hailey retreated with Peg to the kitchen.

"Let's leave them alone for a while," Peg suggested. "Breakfast is in the oven; it'll keep. Sit anywhere. Things are pretty informal in this house."

They discussed moving, the changes they'd each been

through. Peg hid nothing, a trait that Hailey, who had been trained to conceal her emotions, found refreshing.

Through it all, the women could hear Ed's voice and occasionally Willie's curt reply.

"Willie misses her father, doesn't she?" Hailey asked.

"Always. Now she's angry too."

"Maybe I shouldn't have come."

"Oh, no. I'm thankful. It might help her understand that we both have lives and I'm not abandoning her father for Pete. As for me, I'm glad Ed is seeing someone. Maybe if he settles down again I can stop worrying about him, because someone else is doing it. Does that make sense?"

"Oh, yes."

"Willie worries about him too. I suppose that's something she picked up from me. Even now, if Pete calls late at night just to say hello, we both freeze, thinking it's New Orleans and Ed's been shot or worse."

"A lot of ex-policemen are on pensions," Hailey commented.

"I guess I'm just a pessimist at heart."

"Ed told me how much you disliked his work."

"Did he tell you about the time he was shot?"

Hailey shook her head, wondering where he'd been wounded. She hadn't noticed a scar.

"The man surprised him. The bullet grazed him here." She ran a finger down the side of her head. "If it had been an inch further in, he would have died."

"When was that?"

"About ten years ago in Lake Charles."

"Was Joe Morgan his partner then?"

"Yes. They chased a man into an abandoned building. The man didn't look armed but he must have had a gun hidden somewhere. After he shot Ed, Joe killed him."

"He and Joe weren't partners much longer after that, were they?"

Peg smiled. "Ed told me about your book."

"I'm sorry. It must have been terrible for you."

"Don't be sorry. I'm flattered that you'd ask me about it. No, they weren't partners much longer. Joe started drinking— drinking more, that is. I don't think it was related to the shooting, because he'd killed two other people before. I think it was because he thought he'd done something stupid and Ed had nearly been killed. Joe was conscientious, compulsively so."

"Ed says you know his ex-wife?"

"With them being partners, we got pretty close. Denise came over to sit with Willie after the shooting so I could go to the hospital. She was still living in Lake Charles a few months ago when she wrote me. She was planning on moving soon, but if you're lucky, she's still there. I'll write down her old address. She might not have moved."

Peg was jotting it down when Ed and Willie joined them. At fourteen Willie already reached her father's shoulders, and beneath the baggy shirt and jeans Hailey guessed there was a thin, long-legged body. She had her mother's full lips and her father's blue eyes. Only the dark circles under her eyes marred the striking beauty of her face. The girl seemed more at ease with her father now, but she did not look at Hailey through the meal.

Once they were in the car, however, she opened up to Hailey, as if, now that her mother wasn't present, they could be friends. "Daddy tells me that you're a writer."

"That's right. I have five books published."

Willie, it turned out, wanted to be a writer too.

On the way to drop Hailey off, Hailey learned why, what sort of stories Willie liked to write and that she planned to go to college in Milwaukee "because they have the best writer's school."

When she heard that Hailey was from Wisconsin, another barrage of questions followed. The girl's enthusiasm made it hard for Hailey to leave but she pleaded a need to work. Willie pretended to understand and waved good-bye as the car pulled away.

Hailey had set up a work desk on the round lamp table in

the bedroom. Besides the computer, she'd brought a printout of the first two hundred pages of her manuscript, as well as the outline. Usually Hailey wrote in a linear style, but given the haphazard nature of her dreams, she'd begun to fill in the outline according to her inspiration, frustrated by the huge holes in Leanna's early life.

In the book Leanna and Louis were both abused by their guardian, but Leanna, being the stronger one, tried to draw attention to herself to protect her brother.

Hailey had intended the last to be fiction, but from what little she'd glimpsed of Leanna's adolescence, it seemed that it might have more than a shred of truth to it.

What kind of abuse had Louis endured? Physical, certainly.

Sexual? The answer was equally obvious.

Hailey had never shirked difficult topics but this was one she'd never touched on before. Nonetheless, she turned on the computer, found the appropriate place in the story and began to write.

In her book, Henri de Noux had been married once many years before. In the years he'd lived with his wife, the lust had not matured into a loving relationship and he had not been sorry to see his wife leave. By then, her lithe form had thickened, her face had acquired lines. Youth. He wanted youth.

And if he could not have it, he would have nothing.

Hailey grew sleepy, her head pounded. She shut her eyes to rest them for just a little while, lowered her head to her crossed arms . . .

She kneels, the cold uneven stone of the church floor digging into her knees as she holds up her father's photograph to the huge statue of St. Michael the Archangel. It is the last day of the novena, and with her final amen, she rips the picture into pieces, collects the pieces on the floor in front of her and sets them on fire.

"What are you doing? Put that out!" someone screams.

She turns and sees the old nun—Little Sister, everyone called her—rushing toward her. Leanna remains where she is, whispering her father's name over and over as the paper burns.

The nun tries to stomp it out. Leanna grabs her ankle and the nun's thin arms flail, finally finding an anchor in the end of the pew.

The little fire dwindles to ashes. Leanna scatters them on the floor, forcing the nun to stomp out the few remaining sparks before taking Leanna to the principal's office.

She refuses to apologize, to explain, to speak at all. They call her house. No one answers. They decide to call her father at work.

When they leave her alone in the office, she walks home, carting all her books with her. On the way, she thinks of how much she hated that school and how she might never have to go back again. An expulsion—for it would hopefully be expulsion—would mean that next year she would go to the public high school and sit next to colored kids who would have the sense to respect her beliefs. . . .

She finds the hidden key and lets herself in. The house is dark, silent. Jacqueline must be out. Louis sleeping. She goes into the kitchen to fix lunch, moving silently through the house, unwilling to disturb the ephemeral peace.

After, on her way up the stairs, she hears water running in the bathtub, her brother's soft voice.

She knows how he satisfies himself, pounding away to climax. She doesn't blame him but she relishes the occasional times she manages to catch him at it.

Louis is always so superior. His red face and stiff prick are such a great equalizer. And if he is talking to himself, creating some lover to feed his adolescent lust, she'll have another reason to tease him.

She sets her books on the landing and tiptoes down the hall to the bathroom door.

He hasn't even closed it. Why would he be so reckless?

The room is thick with steam and the scent of hand-blended bath oil. The shower curtain is partly closed. She can see her brother on his knees facing the back of the tub, rocking against. . . .

Has he found a lover? Not yet noticed, she takes a step sideways and sees the broad shoulders, sallow skin and dark hair. She watches a moment until she is certain what she sees, then calls out, "My God, are you fucking Belly?"

The water splashes over the side of the tub. Her brother looks at her, his expression savage with hate. "Get out before I . . ." His voice trails off, his expression changes to one she knows too well. She turns. Her father stands in the door.

He came home for her, she knows. Instead he found an unexpected, more potent reason for wrath. She ducks under his arm and runs, not stopping until she is blocks away with the bushes of the park, the picnickers and strollers to give her protection.

There are a hundred different ways to sneak into the zoo. She finds the nearest one and spends the afternoon sitting in front of the cages where the great cats gnaw on their meat and dream of prey.

Long after the zoo has closed, one of the security guards finds her sleeping in the bushes. The police drive her home. Her father's car is thankfully absent.

Jacqueline takes charge of her, promising to keep a closer eye on her. "Come on and eat," she says and leads her into the dining room, where Louis is sitting at the table. One of his eyes is black and puffy. His lip is puffy as well and the empty frames of his glasses are on the table in front of him.

"You shouldn't have left us alone," he says when Jacqueline goes to get Leanna a plate. "I'm not the only one he beat."

And if she had stayed, she could have done nothing to help him. Louis demanded too much. He always did.

"He broke the glasses on purpose," Louis says and starts to cry again. "He told me he would steal my sight."

And he stole something else as well. Leanna sees the

marks on her brother's arms where his father gripped him from behind. It is the same way he once took her, swearing as he used her that she would never have proof of what he had done.

Sometimes, when he was very drunk, he used to call her by her mother's name.

She sits beside Louis and takes his hand, resting it on the side of her face.

As Jacqueline returns with Leanna's meal, somewhere else a door opens, someone laughs.

Ed was bringing Willie back. "Hailey?" he called.

She woke and stifled a moan. Leanna was not a presence in the room in which she'd died, but a presence within Hailey herself.

Ed and Willie had already been to the mall, where Ed had asked her to pick out a Christmas present, and to an early matinee. Now they wanted to swim.

With her hair pinned up and her baggy clothes replaced by a black tank suit, Willie looked terribly thin. The dark circles that Hailey had noticed under her eyes that morning seemed even darker now.

As they swam, Hailey noticed the medical ID on the girl's wrist and asked about it.

"I have asthma," Willie said.

"From allergies?"

"From everything or maybe nothing, my doctor tells me."

Since Willie didn't seem to mind discussing her problem, Hailey went on. "Do you have more trouble in the winter?"

"I used to. Now our house has radiators. Pete's house has electric heat. I'll be OK."

She didn't sound OK. Later, when Ed had gone to the room for sodas, Hailey took the girl's hand and said, "I know we just met but if you ever need anything or just want to talk to someone, you can call me, OK?"

"Pete's such an asshole!" Willie blurted. "I wish Mom had never met him."

Was Hailey so melodramatic at fourteen? "He's more than that. Like characters in books, he has lots of sides. You just haven't seen them all."

Willie hesitated, trying to understand what Hailey meant. "OK, so he's not a *total* asshole. I mean, he likes Mom. I guess that's something.

"But they're getting married in three weeks! I doubt that years will be enough. Do you think Dad would let me come and stay with him while they go on their honeymoon?" She wrinkled her nose as if the thought of her mother and Pete having sexual relations were disgusting.

Hailey wondered what Pete would think of that. "Don't you have school?" she asked.

"I have two days off. I could take the other three."

"Ask."

After Christmas dinner, Willie did. By then, Hailey had mentioned the request to Ed, who had conferred with his ex-wife, who sounded relieved that Ed agreed.

Pete agreed as well, mumbling once when his soon-to-be stepdaughter was out of the room that he hadn't the slightest bit of training in dealing with teenagers.

"She's a great kid. You'll do fine," Hailey said, and noticed how Ed beamed at her compliment.

Ed and Hailey drove back to New Orleans the day after Christmas. They reached the city in midevening. By then, Hailey had nothing but work on her mind; Ed had some errands to run before he went home. They said good-bye in front of Sonya's; then, carrying her valise and the huge poinsettia Peg and Pete had given her, Hailey let herself into the building and went upstairs.

And found her apartment door hanging open, her computer missing, the clothes from her closet and drawers scattered over her bed. She set the plant in the empty place where the computer had been, then checked her hiding place. Her box of backup discs was also gone.

The thieves had what they wanted; she found a certain

fatalistic comfort in that. The loss of the machine would not stop her work. Though she was attached to the old computer, the one she'd buy with the insurance money would serve her just as well, and until she replaced it, she could work on the portable.

Nonetheless, she found herself shaking—with rage, with fear.

Had she really thought a locksmith would solve her problem? Her door was open, not battered in. Professional crooks had their own locksmiths and they were just as skilled as any. She looked out the window at the street. The old man across the way smiled and waved. He no longer seemed a mere nuisance. Now she wondered if he were in on the plot, sitting there watching her apartment, keeping tabs on when she was out.

"Franks says that he's sorry," someone said in a voice so quiet she was certain the intent was to terrify her.

Hailey whirled and saw Norman standing in the doorway, his swarthy skin glowing against the white of his maître d' uniform, his expression still haughty, though less than usual. "Frank sent me up because he's too busy to come himself right now. He found the door open this afternoon. We think that someone broke in during the lunch rush. Frank says to tell you that he'll pay for the new locks."

"That won't be necessary. These still work."

"He wants to know if he should call the police."

This time she'd have to report it or her insurance wouldn't pay for the missing computer. "I'll call them," she said.

"I think you ought to move. There are more secure places to stay," Norman told her.

"And just when you and I were getting along so well," she retorted.

"Apologies, OK? It's just that Frank likes you, so he's worried about this. Everything that's going on is making him think of his aunt too. I've never seem him so upset."

With amazement, Hailey realized that Norman actually

seemed to care for the overweight chef, not just for his money. She'd been unfair to Frank, who might have been huge and far from handsome but who had always been kind to her; unfair to Norman as well. "I'm sorry," she said. "But I can't leave until the book is finished. Tell Frank that I'll try to stay home more often."

"Maybe next time they'll want you at home."

What small amount of affection she'd managed to feel for him vanished just as swiftly. "I know. I intend to be careful," she said.

SIXTEEN

Just after New Year's, Hailey drove across the state to meet with Denise Morgan, and to visit the house that Joe Morgan had purchased a month after his wedding.

The little colonial was in a part of Lake Charles that seemed more suburban than city, the kind of neighborhood police chose when they wanted to start a family. Undoubtedly built in the fifties, the house was distinguishable from neighboring houses only by the buff-toned siding, aqua shutters and the overgrown bushes below the front windows.

During her phone conversation with Denise Morgan, Hailey had pictured the woman with the little-girl voice as petite and shy, a person who would have to be prompted to talk about her husband. Instead, a buxom, big-hipped woman with brilliant green eyes answered the door. Though she'd known Hailey was coming, her sweatpants were coated with dried and fresh paint and her hair was tied back in a ragged cotton scarf.

"I'm so glad you came. I can't stand phone conversations until I can put a face to the voice," she said as she showed Hailey inside. The furniture was pushed to the center of the living room and covered with a tarp. A fresh coat of primer covered the walls, streaks of gold showing through in the corners. "Come into the kitchen, we'll have some coffee while we talk. Be careful in here, there's wet paint on the woodwork."

Also recent paint everywhere else, and no sign of a Christmas tree.

189

"Sorry I'm such a mess. I wasn't sure when you'd get here and I have to get the painting finished."

The room smelled less like paint than cigarette and, Hailey was certain, marijuana. Apparently Denise Morgan was one of those hyperactive souls that found pot energizing. "Remodeling?" Hailey asked.

"Moving. Do you take cream? Sugar?"

Hailey shook her head. "I contacted you just in time," she said.

"Not really. I'll be teaching accounting at a community college in Baton Rouge. My sister and her husband will be moving in here for the next few months while they build a new house. Sometimes everything works out perfectly, doesn't it?" She set the cup down in front of Hailey and scrubbed her hands at the sink. Before she sat down, she arranged a small assortment of Christmas cookies on a plate which she set in front of Hailey, rather than in the center of the table. "You said you're writing a novel about Joe?"

"In a way." Hailey explained the book and the scope of it, emphasizing that Denise would never be mentioned.

"You don't have to sound so apologetic. I wouldn't have minded getting involved. I defended Joe for years after he died. I'd gladly do it again."

"He was a good husband, wasn't he?"

"Fantastic . . . at least for the first few years. He got accepted on the force just after we met. We moved here. And then Joe got promoted and gradually things started to change."

"Ed mentioned that he had a drinking problem."

"Not right away. But Joe always had a problem with being compulsive. He needed everything orderly and precise and perfect. His job certainly wasn't that way. The stuff he saw on the street wasn't that way. But he had control over his wife and his home, he made sure of that."

"What did you do?"

"I coped as best I could. I mean, I loved him so I did what he wanted. The floors were always scrubbed. Nothing was ever out of place. But having to keep things just-so stressed me out.

"We were planning a family. Once we had a baby, I was going to stay home. I like to work, I really do, and I thought that if I could just wait it out, being home instead of working somewhere else would solve everything.

"But I never got pregnant and we finally stopped trying. That was when my control gave out completely.

"You see, I overeat when I get nervous. Even when I was a kid, I'd be the one munching on a candy bar just before the big test. When my marriage became the equivalent of one long test, I went from a size ten to a sixteen-and-a-half in six months. Like I said, Joe was a perfectionist. He stopped having sex with me well before I reached the high point.

"Then Joe tried to control what I ate. When he couldn't, he started not coming home at night. I found out he'd started drinking again after he got suspended for the first time.

"We went to counseling together, then separately. I learned to manage my nervous eating, enough that I lost thirty pounds of what I'd put on. Joe tried to stop drinking. He was succeeding and it looked like we'd even stay together. Then all sorts of things happened all at once.

"Joe and I were in a car accident, nothing serious but I wound up spending a few days in the hospital. While I was there, I had a physical which led to a hysterectomy for cervical cancer. So much for a family.

"Then Ed got shot and Joe seemed to give up trying to stay sober. The few times we made love afterwards were disasters. He was drunk and impotent and probably not physically attracted to me. I was still feeling fat and ugly and less than a woman. Our marriage was over, though I was too stupid to realize it until about a year later.

"I filed for divorce and Joe moved out—in that order, I must stress. With nothing to hold onto, Joe started his downhill slide."

"This isn't easy to ask, but I need to know. How did you

feel when you heard that he was suspected in Leanna de Noux's murder?"

"Furious. I mean, Joe was a decorated police officer. Even when he was drunk and we were having our worst fights, I never felt threatened by him. I couldn't believe he could kill someone he loved. I wasn't surprised that he killed himself, though."

"You weren't?" Hailey asked, amazed.

"When he thought he'd failed me, he started drinking. How must he have felt after that woman was murdered in his bed while he was passed out beside her? No, no surprise there."

"He wasn't drunk; he was drugged. The police thought that someone might have slipped him something."

"So he wasn't to blame. You know it. I know it. Joe? He'd say that he should have been more careful, should have noticed when the first effects of the drug started, should have . . . whatever. Instead, he passed out and some animal stabbed his girlfriend fifteen—no, eighteen times. Maybe someone was really angry, or maybe she put up a hell of a fight. Which do you think?"

"Both," Hailey said. "Or maybe someone wanted the murder to look like a crime of passion."

"That's what Joe thought. Are you surprised that we kept in touch? He begged me to let him come home for just a few weeks after the murder but I couldn't. If I had, I'd have fallen for him all over again."

Hailey wondered if Denise Morgan really believed that Joe had killed himself, or if she had convinced herself of it to avoid any guilt for not taking him in. No matter, Denise was surviving, and from what she said, surviving well. She didn't need Hailey's doubts complicating the truce she'd made with her conscience.

Through it all, Hailey had been sampling the cookies until half were gone. "More?" Denise asked.

"No. They're delicious, but no."

Denise took the plate from the table, replaced the cookies

in their box, put it away, then washed the plate. Apparently, she took no chances with her control.

"I understand that your husband's funeral service was held here?" Hailey said when Denise joined her again.

"Oh, yes." For the first time, Denise Morgan looked as if she mourned her husband. "So many of the local police came. Ed was here, too, of course, and some of Joe's friends from New Orleans."

"Can you remember some of the names?"

"There was a guest book. Pour yourself some more coffee while I see if I can find it."

A quarter hour later Denise returned with dust in her hair, carrying a black leather guest book. Hailey scanned the list. Ed was on it, of course. So were Peg and Willie and Louis de Noux. Frank Berlin also attended, which surprised Hailey since he was always so busy.

"After the woman's murder, Frank closed the restaurant down for remodeling." Denise said when Hailey asked about the chef. "He said there were police all over the building and his business was terrible. Some of the restaurant staff came to the service with him. The names are these with his."

Hailey scanned the list. She didn't recognize any of them. "And de Noux?"

"Louis?" Her expression grew softer. "I'd first heard from him when Joe started going out with Leanna. He was real apologetic about calling, but since Joe was a drinker, he said he had to ask some questions, to be certain his sister would be safe with Joe. I told him about the police force, and what kind of husband Joe had been. I think it made him feel better.

"As for me, I hadn't heard from Joe in nearly a year so I pumped what information I could out of Louis and even called him once a few months later just to see how things were going. The next time we talked was while Joe was being questioned about Leanna's murder. Louis called to tell me that he was doing what he could for Joe, and that I shouldn't worry."

"Why did he call you?"

"Because Joe asked him to. You look confused, but you really shouldn't be. Louis said he never believed that Joe did it. The words meant a lot to me, and his presence at the funeral even more because by then the papers were all screaming that Joe had to be guilty."

"How did Louis de Noux act at the funeral?"

Hailey wasn't sure she'd worded the question well but Denise understood. "Devastated," she said.

There seemed to be nothing else to discuss. "I suppose I should be going so you can get back to work," Hailey said.

"The break was good for me." She took Hailey's pen and jotted down a number. "This is for where I'll be staying in Baton Rouge. If you need any more information, or find out anything more about Joe, call me. I want to know."

"I will. I promise."

They hugged at the door. Survivors both, they sensed the bond.

Though she'd been gone two days, Hailey's apartment had not been invaded again. Hailey considered that a good sign. She found two messages on her answering machine after her absence. One was from Ed, the second from Louis de Noux. Sighing, she dialed Louis first. She would reward herself with Ed's call afterward.

She'd just begun to leave a message on Louis's answering machine when he picked up the phone. "How is the book progressing?" he asked.

"It's going well," Hailey replied. Something seemed definitely wrong with de Noux's tone, as if were expecting otherwise.

"You'll have to excuse my screening my calls. Lately I've been getting some I'd just as soon avoid. Speaking of those, did Carlo Bucci come to see you?"

"Right after the article ran."

"Ah, that. I first learned of it when Carlo roared into my office in all his Latin fury and slammed it on my desk for me to read. I thought you'd wait until the book was finished before publicizing the work."

"I would have. Someone else leaked the story to the press."

"I see." He sounded doubtful. She wondered if he had called Adam Wolfe. If so, what must he think? "Well, if Carlo becomes as great a nuisance for you as he has been for me, don't hesitate to let me know. I can arrange a restraining order," de Noux added, sounding as if he'd be delighted to butt heads with the man.

Hailey doubted that a restraining order would do much good against thieves. "I don't think that will be necessary. He only came here once," she said. "I haven't talked to him since."

"I'm glad to hear that he's leaving you alone. I also called because I'm having a belated holiday party here tomorrow night and I'd like to invite you. You're welcome to bring a friend, if you wish."

Short notice, Hailey thought. Before she could decline, de Noux added, "I admit I hadn't thought of asking you, since we only met that one day, but since the article on your book appeared, a number of our friends have been asking questions about it. I thought I might prevail upon you to come and answer them yourself. Of course, if you have other plans, I'd certainly understand."

"No, I don't. I'd love to come."

"Good. Anytime after nine. I'm certain you must be busy so I'll let you go."

Not busy, at least not yet. But it would come.

Ed would be working the night of Louis's party so Hailey had called Celeste and invited her. The voodooienne buzzed her apartment a few minutes early and swept in surrounded by a miasma of exotic perfume and brilliant colors. Her dress, if the term could to be applied to such fantastic clothing, was made of flowing silk scarves, painted shades of red, yellow and orange. She'd left her hair uncovered and held back with a gold clip. Gold filigre earrings hung nearly to her shoulders, and a matching gold choker circled her neck. She looked like the queen of some exotic foreign land—regal, beautiful. Hailey, in awe of anyone who could wear something so incredible so naturally, said so.

Celeste put an arm around her and pointed to the mirror showing both their reflections. "If I am some ruler from the tropics tonight, you in the cool blue wool against the ivory skin and light hair are the ice princess. What a magnificent pair we make, yes?"

"We do," Hailey said and laughed.

Celeste's fingers brushed her bare arm. "Child, you're so cold. Is something wrong?"

"No. I guess I have mixed feelings about going tonight."

"If you're concerned about me, the de Noux firm has represented me in a number of legal matters. Even so, I called and made sure my presence wouldn't be awkward."

"Because of your race or your religion?"

"One or both, depending on his guest list. But he seemed pleased that I was coming."

"I really hadn't given the matter much thought. I'm more concerned about going there again myself."

"Because of the house?"

"No."

"Because of Louis?" Celeste laughed. "He has a depressing sort of nature, doesn't he? You pity him, in a way, but . . ."

Her voice trailed off. In spite of the invitation, Hailey did not fill in the rest.

They started down the hill to the rear door just as Frank and Norman were coming up the front stairs to his apartment. "Party time?" Frank called.

Hailey turned and he whistled. "And you, Celeste, are as regal as always."

Celeste pressed her palms together under her chin and

bowed with mock formality. "To another successful year," she said as they walked toward the stairs.

Spotlights in pastel shades of mint and rose and blue lit the de Noux house. A silver garland framed the door. One of the guests let them in, motioning them toward the solarium when they asked about Louis.

The guests were the sort Hailey would have expected at one of Leanna's fetes. A pair of young Nigerians in native dress were discussing politics with a couple from Baton Rouge. An old man, his white hair covered by a red beret, was being kissed passionately by a girl young enough to be his granddaughter. The dining room had been taken over by self-styled Louisiana radicals discussing, with apparent seriousness, why the state should withdraw from the union and align itself with the French separatist party in Quebec. One of them recognized Celeste, calling for her to join them.

"In a moment, perhaps," she replied as they passed through. At the solarium door, she whispered to Hailey, "Minnesota is the state with all the Swedes, is it not?"

"And Wisconsin the Germans."

"There's our host," Celeste said. "In what new country does he belong?"

Louis sat on one of the wicker divans. He wore black leather boots and pants and an antique green velvet smoking jacket with a black satin collar. One hand, long-fingered and thin like his sister's, held a cut crystal wineglass, the other a clove cigarette. The rooms were all dimly lit and his gold-framed glasses were only slightly tinted, making his eyes seem dark and huge.

"Sir Percy Dovetonsil, court poet to the king of New France," Hailey remarked.

Celeste laughed.

"There you are!" Louis called to them. "Come and get introduced."

As Hailey had expected, many already knew Celeste. As

for her, though Louis spoke slowly and gave a bit of information about the other guests, Hailey could not remember their names.

Their backgrounds were another matter. One was the owner of a pagan bed and breakfast only a few blocks from the de Noux house. Another ran a small press dealing with Louisiana history and Cajun culture. A willowy, exquisitely beautiful woman ran a haute couture resale shop. There were artists, photographers, an alternative press reporter and an amazon of a woman who, Louis hinted, had an occupation so bizarre that it defied description.

Some of the guests looked familiar, and as a stream of questions followed Hailey's introduction, Hailey realized she must have seen them at Leanna's party. She explained how the drawings and Frank Berlin's story piqued her interest, and how the idea for a novel come from that.

"There's more to it, even though you aren't aware of it," Tashya, the owner of the resale shop, said.

"More?" Celeste asked.

"Of course. Souls that die violently do not leave this world. You especially should know that," she said to Celeste, then turned her attention to Hailey. "When I first went into business for myself, I did not have the money to pay rent for a house as well as the shop so I slept in the shop's storage room. At night, I would hear tiny footsteps moving through the shop and past the daybed I slept on. If I lit a candle, they would stop for a while. Later, they would start up again."

"Tiny footsteps?" someone asked.

"A child's, a little Negro girl who'd once lived in the building. She'd been killed by her mother a hundred years ago. The woman was executed for the crime. Now the girl is still there. Sometimes, I thought I heard her crying, looking for someone to comfort her.

"I don't sense her presence anymore but then I don't sleep there either."

"A pity. She must miss you," an artist said and laughed.

"Don't make fun of me," Tashya retorted. "I felt sorry for the poor creature."

"Do you feel sorry for Leanna?" someone asked Hailey.

"Of course. She died so young and terribly."

"Is she there in that room, walking around while you sleep?"

"Or more like crawling into bed with you. Leanna was always one to make her presence known," someone else added with an evil laugh.

"Please!" Louis cut in with a regal wave of his hand. "You don't need to frighten away a perfectly respectable guest who hasn't even been offered a drink yet." He turned to Hailey. "May I give you a sample of Leanna's favorite? After all, the best way to relate to my departed sister is to try to live like her."

"Forgive me, but from what I've gathered about Leanna, I don't think I have the stamina," she responded.

He laughed. "At least *sample* some pieces of her life. She had such remarkable vices for one so young."

"You make yourself sound so much older."

"Actually, if experience matters, she was older. On the other hand, I had the time and the solitude to cultivate wisdom—a virtue she sorely lacked." He stood and led her into the empty kitchen, where his expression became suddenly serious.

"If I confused you out there, forgive me," he said. "I tend to be a private person. My sister and I shared the house but we kept our own hours, and had our own friends. I really haven't confessed to many of mine about how much she meant to me and how much I miss her. As for hers . . ." He shrugged. "I don't think she had any real friends. In her own way, she was more isolated than I ever was."

"Thank you for being honest with me," she responded, her guard up again. She knew he was sincere, and somehow it made her uneasy. "What are you making?"

He'd taken a champagne glass and laid a mesh tea strainer and sugar cube on top of it, then dripped a pale green liqueur from an unlabeled bottle over the cube. "Leanna's," he replied then filled the glass with champagne. "She always said the liqueur needed drying."

Hailey sipped and frowned. "Herbsaint?" she asked.

"Herbsaint, yes, though Leanna wasn't about drinking the concoction this one mimics so well. He noted her shock and laughed. "Made in Spain, smuggled to her twice a year by a lover who was quite fond of her."

"Is it as dangerous as reported?"

"Few things are, at least in moderation." He poured a second blend for himself, the green bubbles rising in the champagne. "To my sister," he said, holding up his drink.

Hailey took a sip. "Does absinthe really taste like this? If so, it's not at all the way I'd expected," she said.

"You've thought of drinking absinthe. How remarkable!" He rummaged in the cupboard beneath the counter. Hailey heard the clinking of bottles against one another as Louis reached farther toward the back, pulling out a small blue crystal bottle holding no more than two ounces. He laid the used sugar cube on its saucer, found a second and dripped a half ounce from the little bottle over the cube and into a shot glass. After returning the bottle to the cupboard and handing her the glass, he leaned close to her, so close that she had to fight the urge to move away. "My advice is to set that drink down and get just a little tipsy on this. You'll immediately note the difference between it and its tame green imitation," he whispered. "Now, please excuse me."

He left her standing alone beside the pair of bottles and the crystal bowl of sugar cubes. She sipped her drink a moment longer than lifted the second cube from its strainer and touched the translucent drops seeping from it to her lips.

Remarkable. The herbs that gave it flavor must have been infused when fresh, creating a melange of tastes, each one so distinct, so filled with life.

"Anise. Fennel. Hyssop. Wormwood. Delightful. Deadly." Hailey looked up. Celeste stood in the doorway, a splash of warm colors against the dimly lit background of the dining

room. She joined Hailey, dipping her finger into the small
sweet puddle that had collected in the saucer beneath the mesh
straining spoon and licking it.

"You've had it before?" Hailey asked.

"You know me." She held up her glass of ice water. "I've
tasted it, though, just as I have clairin and roots. They're
all too strong, dangerously potent. They pull their energy
from the drinker's power, draining it one ounce after
another. Evian, on the other hand, must be the drink of all
the truly powerful gods. And that is as close to a temperence
lecture as you will ever get from me."

She tasted the absinthe residue in the saucer again and
frowned.

"What is it?" Hailey asked.

"Nothing. A slightly odd taste. I suppose it's just some
quirk in how this batch was distilled."

"The liqueur is so strong, I don't see how you can tell."

"Because the taste is familiar somehow."

Hailey sipped from the glass, but it only seemed more
delicious than a moment before. "Will this little bit hurt
me?" she asked.

"At eighty percent alcohol, only your ego when you feel
your head in the morning."

"Could Leanna have really drank something like this and
kept any of her power at all?"

"Occasionally. Sporadically heavy. But every day, no."

"That's not what everyone tells me about her."

"Maybe that's because she deliberately misled them."

Hailey frowned.

"And she may be misleading you as well. I've warned
you about that."

"Hailey followed Celeste into the solarium. When she
passed through the kitchen some time later, the herbsaint
bottle was gone. In its place was a thermal carafe of chicory
and spiced coffee. She drank it thankfully. Her head had
already begun to spin.

The party had spread to both floors. With her cup in hand,

Hailey climbed the stairs. Celeste was in the upper hall, talking to the elegant woman who owned the resale shop. "A stunning old place, isn't it?" the woman commented.

"It is," Hailey replied, distracted by the square of light falling from Leanna's open bedroom door.

"Have you seen all the rooms yet?"

"I've been in the house before but I've only seen Leanna's."

"Then come on. I'll show you."

"In a bit," Hailey said.

Celeste understood. They stayed where they were until the curious group had moved back downstairs. "I need to see the main bedroom," Hailey said and started toward the front of the house.

This section of the hall was dark but the door was unlocked. Hailey thought of Leanna the child, stealing down the hall to witness her father's perversion. The scene—the tiny child in the hall, confused, concerned—came back to her, clear as her dream or as the night it actually happened.

Celeste hit the switch. In the moment the light touched her eyes, Hailey blinked, and the ghosts of Henri and his crippled wife vanished, not even shadows left behind.

Though the bed was new, the room's decor had not changed. Like Leanna's room, this one was maintained as a tribute to the past. The only other alteration was a portrait of Leanna above the fireplace mantel, her eyes surveying the room, a mischievous smile playing across her face. The room had a familiar smell to it, possibly the same incense Celeste had given her to help her contact the spirits in her room. Did Louis try as well—for his sister? His mother?

"Leanna," Hailey whispered. As she did, she felt a presence she knew well touch the core of her, then for a time . . .

"You feel her here, yes?" Celeste asked.

She straightened the body. She ran a hand through the far too short hair. "I feel . . ." She stopped. To speak would give her presence away.

"Ah! Here you are," Louis said, joining them.

Celeste saw Hailey shudder, her hands clenched into white-knuckled fists. "Hailey? Are you all right?" she asked.

Hailey relaxed and stared, bewildered, at Celeste. An instant later, the pounding headache began and she understood what had happened. "Louis," she said, and walked toward him as he came through the doorway.

"You look pale. Here, sit." He pointed to the table and two chairs in front of the window. Hailey took one gratefully. Celeste arranged herself in the other while Louis sat on the edge of the bed.

"Such a beautiful portrait of your sister," Hailey said. "Who did it?"

"An artist in Metarie who knew her painted it after her death. When we were young, Leanna and I had promised one another that when this house was finally ours, we would live here together. It was a silly thing to promise, of course, but until she died she did live here some of the time. I wanted this reminder of her until we meet once more."

His voice sounded strained. He glimpses her inside of me, Hailey thought. "Once more?" she asked.

"Our family has always believed in reincarnation. Death for us is not an end, but a door to a new life."

"And you'll meet her?"

"We have lived many roles together—father and daughter, brother and brother, husband and wife, sons, lovers. Our souls were united before, they will be united again."

"On a higher plane?" Celeste asked.

"A different plane. A happier one, perhaps. I like to hope so."

"A comforting faith," Hailey remarked.

"One you should know all too well. I read the introduction to your book; I understand your sorrow. You'd met the soul of the child you'd lost many times before. It was meant to be a part of your life and so you mourned."

"I see." Hailey stared at the portrait, certain that the belief would have been a curse in a family such as this. "Would your parents have been a part of your life before?"

"I don't know. But truly, I would love to one day be my father's father." Louis smiled but beneath the innocence of his expression Hailey detected the venom.

"We should be going," Celeste said.

"So soon?" Louis asked.

"We have another stop to make," Celeste replied. "But I was pleased to see your magnificent house." She kissed him on the cheek.

They walked down the hall with Hailey holding Celeste's arm to steady herself. At the top of the stairs, she saw the same tall black man from Leanna's party climbing toward them. Celeste's grip on her arm tightened. Her expression became flat, guarded.

The man nodded politely and paused as they passed. "Maman Celeste," he said in a soft patois. His glance at Hailey implied that he knew her or, more likely, she hoped, knew of her. "Such a beautiful house. I must see it all."

Celeste said nothing, only continued on, eyes set straight ahead as if looking at him would contaminate her.

Hailey managed to get down the stairs on her own. Once outside, she gave in to her weakness and leaned against Celeste. "Are you all right?" Celeste asked.

"Leanna was with me in that room. When I said her name, I felt her presence."

"I should have known."

"I felt her fury."

"The room must have terrible memories for her."

"I suppose," Hailey replied.

"Shall we get something to eat?"

Hailey shook her head. "I just want to go home, take about half a bottle of aspirin and sleep. You'd better drive." She unlocked her car and handed Celeste her keys.

"I warned you," Celeste said as she pulled away.

"This headache was caused by Leanna inside of me, not by the drinks. I felt it before when I let her possess me."

"Inside of you?"

"In the bedroom. I looked at her portrait. I willed her to come for me."

"Into you? So easily!" Celeste drove until she was well away form the de Noux house and pulled over. "Now, child, you are going to tell me everything that has happened. I am not taking you home until you are done."

A car belonging to one of the private security firms that patrolled the area slowed down as it passed them and turned the corner at the next intersection. "He'll be back," Hailey said. "Just take me home."

"No!" Celeste replied. "You must not go back to your apartment until you are fully prepared to deal with her power."

"I am capable. When Louis came into the room, I threw her out of me. I am able to control her."

"Only because it suits her purpose to let you think so. Now we are going to my house. We are going to talk. Perhaps I will even talk to Leanna if she lets me. On the way there you can tell me every small thing you can recall about the times Leanna has come to you."

"I did," Hailey replied.

"Not all of it, I'm sure."

Hailey leaned back in the seat and fought the urge to giggle. Poor Celeste took the whole matter far too seriously.

She licked her lips, tasting the liqueur, the last vestiges of its luscious green infusion, and told Celeste about the perfume and knife.

SEVENTEEN

Celeste's living room walls and ceiling were painted a deep high-gloss gray. The spotlights aimed at them gave them a translucent quality, as if they were veils between the real world and other, more fantastic places. A scattering of primitive African masks with gaping mouths and empty eyes covered one wall. In a corner Hailey saw a staff carved from a pair of branches that had twisted and grown together. Sections of it were painted, others gilded with gold, decorated with colored stones, bits of hair and bone.

None of this would be visible from the street, however. Celeste's windows were cloaked with black velvet, stretched and tacked in place.

Outside of a few colored candles and an incense burner on the brass coffee table, Hailey saw no sign of an altar. "I'd expected your home to be more like the shop," she commented.

"Tacky, cluttered, dusty." Celeste laughed. "Too many practitioners look at the rites as trial and error. If one fetish or chant has small results, add another and another until the results are right. The altar becomes a reflection of the psyche—scattered and distracted. Far better to learn what is correct, then work to make it perfectly effective.

"Now you know that everything in this room has a purpose. Sit down while I brew some tea."

Hailey couldn't. She followed Celeste into the kitchen and sat at the polished teak table. "If it's like the kind you sold me, I can't drink it." She explained about the migranes the brew had caused and was pleased to see Celeste alter the mix.

"If there is any problem with this, I can help you deal with the pain. Just sit and wait."

"I'll go to sleep if I don't keep talking," she said. "Why were you afraid of the man we passed when we were leaving?"

Celeste added another herb to the ball. "Not afraid, wary. Rightly so."

"Who is he?"

"Oba Van, he is a *bocor*."

"A priest, you mean?"

Celeste leaned against the counter. "If Satan can be called an angel, Oba Van is a priest. Have you ever heard of the sorcerer's cults of Haiti, Cochon Gris and Secte Rouge?"

"No. Are they blood cults?"

"Many Vodun rituals have a blood sacrifice, usually of food animals—pigeons, chickens, goats, even a bull when petitioners are truly desperate. After all, without a sacrifice how do the *loas* know a petitioner is serious? However, it is said that members of Cochon Gris eat the dead and those of Secte Rouge get their power by sacrificing men."

"How can they do that?"

"Because in Haiti no one dares oppose them, partly because no one knows exactly who is in the sect, and also because many believe that human sacrifice, the ultimate sacrifice, gives great power. Even the name Secte Rouge is so feared it is rarely mentioned."

"And this man is a part of that group?"

"He is rumored to be one of the leaders."

"Rumored. Do you believe it? Do you even believe the sect exists?"

"That isn't important, at least not to anyone in this country. What is, is that the man does nothing to deny the rumors about him, or to dispel the damage the rumors do to our beliefs. That's what I find monstrous!"

"I saw him in one of my dreams. He was at Leanna's party."

"Why was he there?"

"I don't recall."

"Try to remember."

"My notes were stolen. All I have is the information I stored on the discs."

"It could be very important," Celeste said with emphasis.

"Do you think that killing a man would give great power?" Hailey asked.

Celeste shook her head. "Not from the spirits I worship," she said with disgust.

When the tea was ready, Celeste took a pot and two cups and led Hailey to the back of the house, where doors opened onto a grape arbor. A high wood fence surrounding the yard acted as a windbreak, and the thick vines overhead formed a living canopy over the space. In one corner, caged black-and-white pigeons cooed softly when they saw their owner. "Lie down," Celeste said. "I must prepare the altar. Then I will speak to Leanna through you."

Hailey did as she asked, stretching out on a chaise longue, sipping the cup of tea Celeste handed her.

Celeste turned a dimmer switch just inside the door. Tiny clear lights strung random as stars appeared above her. In the dim light she saw mounted to the vines a huge crucifix with a carved, painted Jesus, his face a rictus of agony; Christ in the depths of the passion, raised to heaven, the lights like angels showing Him the way.

Christ coming, Hailey thought. Coming for those who do good and those who do the best they can. She might have tried to prepare her mind for the ordeal—and it would be an ordeal, whatever Celeste might say to the contrary—but she was so tired. She set down the empty cup and closed her eyes for just a little while and immediately fell into a deep sleep.

Celeste went inside and changed into a bright red caftan and turban, then returned to the arbor and assembled an

altar—the cross, the ritual bowl for sacrifice. Because
Hailey requested it, she would not do an animal sacrifice.
Instead she placed plums in the bowl and, to show the
seriousness of her intent, cut her arm and let a few drops of
her own blood fall on them.

"*Papa Legba, ouvri barrie pou nous passer. Papa Legba
ouvirier barriere pour moi,*" she whispered softly, reciting
the petition opening the portal between the dead and the
living as she turned on a tape of the sacred rada drums. With
the soft drumming emptying her mind of all concerns, she
drained her teacup and began drawing Papa Legba's veve in
maiza flour on the ground in front of the altar. The design
was a simple one: intersecting lines to symbolize the
crossroads between life and death, flourishes to indicate the
two states, and her own personal marks. The work was
simple but important; it focused her energy on the task to
come.

When she had finished, she danced in the center of it, her
feet scattering the pattern. Later, confidently, she turned her
attention to Hailey and called her name. Hailey did not
respond.

Shaking roused Hailey only a little, enough to mumble
that she wanted to be left alone.

Could Hailey have been drugged? Celeste doubted it.
Was she drunk? Celeste doubted that too since Hailey had
given no sign of it just minutes earlier.

No, Leanna had done this.

Challenged, Celeste decided to force the conversation.

She brewed a second, different cup of tea for each of
them, and reached for Hailey.

Sleep. Beautiful, perfect sleep. Beautiful perfect dreams
not of Leanna but of her and Bill and the child they should
have had—an angelic little girl with Bill's dark hair and her
own brilliant blue eyes.

"Hailey."

How dare someone disturb her now! If she'd had the

strength, she would have lashed out. Instead she could only moan, "Nooooo."

"Hailey!"

Someone pulling her upright, forcing warm liquid into her mouth. She batted the cup aside then tried to twist away from the hand that gripped her, lie down and go back to her own perfect dreams.

But all that was denied her. Though her effort was rewarded with the sound of breaking porcelain, a second cup took its place. This time her tormentor was ready for her struggle. Though she sputtered and complained, she had to drink nearly all of it.

The drug slowly energized her, making her alert, sober. Within an hour she was awake, sitting upright with Celeste crouched in front of her, the red cloud of her caftan forming soft folds at her feet. As Hailey stared, trying not to look away, she listened to Celeste's demanding voice speaking to the spirit sharing her body.

"Leanna," Celeste called, following the name with chanting Hailey did not try to comprehend, strings of words flowing on and on, until . . .

"Leanna, you will speak to me?"

Hailey giggled. Come out and play, Eve Black, she thought, and shuddered as if touched by a sudden chill. She rubbed her arms, thinking how silly this all seemed.

And fell asleep, aware of her voice in the same fashion as a dozing old man might note on some half-conscious level the sound of his own slow snores.

Celeste had done all she could to reach Leanna. She had nearly abandoned the attempt when she noticed some barely perceptible narrowing of Hailey's eyes, a stiffening of her shoulders and back: that moment of confusion when a soul materializes and tries to comprehend where it is.

"Leanna, remember me," Celeste ordered. She placed her hands on either side of Hailey's face, holding it still as she moved close enough to kiss her lightly on the lips.

"Leanna. Sister. Speak to me. Tell me how I can help you."

Laughter, rippling laughter, as beautiful coming from Hailey's body as it had been from Leanna's own. The sound of it thrust Celeste back to an earlier time, when Celeste had first heard Leanna laugh. She'd been speaking to a customer in the back of her shop, and paused mid-sentence, suddenly distracted. When others smiled at the sound of it, Celeste focused on its source and thought with a surge of anger and confusion of the rumors about the woman. How could a creature with so much power in the mere sound of her voice waste her life so stupidly?

How could a woman who had spent years learning the beautiful chants, the rituals and beliefs of voodoo, and who acknowledged that belief openly, not make the belief central to her life?

Instead, Leanna had apparently wasted her power on lovers and drink.

Celeste never understood—not until Hailey had begun to fill in the missing pieces of Leanna's sad existence.

"I'm sorry for how thoughtlessly I judged you. Let me help you now," she said.

Denial washed over her, then a rope of mental pain worse than any physical blow tightened across her head. "This woman has been chosen by the gods to help me. Let this woman do her work," Leanna said, the voice Hailey's yet wrong somehow.

"Come into me. I can do so much more," Celeste repeated. "I order it."

"Order!" Again the laughter, higher pitched this time, tinged with fear. "You have no power to command the dead! No more than she, the mare I ride, the mare who does my bidding." An instant later, Celeste was thrust backward, landing hard against the stones that surrounded her little temple.

"Leanna, leave her!" Celeste ordered.

A breeze blew out the candles. The tiny arbor lights

flickered. The pain in Celeste's temples increased—a blinding, terrible agony that grew, eclipsing thought, speech. "Leave her," Celeste managed to say, her voice a jagged whisper.

Hailey's eyes widened, and her hand shot out, slapping Celeste hard. The blow was so unexpected that Celeste lost her balance and fell backward against the table. Eye contact broken, Hailey returned to sleep.

Celeste drank the rest of the tea she'd brewed for Hailey, then paced the arbor, trying to decide what to do.

Hailey had given her specific instructions. Normally, Celeste would not ignore the wishes of a client, let alone a friend, but this was not a normal situation.

Celeste had been raised a devout Catholic and until a few years ago she had attended church regularly. All that changed when the new pastor of her parish had told her, with surprising honesty, that he did not want to see her at mass and that if she tried to take communion, he would refuse her.

Until now, she hadn't missed the Catholic church; but she'd never felt the need of a priest's service before.

Nonsense. She could handle Leanna's ghost; she'd handled displaced spirits before, after all. And no matter what Hailey thought, that room needed to be cleansed. Without an abode, the spirit might lose its anchor with the world and move on.

She hastily changed into a black jumpsuit, then left a note on the table telling Hailey that she'd borrowed her keys and her car. Celeste doubted that Hailey, sleeping soundly and peacefully, would wake to read it before she returned.

Though it was well past midnight, the cold air stole all trace of weariness, from her while the special herb tea made her senses sharper, more acute.

A cat prowling the alley behind Sonya's Kitchen startled Celeste as she left the car. The distant clang of pots in the kitchen as the last of the staff finished cleaning up, and the sounds of people in the street, made her relax. Though her work had to be done alone, there were people in the building, others who would come if she needed them.

She climbed the stairs slowly, listening, certain that she had to remain on guard. As she fumbled for the right key on Hailey's cluttered key chain, she heard a sound like ripping fabric. All her instincts told her to turn, to leave, but she had not come here to abandon the work so easily. "Is someone in there?" she called as she went down the hall and knocked on Hailey's door.

The door swung open. The hallway lamp threw a square of light into the room and in it . . .

"You," Celeste said.

When Hailey woke, shafts of light were leaking from the edges of the black velvet curtains. She called Celeste's name and got no reply.

She found a jar of instant coffee in one of Celeste's cupboards. While she waited for the water to heat, she found the note Celeste had set beside her open purse.

In the last few minutes, I've seen and heard enough. I couldn't wake you to ask permission to borrow your car or use your apartment for what must be done. Stay here until I return. We'll talk then. At the end, she added the time.

Celeste had left before midnight. Why hadn't she returned?

Concerned, Hailey called her apartment. Her machine answered. "If you're there, Celeste, pick up," she said.

Nothing. And from the number of rings, she knew there were no messages.

Hailey tied her coat tightly around her, and with the damp, chilly wind curling around her feet like a hungry cat, she walked home.

Since she didn't have her keys, Hailey walked to the rear of the building, where she discovered her car in its usual space. She borrowed the spare key from the morning help and started up the stairs.

Usually at this time she'd hear the shower running in

Frank's apartment. She'd smell coffee and toast. This morning it seemed as if the odd couple had mysteriously vanished. Even the sounds from the restaurant kitchen were muted, as if she had climbed an extra story or two above it.

Her door was shut. Though it seemed strange to do so, she knocked. As her hand touched the wood, the sense of dread she had been trying to ignore intensified.

She fought it, and pushed open the door.

The drapes were drawn, all lights out.

As she reached for the light switch, she inhaled a smell she knew too well from tragedies and dreams.

The bathroom door hung open. Hailey strained to see the source of the smell, too afraid to expose the secrets of her room to the harsh reality of light.

How much she wanted to run. How right she knew that running would be.

Someone might even be in the bathroom, waiting for her to come, luring her forward.

"Celeste?" she called and, with sudden daring, hit the light switch.

Her little tree was knocked over, its tiny ornaments broken. One string of lights was out; the second twinkled. The string around the outside window glowed for a moment then warmed and began to blink.

The bedspread was ripped down the center, the mattress beneath cut open. Scraps of glass and plastic from her laptop computer littered the floor.

"Celeste?" she repeated and walked toward the bathroom. As she did, she saw a delicate bare foot, so still in the bathroom doorway.

"Celeste, are you all right?"

As she rushed forward, she took in the sight of the voodooienne's body sprawled on her back on the bathroom's tile floor.

Slashed flesh. Slashed fabrics. Bloodstains leaving shiny patches against the black velvet of Celeste's jumpsuit, black as the darkness moving toward the center of Hailey's vision, blocking out sight, blocking out the horror of what she'd seen.

The horror of now; and a glimpse of another murder—older and far more terrible.

EIGHTEEN

"Hailey?"

God no, she wouldn't wake up. Not here, not to see what . . . ?

The light filtering through her closed eyes was too bright to be coming through her windows, and the clean scent of the place was nothing like the melange of spices and blood and ancient wood of her apartment.

"Hailey?"

A different voice, familiar, dependable. She breathed deeply, cracked open her eyes, and shut them again when she saw the brilliance of the light.

Fluorescent. Not more than a few feet above her. "Ed?" she whispered.

"Yeah." He squeezed her hand.

"Where am I?"

"University Hospital. An ambulance brought you here."

"Ah." She tried to nod, felt the padding around her neck. "What is this?" she asked, enunciating carefully. Her mouth felt dry, her tongue thick.

"A brace. You had a fall."

She ran her tongue over her dry lips, felt the swelling in one corner. "I'm OK. Really." She wiggled her toes to prove it.

"Good. I'll be back."

Ed returned with a doctor, who checked her over but did not remove the brace. "Stay immobile until we X-ray you," he said.

"Could you move me someplace a little less bright?" she asked Ed when the doctor left.

He pushed her a few feet down the hallway. "Did I have an accident?" she asked.

"Don't you remember?"

Images returned. Waking alone at Celeste's. The walk home. The stairway. The hall. The broken ornaments. And again, Celeste. "I do." She shut her eyes again.

"I asked if I could stay with you until you woke up," Ed said. "We do that in cases like this. Protection."

"I didn't see anyone, except Celeste," Hailey replied. She paused then asked, "She's dead, isn't she?"

"Yeah."

"When?"

"She died a little after midnight. She was stabbed." He took her hand again. "Craig Linden from Homicide is going to want to ask you some questions. Should I call him now?"

"All right. By the time he gets here, I should have everything straight in my head."

He went and made a call. When he got back, she was ready to tell him everything but he cut her off. "We'll talk after the statement," he said. "I don't want anything I say to influence you."

By the time Linden arrived, Hailey had been X-rayed and was about to be released. Linden took her statement in the chaplain's office while Ed waited outside. Relieved that his skin was dark and his accent that of a Louisiana native, Hailey told him about the previous break-ins, the number dialed from her phone, the possible haunting of her room. She told him everything she could recall about last night. He recorded the likely and the fantastic facts with the same courteous expression.

"Thank you," she said when she'd finished.

"Thanks for what?"

"For not . . . well, looking at me like I was insane."

"Sane or insane makes little difference. People get killed for both reasons and sometimes for no reason at all. Yours ain't the strangest story I've heard, Miss Martin, believe me. This is my town. I'm used to haunts." He began paging through his notes while she sat, not at all certain he was done with her until he looked up. "You can go now," he said. "I'll keep in touch."

Ed drove her to his home and fixed some food while she showered and changed into a pair of his sweats. She'd been hungry when they arrived, but when she sat at the table and looked at the sandwich, her stomach twisted, pushing bile into her throat. She swallowed it down with the beer he'd opened for her, along with one for himself, and picked at her food wearily. Though she knew otherwise, she felt as if she hadn't slept at all last night.

"You can stay with me for a few days until you decide what you want to do. I'd ask you to move in, but with Willie coming next week, it wouldn't be right," he said.

She nodded. No use in telling him that all she wanted to do was get back to that room and finish her book. He'd never understand.

"It seemed like I was the first person Linden questioned," she said.

"Except for the kitchen help that found you, you were. Frank wasn't home last night."

"That's not like him."

"It's the holidays. Nobody sticks to schedule. They probably talked to Frank when he showed up at Sonya's."

"I suppose." She wondered vaguely where Frank had gone, and if explaining where he had been would be hard for him. Poor Frank! In her own way she'd been his most difficult tenant.

"If you want to take a nap or something, I'd understand," Ed said.

"Will you stay with me?"

He nodded.

She lay with her back pressed against his stomach, his

arms around her. While she slept, he lay unmoving, as if afraid that she would vanish if he let her go.

She wondered again what he'd think when she told him that the only thing on her mind—indeed it had become a compulsion—was to get back to her room and finish her book.

The bedside phone woke them in midafternoon. Ed answered and, frowning, handed the phone to her.

"I heard about Celeste a little while ago. I wanted to tell you how sorry I was," Louis de Noux said.

"How did you know I was here?" Hailey asked.

"I called Sonya's Kitchen and explained who I was. Frank Berlin told me where you were. If there is anything at all that I can do to help you in your work, please don't hesitate to ask."

"Thank you. I'll remember that." She didn't want to talk to the man, especially not about the murder, but she had to ask, "Did you hear anything else?"

"Frank Berlin and most of his staff gave their statements to police this morning. The police are coming sometime this afternoon to take my statement as well. Carlo Bucci was taken in for questioning around noon today. This time, I expect the police to be more thorough."

Hailey didn't miss the sarcasm in his last few words, or the way he managed once more to place the blame on Leanna's ex-husband. "You've learned quite a bit," she said.

He laughed, a sound contrived and somewhat sinister. "We attorneys are an incestuous group, although a lot of what I'm telling you is in the early evening paper. Incidently, the medical examiner told me that he's finishing up in your room tomorrow morning. You can move back to it by afternoon."

She hung up, astonished that Ed, who loved her, assumed that she would give up the quest and go home, while Louis, who hardly knew her, expected her to be both stubborn and strong.

"I'm going to make some lunch. Would you like something?" Ed asked.

He tried so hard to make his concern seem casual. Bill had been like that. "Sure," she said and snuggled back into the warmth of the bed, listening to the kitchen sounds until she smelled fresh coffee and joined him, curling her bare feet under her on the padded kitchen chair.

"You're a natural in sweats, you know that, don't you?" he commented.

"It makes me think of all the exercise I haven't gotten since I moved here. I belonged to a gym before I bought the house in Eagle, but there aren't any branches of it there. I walked a lot, though. A lot of paths through the state lands get pretty steep, so an hour walk gives quite a workout."

"You walk here."

"Only because if I take my car, I won't find a place to park. That doesn't count."

"You thinking of going home?"

"Eventually. Not yet." With no real appetite, she ate the sandwich he'd made and tried to recall everything she'd told Craig Linden, and more importantly anything she'd left out. If she could only remember . . .

Oba Van!

She'd mentioned the man, but not his name. She tried to phone Linden, but couldn't reach him. After, she told Ed what she'd remembered.

"By now Craig should have Louis de Noux's guest list. If this man is dangerous, he'll recognize the name," Ed told her. "I'm stopping downtown later. I'll see that he gets the information."

When Ed dropped Hailey off in front of Sonya's the following morning, he wanted to come upstairs with her. She wouldn't let him. She wanted to be alone when she saw the damage in the light of day so that if she shivered, if she cried, if she pounded the wall out of rage—and any or all were likely—no one would see.

The day had been emotional enough already.

As she expected, Ed did not understand her unrelenting need to know the truth about the deaths in her room. She tried to explain, tried to make him see that Leanna's effort to find some means to control her life was no different from her own. Leanna's dabbling in spells and fetishes to keep the evil in her life at bay was so akin to the days Hailey spent after discovering the swastika at her boathouse—with the gun on her lap as she guarded her little domain.

Leanna would have understood her frantic attempts. Leanna would have looked at home in the straight-back chair overlooking the river, watching for vandals, as if vigilence could keep danger at bay.

Hailey approached the room carefully, standing first in the doorway to survey the damage. It wasn't as bad as she'd expected. Her laptop computer lay in three pieces on the floor; the bedspread had been shredded but the mattress beneath had only two deep cuts. The settee hadn't been touched and only one small square of glass in the French doors had been broken.

The newly painted walls were also unscathed, though damage to the drawing was as terrible as she remembered from two nights before.

Paint the color of fresh blood had been thrown over the twins and the snake and smeared to obliterate most of the message. Red rings on the carpet marked the place where the rag and bucket had probably been.

She couldn't put off the inevitable any longer, but even the bathroom held none of the horror she'd expected.

Two small puddles of dried blood, and a broken perfume bottle that filled the little space with a sickening sweet odor, were the only signs that someone had died here.

Could she clean it up herself, knowing the source of it, her own involvement in the death?

She decided she could. As she headed around to the kitchenette to get a mop and bucket, she heard footsteps on the back stairs. Berlin called her name long before he reached her door, undoubtedly trying not to startle her. Nonetheless, she resented the intrusion. If there had been any way to shut the door before he arrived, she would have done so.

He didn't come in. Instead, he stood in the doorway, his face as full of shock as her own had been. "I'll send someone from the kitchen crew up to scrub," he said. As she walked toward him, she saw tears in his eyes and wondered how well he'd known Celeste.

"When did you hear?"

"Norman and I were coming in this morning when we saw the police cars out front. They didn't have to say a word to me. I already guessed the worst of what had happened. I'm glad it wasn't you, but maybe if we'd stayed here last night, Celeste would be OK too." He started to cry openly. "This room is cursed. As soon as you're gone, I'm going to wall this place up and pretend the space doesn't exist."

Hailey couldn't find words to soothe him so she hugged him instead.

"I'll return the month's rent and get the security deposit back to you right away," he said. "It will probably take you a while to find another place if you're staying in the city. You'll need the cash for a hotel room."

"I'm not leaving." He looked so alarmed by her decision that she had to put his mind at rest. "I will be moving out soon, but not yet," she said.

"The person who did that to Celeste was likely waiting for you."

"I know."

"I don't want more blood on my conscience."

"Nothing that happened was your fault, Frank. You know that, don't you?" She still had an arm on his shoulder. Now she used it to steer him back into the hall. "I'm going to be working all night, so if you hear me moving around, don't worry."

"Christ, I thought I was going to come here and comfort

you," he said apologetically. "Then I go and bawl like a baby."

"It's all right."

"No, it's not. Come next door and have a drink with me."

Hailey glanced over her shoulder at the wall clock that had somehow managed to escape the carnage. "Give me two hours to get a start on this mess, OK?"

"I'll send up somebody to help you," he said.

She'd intended to do all the cleanup herself, but Frank was right. Besides, before business shut down for the day there were things she had to do.

Mike, the busboy Frank sent up to help her, was a dark-skinned black whose round face seemed out of proportion on his thin body. She was going to ask him to sweep up the debris in the main room while she concentrated on the bathroom, but he surprised her by volunteering for that job. "Besides, I'm used to blood," he told her. "I live in the public housin' near St. Louis Cemetery."

"It's that dangerous?"

"Yeah. I worked for a butcher for a while, so when my uncle had his throat cut and died on our front stoop, my ma said 'blood's blood' and sent me out to mop it up. He'd spurted everywhere. That was a lot worse mess than this," he told her.

Judging from his tone, murder must have been an everyday occurrence in that part of town. "Why was your uncle killed?" Hailey asked.

"Some fight over a girl, a damned whore if you ask me," Mike replied. He stepped around the bloody puddle and filled the bucket in the sink. "There's an old hoodoo belief that if you taste the fresh blood of a victim, you'll know right away who did the killin'."

"I never heard of that," Hailey said.

"I did it with my uncle's blood and I saw the killer's face like a flash of light in my mind." He laughed. "Not that I learned anythin' everybody didn't know already. The middle's still wet. You think we should try it? Maybe it's not too old."

"You go ahead," Hailey said and made a point of turning her back to pick up the computer pieces.

"Yahhhh," Mike said after a moment. The word was one long exhale, as if he'd had some great revelation.

"What did you see?" Hailey asked.

"Frank tellin' me not to mess with your head no more." He started laughing and kept it up while he scrubbed.

They had the place clean within an hour. In spite of the joke—actually a bet he'd made with someone else downstairs, he finally confessed without explaining exactly what they'd bet on—she tipped him for helping her, then went down the hall to Frank's.

Frank's apartment seemed different. While he fixed their drinks, she noted the changes. Photos were absent from the wall. The entertainment center appeared short a few tapes and CDs and the picture of Frank and Norman wasn't in its usual place. "Norman quit this morning," Frank told her. "Then he came upstairs and cleared out most of his stuff. He's coming back for the rest later."

"I'm sorry," Hailey said.

"We weren't getting along before all this started. I guess he's too young for me."

Hailey thought of Norman's warning, and the reason for it. "Norman said you worried too much about me. It bothered him," she said.

"I can't help it. I worry about everything. I always have."

"That's what makes Sonya's so successful."

"Lady, if I had any interest in women, I'd be rollin' out the red carpet to impress you." He put on some music, sat down in a chair. They listened for a little while, then he asked, "You're really planning on staying here?"

"I am." He looked so disappointed that she added, "Not much longer, though."

"Good. My hair's my best feature, you know. I'd rather not watch it go prematurely gray. And I'm getting disgusted with all these funerals. I ain't old enough to have so many people die."

By the time she left, it was after three. She stopped first at the bank where she'd rented a large safety-deposit box. From it, she took one of the two sets of backup discs she stored there. Even if someone managed to steal the set she carried, another would still remain in the city. She had a third set as well waiting for her to claim it from her post office box in Wisconsin.

Two more stops replaced her computer and bedding and took up the entire line of credit on her Visa card. She'd have to spend carefully until the insurance check came, but at least she could work.

With all of these safely stored in her trunk, she made the stop she'd put off until last.

Carlo Bucci's office was the antithesis of Louis de Noux's. Though she doubted he was more than forty, he was a founding partner of a law firm that, judging from its top-floor offices in one of the better downtown buildings, was thriving.

As she hoped, he would see her. She was taken past a dozen offices and an open area for legal secretaries and assistants, to a private waiting room. Too nervous to drink coffee, too nervous even to read, she sat with her hands folded in her lap and waited.

Fortunately, she didn't have to wait long.

As it had before, something about the man—the way he walked, the way he stood as if ready to pounce, the way he looked at her—made her anxious, though not nearly as much as in the past.

After all, she had initiated this contact. As long as she stayed calm, she would be in control.

He took her into his office. Its wall of windows gave a sweeping view of the city, the lights just beginning to glitter in the darkening sky. A pair of modern paintings flanked the door. A trio of brightly colored wooden snakes slanted up the white wall behind Bucci's desk. "Stylized reproductions of Damballah?" she asked.

"More a statement of my support of young local artists. Please sit down. I'm sure it's been as trying a day for you as for me." When she was settled, he went on. "The police have come, insulted me, and gone, Miss Martin. Louis de Noux has already called to gloat. To what do I owe the pleasure of your visit?"

"I came to ask you if you had anything to do with the murder of your wife,"

He looked as if he'd expected the question but the reply astonished her. "I can only tell you what I told the police after she was killed, Miss Martin. I did what she asked and gave her her freedom. If I am guilty of anything, I am guilty of that."

"I don't understand."

"I can think of hundreds of people I refused to represent who hold a grudge. There are others who, in spite of my best efforts, were found guilty and think that I, rather than the judge and jury, am to blame. Because of this, my home security system is the best on the market. When Leanna and I lived together, I employed a cook and housekeeper. Both lived in the house. Both were armed. Now, do you think anyone would have dared to murder Leanna in *my* bed?"

"You had nothing to do with her death?"

"I swear I did not, nor was I responsible for what happened to Celeste."

He was trained to hide his feelings, Hailey reminded herself. Nonetheless, what feelings he revealed seemed genuine and she doubted that he lied. "Who do you think did killed your wife?"

"Every shred of evidence, and they are shreds, which is why he was never formally charged, says that Joe Morgan did it."

"Do you believe it?"

"Not entirely."

"And Celeste?"

He shrugged. "Sometimes things like that sort themselves out at funerals. I'm planning to pay my respects tomorrow. Are you going to the wake?"

"I am." And at the insistence of Celeste's sisters, to Celeste's house afterward.

"Then perhaps I'll see you in church."

It was a polite suggestion that she go but she wouldn't just yet. "When you came to my apartment, you said that Leanna was always leaving scraps of paper around your home to ward off evil. Who frightened her?"

"Everyone."

"Really?"

"She was raised on fear. The state was natural to her. She devised the most elaborate rituals to allay it, and the little scraps of paper were just one part of it. She would do anything for someone who could offer her some new ritual, some hint of new power. I think it showed her real courage that few who knew her suspected the terror with which she lived her life. People used to think she was a loose woman, when in truth she was simply afraid to sleep alone." He hesitated, as if the memories were too painful. "Have we discussed this enough?" he asked.

"You sound so understanding."

"I understood. I was raised by violent people. Now I defend violent people, but I have never taken a case for a man who I believed was guilty of harming a child, and I never will." He opened the office door for her and followed her down the hall to the elevator. "If there is anything you need from me, call," he said.

The pastor of St. Agnes Catholic Church allowed Celeste Brasseaux's funeral service to be held in his church out of respect for Emalie Brasseaux, Celeste's mother. Emalie, the matriarch of the huge, tightly knit family, had worked for the parish as a teacher, an assistant principal and, since her health had begun to fade, the parish secretary.

But it was not Emalie Brasseaux who caused the crowd to

form in front of the church a full hour before the service. Emalie had never known such a cross section of New Orleans society, from the wealthiest to the poorest. Even the mayor made an appearance, arriving with his wife, who had consulted Celeste often.

By the time Hailey arrived, every church pew was full, so she stood in the back through the service. Afterward, the casket was opened, and the flowers laid over the body again. A pair of chocolate-skinned women took their places at the head and foot of the casket, like imposing statues set in place to guard the dead.

And while Celeste lay in state, one person after another went to the casket to say a private prayer. After, many took the microphone and shared a memory of Celeste, most to describe how much she had helped them.

It was a touching, dignified service, not at all the sort of wild ceremony Hailey had envisioned.

When her turn came, she stared at the body curiously, as if Celeste's beliefs should somehow have altered her corpse. She saw nothing out of the ordinary except that Celeste's arms were crossed over her chest beneath the covers and her right hand seemed to be holding something. As Hailey knelt to say her prayers, she glimpsed the hilt of a knife, the body watching over the soul even in death.

Hailey's prayers were genuine. Someone, recognizing her from her picture in the paper, held the microphone out to her but she did not take it. She could say proper funeral words for every one of her characters, but speaking from her heart in front of so many strangers would be impossible for her. She waved the mike away and took Emalie Brasseaux's hands instead. "I am so sorry," she said. "Celeste died helping me. I will never forget her."

"I never thought I would bury one of my children," Emalie replied.

That simple declaration of her loss brought tears to Hailey's eyes. Later she learned that Emalie had been in state of near shock since her daughter's murder. Those were the only words she had said to anyone.

As the last person in line stood before Celeste's body, the crowd grew silent. The man bent over and kissed Celeste's cheek. Holding the microphone in front of him as a priest might a chalice, he began to sing an African song. His bass voice, soft at first, grew louder. Many in the church joined in, the number growing when the refrain was repeated after the second verse.

From what Hailey could make of the song, they called on God and his angels and all the saints to overlook Celeste's shortcomings and lead her spirit to heaven.

In this magnificent blending of two ancient faiths, even the priest sang.

After the service, most of the clients went home. Many of Celeste's family did as well, but Hailey took a place in the line of cars going to the cemetery.

Once there, she stood on the edge of the crowd and listened to the last prayers of the priest. In a custom she'd never seen before, the casket was opened one final time so the family could kiss Celeste good-bye. Emalie bent over her daughter, her tears falling on Celeste's face, as she cried for her daughter, her lost life. Lisette was last. As she leaned over her sister, she took a pair of scissors from her pocket and clipped off a lock of Celeste's hair, wrapping it in a piece of red flannel, and used the packet to dry the tears that had fallen on Celeste's face.

A moment later, the casket, covered once more, rolled into the white stone crypt.

By tomorrow, there would be offerings. Within a week, there would be crosses hastily drawn on the stone door and sides. Petitioners would not let Celeste's spirit rest.

Lisette joined Hailey. "Are you coming to Celeste's tonight?" she asked.

Hailey glanced at the crypt, where Emalie and Marie sat on the stone steps. She wanted to talk to them, to say something more than just a hurried condolence. "Will they be coming?" Hailey asked.

"Their place is with my sister, guarding her soul from her enemies."

From her reading, Hailey knew that mother and sister would remain at the grave throughout the night, as others had remained with the body through the autopsy, the preparations for the funeral and the hours before the wake. No one would be able to steal Celeste's soul, or to tap her power, with them on guard. And yet, if such a thing were possible, perhaps it had already been done by the one who killed her.

As she walked toward her car, Hailey noticed a woman waiting beside it. As she came closer, she recognized Jacqueline Menieur.

Hailey held out her hand. Jacqueline took it and did not let it go. A look of pain crossed her face but she gripped Hailey's hand even harder, not seeming to care that Hailey looked at her as if she were mad.

"My mother used to know things about people by touching them," she said. "I sometimes try to do that. Usually I can't." She hesitated then added, "But now I see another death if you go on."

The woman was trying to frighten her, Hailey knew, and perhaps she even believed her vision. Nonetheless, Hailey would not allow herself to abandon her search for the truth. She asked the question that had been on her mind for some time. "How did you know that Leanna's mother tried to kill herself?" she asked. "The doctor said he found the bottle, and that he never mentioned it to anyone."

The question was so unexpected that Jacqueline could not hide her shock. Hailey watched her struggle to find composure. "I took care of her," Jacqueline finally replied. "I found the pills missing. Later, I asked Leanna about them and she confessed."

"The cause of Joanna's death was asphyxiation, not a drug overdose."

"The doctor was a friend of the family's. He lied to save their reputation."

"I talked to him. I doubt he ever lies about anything." While Jacqueline tried to absorb this new information, Hailey repeated the question she'd asked earlier, "Does Leanna ever come to you?"

"Never." Jacqueline let go of Hailey's hand, intending to leave. "If you won't listen to me, there's nothing more to say."

"Does she?" Hailey repeated more insistently.

"Sometimes I dream about her," Jacqueline replied, as casually as she could, then turned and left.

Hailey watched her go, stared back at the grave for a moment, at the mourners standing for their silent vigil, then got into her car and drove away.

By evening, the cold rain that had plagued New Orleans for the last week had started again. The houses on either side of Celeste's were dark, seemingly deserted, as if the owners, knowing they would get no sleep tonight, had moved to quieter quarters.

Many of the guests arrived bearing pairs of dishes. The women set one on the kitchen table to serve to the other guests, and carried the second outside. Hailey watched the women kneel in front of the cross and say a prayer, undoubtedly for success, before laying their dishes in front of it, where they would be left as a sacrifice to the gods.

Hailey returned to the kitchen where another guest was pouring shots into tiny plastic glasses. *"Pour chance,"* she said as she handed one to Hailey.

"Poor chance," Hailey repeated and looked down at the concoction, the color of molasses, and the consistency of a thin liqueur. Like Alice, she was being asked to drink a great many things of faith. At least the woman who had given her this did not have the sinister edge of Louis de Noux. Hoping she could keep it down, Hailey swallowed it.

Fire. In her mouth. Her throat. "What is it?" she said when she was able.

"Clairin," the woman replied. "Rum."

Ronrico dark never tasted like this, nor did it burn with quite this lasting a flame. Had Celeste, who thought Evian the water of the gods, really consumed something so noxious?

"They'll be more later," the woman said. "You'll need it. This is such a cold night."

As she spoke, the drumming started. This was no tape, Hailey knew, and for the moment the drums were softly played, out of respect for the city, in the hope that the city would respect the beliefs of Celeste's people.

A few dancers answered the pounding of the huge drums and began moving in front of the altar. The tempo increased. A pair of smaller drums were added. Other guests began to move, until nearly everyone was participating in the ritual.

The drumming seemed to merge with Hailey's heartbeat, quickening it, beating down her defenses. Her feet began to move in time to the ritual rhythms, her hands to rise and sway. She didn't notice when Lisette placed the little pouch containing her sister's hair, and their mother's tears, in a bowl in front of the altar, soaked in with *clairin* and lit it.

The smoke wafted on some unfelt breeze toward Hailey's face.

As the smoke touched her, her eyes smarted. She shut them and the blackness rolled over her. In the center of it, she felt the drumbeats drawing her forward.

Her arms and legs began to twitch and she tumbled backward before she reached the dancers. Someone caught her before she hit the ground. In her last lucid moment, she looked up and thought she saw Louis de Noux staring down at her, as if not certain of the identity of the body he held.

He might have been Ed or her husband or any one of the lovers from her past as she raised her arms, pulling herself up so she could kiss him.

She felt his hand on her breast, his breath warm against her ear as he whispered the question, "Leanna?"

Blind, unfeeling, one with the gods, she begins to dance.

NINETEEN

Images of reality, insubstantial as dreams, gave Hailey some glimpse of the present her body inhabited.

Fleeing Celeste's voodoo wake, the rain beating against her face the gods weeping for their lost priestess.

Meeting Norman in the hall outside her apartment, his expression more sullen than usual as he carted his boxes down the back stairs to his truck.

A phone call to Lisette Brasseaux for help. A busy signal.

A hasty packing of her things. Scribbled notes—to Frank. To Ed.

Had she been allowed to sign *I love you* to the last?

So much of those hours were lost to her. She could only hope so, and hope that someday she would be allowed to explain.

And then the blackness became complete. . . .

She woke—if such a word could be applied to the moment when she was allowed to take control of her body—in front of the old computer she had left behind in Eagle when she'd begun her long drive south. The backup discs she had kept in her post office box were neatly stacked on the worktable. The machine was already on. If date at the top of the screen was accurate, four days had passed since Celeste's funeral. No wonder her head pounded. No wonder she felt as if she had spent the last days sedated.

Leanna had fled—her past, her city, all but the memory of her life. She had brought Hailey home to this safer, quieter, place, to finish the work they had begun.

235

Hailey looked out the huge pane of glass in her second-floor workroom. The snow covered the ground as it had when she'd abandoned the house. The way it shimmered in the early morning sun, as well as the tendrils of frost forming between the triple-glazed window glass, gave her some idea of the temperature outside.

Well below zero. Inside, however, it was over seventy. Leanna, poor Southern belle, had been cold.

"You brought me north. You'll just have to deal with the weather," Hailey said aloud to the spirit within her as she pressed her hands and forehead against the window. The cool glass soothed her pounding headache, and she breathed slowly and deeply until calm returned.

When she pushed away from the window, she noticed that her nails were longer, filed and painted. Leanna, at least, had different bad habits.

What other changes had there been? She went into the nearest bathroom and looked at her reflection in the mirror.

She'd been prepared for changes. But not to this extent.

She choked back a scream. Hadn't she welcomed the dreams? In a way, she'd asked for the possession. She refused to admit her terror even to herself.

Her white-blond hair was still the same length, but it had been permed into soft curls. Her makeup had been thickly applied; the foundation seemed paler than her usual tone, and her lipstick was bright red.

The silk shirt she wore plunged between her breasts. Even they seemed fuller. She unbuttoned the shirt and saw the skimpy lace cups of the bra, felt the padding beneath—artificially voluptuous.

The full-length mirror in her bedroom showed the rest of the changes: the tight jeans, the black leather lace-up boots.

She checked the closet: more silk blouses, tight skirts and a crushed black velvet sheath, low-cut and slit to mid-thigh.

Hailey held it up to herself, feeling the softness of it against her bare chest. Where could she go in such a revealing garment? Would she dare even to try it on?

Not now, at least, when Leanna was so much a part of her.

As she returned it to the closet, she noticed a box on the shelf. She might have missed it altogether but the color was not the usual white or green of the local stores. She pulled it down and opened it.

Inside was a wig, human hair it seemed—thick and dark and softly curled. What poor woman had been desperate enough to sell hair as beautiful as this? Had she a husband, a sweetheart, a family? Had they mourned the loss or only accepted it as a price they all paid to survive? Hailey lifted the wig, but did not put it on. Instead she held it up to the side of her face. As she did, she caught the scent of perfume.

Leanna must have found Hailey's thin hair a disappointment, enough of one that she did not bother to dye it. Instead she had purchased someone else's beauty. The receipt was still in the box. Of course, Leanna had used Hailey's credit card; ghosts weren't known to be long on cash.

The store had been in Jackson, Mississippi, not exactly close enough for an easy return. Leanna had probably planned that too.

Furious, Hailey began an inspection of her house.

Though the home was solar heated, Hailey had not dared rely on that in the unpredictable Wisconsin winters. The furnace's maintenance setting had kept every pipe from freezing except the catch drain in the utility room, which had frozen then cracked. She discovered that out only after she'd turned on the stationary tub faucets and felt the splatter of frigid water on her feet.

She checked the flue in the living room fireplace, started a fire and went upstairs to change into warmer clothes. Later, as she walked into the kitchen to brew a pot of coffee, she found the special teas and oils and candles she had purchased from Celeste carefully laid on her counter. She avoided touching them, or even looking at them, as she went about her work.

With her feet curled under her, a cup balanced on her lap, she stared into the flames until she found the calm and the courage to open her mind to Leanna. "How can I trust you after this?" she asked.

How can you not? The voice speaking in her mind sounded much like her own.

"Will you release me when you're done?"

No reply. Perhaps Leanna was not sure. At least she had the courtesy not to lie.

If she weren't released, Hailey had no way to prevent the possession. She couldn't stay awake forever and she didn't have the knowledge to ward off Leanna's spells. Now that she was in Wisconsin, she didn't know whom to contact to help her, either.

No one will disturb us here. No one will harm either of us.

Not yet, Hailey thought, her own pessimism seeming so out of place next to Leanna's confidence.

But how could Leanna be confident? After all, what in the hell did Leanna have to lose?

Not my sanity if we don't finish this.

Her thought or Leanna's? The voices in her mind sounded so similar that she had no way to be certain anymore.

She had another cup of coffee and wandered the house, putting off the inevitable. Every window showed the emptiness of winter, lonely as Celeste's white tomb.

"I yield," she said, her whisper sounding harsh in the sun-drenched silence of her house. "Let's finish it together."

She went into the kitchen, where the water was still warm enough to brew a bitter, potent tea. When she finished the cup, she built up the fire then lay down on the couch, exhausted by the drive she couldn't remember, by Leanna's frantic demands to go on with their search for the truth.

Always, in the moment between waking and sleep, the past comes back to her—all the pain, the terror, the sadness relived. Death must be like that, she thinks as she looks down at her father's body. If so, how did her father, always ready to blame others for every defect in himself, judge his life?

In death, he seems so shrunken, so impotent, not at all the tyrant he was right to the end.

After a two-month stay in the hospital, doctors had told him that there was no hope, and at best his life was measured in weeks. They suggested a hospice. Instead, he ordered Louis out of the house and, accompanied by round-the-clock nursing care, moved into his old room.

Afterward, he sent for her, or for Louis, more than a dozen times before he died. Sometimes he would lapse into delerium before they got there; at others, he would stare at them, his eyes deep-set, his expression vague, as if he could not quite remember who they were. On rare occasions, he would be alert and waiting, railing at them separately or together before lapsing into the inevitable confusion. Each time Leanna went, hoping to witness that last moment of lucidity before death claimed him. Finally, exhausted and certain that he was using his deathbed to torment her, she stayed away.

So only Louis was there to see him die. He told her how Papa had screamed from the pain, then, after months of morphine-induced fog, refused any painkillers that would have dulled his final battle with death. The nurses left Louis and his father alone out of respect for their last moments together, never guessing how Louis stood by the bedside watching, simply watching, not saying a word through the last minutes when his father's eyes glazed over. He stayed there for some time before summoning a nurse.

Papa went to hell with eyes wide open, Louis said. She'd expected that of him.

As she stands between Louis and Joe and watches the casket close, the body slide into its niche beside their mother, she feels a curious lack of triumph. She finds it so disappointing that the real mourners (a surprising number of them, she notes) must think she grieves.

"Come home tonight," Louis whispers to her.

She shakes her head. That house is the last place she can bear to be.

"Please. Just tonight. We have to talk in private."

She wants to refuse but he has been through so much for her sake. "All right," she says, softly so as not to disturb the priest mumbling his last futile prayers.

Louis arrives ahead of her and waits at the door to hand her a copy of the key and show her how to turn off the security system. With that done, he goes to the bar and pours them each a shot of brandy. "To freedom," he says and raises his glass.

She drinks, though she knows she is hardly free. "You said we had to talk," she says.

"In here." He takes her hand, leads her to the dining room. There, spread across the table, are drawings of this house, lighter, more open, with color swatches for each room arranged beside each sketch. "I wanted you to see the plans. You can change them if you wish. The solarium is going to be across the back, just as we discussed so many times."

"Are you as mad as Papa was? I can't live here."

He looks at her, dull surprise so clear on his face. "We always swore that it would be ours, and he left it to us both."

"Buy my share. No, better yet, I'll give it to you. Louis, I'm sorry, but I can't live here."

"Leanna, you don't mean it."

"Here we stand in the room where he belittled us each night. The memories don't lie. And here . . ." She runs into the foyer. "Her are the doors where they carried in Mama. And up there is the bathroom where he raped you. The bedroom where he raped me. The room where Mama killed herself—no that isn't right, the room where *I* killed her! Louis, this house is as cursed as the ones who lived here."

"It's ours."

"No, Louis. If you want it, it's yours."

"Stay with me tonight. Please, just tonight. Think about it one last time before you make your decision."

She wants to say not, but perhaps he's right. They did dream of this when they were young, and as adults made every effort to stay here together when their father was gone. She should try it for his sake. "Tonight," she says.

Louis cooks for them, and they eat the meal standing in the kitchen—the happiest room. Later, after dessert, they take their brandy into the yard, light the citronella candles and sit without speaking, reveling in the quiet, the night.

"It's late," he says.

She nods and follows him inside. The climb up the stairs seems to take forever. At the top, she pauses. Can she sleep in her room, face the nightmares that are sure to come now that Papa is gone?

He takes her hand, leads her to the main bedroom, where candles burn on the white marble mantel, below their mother's picture.

In the last few years, Louis moved from his old room into the downstairs one that Jacqueline had used. It has a private entrance and a private bath, so he could come and go as he pleased. As soon as their father died, he moved himself into the master bedroom. Leanna saw the change as a sign of confidence—the old man had died; their lives would be at peace.

As if, after Henri, they could ever really know peace.

"Sleep here, like you did when we were young. You said you slept in Mama's bed, hoping to dream of her."

Leanna has forgotten that. Now the memory comes back. In her dreams, Joanna de Noux would be whole, and happy. Always, they would go somewhere together, some faraway and exotic place where no one could find them.

"I'll sleep downstairs," he adds.

This room is preferable to her own. She goes down the hall to her room, where so many of her things are still kept, and chooses a plain white cotton nightgown, a little-girl design with ribbons at the collar and a lace-trimmed hem. She undresses quickly, and pads across the hall to bathe. The warm water soothes her. She leans back in the tub and closes her eyes.

Get away.

The sort of trick a draft plays, touching the hair, whispering with almost speech. The sort of trick the noise of running water plays—the beat like some song, the mind filling in the melody.

Get away.

No, none of that. Her own fears, magnified by the height of the ceiling and the darkness of the tile walls are speaking to her. One night would mean nothing in the course of her life. She could give Louis that.

She hears the words again, ignores them.

Faint light puddles onto the hall carpet from the main bedroom, lighting her way as she walks to the bedroom door. At it, she pauses, looking from the mantel candles to the bed, folded back, waiting.

Get away!

This time she can not ignore the warning. She goes to the stairs and looks down at the open door to the brightly lit parlor. The rum-and-sugar scent of his pipe tobacco fills the air. She cannot leave without his knowing. Making the choice between instinct and love, she returns to the bed.

And dreams.

Papa, his face yellow, his naked body bloated, a knife in his hand, stands above her bed. "You will come with me," he tells her, his voice deep, weighed down by death.

While she lies, unable to escape the dream, he moves up the length of the bed, sits beside her. His hands press against her shoulders, his lips against hers. His breath is fouled by death, hers so sweet. He inhales—pulling life from her. Exhales—filling her with the chill of the grave. "Take my place. Let me live again," he tells her as he rips the covers back, tears the gown she wears from neck to hem.

She's fought him off since she was twelve years old. How can she be so weak now?

It's death that takes away his fear and doubt, death that makes him strong.

Then he is on her, the sweet scent of funeral soap and

preservatives, wax and decay sickening her as he pounds into her. "Fucking bitch! You're coming with me."

"No! Leave me. I call upon Legba, who shows the way to death, to banish you, to send you to the darkness, to—" The words are stolen by fear. She screams, pounds her fists against the empty air.

Hears Louis's voice, calling to her, growing louder until he is sitting beside her, holding her, begging her to wake.

In his hurry to come to her, he left his glasses in his room. His silk robe is loosely tied, and she notes the fine hairs on his chest. She brushes them with one shaking hand then presses her palm over his heart, as if the steadiness of it can slow her own.

"I saw Papa. He touched me."

"Shhhh, Leanna. It's all right. Here." Without letting go of her, he reaches behind him into the nightstand drawer and pulls out a half-pint bottle. The label has been soaked off, and the bottle filled with a thick green liquid. "You made this tonic for me, remember? You said it brings sleep without dreams. Drink it."

"Louis, I'm afraid."

"You've never been afraid of anything. Here." He uncaps it, holds the bottle out to her.

"Will you stay with me?" she asks.

"All night."

She takes the bottle from him, drinks what little is left in it, then leans against him. Her breathing slows. Her eyes close.

On the edge of sleep, she feels Louis release her, lay her on her back, her head propped up by the pillows. "Louis?" she whispers.

"I'm not leaving."

She trusts him, relaxes as he lies beside her, propped up on one elbow, staring down at her face.

Hailey can only see what Leanna sees, can only feel through senses dulled by exhaustion and the drug his hand parting Leanna's legs, moving up her bare thigh, coming to rest on the damp warmth of her sex. . . .

The smells of coffee, cinnamon, oranges and fresh-baked bread bring in the morning. Louis stands beside her holding a tray. "Breakfast, mademoiselle," he announces.

"Actually, I think it's madame, even now that I'm divorced."

"Poo!" He wrinkles his nose. "I met Madame Bucci at your wedding. She's old and fat. Not at all you, Mademoiselle de Noux."

"All right," she says and smiles. "Put it on the table."

He does as she asks, hands her a robe and turns while she puts it on—the dutiful brother, a bit embarrassed by his sister's too obvious charms.

"Pour the coffee," she says, goes into the bathroom and shuts the door.

The inside of her thighs are wet; her womb feels swollen. She may not recall it, but she has dreamed. Splashes of cold water on her face do little to shake off her weariness. Her eyes are puffy and red, as if she hasn't slept at all. When she joins her brother, she drinks the coffee eagerly, then pours another cup. She devours the oranges, the little morning buns, but her eyes still feel heavy, and the vague fog that settled in last night refuses to dissipate.

"You look terrible," Louis says.

"I feel about the same."

"Go back to bed and get some more sleep."

"But Joe will be—"

"Joe's working, remember? I'll call the TV station and tell him where you are."

She agrees because she doesn't have the strength to argue. As she tries to stand, her legs buckle. He catches her and carries her to the bed, arranging the covers over her, plumping the pillows before laying back her head.

"Poor dear Louis," she says. "We've grown so apart."

"Never! Never say it."

"Your strength is that you can live in these walls in peace. Mine is that I can leave them and never look back."

"Sleep, Leanna. We'll talk later," he whispers and kisses her on the lips.

"Ah, Louis," she replies, her arms circling his neck, pulling him closer to her. "I love you so much."

Darkness. Hours of it. The phone rings, stops, rings again. Someone pounds on the front door. She hears these things but they do not rouse her completely. In the silences between them, she sleeps on.

Her mother comes to her, dragging herself through the doorway, toward the bedside, each movement of the crushed pieces of her spine making her cry out in agony. When she reaches the bed, Leanna grabs for her hand as if she is still real, still alive. And in the dream, for a moment only, they touch as they never could in life.

And the tragedies of her past mingle with those of her mother.

The screech of brakes on wet pavement sending the car skidding sideways. The impact against the passenger door more feeling than sound.

Henri, blood flowing into his eyes from the cuts on his head, tries to pull her out the driver's door. "You could burn," he cries frantically, oblivious to his wife's screams that he please, please stop.

Ah yes, he was drunk. And he lived with the guilt of it all her life.

"Beautiful, stubborn child," Joanna whispers. "No wonder he loved you. We were so alike."

"Stay with me," Leanna begs, but the ghost, the spirit, the *loa* of her mother is fading.

She recites the prayers, the chants—uses any ritual, calls any god from any belief that might hear her. "Help her to stay!"

They do not hear. The vision thins to clouds, to mist, to air.

TWENTY

Three days! Leanna has been gone three damned days and all he hears every time he calls the de Noux house is a ringing phone. Louis did talk to him briefly the day after the old man's funeral. "She's resting. She doesn't want to see anyone, even you," he said.

Louis seemed so filled with concern for him and his feelings that Joe almost believed him, almost forgot the truth of the situation.

Leanna hadn't wanted to go to the house in the first place. If she'd really wanted to be alone, she'd have gone somewhere else, maybe to her condo or up to the summer house west of Mandeville.

And she sure as hell would have told him her plans, not left it to Louis to do so.

It galls him to have to rely on someone to help him, but if he must, old friends are best. He calls Ed, explains the situation.

"Has she left you before?" Ed asks.

"A couple of times after an argument she left to cool down. But we didn't argue this time."

"You think she's being held there against her will?"

"I don't know. I'd feel a hell of a lot better if I could just talk to her and make sure things are all right." He expects Ed to say that things hadn't been right all along, and in a way he'd be correct. How could he expect any future with a woman like that?

"I'll pick you up in an hour," Ed says.

The room seems too empty without her. Joe goes downstairs to wait. The restaurant is closed between lunch and dinner. As usual, Frank tends bar. "Beer?" he asks.

Joe nods.

"Still no word from her?"

"None."

"What are you gonna do?"

"I'm taking the cops to the house. A friend on the force is coming to pick me up."

"If she really wants to be left alone, that's gonna piss her off."

Joe looks down at his beer. "She's been pissed off before. At least this way, she'll know I'm worried."

"I suppose." Frank serves a pair of new arrivals, and turns away someone hoping for lunch. "Keep an eye on the register for a minute? I got to get some stuff out of the back," he says to Joe.

"Sure."

Frank returns with a case of beer and starts stacking bottles in the cooler. He hands Joe a second one from the stock, then takes one for himself. They face each other, saying nothing until a squad car pulls up outside.

"Good luck scaling the walls," Frank says to him.

In the car, Ed catches the beer scent, eyes Joe suspiciously. "Just two, so help me," Joe says.

Ed pulls out, looking straight ahead.

"Jeez, Ed. I'm all right, OK?"

"OK. Left by the park?"

Joe supplies directions.

Louis's car is parked in the drive. The gates are locked. Repeated ringing finally brings Louis to the door. His tie hangs loose on his open collar. He carries a drink. "Joe, is something wrong?" he asks as he unlocks the gates.

"Where's Leanna?"

"Upstairs resting. Who's this?"

"Ed O'Brien, New Orleans Police Department."

"Police?" Louis eyes him suspiciously.

"I want to see Leanna," Joe says.

Louis looks at him and smiles. When he speaks, his voice is soothing. "Of course you do. Go on up. She's not dressed so maybe . . ."

"I'll stay here," Ed suggests.

"If you're not on duty, perhaps you'd like something?"

"I am. Ginger ale would be fine," Ed responds.

Joe pauses on the stairs to listen to the conversation below.

"How's your sister?" Ed asks.

"You know how funerals are. We have a lot of catching up to do." His voice reveals no caring, no sympathy, no loss. The sound of it always makes Joe feel like he's in the crosshairs of someone's rifle sight.

Louis cares about Leanna. He'd never hurt her. Nonetheless, Joe senses a terrible wrongness in the silence of the upstairs hall. The walls speak, Leanna once told him. If so, they are speaking now. "Leanna?" he calls, and opens her bedroom door, her brother's old room, and finally the last—the room her parents shared.

She is there, a thin, pale form in the big bed, the covers pulled just past her waist, the little-girl cotton gown wrinkled over her breasts, which rise and fall slowly, peacefully. Now that he has found her, he is less certain he should wake her. "Leanna?" he whispers and sits beside her, taking her hand.

Her eyes slowly open. Their brilliant blue is faded, her expression dull. "It's Joe. Are you awake?" he asks.

"Joe. He sent for you. I'm glad." Until that moment, he wasn't entirely certain what she would say. He helps her to sit up, wraps his arms around her, holding her—loosely, as if she might break were she to guess his passion, his concern.

As he does, he notices the prescription bottle on the nightstand. "Were you sick?" he asks.

"Nightmares. Louis gave me something."

Joe notes today's date on the bottle, Leanna's name, and the doctor's. "I was so worried about you," he said.

"I told you I was staying the night."

He hesitates, decides it's better she learn the truth from him. "You've been here three days."

"Three?"

No shock. No surprise. Indeed, she looks as if she were expecting to hear that. "The doctor must have been here. Do you remember?" he asks.

"No."

"Do you want to leave?"

"Oh, yes." She grips him, unwilling to let go.

"Before you go, I must talk to Joe." Louis stands in the doorway, Ed just behind him.

"Don't," she whispers.

"I promise I won't leave the house without you." He follows Louis into the hall.

"Pick up the phone. Her doctor wants to talk to you," Louis says.

Joe has some knowledge of psychiatric terms but he can't understand how the doctor could believe that Leanna was hysterical, or unstable due to grief, how she could have suffered any breakdown at all, or why she needed to be sedated. He says as much.

"She suffered a terrible loss."

"A loss!" If the man didn't sound so serious, Joe would laugh. "Henri de Noux was a sadistic son of a bitch. She doesn't miss him. If anything, she's glad he's gone."

He expected that what he said would shock. Instead, the doctor replies, "How do you think living with that makes her feel?"

"Relieved."

"I think I should see her again soon."

"That's for her to decide."

"She should be constantly watched for the next few days."

"I'll take some time off from work." Damned straight he would, though it would likely mean his job. If he didn't,

he'd come home some night and find her gone again,
spirited off by her brother, or her father's ghost.

If she had been wider awake, Leanna would have been
able to understand Joe's phone conversation. With her
senses muddy from tranquilizers and sleep, she simply took
comfort in the sound of his voice. His presence gave her
strength, enough that she sat up and piled the pillows behind
her. "Hand me my hairbrush," she asks Louis.

Instead, he moves beside her. "Lean forward," he says
and begins brushing out the tangles.

Joe joins them, standing in the doorway. As always when
she and Louis are together, he appears ill at ease.

"You can both stay here, if you like," Louis suggests.

She takes his hand. He must know the sorrow she feels,
but she can say nothing but a simple "I can't."

Joe moves beside her, too quickly she thinks, as if her
affection for him and for her brother must be weighed and
measured, evenly divided, when the feelings are so different. Joe was an only child. How can he understand the bond
of siblings, let alone the inseparability of twins?

"I'll take her to the condo. It's her home, after all," Joe
says.

"I'm sorry, Louis," she whispers to him, holding him
close. As he touches her, she feels him trace a pattern on the
back of her neck.

She taught him that trick, the little spell to use when you
want to hold onto a loved one. Did he really think it would
work on her?

"If you leave, I can get dressed," she tells him, and throws
back the covers, standing so that Joe will feel relieved, less
protective.

"Did you dream of Mama?" Louis asks before he goes.

"For a moment only, I think," she replies sadly.

Even though they have only stepped out of the room, the
walls suddenly take on a sinister quality. As she slips off the
cotton gown and reaches for her slacks, she hears music,

something by Bach or one of his contemporaries—a sharp-edged harpsichord, a mellow flute. It brings back memories of when she was very young, and her mother would read to her, asking Leanna to turn the pages, while music such as this played softly in the background.

Later, when the book was finished and stacked with the others in the old chest in the hall, Leanna would go to the phonograph and turn up the volume until the music drowned them both with its complexity, bringing tears to Leanna's eyes, a tightness to her throat.

"People would dance to this in vast ballrooms with marble floors. The women wore high, powdered wigs in shades of silver and peach and their dresses were cut," Mother slid the side of one hand across Leanna's chest just above her nipples, "to there."

"Wicked," Leanna would say.

"Not wicked then, stylish. Beautiful."

The music grows louder. The dark paper seems to move. Its pattern blurs. "You can leave me?" Her mother's voice, reproachful, filling her with guilt.

"I have to!" Leanna whispers frantically, her control dissolving into tears.

"Stay."

Leanna's legs fold beneath her. Her fall brings the men rushing in. "Are you all right?" Louis asks while Joe, always one to act, lifts her and lays her on the bed, covering her bare chest.

"Do you still want to go?" Joe asks.

She looks from him to Louis—ah, the anguish in her brother's expression that she could go now, in such haste, when she was so obviously ill. He judged their relationship by their proximity to each other, and she saw no way to explain that distance made no difference.

Explain gently, her mother might say. Explain slowly. Make him understand.

"Not tonight, unless you won't stay with me," she responds, taking Joe's hand.

"I'll stay," he replies.

"What about the officer who came with you?" Louis asks.

"Ed! I forgot all about him. I'd better go down and explain."

"You go too, Louis," Leanna says. "Leave me alone for a while."

She lies in bed a few minutes longer, long enough certainly for the policeman to go, then she kicks off the covers. No matter how much effort it takes, she will not be an invalid any longer.

Decision made, some of the dizziness leaves her. She dresses slowly, holds carefully to the bannister as she descends, while the stairs and walls sway around her. It's a good thing she has experience in being drunk, she thinks. This is hardly different.

Louis and Joe are in the parlor, where Louis is explaining her condition. She stops in the doorway to listen for just a moment.

"There's a terrible void in our lives," Louis tells him. "The great villain is gone. The emptiness is depressing."

"If Lucifer died, would God have a reason to exist?" Leanna adds as she joins them, her step even as she orders her legs to be firm. "Fix me a gin and tonic and stop looking so surprised, brother dear. There may be a void in our lives but it should be a cause for rejoicing, don't you think?"

She falls into the chair, her arms outspread to make the sudden move look more like exuberance than what it was—another moment of weakness, a spasm in the center of her brain radiating out to her limbs.

Louis hands her a glass. The drink is strong, the way she likes it. Apparently Louis took her at her word.

There is little to do in the house, one long hour giving way to another as the afternoon moves slowly on. They all drink far more than usual, but it brings no joy, or even any relief from the uneasiness that plagues them all. At best, it dulls the sharper edges of their anxiousness.

Tomorrow, definitely, she will leave here. Even if Mama

and all her ancestors appear before her and beg her to stay, she will ignore them.

No one can ask her to make this sacrifice for Louis.

By evening no one has the energy to keep up the pretense of conversation. When Leanna decides to retire early, Joe accompanies her upstairs.

As soon as they are alone, she kisses him and says, "I promise that we'll leave tomorrow." He doesn't ask why she's decided to stay one more night and she is thankful. How can she explain what she doesn't understand herself?

Each room in old Southern houses seems to have its own distinct scent. A connoisseur of such things could probably tell that this room had once belonged to an invalid, had once been the home of a beautiful woman, had been used as a center of perversion by an aging, bitter man.

Perhaps scent was the source of last night's dream, this afternoon's vision—olfactory-induced hallucinations. She snuggles close to Joe, her face half-hidden by the covers, breathing in the warm male scent mingling with the faint hint of spice aftershave, cognac and cigarettes.

Such a perfect man to keep the demons of her past at bay, she thinks as she runs her hand up the side of his thigh and feels him shudder, with surprise, with delight.

"Leanna, are you. . . . ?"

"Shhh. It's all right."

His chest shakes in a silent laugh, the sort a well-bred Catholic father might use when his children are sleeping just down the hall. "It should be more than that," he says.

"It is." She tilts her head up so he can kiss her, then rolls on top of him. She long ago told him the story of her mother's illness and death, her papa's brutality and bitter grief. Only Louis knew all the rest her father had done to her. Their strongest bond is the horror they have shared.

"This was Mama's room," she says, kneeling above him, pulling off her gown. "And Papa's as well. If we make our own memories here, we exorcize their ghosts."

Once again, the inevitable passion takes control of Joe.

He forgets the brother sleeping downstairs and pounds into her while the bedsprings creak and the headboard rattles.

When they are finished, and lie apart, he twines his fingers through hers and whispers, "I love you."

Perhaps someday, when she can feel something beyond relief that the worst of her life is over, she will say those words to him. Until she can she will not lie. "I know," she replies.

Later he tries to fall asleep as easily as she has but that relief eludes him.

He hates this house, hates how she defers to her brother as if Louis is still the invalid, she the devoted sister. He has no reason to resent these roles, save for the vague instinct, born of years of police and investigative work, that Louis de Noux is not at all the man he seems. If Joe can somehow spot the nature of the deceit, he will feel far more comfortable in Louis's presence.

He spent the long hours of the afternoon looking for hints in the way Louis watched his sister, as if she were an apparition that ignored would vanish; in the way his hand would lie on her shoulder as he stood behind her; in the way each change in her expression, each small sigh would cause him to make some comment.

Louis notices everything about her. How can Leanna stand to be near him? How can she say that he makes her feel safe?

But Louis does not appear to look on Joe as a rival, or even as a threat to his sister's well-being. Joe is no fool; this astonishes him. Considering what little he's done with his life, he is a far from ideal in-law, especially for a family as wealthy as the de Noux.

Yet Leanna does more than sleep with him. She seems to need him, to cherish him. How has he become so lucky?

Joe buries his face in her hair, reveling in the softness of it, in the scent of her perfume. Any sacrifice she would ask him to make would be worth it, even if it means living the rest of his life trapped within these walls.

Not a comforting thought. He's hardly surprised when he finds he still cannot sleep.

He hears music downstairs. Louis undoubtedly cannot sleep either. Joe recalls how many times Louis has tried to speak to him, and how many times Leanna has interrupted them. Now is as good a time to face Louis as any, he thinks, and carefully moves away from her. She does not stir as he slips on his pants and leaves.

The hall is dark, the path to the stairs lit only by the faint light coming from somewhere below, a light reflected in the tall cheval mirror across from the landing, in the brass sconces that flank it. Joe pads down the hall, but at the top of the stairs, he sees motion from the other wing of the house, where Louis and Leanna's rooms were. "Is someone there?" he calls.

"Is that you?" Louis responds from below. "Come down."

Before he does, Joe checks the hall. The doors are closed. Shadows, he thinks. I'm frightened of fucking shadows. That's what this house has done to me.

He goes down to where Louis waits, moving a little too quickly it seems.

Louis has changed into a red bathrobe and sandals. As soon as Joe joins him, Louis goes to the wet bar and fixes him a drink. He doesn't ask what Joe wants or even if he wants anything, just thrusts the glass of ice and liquor into his hand.

It is a strange concoction of herbs, honey and bourbon that burns as it goes down, burns in his stomach as well. He takes a second, larger swig.

"My sister is sleeping?" Louis asks.

Joe nods.

"Good. She hasn't slept well in all these days."

"Then why didn't she know she'd been here three days?" Joe asks, not able to keep all of the anger out of his voice.

"She hasn't slept *well*. There were dreams, terrible ones.

She raved. Once when I tried to wake her, she did this." He pulls back one flap of the robe to show the red scratches on the smooth white skin of his chest. "Can you really give her the care she needs?"

"She wants my care." Joe takes another swallow, holds out his glass for more. God, it tastes good, better than any drink he's had in years.

Louis seems to know he's lost the battle. He frowns then says, "Of course she does. That's as it should be—a woman and her lover." He pauses, emphasizing his capitulation, then adds, "I can arrange help for you. You'll have to leave her sometimes."

"I'd appreciate it, but later, after she's had a chance to recover on her own." And after I have her well away from here, and can see for myself what sort of delusions she shows, he adds to himself.

The mantel clock strikes the hour. Midnight. The sound echoes through the quiet house. As he listens to the empty air, Joe realizes that sometimes between his arrival and this moment, the music has stopped. He didn't notice.

"It's late. I'm surprised we aren't both exhausted," Louis says.

Actually Joe is exhausted, so much so that the drink has gone right to his head. He mumbles something about the hour and leaves, catching himself on the stairs when he trips.

By the time he reaches the top, the music has begun once more. Such a strange blend of sounds—drums, discordant notes, a high-pitched voice wailing above it. A song without rhythm or substance, all so soft that it seems as if the music comes from within himself.

Shadows again, shadows curling like cats around him. And in their center is a core of darkness more complete than that of dreamless sleep.

"Louis," he wants to call, but pride makes that impossible. Whatever he feels, whatever he sees is caused by the alcohol, his own exhaustion or Leanna's unfathomable fear.

A few steps, just a few steps through that blackness and he will be in the room with Leanna. With that thought to steel him, he walks confidently forward.

One step. Two. Three.

He glimpses a reflection in the hall mirror. It should have been his but instead he sees the face of a dead man—Henri de Noux. Younger. Stronger. Angry.

The vision fades to nothing at all, and Joe cannot tell whether minutes or hours or days have passed. He only knows that his heart pounds, his breathing comes too fast and his limbs are heavy and numb as if they, like his senses, have gone to sleep.

Shouldn't he have fallen? Perhaps this is all a dream, nothing more.

That last, comforting thought vanishes with the rest as the darkness steals his last shreds of self-awareness.

Leanna wakes when the bedroom door opens, and sees the shadowy figure standing there. "Joe?" she calls.

The figure moves toward her, saying nothing.

She flips on the light, and is blinded for a moment as she says, "Joe, did Louis get you drunk?"

Joe's eyes are open and staring at her with an expression she's never seen on her lover's face, though she knows the fear it brings all to well.

Pulled from sleep, her eyes tearing from the sudden light, it takes a moment for her to recognize the source of the fear. When she does, she freezes, as she did when she was a small girl and thought that stillness would render her invisible.

Her fear only excited Papa. Then he would pounce, and what he gave after—pleasure or pain—depended on his whim. Unpredictability was the main horror of Henri de Noux.

For a few years she actually reveled in the moments of pleasure, the shame of that passion making her his prisoner more surely than fear had ever done.

She manages to speak. "Joe, fight his presence," she says.

He does not hear. One hand catches her wrist, squeezing it so hard she expects it to break, while the second grips the bodice of her gown, ripping it open down the front.

Joe has never looked at her with such monstrous desire. Joe has never hurt her, and never would.

She considers screaming for Louis, decides against it. Instead, drawing on some reservoir of power deep within her, she places her free hand on Joe's forehead and begins to call his name.

He kneads her breast, squeezing painfully, but does not try to push her arm away. Certain she's made the right decision, she wills herself calm and repeats his name while the creature inside her lover runs his hand down her stomach, thrusting it between her legs, the fingers moving savagely, trying to force her to respond.

If she breaks her hold on Joe now, her father's ghost will triumph. She ignores the pain, turns her head sideways when he tried to kiss her.

"Joe . . . fight him. Joe . . ."

She repeats the words a dozen times before she sees some glimmer of response in his eyes. When she does, she speaks firmly, "Spirit, leave this body. I order it."

Her hand on his forehead seems to draw the madness from his brain. He blinks and falls against the side of the bed. He looks at her sitting above him, fingers the ripped fabric as he stares at the cut on her cheek, the tears she cannot control. She can read clearly in his expression how hard he is trying to account for those empty few moments. "Did I do that?" he finally asks.

He has a right to know that much at least. She nods and he kisses the bruise, the cut, tasting her blood with the last. "How could I have done that?" He looks at her, begging for some logical answer.

"It isn't over," she says, wishing there was some way to make him understand that he had no control over what his body has done. "You weren't responsible. That's all you need to know," she finally says. She rises and begins to pack. "We're leaving now. Louis is going to say that I've gone mad but I don't care. I won't stay here and be subjected to his torment. He's dead. I survived him, and I won't let him touch me anymore."

She speaks of her father, not her brother, and her anger is a crutch, he knows. As long as she keeps it up, she will not have to give in to the fear that could paralyze her. He has seen too many victims over the years; he understands the danger all too well.

Without a word, he helps her.

The house is dark when they leave the room and feel their way to the stairs. Halfway down, he hears a shuffle in the hall below. Leanna cries out and reaches backward for him.

The hall light switches on. Louis stands at the foot of the stairs looking up at them. "The old man was here, wasn't he?" Louis asks, his eyes blinking behind the round glasses. When he sees his sister's face, he rushes up the stairs, ready do defend her. "Who did this?" he demands, looking at Joe as he speaks.

"Leave him alone, Louis. It was Papa who attacked me, no matter whose body he used." She pushes him aside, continues down. "I told you it's foolish to stay here. You can live with his ghost, if that's what you want."

"In the four days you were here with me, did he ever appear to you, much less harm you? Let me protect you. I know how," Louis tells her.

She lets the anger loose, focusing it on her brother. "I'll never set foot in this house again, do you understand?" she screams at him.

Louis sits on the stairs, saying nothing until she reaches the front door. "What makes you think the spirit is confined to this house?" he asks.

"I'll have to take my chances with that, won't I?"

"Leanna, you dabbled in voodoo. You never learned what you need to know. I do."

"I'll find someone. I'll go to Celeste. I have money. She'll help."

"You would tell our secrets to a stranger?" he inquires; he does not sound concerned.

"I'll tell just as much as I have to," she replies, and pulls open the door.

The night itself is her first real indication of how many days she has spent in that house. Though the thick air obscures the stars, the almost full moon is visible through the branches of the trees lining the street. Joe puts her bag in the trunk while she stands beside the car breathing deeply, inhaling the dampness, the fragrance of the honeysuckle that everyone in the area cultivates so diligently it seems their vines have always been here.

When she was young, she would go outside late in the morning when the new blossoms had just opened and the fragrance was at its peak. She would find the newest shoots and snip them off, then carry the branches upstairs to her mother's room. Often, her mother would be sleeping and she would lay the vines across the bed and wait for the smell to wake her.

In those moments between sleep and awakening, between unconsciousness and pain, her mother smiled.

Moments of peace. Brief, happy moments; as brief as the life of these fragile blooms.

"We should go," Joe says.

She gets into the car, but after they've gone a few blocks, she asks him to pull over at St. Charles Street. "I feel like I've been a prisoner forever," she says, leaves him, and walks alone under the huge ancient oaks.

Joe follows her. She spies him keeping his distance, not wanting to intrude on her freedom or her solitude.

Tonight she defeated a ghost. What concern does she have for mortal threats?

She stops in a place where the branches aren't so thick, sits down on a bench and looks up at the night sky, tinged mauve by the city's lights.

The nightmares are over. She will never go back to that house, never let her father's ghost trouble her again. The dampness of the night makes her face wet, forms beads of water in her dark hair, but still she remains where she sits.

A sound breaks the stillness around her, a droning like a prop plane, but it does not pass over, but rather grows in intensity. It is a gray noise, discernible only because there is no silence, not in the world around her, or in her mind. And through it all, like a shape moving through fog, she hears her papa's terrible laughter.

Joe walks toward her. For a moment she isn't certain if she should stand her ground or run. She hasn't the strength to defeat the monster again.

"We ought to go," he says.

Joe's voice, steady, concerned.

"In a minute." She holds out her hand, and when he's pulled her to her feet she kisses him, slow and passionately, as if they hadn't coupled just hours before. Ah, she was so hungry for him—for the pleasure he gives, and the moments when they are joined and she can forget the fear.

A storm, so sudden and strong it could only happen in dreams, roars down on her. And as she turns her face into the gale, Hailey woke.

TWENTY-ONE

The fire had burned to a few glowing cinders among the ashes. Outside, the sun that had warmed the room had vanished behind a dense covering of clouds, and a thick, wet snow fell. Hailey built up the fire, turned on the blower that would distribute its warmth through the house and went upstairs to record the events she had been allowed to witness.

She typed quickly, not stopping to judge or try to understand what she had been shown. By the time she'd finished, she'd begun to feel sleepy again. Not yet, she thought; at least not until she'd sorted out what she'd learned. Thinking that a walk would clear her head, she put on boots and her hiking clothes and went outside.

The Ice Age Trail that linked much of the southern Wisconsin state forest land cut through the back of her property. She followed it through high meadows covered with drifted snow, past winter-bare oaks and maples that the snow had turned into an artist's stylized winter, and the rock-strewn moraines and drumlins left by the retreating glaciers centuries before.

The spirit that shared her body seemed to be asleep or occupied elsewhere. An ideal time for Hailey to reflect on her situation without having her ghost try to direct her conclusions.

A shelter had been built on the rise overlooking the area's largest inland lake. She stopped there, as countless hikers and cross-country skiers always did, and sat looking past the

263

steep drop-off and the road beneath it, to the gray horizon, the gray snow, the dead land.

When she had been here before, she'd often walked this path and stopped in this place, mourning the child she had lost. Now, in a sense, she felt as if she mourned another child, the Leanna who had carried honeysuckle to her mother's room.

Then lost her mother and, soon after, her innocence, to a monster.

Ed had asked her why she had chosen to unravel the mystery of Leanna's life. The bond between them and the blessing that came from it seemed all too clear. For the first time in her life, injustice did not make her cry, or weakly hope for someone stronger to end it. Instead it made her angry, and ready to die to do what she could.

She analyzed everything she had learned in today's vision. When she had a course of action ready, she hiked back to the house, got her keys and drove into town, where, among all the other errands she ran, she arranged to have her phones reconnected.

When she returned, she unloaded her groceries, and cleaned up the mess beneath the frozen drainpipe, biding her time until her phone rang, signaling that service had been restored.

Ed would be getting ready to go to work now, an ideal time to reach him. She wondered if he wanted to speak to her, or if they'd argued before she left. She could only remember starting his letter, not delivering it or sending it out in the mail. He might have never received it, in which case he'd likely be frantic.

The day after Celeste's funeral, Ed had stopped at Hailey's apartment for their breakfast date. When she didn't answer, he'd tried calling. The phone company told him that her line had been disconnected.

He went to the restaurant and found Frank Berlin, who told him that Hailey had left, then added that he wasn't sorry to see her go. Ed supposed that he'd feel the same way about a tenant who had, innocently to be sure, caused so many tragedies.

"Did she say where she was going, or leave a note for me?" Ed asked.

"Note? Oh, yeah. Come on upstairs." In the past, Ed had noticed that Frank moved surprisingly quick for a man his size, but today his steps were slow, plodding. When he handed Ed the unsealed note, Ed saw that his eyes were red-rimmed, as if he'd been crying, and his hand shook.

Hailey had mentioned Norman's defection. Apparently Frank wasn't taking the breakup well. "She paid her rent through the end of next month and said I should hold onto her stuff," Frank told him. "Just as soon as she moves out, I'm spreading salt from one end of that room to the other and boarding it up. The room is cursed, that's what it is. All these deaths."

"Can I see it?" Ed asked.

"See it? I suppose." Frank let him in and left him there alone. From the expression on the man's face, Ed suspected that he'd have someone else spread the salt while he waited outside.

Hailey hadn't taken anything but a few clothes. She'd even left dirty dishes in the sink. Ed washed them before they could attract any stray roaches hiding in the walls, then sat on the bed they'd shared and opened her note.

I'm taking your advice and going home to finish the book, she'd written. *I'll call when I'm able.*

Not a hint of what made her run so quickly. Not a word about Willie, or anything about how much she cared for him. None of this was like her.

When he left, he knocked on Berlin's apartment door. Berlin invited him inside and he followed the chef into the kitchen, where he was chopping vegetables. A cookbook lay open on the counter. "I experiment on my dinner guests. That's better than using the customers," Berlin said. He offered Joe a beer, and opened one for himself as well. "Did you hear anything about Celeste's murder investigation?" he asked.

He sounded concerned, which was understandable, especially now that Norman was gone. Nights alone had to be hard on the man. "No. I'm a witness," Ed replied. "Under the circumstances, I'm kept in the dark as much as you are. But when they arrest a suspect, it'll be in the papers."

"The police keep coming back to me with new questions. The help is on edge, not to mention the customers. I watch people coming in, thinking could it be him, or him?"

"Do you have any ideas?"

"Believe me, I'd feel better if I did and a whole lot better if I didn't think that just maybe it was Leanna defending her space."

"The murderer was human, and alive," Ed told her.

"You sure? With everything that's been going on, can you really be sure?"

Hailey wouldn't think so, Ed thought. And fantastic though it was to contemplate, he wasn't sure either. He finished his beer and left, going home instead of running errands, hoping to see the light flashing on his answering machine, to hear Hailey's message that she was all right.

He'd waited two days, to give her a chance to get home, then tried her house a half dozen times. Each time, he got a phone company recording stating that her phone was not in service.

He felt both relief and anger when Hailey finally called. "You scared the hell out of me," he told her.

"I had to go. I'm sorry but I couldn't help it."

"Christ, don't apologize. Most people would have run screaming from that apartment as soon as they met their roommates. You stuck it out a long time."

"Leanna, at least, came with me," she said. "She was the one who made me leave. I think she's worried about what could happen to me if we stayed. And I think she was the one who wrote the note too. Did you get it?"

"Yeah. I thought it was a little cold coming from you."

Did he actually believe what she'd told him? He examined his thoughts a moment and realized that he did. "Hailey, listen. You can't keep going on like this."

"I don't seem to have much choice."

"Do you want a choice?"

"I'd be happier if I had one, I suppose, but I'd probably do just what I'm doing. I'm calling so you'll know I got here all right and to ask your help. There's a man called Oba Van; a Haitian, I believe. Celeste said he was rumored to be in some murderous cult, Secte Rouge. Find out if he has a criminal record in this country."

"Why? What did you discover?"

"Nothing definite. Just a feeling I have about Louis de Noux. As soon as I finish typing my notes, I'll send you a copy."

"All right, I'll do what I can and call you."

"If I don't answer, don't worry. I usually turn off the phone when I'm working and let the machine pick up the calls." This was only a half lie, she reasoned, since it was exactly what she intended to do this time so no one would disturb her dreams.

"Willie is coming in on Sunday and I'm taking three days off next week. She'll be sorry to have missed you."

"Who knows, in the next few days I might solve this thing and join you both there. If not, tell her I'm sorry I missed her too."

"How's the book?"

"I'm in the final stretch. I can't wait for it to be done, Ed. I want my life back, and soon. When this is over, I'll take it back and no ghost will stop me, I promise." A pause, then, "I love you, Ed."

"And I love you."

As soon as Ed finished talking to Hailey, he left for work, and got in almost an hour early. Administration might get down on him for an unauthorized investigation but at least he'd conduct it on his own time.

Background checks on Oba Van revealed no records on any level. A call to Harold Neale, a friend at the FBI, added nothing to nothing, but the man did have some information on Secte Rouge.

Hailey was right; it was a blood cult. Its origins, like those of voodoo, were in West Africa, and as with voodoo, the belief had been carried to the New World by slaves. The rituals were similar but the addition of human sacrifice and cannabalism made the cult both dangerous and feared.

Strangers apprehended after dark were the usual victims. But anyone who wished to join the sect had to provide a sacrifice—and it was believed that the closer the relationship between initiate and victim, the greater the power the initiate would obtain.

"We've had reports of rattles made from human bone, of spellbooks written in blood and bound with human skin, of mementoes from an individual's victim kept close to give the sect member special power."

"Power to do what?"

"The usual things—to make someone love them, to harm their enemies, or for luck in business. But there's more to it than just that. A real believer might seek the power to raise the dead, or to control a spirit—human or otherwise."

"Are they active in this country?" Ed asked.

"There have been a few rumors but none of them have been substantiated. The same is true in Haiti, but there it's because people just don't talk about it. It may be that the sect doesn't exist there at all, except as a sort of rural legend parents use to get kids in by dark."

"They why keep the information?"

"There have been cases where people have believed in the sect enough to start do-it-yourself groups. Those drug smugglers in Texas were a good example. There's also been ritual murders by a street gang in Chicago, and some prison inmates in New York. The more we learn about the sect, the more we're able to distinguish between ordinary psychopaths and an organization of them."

"Oba Van is believed to be a priest in Secte Rouge. Could you dig a little further, and see if you can find out anything at all about him?" When Neale agreed, Ed gave him his home address and phone number.

For the rest of his shift, Ed's mind kept moving back to thought of Secte Rouge. Could Leanna have been involved? No, that was foolish. Leanna broke hearts, but now that he considered her in light of her past he found her less frightening than frightened. Her power, if indeed she had any, had been entirely defensive. She didn't have the soul of a murderer.

The snow increased throughout the afternoon, coating the brush and trees as it had coated the lawn earlier. The tracks Hailey's car had made in the front driveway when she'd gone into town to mail her notes to Ed had filled in and drifts were forming near the road.

The fatigue Hailey felt seemed to return the moment she stopped being busy, or glanced out the window at the winter landscape. As she prepared her dinner, she tried not to look outside but to concentrate only on the task at hand. But as she began chopping vegetables for soup, a gust of wind picked the snow off the garage roof and flung it against the kitchen window. Startled, Hailey peered out the window to see if anyone had come into her drive.

It was foolish to think so. Her friends wouldn't know she was back, while her car and the house lights would make it clear to any prowler that the home was occupied.

Nonetheless, the feeling that she was being watched would not go away. Finally, Hailey put on her coat and loaded the rifle that her father had made her buy when she moved out here. With the weight of it reassuring in her hand, she went outside.

The wind blew into her face. The tried to catch her breath in the cold, and squinted in the blowing snow. Something was out there, moving in the trees whose dark branches provided the only distinction between snow-covered land and snow-filled sky.

She pulled the jacket's hood forward so it would shield her face from the wind and wondered if she should call out or go inside and lock the door. As she paused, waiting for instinct to make the decision, two does and a buck bounded from the trees and across the lawn, disappearing on the side of the house.

They had glimpsed her as she had them. And they had run, as she had run, from danger. Her world and theirs were so different, yet their reflexes were so alike.

She looked up at the sky, took a deep breath of the damp evening air and went inside.

Hailey's hand shook as she built up the fire, hoping that its warmth would dissipate her fear, that the act of building it would give her energy. Neither worked. Instead the familiar dark cloud descended on her, muting her thoughts as well as her senses. The fatigue she knew so well grabbed hold of her, the weight of it pulling her down.

If she slept now, would she dream?

The teakettle began to whistle, drawing her back to consciousness as her feet drew her to the kitchen, where she stared, bewildered, at the kettle, the tea she had brought from New Orleans waiting beside the cup and saucer on the counter.

As the world closed in around her, someone else prepared the brew.

. . . Joe goes to sleep listening to her voice droning on. He wakes and she is chanting still. The room reeks of incense. His nose is perpetually stuffy and the only thing that keeps him from leaving in search of peace is Leanna's fear.

She refuses to acknowledge that her fear even exists but he sees it in the intensity of her ritual, in the way she glances at the door or the window each time a sudden noise—and there are so many!—startles her.,

She takes strands of his hair and braids it with her own, winds it around some pieces of red twine, finds a loose splinter in the door to stick it behind. She creates a second bundle for the door leading to the balcony.

Such tiny fetishes, but she swears they are potent, though she hardly appears relaxed with them in place. Instead, she brews him tea, bitter herbs that she allows him to sweeten only with molasses.

"How do you feel?" she asks when he's finished, her voice so intent that all he can do is mumble some reassurance that seems to please her.

Later that afternoon, she sends him out for supplies— things that can be purchased at normal stores, such as peppercorns, mustard seeds and coarse pickling salt from the grocer's; brushes, acrylic paints and glue from an art shop; sulfur from a druggist.

When he returns, he finds that she has stripped off two loose sheets of the fading wallpaper and washed the wall beneath.

"Redecorating?" he asks.

She doesn't answer, only takes his hand and pulls him down to the floor beside her, repeating her chant until he finally gets it right. He sits for hours, trying to concentrate on the senseless strings of words—a matra to some pagan god.

"*Aisan hey. Onape laisse coule. Aisan hey. Onape laisse coule . . .*"

They chant it over and over until she feels the time is ready, then she sprinkles the spices under the carpet in front of the doors and throws the remainder into the hall.

And with him continuing the chant, she picks up a brush and begins to paint.

The first hesitate strokes grow bolder as she continues. At the end, she is flying through the work, laughing as she goes, the sound of one whose death sentence has been commuted in the last hours.

Finally, she turns to him, her face paint-speckled, holding

out a brush and jar of black paint. "Finish with me," she tells him.

With both their hands holding the brush, they write the final strokes of the spell, the words that all her hours of concentration had made powerful: *Protect the Innocent.*

"His spirit cannot harm us now," she whispers and wraps her arms around him, kissing him, pulling him down to the floor.

He makes love to her, his eyes on the twins with their huge erections, on the tail of the snake coiled around their feet. . . .

"I'm hungry," she says later and laughs. "Famished."

He goes to the store. When he returns, she is still undressed, sitting cross-legged on the bed, her pale body even lighter against the deep blue sheets. She points to the wall where the drawing was. The paper has been reglued, the seams carefully matched.

"Would anyone notice it there?" she asks.

"I don't think so."

"Good. Don't tell Louis or Frank, or anyone else. It's our secret protection. Don't even think about it when you're outside this room if you can help it."

He can almost hide his smile. "It's serious," she says. "What happened to you at the house can happen here or anywhere. Spirits read thoughts."

"What about now?"

"The room is protected. They have no power here." She spoke with only the tiniest bit of doubt, of fear.

Harold Neale's report came by fax the following afternoon. Ed found it on his desk when he got to work.

Oba Van had been born in Haiti in 1944. His father had been a follower of Duvalier, occupying a high position in the dictator's government. Van had been educated in France and Berlin, moving from philosophy to business, eventually earning an MBA. He worked in New York for a time, then returned to Haiti to become president of Prince Island

Investments at the age of thirty. After Duvalier's son was removed from power, the firm moved its main offices to St. Thomas and opened a branch in New Orleans.

Curious, Ed ran the firm's name through the police computers and discovered that their New Orleans branch manager, Oba Van's brother, had disappeared sixteen years ago after apparently embezzling half a million in investors' funds.

Most of the funds were recovered, but the man was never sighted again. It was rumored that the family-run firm had allowed him to escape.

Principal American clients of the firm included the de Noux family. That explained the man's appearance at Louis's party, though Oba Van hardly seemed the sort of man who would dine on human flesh.

As if there were some specific type who would, Ed reminded himself. Nonetheless, it all seemed improbable. He wrote Hailey a brief note, sent it and the information to her via overnight letter, then tried to forget about the matter. Hailey was well away from danger and Willie was coming in soon. If he wanted those days off, he had a lot of extra hours to put in.

TWENTY-TWO

Two weeks have passed and her father's spirit is still watching her. She senses his presence beside her in the car, senses it lurking in the hall outside of Joe's apartment. So far, at least, the spells she has laid on the doors have held, but she has no idea how long this will last.

As for Joe, he drinks the tea she brews for him, a dutiful lover, though she can tell by the way he looks at her that he thinks she is losing her mind. Louis is no help, with his hints that she's had some sort of breakdown, his constant attempts to get Joe to bring her home.

Home! Has Louis forgotten everything he learned? There, in the house where he died, his father's spirit would be at its strongest. That didn't seem to plague Louis, but then Louis always welcomes a challenge, especially a fight with someone he hates. He is so like Papa that way.

She tells him that when he calls to invite her and Joe to dinner, saying emphatically that she will never set foot in that house again.

"Then let me take you both out. We can slum and eat at Sonya's if you like, so you won't even have to leave the building, though I'm more in the mood to celebrate somewhere else."

"Why would Sonya's make a difference?" she asks.

"Because I hear you've become a hermit, sister dear. It hardly becomes you. Now, get dressed."

She tries to decline but he insists that she put Joe on the phone. Whatever he says to Joe has its intended effect. With both of them against her, all she can do is agree to drinks and dinner at Broussards.

Once she does, she feels much better, so much so that she ignores her fear. A week has passed since the night she saw Henri inside of Joe, and nothing more has happened. A night out may be exactly what she needs.

She plays with combinations of clothing. None of them work. So much is still at her condo that she decides to walk there to dress.

When she tells Joe where she's going, he asks, "Do you want me to go with you?"

"I'm not an invalid, dearest. Wait here for Louis. I'll be fine." His silent concern fills her with sympathy. "I'll call when I get there. You call before you come to get me. All right?" She kisses him playfully on the cheek, then, with more passion, on the lips. "And drink your tea," she reminds him just before she goes.

When the door shuts behind Leanna, Hailey stays behind. A voyeur for a moment, watching Joe shower and dress, watching him brew his tea, his expression of disgust when he tastes it. An instant later, she is sharing his feeling, the nausea the bitter herbs give him.

Someone knocks at the door. Before Joe can answer it, Louis opens it and steps inside, blinking from the bright sunlight streaming through the windows. "Could I close the drapes?" he asks.

Joe pulls them shut while Louis surveys the room. "It's changed quite a bit," he comments. "Same ugly wallpaper, though."

"You've been here?" Joe asks.

"Years ago. Frank and Leanna and I went to school together. Before the now legendary Sonya had her stroke, this was her room." He glances at the fetish above the door, at the tea in Joe's hand. "How's my sister?" he asks. "Still frantic?"

"Much better, actually. She went to her own place to change."

"Her own place. How odd it seems to hear that. Ah well, I guess I'll have to learn to get along without her."

They don't know each other well, so perhaps Joe should overlook the comment. Nonetheless, he has to ask, "After everything that's happened in that house, why do you want to stay there?"

"Because I cherish it. And to let the memories drive me away is admitting defeat. I won't let Henri win. I despite him too much for that."

He speaks as if the battle still rages. Perhaps in his mind, as in Leanna's, it still does. "Would you like something to drink?" Joe asks.

"Beer if you have it."

Joe pulls out one for himself as well. Later, as he puts on his tie, Leanna calls to say she is ready. He glances at the half-full cup of tea on the sideboard. It's always more bitter when cold. With some guilt, he leaves it and follows Louis out.

Leanna decided to wait for them outside. Joe spots her from the corner—the fuchsia silk blouse and gathered floral skirt impossible to overlook. While she was waiting, one of the Quarter's most infamous mashers spied her. Now he kisses her hand then her cheek before reluctantly letting her go. "If Joe don't treat you like a lady, you come runnin' to me," he tells her, then he spies another unattached female and moves on.

"I'm truly amazed the man is still alive," Louis comments.

"Who could kill the last living legend of Rampart Street?" Leanna laughs and links arms with her brother and Joe as they walk on.

It pleases Joe to see how lighthearted Leanna has become—how she flirts with the waiter at Broussard's, then, even more openly, with the help at Sonya's where they go after dinner. As for Frank, he keeps his distance. Odd, considering that he knew Louis, but Joe had to admit there are plenty of old school friends he'd just as soon avoid.

When Louis walks to the bar to order a second round of drinks, he says a few words to Frank. Frank fills the order himself and joins them.

"Long time," Leanna says, smiling. She and Joe were in the day before.

"For some of you," Frank adds, looking at Louis as he speaks.

"Louis said you went to school together," Joe comments.

"They were best friends." Leanna's smile turns into a laugh. "Best and only friends."

"I believe nowadays we'd be called the 'geeks,'" Louis adds.

"Friends by elimination, you could say." Leanna grasps the hands of Louis and Frank. "Witch Woman, Owl Eyes and—"

"Don't say it. The help might overhear," Frank mumbles.

She leans toward Frank. ". . . Belly," she whispers, her mouth close to his ear. "Belly. Belly. Belly."

Louis smiles. "Never do that again, sister dear, or Frank might double Joe's rent just to be rid of you."

"Our school years were less than ideal," Leanna continues, speaking to Joe. "But we survived. Isn't it amazing?"

They sit together awhile longer, making jokes about their past that are never explained to Joe. When he and Leanna leave, Louis and Frank remain together, talking softly.

"You never mentioned that you knew Frank," Joe says when they're alone.

"I knew him because Louis did. He was my brother's friend, not mine."

She pulls her skirt over her head, unbuttons her blouse. It amazes him how, after seven months together, he still finds watching her undress so arousing, her body still so much a gift to him.

Later, when Leanna lies sleeping in his arms, Joe hears someone walking up the front stairs, the jingle of keys, Frank's laughter as he opens his apartment door. Soon after, he hears Frank come into the room on the opposite side of the wall to check on his aunt and dole out her evening medication.

The other usual sounds follow—their low voices, her cane tapping on the tile floor in her bathroom, the toilet flushing.

Then, as always at that hour of the night, the music begins. When Joe moved in, Frank explained that he played the cassette to help his aunt get back to sleep. Tonight, the music seems a little louder.

But then tonight Frank has a guest.

Tall, thin Louis and big Frank—Owl Eyes and Belly, what a pair they must have made!

And Witch Woman, sleeping beside him. Though he feels no return of that strange disjointed anger that made him lash out at her, he can make a small sacrifice to her. He slips out of bed, pads to the sideboard and finishes the brew, gagging from the bigger, astringent taste. . . .

Quick scenes follow as Hailey's dream grew disjointed.

Louis leaving Frank's apartment just as Joe is coming up the stairs . . .

Leanna and Joe sitting at the old bar in Sonya's. Though the tavern is nearly empty, Frank speaks only a few words to them. "Uneasy?" Joe comments to Leanna and she laughs. At the sound of it, Frank looks up from the paper he is reading, and Joe sees a brief wave of pain in his expression. . . .

A storm blows sheets of water against the balcony door. Joe wakes at the first flashes of lightning and sees Leanna sitting up in bed, her eyes fixed on the thin trickles of water that have seeped through the door frame. His expression is troubled. When Joe reaches for her, she flinches, then, seeing his concern, lies back down, kissing him, pressing close. "It's all right," she whispers, sounding as if she almost means it. . . .

Leanna and Joe downstairs after Sonya's has closed, celebrating Frank's birthday with champagne and cake. Though Sonya rarely leaves the apartment since the stroke,

Frank has insisted that they carry her down. She sits in a folding lounge chair, the back at half-mast, balancing the cake on her fork and bringing it to her mouth with a trembling hand. Someone has spread a napkin over her still ample chest and crumbs litter it. Leanna looks away in distaste.

"Happy birthday," she calls happily to Frank. "A hundred more."

Leanna has a sudden vision of Frank at seventy, at eighty. The bulk of the man would have ruined his ankles and knees by then. He would use a cane or a walker, if he could walk at all.

No, not eighty. Certainly not for Frank, not even for her. And the alternative?

What difference does it make? She'll be born again; she believes it, has always believed it. Sometimes, if she concentrates, she can even get a glimpse of a past, always happier than this life.

Joe fills Sonya's glass with champagne, holds it to her lips so she can drink. "A good man. I always thought of him that way," Sonya calls to Leanna. Sonya hardly knows Joe and Leanna wonders if the old woman has him confused with a cousin or a brother, someone long since gone from her life.

Is it the fear of death or of the next life that makes Leanna so terrified that she can only look in Sonya's direction with her vision deliberately unfocused, all the better to ignore the lines in Sonya's face, the palsy in her hands?

She wants to leave but Joe is at the bar with Frank, drinking slammers of tequila and warm seltzer with wedges of lime for the chaser. "I'm going to take a shower," she whispers in his ear. "Join me?"

"I'll send him up after one more round," Frank says. "I'll send him up good and ready."

Leanna laughs, hiding her uneasiness too well, not wanting to confess in front of so many how much she needs him tonight, and how troubled she is that they will be separated for even a little while.

Upstairs, as she strips off the tight jeans and sweater, she thinks again of Sonya and the strange, persistent feeling she has that for all the old woman's strength, death will claim her soon. She brews Joe's tea and undresses.

The rushing water beating against the shower walls and curtain blocks out all sound. She cannot hear the music from the tavern or the phone or even if someone comes into the apartment. Anyone could be standing on the other side of the closed curtain, spying on her, waiting for her to finish before striking the first blow.

A shadow falls between her and the light above the sink. She pulls the curtain back.

Joe sits on the closed toilet seat, a lopsided grin on his face.

"Frank sent you up just fine, I see," she says.

"And ready." The smile broadens, inviting her to come within reach.

She refused to oblige him, and after the alcohol he's consumed he cannot comprehend why. "Your tea is on the counter," she says.

He makes a face, and stands, one hand on the door frame for support as he goes.

The tea is sitting in its usual place, in its usual cup as if the container itself was part of some ritual. He hadn't even managed the first swallow when the taste made him gag, bringing alcohol and bile into his throat. He rinses his mouth with water, pours the tea down the drain with no feeling of guilt.

It has been weeks since the funeral. Nothing has happened. Nothing will. "I'm famished," he calls, and lumbers to the bed.

By the time she joins him, he is sleeping so soundly that she has to listen to be certain he still breathes.

She might as well be sleeping alone, she thinks as she lies down beside him. The doors are protected, the room is blessed. Nothing can harm her. With the thought firmly in the center of her mind, she is able to sleep. . . .

Hailey forced herself awake just after midnight, with her heart pounding, not from terror she had witnessed but from anticipation of the visions sure to come. She turned on her computer and recorded the dream in one quick effort, then went back and filled in the hazier scenes as she recalled them.

Something Celeste once said had a bearing on this dream, but Hailey couldn't remember the exact words. If Celeste had been still alive, she would have phoned her, read the description and asked.

She read what she'd recorded three more times before it struck her.

Spirits could go through doors but not walls!

She recalled her room, and the one bit of new woodwork that had framed her entrance. At one time the closet door must have joined the room to Frank's apartment. In her haste to protect Joe and herself, Leanna had overlooked it.

Frank had been so helpful to her, so kind, and her instincts said he was not a violent man. Yet, he had become so concerned when he'd heard about her novel, and it had affected him strongly enough that he had apparently lost a lover as a result.

Could Frank have knowingly let Henri's ghost into the room?

If there had been any justification at all for calling Ed at this hour, she would have done it, but she could see only one—to put off the inevitable.

Had Ed been here, sleeping beside her, he could not have saved her from it.

The cuckoo clock she'd bought on a trip to Germany and hung in the downstairs foyer called out the hour. Four A.M.

Four-thirty. Five.

She could close her eyes, but how would she sleep, knowing what was coming?

Finally, desperate to merge with Leanna once more, she padded to the kitchen and washed two antihistamines down with a glass of wine. Not certain the combination would be enough to assure success, she followed that with a cup of Celeste's tea.

The cuckoo called six times.

She did not hear it.

. . . Leanna sits upright in bed, awakened by a sound softer than Joe's deep breathing, softer than the breeze curling around the corner of the building and through the slightly ajar door, brushing against the curtains.

A whisper. A motion of air past tongue and teeth and lips.

She woke when the breeze was still outside but before she could recite some prayer for protection, it had gotten past her defenses. Now it is all around her. Because of it, unseen, there is no use in trying to detect it until it strikes.

"Papa," she calls softly, staring down at Joe all the while, not certain she should wake him; not certain who will wake in his body if she does.

"Papa, leave us. Leave this world. I call upon . . ."

Fear steals the words as it has already stolen her power. She looks toward the kitchen, thinking she needs a knife or a club, paltry defenses against the spirit demanding flesh, demanding the fulfillment her body has given his in life.

The phone is on the beside table next to Joe. She'll call Louis. He'll know what to do. He knows so much more than she does, and he loves her. She reaches over Joe, but before she touches the receiver, Joe's hand closes around her wrist.

How could he wake without her noticing! She finds some small bit of calm, lays her hand on his forehead. "Joe," she calls. "Stay with me. Stay with me."

The grip loosens. She pulls free and runs to the sideboard. There's a paring knife on it but she prefers something hard and flat, something that will knock Joe out if need be and hopefully do no lasting damage.

"Stay with me, Joe," she repeats, turns on the light and

gropes in the cupboard, keeping her attention on him all the while.

Joe's body sits up. With eyes open, expression flat, it gets out of bed and staggers toward her. "Joe," she calls again. "Joe, stay with me. Joe . . ."

Can she weaken Papa's hold on him again as she did a moment ago? Dispel the spirit in Joe again as she did so recently in her mother's bed?

The fry pan is heavy, and her fear far too strong for her to muster any real mental power. She decides on the weapon and swings, striking the shoulder rather than the head, love making a hard blow impossible.

Her attack increases his rage. He slaps her and she falls backward against the sideboard. As she slips down, she manages to grab the knife.

"Joe!" Her voice is louder now, as if volume could bring her lover's soul back to her. "Joe, fight him! Help me."

Joe's expression grows softer, confused. For a moment he seems to take control. Then Henri returns, more furious than before.

He buries a hand in her hair, using it to drag her back to the bed. With no choice but to fight, Leanna slices the blade across the back of his wrist, stabs down at his hand, backward at his leg.

He does not make a sound, only reaches down and, seemingly oblivious to the pain, pulls the weapon away from her.

Still screaming Joe's name, her hand trying to find a grip on his bloody wrist, Leanna is jerked upright, flung across the bed.

She kicks. With a bellow of rage, he slices the knife down.

Pain. Pressure. A deeper pain, radiating out. Hailey, caught in the dream, feels it all, and is amazed at how it ends so quickly, how she is flung out of Leanna's body along with Leanna's soul, to look in horror at her flesh being sliced open by the monster inside her lover.

At least they can't feel it. At least, thankfully, Leanna is already dead.

And yet, in this space between life and eternity, they sense another terrible anguish. Physical limitations have no meaning any longer and Hailey's consciousness, merged with Leanna's gravitates to the source. The hallway where Sonya lies, holding onto her last terrified thoughts as her mind slowly drowns in her own blood. . . .

Sonya drank too much champagne for sleep. The bed spins when she closes her eyes and her mind is playing its little tricks again. She is certain that she heard the floor in the hallway creak. Thinking it must be Frank, she waits for him to return then calls his name.

No response.

She listens. Yes, someone is definitely close by, droning softly on. She hears the rasped gutturals, the moaned long vowels, trying to determine if the sound is coming from her apartment or Joe's.

Car . . . re . . . fo . . . ur . . . mi . . . hau . . . oot . . . mi . . . ba . . . se . . ."

It certainly sounds like something Leanna would sing but this is not a woman's voice; it scarcely sounds human at all. "Frank?" she calls again, louder. No response, but the voice continues, a sort of chanting or singing by a creature with no sense of music.

"Car . . . re . . . fo . . . ur . . . mi . . . hau . . . oot . . . mi . . . ba . . . se . . . tin . . . gin . . . din . . . gue . . ."

Frank is probably still downstairs getting drunk with the help. She doesn't grudge him that; in her opinion he works too hard and takes care of her with more concern than she would have expected from her own child. She finally requests an alarm pendant that she could press, alerting Frank if she had a problem. It galls her to have to be so dependent but at least the alarm made Frank relax a little, enough that he stopped checking on her once every hour.

Such a dutiful boy. She decides not to disturb him. Instead she'll see what the sound is herself, and call him if necessary. Her cane is in easy reach. Balancing carefully, she pushes herself to her feet. Moving forward with her good leg, draggin the dead one behind, she begins the slow shuffle toward the door.

The noise is louder in the hall, but as she is about to turn toward the closet, she hears Leanna scream Joe's name, her voice full of terror.

The keys are on the hook beside the entry door. She presses the button of her alarm and reaches for them.

Leanna screams again then falls silent. Sonya moves as quickly as she is able into the hall.

She expected to see Frank there. Perhaps with the music coming from below, he hasn't heard the buzz. She presses the alarm again and shuffles toward Joe's locked door, pounding on it. "Is everything all right?" she calls.

The bed creaks. It occurs to her that she may be interrupting an intimate moment, but if so why didn't they just tell her to go away?

As she stands there, uncertain what to do, she hears another sound—a low, terrible moaning like someone in pain. But she cannot pinpoint the source.

"Frank!" she yells down the hall. The one time she really needs that boy, he is nowhere to be found. "I'm coming in!" she calls through the door, unlocks it and pushes it open.

The old brass chandelier with its flame-shaped amber bulbs sheds a soft glow on the carnage below. She looks from Leanna lying across the bed, her body covered with cuts and blood, to the creature hulking above her body.

It has Joe's features, yet if she were asked to swear to it, she would say it was not Joe. Joe has never looked so enraged, so dangerous and, in some strange way she cannot fathom, so inhuman.

She can feel her heart pounding hard in her chest and fights to catch her breath, to find the strength to retreat.

Before she can put a wall between her and the horror, the

killer flings the knife at her and collapses beside the body. It was less an attack than a final burst of rage, and the knife strikes her sideways and falls at her feet.

She looks from the blood on her robe to the weapon beneath her. As she does, her apartment door opens and someone runs down the hall. "Help!" Sonya says, her voice unable to rise above a whisper.

She starts to turn to face the intruder. Before she gets a look at him, he shoves her forward and runs past and down the back stairs.

Dark hair. A thin form. Familiar somehow. She's almost attached a name to the man when something explodes in her head. With her last bit of consciousness, she presses the buzzer again then falls on top of it. . . .

"Auntie?" Franks calls up the stairs, then starts slowly up, the alarm beeping quickly, growing louder as he approaches its source. When he reaches the end of the hall, he takes in the scene—the open doors, Sonya lying unconscious in front of Joe's apartment.

"Aunt Sonya!" he screams and moves to her side. As he crouches beside her, he spies the bloody knife, looks from it into Joe's room and begins a slow chant of his own— half prayer, half raw terror. "Jeeesus . . . Jeeesus . . . Jeeesus . . . Jesus. He did it. Jesus, help us. He did it. He . . ." Shaking, crying, calling his aunt's name, he finally composes himself enough to check for a pulse, and laughs when he finds one.

"Aunt Sonya, I'm sorry," he whispers and reaches for the knife. Carrying it carefully so he gets no blood on himself, he goes into his apartment and throws it in the dishwasher. As he reaches for the phone to call the police, he checks the hall closet, the bedrooms. By then a dispatcher is on the line and Frank leaves the address.

"Jesus," he mumbles again as he washes the knife, dries it carefully and places it with the others in his cutlery drawer.

By the time the ambulance and police cars pull up outside, Frank is kneeling beside his aunt, alternately sobbing and calling her name.

"They're dead, I think," he says, pointing to Joe's room. "She must have seen . . . Aunt Sonya, I'm so sorry. . . ."

TWENTY-THREE

Hailey hated the thought of disturbing Ed when his daughter was coming into town in two days, but she saw no choice. She called him around noon.

"I discovered who killed Leanna," she said. "It isn't easy to explain but it was Henri de Noux. I saw exactly how it was done." She described her dream, often reading aloud from her carefully assembled notes.

"But the room was protected," Ed protested.

"There was a door Leanna missed."

"You'd know if there was an extra door in your apartment, Hailey," he said, his voice overly calm, as if he were soothing a child after a nightmare.

"The closet door had old woodwork. It was probably the main door into the room, and the closet added later. Don't you see?"

"And the killer went right through the wall? Hailey, that's ridiculous."

"I know what I dreamed."

"And maybe that's just what it was—*your* dream. That's possible too, isn't it?"

"It could be," she admitted.

"Someone very much alive killed Leanna de Noux."

Joe Morgan's very much alive body, she thought, but did not say so. "Louis knew Frank Berlin from grade school. He'd been in the old apartment and told Joe that Sonya had to divide the space to meet expenses after her stroke. If that's the case, where did Frank get all the money to remodel Sonya's Kitchen?"

"Insurance most likely."

"Can you look into it, just to make certain?"

"I'll do what I can," he said when she'd finished.

Ed had meant only to placate Hailey, but after he hung up, he considered how on the mark her dreams had been and started making calls.

In two hours, he discovered that Sonya had signed the tavern over to her nephew, and that it was all she had to give him. There had been no insurance, no estate, but four months after the deaths, Frank Berlin had begun an extensive remodeling of Sonya's Kitchen.

A loan for the work had been obtained through Prince Island Investments.

Now Ed's options were tricky. There was no ongoing investigation into the murder/suicide. The information he had was circumstantial at best, certainly not enough to obtain a search warrant. Since it seemed that the entire department had learned of his affair with Hailey Martin, using her dreams as evidence would only earn him a new round of laughter. He couldn't blame anyone for that. Hell, if someone else were in his position, he'd be laughing too.

On the other hand, he had a relationship with Hailey. If he asked, Frank would probably hand him the apartment key.

He drove over there an hour before he was due at work. It might have been the slow time in the dining room but the kitchen work was in full swing as the staff prepared the side dishes and soups for the evening menu. Overpowering the smells of onions and garlic and cayenne found in every Cajun kitchen were the scents of vanilla, cinnamon and chocolate as Frank personally prepared the wickedly rich desserts Sonya's had become famous for.

Ed had counted on Frank being busy. The chef hardly seemed to listen as Ed explained about Hailey's missing sapphire earring. "Keys are on the second hook," Frank said and added another egg to his mixing bowl.

Judging from the age of the woodwork, the long hall

outside Hailey's apartment was part of the building's original design but the door to her room had been added in the last decade. The framing was cheap wood, the door a salvage, both paid for by a man obviously short on cash.

He let himself in. As Hailey had described, the woodwork around the closet was original. When he opened the door, he saw that the back was nothing more substantial than a piece of painted pressboard, though the side walls were old.

A new addition. A way in for a spirit determined to have its revenge.

Damn it! Now he was thinking as strangely as Hailey, and he admitted he was going to continue to do so. His instincts told him they were on the edge of solving this murder. Even if it never came to trial—and he doubted it could—he wanted to know for his own sake, for Hailey and above all for Joe.

He locked up, then stood in the hallway above the stairs listening until he detected Frank's voice in the kitchen before trying the second key in Frank's apartment lock. It opened as he'd expected, and after one last moment of indecision, he stepped inside and moved silently down the hall. Though the space had been remodeled, the old woodwork remained. The closet was exactly where Hailey had said it would be and its woodwork, a near-perfect match to the original, was also new.

He opened the door, gauged the depth. Plenty of space for someone to hide and conjure.

And he had a pretty good idea who it had been.

"Breaking and entering is a felony, you know." Frank called to him. Swearing, Ed turned and saw Frank standing at the end of the hall, holding a .38. "But I wouldn't want to call the police, not until we've talked at least. Come here."

Resigned, Ed walked toward him. Frank moved his bulk aside so Ed could pass. As he did, the gun butt came down hard on the side of his head. Stunned, he felt his arms pulled back and his own cuffs jerked from his belt and snapped around his wrists. Ed wasn't a heavy man, but he was surprised at how easily Frank pulled him down the hall.

Frank's skill with ropes and gags amazed him as well, though he had to admit the man's amateur sense of overkill was painful. His hands and feet were numb by the time Frank arranged him in one of his dining room chairs and secured him in place with another few loops of rope.

If Frank had shot Ed when he first saw him, he would have had a valid claim for the killing. In breaking and entering, Louisiana law favored the owner. Frank would probably have gotten off.

Instead, Frank had gone to all the trouble to immobilize him. Ed considered this a hopeful sign. He watched as Frank locked the outer door and closed the curtains, then paced for a while before going behind Ed and checking the knots on the gag and ropes.

"Tight?" Frank asked.

Ed nodded. The piece of cloth in his mouth was pushed in too far. He tried not to swallow, certain that if he did, he'd choke. Would Frank take the cloth out of his mouth if he did or let him die?

Perhaps he'd never know, because Frank left him alone, locking the apartment door behind him when he went.

Ed saw a phone was on the wall next to the kitchen door. There'd be knives in the kitchen as well. As quickly as he was able, he began to push himself toward the door. His bound feet gave him little leverage but the castors on the chair bottom made up for it.

He'd gotten about all the way when Frank returned, carrying two pieces of pie, two crocks of gumbo and a plate of cornbread on one of the restaurant serving trays. He laid out place mats, then the food, before retrieving Ed from the kitchen and pushing him back to the table.

Frank set the gun on the table beside his place mat. "I really hate to eat alone. I suppose that if we're going to dine together, I ought to take the gag out of your mouth. If you start to yell, you'll never hear what I have to say, you understand? And since you and Hailey have been digging around trying to discover what happened in this room, I suppose you want to hear all of it."

He walked to the kitchen, and returned with a bottle of red wine, some glasses and napkins. "You see, I know most of the story," he went on. "I think I owe it to Joe to tell it to somebody."

Ed shifted in his chair, pulling his arms farther back, flattening his body against the chair back to loosen the ropes across his chest.

"You'll only make 'em tighter if you go on like that," Frank said. "Don't worry. You won't be there too long."

Ed stared at the gumbo, hoping Frank would take the hint and at the very least remove the gag. He didn't.

"Ignoring me isn't going to do you any good, you know," Frank said. "When you've got somebody in one of the little interrogation rooms, can you really get them to shut up once they start to spill their guts?" Frank pointed the gun at him, and cocked it. Ed took some consolation in the fact that when it went off, it would make a hell of a sound. First shots often missed the mark, or at least missed being lethal, and the man's hand looked a bit shaky.

As Ed had expected—no, hoped—Frank put the gun back on the table, then reached for the wine instead. He poured two glasses and set one in front of Ed, though he was hardly in any position to drink it.

"Start where it started, Aunt Sonya used to say. And it started when I was just a kid.

"People think I got huge because of what I do, but actually it was the other way around. I was born fat; ten plus pounds, they say. Wide-angle lens for the baby picture, those sorts of jokes stuck to me right from the beginning. By sixth grade, the class game was making up nasty nicknames for me and anyone who dared to talk to me. If the teacher was feeling generous, I'd get to stay in the classroom and read through recess.

"Most every kid at the school came from poor stock, and our parents had to scrape to send us there. Leanna stood out like a movie star in her fashionable clothes worn so fastidiously.

"That might have made her well liked except that by eleven, she already had a reputation for being a bitch, somebody to avoid. Her brother, the brilliant student no one had ever met, only made things worse for her with the other kids.

"You see, the teachers adored Louis. You could see it in the way they posted his papers on the bulletin boards— always the neatest, always the top grade. They'd tell us about going to see him, raving on about the little desk and bookcase he had in his dark room. I think that Louis was lucky that he couldn't come to school. The other kids would have jumped him the first chance they got.

"Instead, they made fun of him the same way they did me. Only I didn't have someone like Leanna to stick up for me.

"She wasn't a fighter, at least not in the sense that she bloodied anybody's nose. But once, Brian Foster started really going on about Louis—Glass Eyes, he called him. Leanna told him to cut it out but that just made him louder. Then Brian came in one Monday and opened his desk. I heard him make a strangled sort of sound, then he started to puke, first on himself then on the floor. The teacher ran over to him, looked in his desk and screamed.

"I was sitting two desks behind Brian, in the back where I always liked to be. I went up behind the teacher, and got a good look at what was inside.

"Someone had put a dead rat in there, and had arranged it so it lay on its belly, snout toward the seat. That would have been bad enough, but the eyes had been cut out of it and replaced with little glass balls.

"A couple of the kids who saw it screamed too. The others started to giggle. I looked across the room at Leanna—of course it had been Leanna who had done it. She sat reading her English book, a tiny satisfied smile on her face.

"All of us were waiting to see what would happen after school. But nothing happened. Leanna made sure of that at recess. When she walked up to Brian, even I moved in close. We all wanted to hear what she said, and see what he did, since he was ready to slug her on the spot. She just looked at him, smiled and said, 'What made Louis blind can be passed on. There are ways.'

"Then she held out her hand. In it were three white-blond hairs. Nobody in that class had hair that color but Brian Foster. She said, 'Never touch me. And never say a word about my brother again.' Then she whispered something in his ear that made his face go slack, and turned and walked away.

"If they'd been alone, I think Brian would have run. With the crowd around him, he had to save face so he just laughed. But he never did make fun of Louis again. And he never repeated what Leanna told him.

"One January Leanna was off school for six days. I'd been staying in for recess, so I guess I was the handy one.

"'You live on Broadway, don't you?' the teacher asked.

"I mumbled yes.

"'Can you take lessons to Louis de Noux?'

"Now, I lived on Broadway, sure, but way down by Clairborne, which meant I'd have to walk, or bike, a good twenty blocks. I didn't say anything, though, because I was so damn curious.

"I went right after school. On the long walk, I kept thinking how I was going to be *the* kid to know the next day because I had seen Louis de Noux with my own two eyes.

"That house! Christ, that place alone would take the lunch hour to describe. Then there was Jacqueline. A colored housekeeper! I mean, who in the hell had help like that?

"'Would you like to take the work up to him?' she asked.

"I went up. The room was dark, just like the teacher had described. Louis was in bed, lying on his back with his hands crossed behind his head. I heard some sort of classical music playing. I don't remember what. And he wore a kind of mask over his eyes.

"I thought of Brian, the glass-ball eyes on that rat.

"'I brought your homework,' I said.

"He took off the mask and sat up, crossing his legs. 'Do you have notes?' he asked.

"I shook my head, and explained that my coming was only because his sister was sick.

"'Do you like it at school?' he asked.

"I shook my head again.

"'Is that all you can do?' He shook his head, mimicking me.

"'You're lucky you can't go. It's that bad,' I just blurted out.

"He laughed. When he laughed, he sounded a lot younger than me. That put me a little more at ease.

"'What was that thing on your face?' I asked.

"'It's for headaches. I get them when I use my eyes too long.'

"I looked around his room. I'd expected to see a TV, maybe some games, but there wasn't anything but the record player. I looked at that, and the stack of records next to it. Nothing new, nothing popular. 'Do you have a radio?' I asked.

"Now it was his turn to shake his head.

"'What do you do when you're not studying?'

"'I read.'

"'Bad for the eyes, ain't it?'

"He laughed again. I swear, to this day, I never heard a laugh so beautiful, except maybe for Leanna's. They were the same that way.

"I started feeling sorry for the kid. I mean, here he was trapped in this room. Sure he had money and a great house but from the look of him, so thin and pale, I didn't think he went out much, if at all.

"I suppose you could say that I finally found somebody more miserable than I was. It was a liberating experience.

"'Do you have any games?' I asked.

"We played checkers for an hour. Jacqueline brought us some lemonade. Fresh squeezed, I recall. Funny how what

you're going to do with your life is so clear so early. Did
you play cops and robbers when you were a kid?"
   Ed shook his head. As he did, the corner of the gag
slipped farther back in his throat. He started to retch. Tears
filled his eyes and nose. He sniffed them back and tried to
breathe. The thought crossed his mind that being talked to
death was a hell of a way to go.
   "You all right?" Frank asked.
   Ed shook his head again.
   "If I take off the gag, will you keep quiet?"
   Ed nodded just as vehemently. It seemed to take Frank
forever to decide. When the tape was removed, Ed took a
few deep breaths while Frank stood there, the wet cloth in
his hand, waiting. "Keep talking," Ed said when he was able.
   Instead, Frank lifted Ed's wineglass and held it to his lips
so Ed could take a drink, followed that with a spoonful of
gumbo, then another drink. He continued doing so until the
soup was gone, then sat down and sipped his own wine,
rolling it around in his mouth before going on.
   "Later Leanna joined us. I don't remember much about
how she looked except that she was wearing a chenille
bathrobe. She sat next to Louis on the bed, and the
resemblance between them was fascinating. I couldn't not
compare their mouths and eyes and hair.
   "Louis and I had been laughing a few minutes before, but
when she came into the room, it was like I wasn't there at
all. I felt more and more uneasy, though I couldn't figure
why. 'I got to go,' I finally said.
   " 'Will you come again?' Louis asked.
   " 'I'll bring your work if Leanna isn't in school on Friday.'
   " 'I mean, will you just *come*?'
   "Leanna smiled. I knew the sort of smile all too well. It
was the look I got at recess before the teasing started. 'Yes,
do come back, Belly,' she said.
   " 'Belly?' Louis looked from her to me. 'Is that what they
call you?'

"'On my lucky days,' I said, feeling god-awful by then. I mean, what if he asked for the rest of the list?

"'What do they call me?' he asked instead.

"'Glass Eyes,' Leanna said. 'On your lucky days, that is.'

"She looked at me, and smiled that teasing way again.

"'I can come Friday whether Leanna's at school or not,' I said.

"I did. And I kept going there. Not regularly, but when I could. When Louis finally managed to come to school for a few months at the end of the following year, well, at least I'd prepared him for the worst."

Frank paused to give Ed another sip of wine, then finished his soup and filled their glasses once more. "The best merlot in my cellar. Aged to perfection. I'd been saving it for a special occasion. I guess this is it—Frank Berlin Tells All Day. What do you think?"

"It's worthy. But the meal would be a whole lot better if I could eat it myself."

Frank shook his head. "Better I think about my story than about getting jumped by you. If I thought you'd behave, I'd take you downstairs and give you the five star treatment a last meal deserves." He buttered the cornbread, and ate it slowly.

"That summer, everything changed. Leanna matured, not in the slow, awkward way most girls do, but suddenly. In May, she was a pretty girl; by July, a beautiful woman. She didn't hang around with Louis much anymore; instead she was always with Jacqueline or off on her own somewhere. Louis was lonelier than usual and I was spending a lot of time at the house.

"Louis and I were changing too. We'd both had our growth spurts. Mine added six inches without a weight gain and for the next few years I'd be a big kid rather than a fat one.

"Louis changed the way Leanna had—went right from little boy to man. And what a beautiful man! I loved watching him—the way he walked, and moved his hands when he talked; the slow, syrupy way he spoke. Even now, I'll be stirring some thick sauce and think of his voice.

"Christ, I loved him but I never told him. I mean, how could I confess that to my best and only friend? I would've lost him, completely.

"Then one day we'd gotten some meat pies from a vendor in the park. We were sitting on the riverbank not far from his house. Nobody was around, and without warning, he leaned over and kissed me. I must have blushed six shades of red. I mean I thought I'd been found out and he was teasing me, but then I felt his tongue moving between my lips, his arms circling me." He paused.

"You look disgusted. Are you?"

"No."

"Amused, then? I sense some vague emotion running below the fear. When you kissed Hailey Martin for the first time, how did you feel?"

"Elated," Ed admitted.

"Then you felt the tiniest bit like I did when I kissed Louis de Noux. You see, that was my first kiss and I loved him. Believe me, love is not confined to men and women, boys and girls. Mine was just as real, only a bit more pathetic.

"Pathetic," he repeated. "You see, I was too young to recognize an experienced kiss. If I had, I might have wondered where a boy who rarely went to school, and who had no friends, had learned how to kiss like that. Later that night, after he smuggled me up to his room, I might have wondered how he learned to fuck like that. Only I never would have called what we did anything as crude as 'fucking.' It was growing closer, making love. 'Fuck' is a word the kids today use. They're more honest about their feelings, or lack of them, I guess.

"For the next year, we were on one another every chance we got, and there were plenty of them. Louis and I got bolder but it wasn't boldness that ruined our affair; it was the heat.

"That August set records in a town that's used to heat, and the window air conditioner in Louis's room made the temperature just bearable. After a few hours in there, we decided to take a shower, then changed that to a bath.

"Henri had a huge claw tub in his bathroom. We ran it deep and cool, filled with bubbles we stole from Leanna. Henri wasn't expected at home at all that day. Leanna and Jacqueline were off somewhere, so we relaxed. We fooled around, soaping one another, that sort of thing, until we were both really excited. We were just getting started, both of us hard and ready, when the door swung open.

"Leanna stood there. I leaned back behind the shower curtain but she paid me no mind. Instead she was looking at her brother. Something in her face—I don't know what. But I knew then that she had been intimate with him, far more than once.

"She said something, and as she turned to leave, Henri de Noux came up behind her and pushed her aside, not caring that she hit the wall hard.

"She ran and left us alone with him. When Henri left, I had a bloody nose and a couple of bruised ribs. I didn't notice, though, because Louis was on the floor, one eye already darkening, his knees pulled against his chest moaning. I reached for him, but he slapped my hand away. "Just go," he said.

"By then, Louis could come to school regularly. We still sat together every day at lunch but I never went near him outside of school. He understood, I guess, because he never asked why I stayed away.

"I'm an only child so I guess that I can never fathom the love and hate relationship between brother and sister; but the sin of incest seemed terrible to me, maybe because my own sins needed something to make them look minor.

"After graduation, we went our separate ways. I started working in my aunt's tavern, taking on more responsibility downstairs. I thought of Louis sometimes, but I never dared to call him."

He paused and drained his wine, then poured another glass. He almost seemed to have forgotten Ed was there.

"Aunt Sonya had the big stroke that left her with blurry eyesight and a nearly dead right leg. Money got tighter because of doctor bills so I moved her into a smaller bedroom, remodeled her big one and rented the place out. I had a whole string of derelects in there until Joe showed up. He paid rent on time, even helped out when I had a problem. He kept his place as spotless as I kept mine and turned into one of my best customers. That last bothered me because if it hadn't been for the booze, he could have made something of himself. Instead he just scraped by.

"Then out of the blue, he walked into the tavern with Leanna. I looked at her, thought of Louis and spent the night avoiding her. She had a reputation for one-night stands and I figured that after she left I'd probably never see her again.

"She surprised me. She stuck with Joe, and pretty much moved in after he lost his job. I heard some rumor that old Henri was behind his getting canned. It didn't surprise me.

"Henri died. Small loss, I guess. A few weeks later, Louis showed up downstairs with Leanna and Joe. We had a drink together. When the couple left, Louis stayed.

" 'I think about you,' he said. 'All the time.'

" 'Why?' I asked, genuinely amazed.

" 'Because you are the only person who ever loved me,' he said and gripped my hand.

"I knew what he wanted. I took him upstairs because I wanted it too. When he undressed, I saw that he hadn't changed at all. His body was as lean, his motion as fluid, as it had been when we were teenagers. That brief moment of being just a big kid, not a fat one, had passed years before. I felt huge and slovenly and I decided not to take off my clothes and show him the lard I'd let return to my stomach and thighs.

"I think he understood because he sat in a chair and pulled me down in front of him. I took him in my mouth, and gave everything I could while he sat with his drink in one hand, the other brushing the back of my head. Everything we did was done in silence. He didn't even breathe

fast when he came. When I'd finished, he leaned forward
and kissed me. His lips were sweet from the Benedictine
he'd been sipping and I thought of the first time by river.
Everything we had done came back to me. It was like we
took off right where we were before.

"A couple of weeks later, he told me how concerned he'd
become about Leanna. He said that the money from her
divorce settlement was about to run out, and that she
wouldn't listen when he told her that she had to cut back on
her lifestyle. He wanted her to come home, where he could
manage her moods and finances, and maybe direct her into
doing something constructive with her life. He flattered me,
saying I would understand how he felt because of how well
I cared for Aunt Sonya. You've met Louis. You've heard
how he talks. He can be so damned persuasive that it seems
like you're being hypnotized.

"Don't think I was all that gullible, though. I saw Leanna
almost every day so I knew how paranoid she'd gotten.
Even Joe was worried—so much so that he stayed with her
as much as possible. And sometimes at night I would hear her
chanting or smell the incense when I passed by Joe's door.

"Voodoo shit, I thought. A lot of my help were into it. Even
me, a little. I mean who doesn't want a little protection for
the car or the restaurant? But the really obsessed spend all
their money on charms and mojo bags and sacrifices. I knew
Leanna wasn't supporting Joe so I figured she was spending
on stuff like that. Anyway, I told Louis I'd help him.

"My part was easy. All I had to do was get him a key for
Joe's apartment and for mine. Then, one night when Leanna
and Joe were downstairs, I had to slip something into Joe's
drink that would make him pass out within an hour.
Upstairs, Louis was going to go into Joe's apartment and
remove her little charms and fetishes then sneak into my
place, down the hall and into the closet. When she was
ready for bed, he was going to start his own chant, a
frightening one. With no Joe to come to her aid, she'd lose
faith in him and turn back to Louis.

"It all sounds pretty lame now, but I knew that Louis's knowledge of voodoo was probably broader than hers. He made me believe that he could pull it off."

Frank had nearly drained the wine bottle and stopped to devour the first piece of pie. When he held out a forkful, Ed shook his head. The whole situation was bizarre and frightening and sickening to him. He tried not to think too far ahead, to wonder whether Frank would fire one bullet or two when the time came.

"Louis got his chance the night of my birthday party," Frank went on. "Drinks were on the house, so I knew Joe would have least a couple. But they kept hedging on where they were going after the party. I didn't want to slip Joe the drug until I was sure they were going upstairs, because Joe always drove when Leanna drank. I could picture him passing out at the wheel and killing both of them and someone else besides and I couldn't be responsible for that.

"Finally Leanna went upstairs. Joe was going to have one more drink and follow. Louis had given me enough liquid for two doses, just in case. I put both doses in the drink because I didn't think he'd finish. He did, though, then had another. By the time he left, he was already woozy so I didn't figure he'd stay conscious long.

"Me and a pair of the kitchen guys carried Aunt Sonya upstairs just after midnight. By then Louis was already in place.

"I wasn't worried. I figured if anything went wrong, Leanna would be furious with her brother, not me. But of course everything went wrong.

"My aunt's alarm went off once. I went into the kitchen, where things were quieter, and listened. I heard a thud, then the alarm again, a constant buzzing. This time, I couldn't ignore it.

"I ran upstairs and I saw her lying in the hallway by Joe's open door. I think I spotted the knife first and then . . ."

Frank paused. He took a deep breath and went on, skirting over the worst of what he'd seen. "I loved her more

than I had my own mother so I did what I had to do. I picked
up the knife and went into my flat, washed it then called the
police."

"Why did you wash the knife?" Ed asked, his cop
instincts coming out.

"Because I was afraid that Louis had killed her and
dropped it when he ran. If so, his fingerprints might be on
it. I'm glad I got rid of it, because the absence of a weapon
took suspicion off of Joe. So did the drug I'd slipped him.
The police talked to my staff but nobody saw anything out
of the ordinary. Joe was questioned and released. At least I
didn't have his arrest on my conscience; living with his grief
was bad enough.

"I told Hailey how he drank after Leanna died, and how
I'd hear him talking to Leanna at night, like she was still
alive and in the room with him. It was the only time he
spoke. All the soul seemed to have gone out of him.

"My aunt hung on a few days then died from the stroke.
Louis waited a couple of weeks then showed up at Sonya's
one afternoon. He sat at the bar, ordered a drink and held the
glass hard, saying nothing for a long time. 'I lost control and
he killed her,' he finally blurted, loud enough that I was glad
the place was empty.

"To this day I can't figure out how I feel about what he
said."

If Frank intended to confess then shoot him, Ed knew he
was already dead. He decided to take the risk. "When did
Louis give you the money?" he asked.

"I suppose you would know about that. He slipped a
business card across the bar and said I should call the
number on it and mention his name. I didn't. I stuck it in my
wallet instead.

"You see, I didn't want to be paid for my help. I didn't
want anything to remind me of what happened. Then Joe
died and the murder case was closed. The bills kept rolling
in from my aunt's doctors, the hospital, the funeral home. I

knew it was only a matter of time before I lost everything so
I gave up and made the call."

"How did Joe die?" Ed asked.

Frank shook his head. "I'm glad I don't know," he said.

"And Celeste?"

"Don't make me jump around, all right?" Frank finished
the first piece of pie, then went into the kitchen and poured
them each a glass of cognac, warming the snifters over the
gas burner on the stove before returning to the table. The
snifter was a bit harder for Ed to drink from and some of
the brandy spilled on his shirt. Frank mumbled an apology,
wiped it away, then sat down and went on.

"I tried to forget about the murder, and Louis too, since he
seemed to have forgotten about me. But I started hearing
things about him—like how he'd redone the old house, and
how he sold his partnership in the law firm and became
something of recluse. I guess he loved her. I don't think he
loved anyone else.

"I didn't rent Joe's room out for a long time, then I found
an old lady who liked the wallpaper. So I left it. Hailey came
next.

"I should have known better. A writer, for Christ sake!
And then she found that drawing, and started to pry. I called
Louis after she went to see him but by then he'd already
given her permission to write the novel.

"'Let him pay,' he said.

"I asked him what in the hell he was talking about.

"'Carlo,' he said. 'Let him pay.'

"His attitude made me nervous. Hailey started digging
and I knew it was only a matter of time before she found
something damning on me or Louis.

"Louis wasn't concerned until I told him about Celeste.
This made him listen, and one night when Hailey was
somewhere with you, I let him into her apartment and he sat
at her computer, reading over her notes.

"'It's all right,' he kept telling me. The more he said it the
more nervous I got and the more bitchy Norman became.

"Finally, Norman took matters into his own hands. On the night of Louis's party, he whined until I went back to his place for a change. Then he waited until I was asleep and left me. I heard him go. I was feeling jealous as hell because I thought he was going to meet someone else, so I followed him. By the time I got upstairs, he'd already ruined Hailey's computer and the drawing and was starting to shred the mattress on the bed.

"I stood there a minute, watching him, amazed that he would do this for me, I guess. 'Give me the knife,' I finally said. I was taking it out his hand when Celeste walked in on us.

"The hall has a little night-light that goes on automatically when it gets dark. It threw just enough light that I could see the person wasn't Hailey. For a minute, I thought Celeste was a man and I panicked. I struck. One cut and she was gone."

He probably didn't recall the other three cuts he'd made. Ed had seen and heard that often enough.

"I would've confessed but then they'd have started digging and discovered the rest. I couldn't do that to Louis."

With the last few words, Frank wrapped his hand around the gun butt, fingering the barrel. "I had to tell my story first," he finally said. Then he added with real anguish, "It's a hell of a whopper, though. Everything I said about Leanna's murder was a lie." He picked up the gun, cocked it. "All a lie. Since then, I've learned enough to know that her death was all my fault."

Ed shut his eyes and mumbled the prayer he thought was the one that guaranteed you heaven. Then he prayed for something else.

Let him miss. Let him miss.

"Funny," Frank said. "I thought the end of the barrel would taste more like gunpowder."

What in the hell—? Ed opened his eyes just in time to see Frank pull the trigger.

TWENTY-FOUR

The bullet went through Frank's head, the window and the balcony door of the man's apartment on the opposite side of the street. The sound of the gun brought the kitchen staff and a couple of guests scrambling up the stairs, where they congregated in the hallway, too shocked to do anything until Ed ordered them to call the police.

One of them ran downstairs to phone. A busboy started to come into the room to untie Ed. "Wait outside," Ed told them. "Let the police handle it."

"You want to stay trussed up like that?" the busboy asked.

Actually Ed didn't, but the last thing he wanted was for anyone to have any doubt about the strength of the knots or the skill of the one who had tied them. Nor did he want anyone contaminating the suicide scene. So he sat, facing the body, listening to the sounds of police cars moving cautiously down the narrow Quarter streets, trying to figure out how much to put into his statement.

As Ed had expected, the patrol officers called in Homicide as soon as they arrived on the scene, then untied Ed, cursing at the disorderly knots and how tight they'd become. Ed pulled up his shirt and fingered the rope burns across his chest.

"Jeez, how'd you breathe?" one of the cops asked.

"I panted," Ed responded.

"Tied up long?"

"An hour or so. He wanted to talk."

"Confessions?" The cop was leading now, his curiosity only natural. The history of the building was common knowledge on the force.

307

"Sorry, I got to save it for the statement."

They heard the downstairs door slam, a familiar nasal voice. The officer talking to Ed rolled his eyes and looked toward the door. "Good luck giving it," he said.

Ethan Collings ran his hand over his bald head, scratched his hook nose and looked at the crime scene as if it were an annoyance designed solely for him. "Fuck it, does this place never quit?" he moaned then saw Ed. His expression hardened. "The goddamn black hole of murders and whenever one happens you turn up here. Now, why the hell is that?" He glared at Ed.

"Murder?" he asked.

"Suicide," Ed corrected.

"Two and two, huh?"

The beat cops explained what they saw when they arrived. "I want to see you at the station in two hours," Collings said to Ed.

"I think we have to talk now," Ed responded.

"He killed himself, it can wait," Collings replied with obvious irritation, as if Ed, not he, were stalling for time. "Now, get out of here."

Ed reminded himself that it was a common belief that Collings had incriminating photos of at least three captains and probably the chief's illegitimate brother. Nothing less could explain how he kept his job.

By the time Ed gave his statement, radio and TV news would have picked up the story of Berlin's death. Louis de Noux would have ample opportunity to prepare a statement of his own.

If he even needed to give one, Ed reminded himself. He had to admit that Frank's confession was hardly one to take on face value, especially considering Frank's final admission that the whole thing was a lie.

Ed stopped at home and took a shower, scrubbing off the scent of fear that clung to his body. As soon as he was dressed again, he went downtown. Collings was waiting for him, his expression far from pleasant.

By the time he finished his statement, Ed knew he was in for one of Colling's famous tirades—one that seemed all the more galling because the idiot was probably right.

"So what in the fuck do you want me to do, get a goddamn search warrant because some suicide tells you a story that only proves he was insane when he pulled the trigger?" Collings yelled as if Ed weren't sitting right across the desk from him, and were some stranger off the street instead of a fellow detective on the force.

"A minute after he told me this, he shot himself. Why would he lie?" Ed retorted as calmly as possible.

"You said he said he lied. Was he lying about lying? Maybe that's when he was telling the truth. After the story he told, that's pretty likely."

"Look, the de Noux murder was never officially closed—"

"Never officially counts for half the solved murders in this town. It's over. Your friend did it. Get it through your head or get out."

"Not until I get to sign my statement."

"Not until! You want to commit suicide? All right, sit here. Sit for a goddamn hour while I have somebody transcribe the drivel on this tape. Then you sign that Joe Morgan killed his lover because he was under some kind of voodoo possession caused by Louis de Noux."

Collings had just started gearing up, Ed knew, as he sat, mentally counting to ten while Collings railed on.

"Louis de fucking Noux! Yeah, you sign. I'll witness. And then what? You and I get a search warrant? What judge will issue one? None of the ones I work with, I can tell you that. Do you know one? Maybe some haunt we can conjure up to sign it? Or maybe some back-of-the-bayou voodoo judge?

"Better yet, let's haul de Noux in for questioning. How fast do you think he'll get us canned? Correction—*you* canned. I'm not touching this one, you hear me?"

"Transcribe it. I'll sign it tomorrow. Make sure I get a copy of the tape," Ed had replied quietly, got up and headed for the door.

"Where the hell are you going?" Collings said.

"I'm taking an extra day off. I think I earned it."

He left before Collings could say any more and went home. He phoned Hailey, got her answering machine and left a message asking her to call.

Then, curious, he called de Noux's office.

"Do you want to make an appointment?" a secretary asked.

"As soon as possible," Ed replied.

"You'll have to wait at least two weeks. Mr. de Noux is out of the country. I'm canceling his appointments now."

"Two weeks, you say."

"I can refer you to another lawyer."

"That's all right. This isn't a pressing matter."

So Louis had run. At least there was some satisfaction in that.

The ringing of the phone touched Hailey on some subconscious level but she did not answer. She didn't want to leave the comfort of her own little room, the sorrow into which she had been dragged so willingly when she merged with the spirit of Joseph Morgan.

Leanna has not abandoned him. He dreams of her then wakes with the smell of her perfume lingering on the pillow. It is enough to send him back to sleep again, and to take pills to keep himself asleep, rousing only when necessary, trying not to get too conscious, for to do so is to lose the reality of her presence.

In that state, he talked to the police through the endless grillings in which he could do nothing but admit his guilt for having failed her.

Now, in that same state, he goes to Leanna's funeral mass. He sits in one of the back pews, next to Ed, looks at the coffin, closed because of the nature of her death, and sheds few tears. The death of her body means little to her soul. She is waiting for him, back in his room.

In the nine days since her death, her friends seemed to

have formed two distinct groups—those completely certain of Joe's innocence and those just as certain of his guilt. They sit on opposite sides of the church as if this were a marriage and those around him friends of the groom.

Louis was outside, greeting guests. Now he enters, sees Joe and slides into the pew beside him, clamping a hand on Joe's arm in a gesture of camaraderie and support so unlike his usual reserve. "I'm glad you came," he says and moves forward to the front pew reserved for close family.

The music begins, soft at first, drifting from the choir loft. A flute joins the voices. A harp. Joe turns to look up at them and notices Carlo Bucci just taking a place in the back.

He met the man only once, on the night Leanna died. Now they eye each other with mutual suspicion. Later, Joe looks back at the pew and notices Carlo leaving.

"I'll be back in a minute," he whispers to Ed, and follows the man.

Carlo leans against his car, smoking a Djarum cigarette. The scent of cloves and tobacco hangs in the dense air. Joe thinks of Leanna's incense and wishes he hadn't come here today, hadn't left her spirit alone in that little room. Today of all days, she might need him close.

Carlos holds out the pack. Joe shakes his head. He isn't certain why he came out here to face the man; nonetheless it has to be done.

"Louis made a nice display of support for you in there, didn't he?" Carlo says.

Joe doesn't answer.

"He can't handle your case, of course."

"If there is one," Joe replies.

"From the rumors, I'd say you might be right. But I am curious about one thing. Chloryl hydrate is a common drug but what about the rest of that arcane mix? Where did the ingredients come from? Did Leanna give you something to take?"

Carlos seems too cordial. Nonetheless, Joe sees no reason not to tell him what he told the police. "She had me drink some kind of tea every night before we went to bed."

"That might account for them." Carlo hesitates, looked evenly at Joe. "You drank it that night?"

"Yes," Joe says.

"You can't remember anything?"

"No."

"I suppose that's a comfort."

"If you're implying—"

"I'm not, believe me. But I'll leave you with something I learned in my years of marriage to Leanna. In Haiti there are said to be priests capable of animating dead men's soulless bodies to use as their slaves. The bodies are called zombies, and perfectly sane Haitians believe they exist. But why must a man be dead to be used that way? Knockout drops combined with booze are very much like death, don't you think?"

Joe recalls the night in the de Noux house, how he hit Leanna without intending to. Since he learned the details of how she died, he has thought about that moment of rage all too often.

"In the last few days, I've made some inquiries of my own," Carlo continues. "It seems that the week you met Leanna, her beloved brother was in Haiti. Louis has made a number of trips to Haiti in the last few years, and soon after he arrives there, he usually disappears. Once he was seen in Aux Cayes, not exactly a comfortable tourist stop. You might ask him what he was doing there." Carlo tosses his cigarette away and pulls keys from his pocket.

"Thanks," Joe replies.

Carlo stares at him thoughtfully. "If you do find out the truth, you'll regret thanking me."

"I didn't kill her. I couldn't."

"Your hand is incapable of raising a knife?" The affable facade dissolves and Joe sees the depth of anger the man has been hiding. Carlo loved her, loves her still, with the same incredible passion Joe feels.

"You knew how terrified she was, yet you took her out, you both got drunk, you let someone slip you drugs. If I didn't understand the hell you're going through, I'd see that you paid if only for your carelessness. I might do it anyway," Carlo adds, "if I wasn't certain that's exactly what Louis expects me to do."

He leaves, the car's taillights blinking at the corner as he makes a smooth, sharp turn.

Joe goes back inside just as the priest is finishing his sermon. He isn't sorry he missed it. As far as he knows, Leanna never met the man.

Through the rest of the mass, Joe kneels and stands and sits with the others, watching Louis's back. The only close family left is Louis's aunt, Henri's oldest sister, who rests her hand on his forearm. Louis's reserve had crumbled hours ago. Now his shoulders shake. Joe sees him wipe his face, undoubtedly brushing away tears.

His grief increases through the interment, until by the end, when Leanna's coffin is slipped into the space below her father's remains, Louis sobs openly.

After, he returns to Joe's side, grips his arm and whispers, "I wish I'd had the courage to defy tradition and inter my sister somewhere else, far away from our father's body; someplace where I could plant a tree on her grave. She would have liked that."

Joe held Louis's hand with both of his and says nothing.

"You must come to the house now," Louis tells him. "You loved her. You belong there with the family."

Joe wants to decline but he can't. There is something too out of character about the intensity of Louis's grief. Its presence, combined with his brief exchange with Carlo Bucci, concerns him.

"All right," Joe says.

"I have to get to work," Ed reminds him when they're alone.

"It's OK. Really. Just drop me off at the house."

"You're sure?"

"Christ! Who the hell are you, my mother!"

Ed looks shocked, a bit hurt. Later, perhaps, Joe will explain. They say little as Ed drives him over and drops him off in front of the place where a handful of black-clad mourners are assembled on the sidewalk like a flock of crows. Someone has hung a mourning wreath of black crepe and dried roses on the door and the streamers blow in the gentle wind.

Louis arrives just after Joe and leads them inside.

He's arranged a buffet laid in all its Southern splendor by caterers who did their work and left. The mourners eat and drink and talk of the past while Louis sits in the chair, staring at some place between his eyes and the far wall.

Joe understands. He goes and sits beside him, their silent presence together keeping the other guests at bay.

Gradually, friends come to Louis, mumble some final condolences and leave one by one, until only a few are left.

Joe picks at what is left on the sideboard, eating only for sustenance, drinking only coffee. Indeed, after Carlo's accusation, he thinks he may never drink again. The downstairs bathroom is occupied, so he heads for the upper level.

He pauses in the upstairs hall, thinking of what had happened here only weeks ago. How concerned Leanna had been and how frightened. He stares into the mirror, half expecting the ghost to reappear. But there is nothing, only a guest coming down the hall from the bathroom, smiling uneasily as she passes him by.

In the bathroom, he pauses at the white pedestal sink, splashes water on his face, which clings to the day's growth of beard like tears. He whispers her name, certain he will find her here as he does in his little room. If she is present, she does not respond.

He pauses in the hall. This may be the last time he will ever be in this house, walking through the rooms in which she grew. He will say good-bye to them, take them all in, make a memory, as they say in the hill country in which he was born.

He goes into her room, thinking how she stood at the window only weeks before and told him about seeing her mother carried inside. He inhales the scent of rose sachet and old incense, takes a scarf from the crystal bowl on her dresser. Louis would not begrudge him this, but he will not ask. Instead he hides it in his coat pocket.

Outside, he pauses, then opens the door to the room Louis used for so many years.

Leanna showed him this room only weeks before. Then it smelled of mildew and age, the smell of all unused rooms in the delta. Now the scent seems stronger, stranger, far less pure. Though he cannot place it, it makes him wary and he glances down the hall before stepping inside and closing the door behind him.

As before, there is dust on the floor, cobwebs on the walls and ceiling. But now a path leading from the entrance to the closet door has been formed in the dust on the floor, as if someone has walked from one door to the other many times.

He follows it, tries the door and finds it locked.

The lock is not one of the old ones, opened with a skeleton key, but a new one, one far more sturdy than a closet in an abandoned bedroom merits.

He has Leanna's key to the house but nothing more. He studies this lock, certain he could pick it if he had the tools.

He'll come back, he decides, hoping to find nothing, then cursing his moment's weakness—the fleeting thought that it would be better if he never opened the door, never learned the truth.

He retreats carefully, closing the door behind him.

Downstairs, he joins the last group of departing guests.

At the stoop, the old aunt turns and asks Louis, "You're certain you want to stay alone tonight?"

"I've been alone a long time," Louis responds vaguely. "I'm used to it."

A woman offers Joe a ride. He shakes his head. "I'll take the trolley," he tells her and heads down the street, then through the park. By the time he reaches the trolley stop, he's decided to walk.

An hour later, he closes the door to his room behind him.

"Leanna," he moans.

And she is with him—the scent of her hair, the tinkle of

her laughter, the whispered brush of spectral hands against his face. . . .

Joe has four days left to his life, Hailey knows. As she watches him, leaning against his door with the joyful tears falling from his eyes, she senses the inevitability of it, and the mercy.

As the vision fades, Hailey can almost see the woman— more beautiful than in life, perfected by her lover's memory.

"Together then, now, forever," Hailey said aloud, a prayer, a plea.

There seemed to be an agreement between Hailey and her ghosts. They allowed her time to make her phone calls to her agent and to tell a couple of friends that she'd returned. They let her eat, and clean, and bathe.

They waited patiently until she was ready, then began their soft, insistent pleas.

Finally, as anxious as they were to end the dreams of death, she brewed the tea, drank it and slept again.

On the morning of the thirteenth day after Leanna's death, Louis phones Joe and asks him to lunch. "I'm at my office today. It's an ideal time to give you some personal things I know my sister would want you to have."

"Personal?" Joe asks.

"A few photographs. Some mementos."

"I'd like to have them but I do have to be somewhere else. If I stop at your office after two, will you be there?"

"I'll be in until five at least."

They talk a little longer. As soon as the conversation is finished, Joe reaches for a felt bag on the sideboard, sticks it in his back pocket and heads for his car.

Louis will be on Royal Street all day. What better time to open his closet?

Leanna not only left him a key, she also told him the code to deactivate the security system. Praying that Louis hasn't changed it, Joe presses the numbers on the security panel

inside the door, an easy code to remember, she said with a
sneer when she told him the numbers: 701, the first digits of
the zip code. This kind of system gives no warning but
instead summons police. He stands at the open door, listens
and waits.

When he is convinced that no one is coming, he moves
slowly through the house, alert for some sign of life.
Satisfied that he is alone, he goes upstairs and into the old
room where the child Louis spent so many years.

Years alone save for Leanna.

It's inconceivable that Louis would kill someone he loved
so much. Yet Joe knows all too well how easily passion can
be twisted into rage.

He picks the lock carefully, trying to leave no sign he's
done this. When the knob turns in his hand, he pauses before
pulling open the door.

For a moment he is not certain what he sees. When
understanding hits, he reels back in horror and revulsion,
then steadies himself and forces his eyes to examine the
dark space.

The shelves and clothes bar have been removed from the
closet. Replacing them is a rough wood cross of seven feet
or so, the top of which disappears into the darkness above
the closet door. Someone has draped scarves and necklaces
on the crossbeam, along with a length of thin blue nylon that
looks like the hem of a skirt or dress. Below the dangling
scarves is a shelf with a basket, a bowl and a pair of candles.
Stacked neatly on the floor beneath these is a pile of bones.

Not old bones, but those from a death not more than a few
weeks old. Shreds of gray dessicated skin still clung to
them. The odor in the little room is overpowering. Joe steps
back and pulls a cigarette from his pocket. Sticking it unlit
in his mouth, he breaths through it while he crouches down
to study them.

They have been arranged by size then bundled and tied with
red twine. The longest bones of the legs are in one pile on
the bottom. The arm bones rest above them. The piles above

lose some of the neatness. The smallest bones are collected
in the basket on the shelf, the top webbed with the same
red twine. Joe brushes the scarves aside, lights the candles
and looks down into the basket. He already guessed the
bones were human, but the sight of human fingers and toes
with their nails still in place nonetheless shakes him. Beside
the basket, an earthen bowl holds chunks of dark colored
flesh almost invisible beneath a velvety carpet of mold.

"No," Joe whispers, but even as he does, he understands
what he sees. Brother and sister shared everything. How
could he have been so naive as to think they hadn't shared
belief too?

But if so, Louis's beliefs are far darker than his sister's.
Leanna would never have robbed a grave or, assuming this
was murder—a possibility Joe could not rule out, though he
doubted it—killed a man for power. She'd once confessed
to him that she found it abhorrent that the *loas* would
demand that she kill anything at all.

He looks up and sees that upper portion of the cross is
obscured by a black scarf fastened from it to the top frame
of the door. He bats at it, feels nothing resting above it, then
carefully unfastens it from the door and pulls it down.

And there, mounted on the pointed top of the cross,
staring down at him is the head. Red glass balls have
replaced the eyes, and the lips are sewn together with the
same red twine that ties the bones. The head's expression is
no less pleasant in death than it was in life.

Joe whispers the name of the dead man. "Henri de Noux."

One of the scarves, dangling too close to the candle
flame, flares. Joe pulls it down, beats it out on the floor. This
jerking on the cross causes the head to wobble, and one of
the glass eyes falls and shatters on the floor. As it does, the
room seems to alter, becoming colder, darker.

Joe turns, looking for the door, but it has vanished in the
growing blackness. The only points of warmth and light
seem to be the flickering candle flames, and as he stares at
them, he sees his breath fogging in the sudden chill.

This is no trick of the sun sliding behind a cloud, a shadow falling over the heavy, closed drapes. There is a presence here, not Leanna's, for Leanna would never frighten him. No, this presence can only be the spirit of Henri de Noux.

Even thinking his name gives the presence more power. The air roars around Joe, the candlelight dies in its wake. Joe staggers, falls. The darkness increases and thickens until there is no closet door to orient him and the air itself is so heavy that moving through it would be akin to swimming through quicksand.

Joe had never believed in voodoo, never even believed in God. Leanna's presence in his room for so many days has convinced him of an afterlife. Now he has a glimpse of hell.

And something from it desperately wants him to pass out, wants to claim his body, to use if for some terrible purpose, as it has before.

He forces air into his lungs and whispers the name of the only creature he thinks can save him.

"Leanna." He repeats it again and yet again, letting the beauty of that name, the warmth of his memories, keep the darkness at bay.

It isn't enough. He feels his consciousness slipping away, feels the presence of Henri de Noux growing within him.

"Joe!"

Leanna screams his name with all the force she should have used so many times when she was still alive. Screams it so hard that for a moment the veil between the living and the dead is lowered and he looks into her face—so magnificent, so frightened, so very sad.

She holds up her arm and moves aside. Behind her is the bedroom door. He runs through it and down the stairs, not pausing to breathe until he is on the sun-drenched porch outside.

His clothes are wet and stuck to his body. In spite of the day's warmth, he shivers. Not caring who might take the open door as an invitation, he finds his car on the side street and leaves.

Before he takes his story to the police, he has to face
Louis and tell him what he's discovered. He owes Leanna
that. . . .

Henri de Noux founded the downtown law firm thirty
years earlier, but in the last five years, his son gradually took
charge, throwing out the good old boys with graduates from
the better schools of both the North and the South. Criminal
law eventually became only a small part of the firm's
business. When it does come in, Louis, true to the de Noux
roots, is the one who handles it.

Louis has apparently told the receptionist about Joe,
because she recognizes his name immediately, announces
him and waves him down the hall. Joe suspects that another
client would be personally escorted to Louis's office but he
understands the woman's distance. He saw his reflection in
the polished metal walls of the elevator—his expression
still dull with grief, his eyes haunted by the assemblage he'd
just discovered.

And he saw how people on the street reacted to him on
his long walk here—a glance, a fascinated stare, a sudden
look away when his eyes met theirs.

The reason for their fear is so simple. An hour ago, he left
the world of the living and joined the ranks of the dead.

The main offices appear to be on the window side of the
building, with windowless private secretarial offices inside.
Louis's layout, however, is shifted. The secretary's desk
overlooks the Quarter and the river, while Louis's office is
in the center of the space.

A secretary sits at her clean desk, changing into walking
shoes. She looks at Joe warily. "He's expecting you, Mr.
Morgan," she says and points to Louis's office.

The spaciousness of the room is diminished by the
sienna-colored walls lit solely by a pair of green-cased desk
lamps. Joe pauses to let his eyes grow accustomed to the
dim light then walks to Louis's desk and takes a seat.

Louis sits across from him, nearly immobile, looking

through his glasses, waiting for Joe to say the first word. The scene uncomfortably reminds Joe of a confessional, with the devil sitting in the place of the priest.

"I was at your house . . . ," Joe begins.

"I know," Louis replies calmly. He walks around the desk to lock the door, then returns to his seat. "The alarm is wired to my pager, not the security firm. I've been expecting you."

"I was at your house," Joe repeats, not certain how Louis can be so calm.

"I know. And from the look of you, I'd say you've discovered the contents of my closet as well."

Joe covers his face with his hands. "Why did you do it?" he asks.

"I owed it to old Henri for a lifetime of torment to Leanna as well as myself. Now I have my revenge."

"His body?"

"I'd considered that. Reanimating a body is a simple thing, any *bocor* can learn it. But there is so much more vengeance in controlling his soul, his *loa*, if you wish to call it that.

"So I breathed in his soul just before he died, then stole his body and bound his spirit to this earth. As long as that altar exists, he can never be reborn to torment us again."

"He haunts the house?"

"When I allow it. When I don't want his presence, I banish him. I have no idea where he goes—to hell I hope. You see, I am finally stronger than the old man. I find that remarkably satisfying."

"But you're not stronger than him all the time, are you?"

The box in which Louis stores his emotions cracks. "No," he admits, then stands and leans over his desk on tightly clenched fists. "Not when the man who said he would protect my sister gets so stinking drunk that he loses his will completely. You were supposed to fight the *loa*, damn you. Instead you did nothing but sleep."

"I was drugged."

"You allowed yourself to be drugged."

"Who drugged me, Louis?"

Louis ignores the question. "And because of it I couldn't hold him back."

"Did you try?"

"Do you think I didn't love her?"

"Not if you couldn't have her," Joe retorts.

"I loved her. I fought for her with every bit of power I possessed while you just lay there and let his spirit ride you. I called on every spell I knew. I even tried to draw his spirit into me, but he would have his revenge on her and me because you made it possible. I should have trusted my first impression of you."

"That I was no better than Leanna's other lovers? The only one you truly seemed to hate was the one most likely to last."

Louis's entire body shakes with rage. "She promised me that we would always be together! You took her from me and now you can't even remember what you did to her! Damn you!"

He takes a deep breath and stares at Joe, a mad, twisted smile growing on his face. His calm returns as abruptly as it departed. "But he remembers. When you opened the closet door, did you light the candles before the cross of Baron Samedi? When you recognized my father's remains, did you say his name aloud?"

Joe sits, stunned. As he hears the questions and gives a silent assent, he feels something terrible uncoiling inside him. His mouth goes slack, his eyes, half-focused, watch Louis take a small leather pouch from an inside coat pocket. Louis holds it, squeezing it tightly, and recites words in French so quickly Joe can hardly hear their syllables, let alone understand them.

"Go inside of him. Show him what his body did, Papa Henri. I order it."

"Nooooooo," Joe moans, closing his eyes, opening them, rubbing them, trying to wipe out the sight of Leanna on her back begging him, screaming, as the knife rises, slashes, slashes, slashes.

"No!" he screams this time, stands.

The door he came in has vanished in the darkness surrounding the vision, but another is open, waiting. He runs through it to the hall. Too terrified to wait for the elevator, Joe bolts down the service stairs, running as if the spirit and the vision it brings were in pursuit instead of inside him.

Blood is all around him. Her screams assault his ears as he scrambles through the traffic and the evening crowd, rushing to the only safety he knows, the protection his lover has given to his little room.

He wedges himself past Frank on the stairs, locks himself in the room and stares in horror at the vision of the bloody mattress and carpet, the body of his lover slashed and bleeding, at someone who looks very much like himself stabbing again and again.

"Leeeannnnaaaaah!" he howls, covering his eyes, his ears. "Please, God. Please show mercy and let her come to me."

The vision fades enough that he can feel her presence, the almost-touch of her body as she comforts him. He senses her terror as well—a terror that came when she realized that death had not ended her struggle, that the spirit of the one she feared in life now shared this room.

"Leanna," he whispers as he slides slowly to the floor, his back to the wall, his knees touching his chest. "Leanna, I'm so sorry. So sorry."

He stays in that position until exhaustion claims him.

When he sleeps, he no longer dreams of her, but of the murder. He wakes screaming.

The hours wear him down. He paces the little room, murmuring her name. Sometimes he feels her, so near she almost seems alive; at others he is too distraught to sense her at all.

The sight of her, all the beauty of her features twisted with pain and fear of him, waxes and wanes. He pounds his fists on the walls, the floor. The pain steadies him, but when he picks up the phone to call Ed, or the police or someone to come to help him, he forgets the number, forgets everything but the truth of what Louis had said.

He failed her. He killed her. She can never come back to him. He can only go to her and try to protect her in death the way he never did in life.

Now that he believes, the decision is so easy.

With his fate decided, the spirit of Henri de Noux allows lucidity to return.

The sisal twine and the brown paper wrapping from his new mattress are still in a pile in the corner. Poor Frank has been through too much already, he decides, so he spreads the paper on the floor then places a kitchen chair in the center of it and begins braiding the twine into a rope heavy enough to hold him.

When it's finished and looped through the brace on the ceiling fixture, he finds the bottle he keeps in the sideboard, sits at the table and drinks it, one quick shot after another.

There is still time to call Ed and tell him what he's learned, but it seems so pointless somehow. If the authorities find Henri's body in the closet and learn the truth about how Leanna died, she and her brother will only become two more macabre legends in a city already filled with them. He cannot allow it. Besides, the real revenge is to let Louis live out his life in the company of the demon he refuses to exorcize.

His expression serene, Joe finishes the bottle and picks up a pen.

I love her. I will always love her. I'm so sorry, he writes.

The chair is ready, the rope is ready. No use putting it off any longer. . . .

Later, as the body hangs swaying, the souls are united. Hailey cannot see beyond the veil of death but she senses the calm they share, the love. . . .

The door clicks open. "Oh, hell," Frank says.

He makes a wide circle around the dangling body, reads the note on the table. Satisfied, he leaves, closing the door behind him. When he returns, he carries the knife he took. Wincing, he wraps Joe's hand around it, pulls it loose and lets it fall, then leaves to call the police.

TWENTY-FIVE

For a moment the horror Hailey had shared made dream and reality merge. She looked at the rough wood that bisected her ceiling and expected to see Joe Morgan's body hanging from it, or Frank making his swift, terrified exit from her bedroom.

She almost wished that someone were there—a human intruder would be a diversion from the despair she had been allowed to share. Suddenly in need of the sound of a human voice, she wrapped herself in a bathrobe and padded barefoot across the hall to her workroom.

The answering machine showed two messages. As she listened to the first, from Ed, she managed a relieved smile and reached for the phone. If he weren't home, she'd call a friend, anyone at all who was alive and sane.

As Ed's phone rang, she heard the second message, an equally familiar voice talking not to her but to Leanna.

"Sister, dearest, come home." This was followed by a string of words, probably in Creole. She didn't know them, but she didn't have to. Her knees shook. She slammed down the phone just as Ed picked it up, and folded into a tight ball on the floor, her fists clenched hard, her nails digging into her palms.

Louis knew where his sister was; more than that, he knew exactly the right words to say to drain all will from her.

Fighting the fear of the spirit inhabiting her body, Hailey reached up and turned off the volume of the answering machine.

"It's all right," she whispered. "He can't hurt you anymore."

She felt like a mother comforting a child with a convenient lie, for it wasn't all right, would never be all right. Louis de Noux controlled the soul of his father. She recalled the de Noux crypt, close to the gate and the main road. All he'd had to do to take his father's body was ask to remain after the other mourners had gone. It was a natural request, one the sexton could certainly understand, and Louis would have tipped him well for the favor. An hour and darkness were all he would have needed.

Could he do the same with his sister's body even after so many years?

Perhaps even that made no difference. There were other ways to bind her spirit to him. If he didn't know them yet, he would learn them. And Leanna could run, could hide, but he would always find her, then use some means to call her back.

"You have to face him, Leanna," Hailey whispered. "Your soul will never be at peace until you do."

Hailey felt the denial. The terror.

"I'll help you. I'll do whatever it takes to be certain Louis doesn't claim you again."

And if he did, whose body would Leanna inhabit? Whose breasts would he kiss, whose body would he touch? Hailey shivered with the horror of the thought. "For my own sake as much as yours," she added truthfully.

The phone rang again. Hailey waited until she heard Ed's voice before picking it up.

"Frank's dead. Louis is apparently in hiding; not that he needs to be. No one's even suggesting we bring him down for questioning," he told her. Then he described the suicide. He spoke quickly, evenly, surpressing any emotion he felt. She sat and listened to the story unfold, less surprised than saddened by the outcome.

Poor Frank! He'd been drawn into the struggle, just as Joe

had been, and manipulated as easily. Her hatred of Louis increased.

When Ed was done, she told him what she'd learned— how Joe had discovered that Louis had caused Leanna's death, then killed himself anyway because of how he'd failed her. Because she didn't want Ed to continue on the case, she didn't mention the evidence that might still be in the closet.

"What about Joe and Leanna?" Ed asked. "Are their spirits still with you?"

"I don't know," she said, hoping the lie would keep him from worrying about her. "I think they left me when the story was finished. I feel as if I've lost a pair of eccentric friends, but at least I have my life back."

"So what do we do about Louis?" Ed asked.

"We'll decide together later. In the meantime, you have a wonderful week with your daughter. As soon as I'm finished with the rough draft of the novel, I'm driving down, so I may even be there for the tail end of her visit. If not, give her my love."

As soon as she hung up, Hailey went outside and made her way through the thigh-high drifts from the winding drive to the road. Though the county plows had already made their pass through, sections of the road were icy and treacherous. It would be so easy to wait another day or two, until the weather improved, but she wasn't certain she had the luxury of time. If she slept, Leanna might run again, or Hailey might lose her nerve, or she might hear a pounding on her door and find Louis himself standing outside armed with a more potent spell to force his sister's obedience.

Better he think the first incantation worked. Better that she go now.

After phoning the firm that plowed private drives and being assured that they'd get to hers by noon, she contacted a travel agent to arrange a seat on the next available flight to New Orleans.

One was leaving early that evening. Given the state of the

roads, she'd need at least three hours to get to the airport. She went upstairs to pack. She chose her clothing with deliberate care.

Afterward, she sat down at her computer and began the final chapters of her novel. As she worked, she sensed Leanna waiting on the edges of her consciousness, not disturbing her but not hiding her presence either.

Leanna had unfinished business, Hailey thought, certain she knew whom Leanna expected to face.

I'm not strong enough, Leanna's voice in her mind, its doubt and uncertainty so real.

"We'll face him together," Hailey responded and returned to work.

In the hours between her last dream and the time she had to leave, she finished almost all the first draft. She worked with compulsive speed, as if any procrastination now would mean the novel would never be finished at all.

Louis will want them. Don't give them up.

When it was time to go, Hailey backed up her files and stored the discs behind a loose board at the back of her closet. Her mother knew she kept valuables there when she traveled. If Louis did come after the files, these copies might stay safe.

Before she left the house, she added a second battery pack to the laptop case and took the last chapter with her. She typed at the airport, and on the plane; working, always working, afraid to sleep, afraid that if she did, Leanna would take control of her body and run again.

"It will be all right," Hailey reassured her as she opened her suitcase hours later in the New Orleans hotel room. "I think it's time you learned to trust *me.*"

Some time passed, and she stood in front of the mirrored closet door and admired the result of her work. Her hair had been dyed black, the short curls teased and blow-dried until they looked thicker, more like Leanna's hair would have been if cut short. The wig Leanna had purchased had looked beautiful but seemed too much like a costume. This, on the other hand, was a radical change, the sort Leanna would have made had she taken permanent control of Hailey's body.

Hailey had dressed in the clothes Leanna had purchased, the black silk shirt so sensuous against her skin, the tight jeans and high-heeled boots shaping her muscular legs. Her nailed, filed and polished, were bright red against the dark shirt, and the drop of Norrell between her breasts gave the perfect finishing effect.

Now that she studied herself calmly, she saw that the resemblance between them was more than superficial, more than accidental. Perhaps Leanna had sensed her strength, her resolve, and led her to that room, that first marvelous discovery.

"You protected your room from him, Leanna. You called Joe back into his body twice before your confidence gave out. You have the power to free your soul from his hold, find the courage to tap it."

Before her own courage gave way, Hailey had to act. She called the concierge to arrange a cab, then made a second call to the de Noux house. As she expected, the answering machine clicked on. "I'm coming home tonight," she said in what she hoped was an accurate accent and hung up just as someone who had been screening calls picked up the phone.

With her black leather coat draped over her shoulders and the knife Leanna had bought for her pressing against the side of her calf, she went downstairs to find her cab.

The driver was uneasy about letting her out on the edge of Audubon Park but the danger the nighttime walk presented was minor compared to what she'd face at the house. Besides, even at this late hour, there were people in the park, walking the paths through the huge ancient trees, enjoying one of those balmy Delta nights that gave hints of the approaching spring.

Hailey's own fear intensified as she approached the

house, but the spirit inside her seemed calmer. Perhaps Leanna was hiding her fear, as she had in life. Perhaps she'd become resigned to whatever fate waited for her. Perhaps— such a hopeful thought!—Leanna was absorbed in building her strength, her power.

Hailey hoped so, *prayed* so. If she thought it wouldn't be distracting to her ghost, she would have recited some formal prayer. Instead she walked faster, turned the corner and saw the house.

As she'd expected, only the outside lights were burning. She rang the bell and waited. When no one answered, she hesitated.

Leanna would . . .

Without further conscious thought, she pulled open the garage door, and found a key hidden beneath the garden pots. She let herself in the back door, then went directly to the security box and punched in the code. She paused a moment.

"Louis," she called.

No response save a growing dread, as if someone or something were watching her dispassionately, curiously—a dark force that had moved beyond most human concerns.

But not all of them, Hailey reminded herself. Even Henri de Noux for all his perversity would benefit from what she did here.

Her heart pounded; she felt dizzy from fear. But taking her stance from Leanna's life, she walked with apparent confidence toward the pool of light coming from the kitchen, the high heels of her boots making sharp sounds on the hardwood floor.

Jacqueline sat at the kitchen table, a loose cotton bathrobe wrapped around her thin frame. As Hailey stepped into the light, the woman stared at her with an expression of mingled astonishment and resignation. "Monsieur Louis told me to expect someone. Even after the message on the machine, I never really thought it would be you," she finally said.

Hailey laughed, trying to make it sound the way Leanna's

laughter had sounded the night Joe first glimpsed her. The result seemed contrived, but Jacqueline appeared convinced. "How could I stay away from here?" Hailey said. "Louis has called to me so persistently."

"Called?" Jacqueline looked faint. Under the circumstances, Hailey could well understand the shock.

"You don't know what he has done? The terrible altar that he keeps upstairs?"

Jacqueline shook her head.

"Then I'll show you." Again, with no conscious effort to retrieve the knowledge, she reached into a kitchen drawer and took out a hammer and screwdriver. "Come with me," she said. When Jacqueline didn't move, she gripped the woman's wrist. At her touch, Jacqueline cried out and jerked her arm away. Hailey looked at her with disgust. "Come up when you're able," she said and went up the stairs. She wasn't surprised when Jacqueline followed, keeping a safe distance, undoubtedly ready to retreat if necessary.

Leanna's presence returned full force on the second floor. Hailey felt the spirit's uncertainty, the mounting terror. "When we destroy the altar, we destroy Louis's power over your father," Hailey whispered, softly so Jacqueline would not hear.

Louis himself had told Joe that. Why did Leanna seem so concerned?

Ignoring the ghost, and the visions the dark hall evoked, Hailey went down the hall to Louis's old room. Even with the light on, the space seemed dimly lit, the flat dark green walls absorbing all light, all warmth. The floor was as dusty as it had been when she'd first seen the room. Certain of what she would find, she headed straight for the closet.

The lock was new. Hailey pried the molding loose and slipped the bolt, cracking the door open. "Do you know what's in there?" she asked Jacqueline.

The woman shook her head.

"Then prepare yourself," Hailey said and opened it.

The sight was little changed from the one Joe had seen,

though less grisly now that the bones were older, the flesh completely dessicated. The putrid odor had all but gone, replaced by a more familiar smell of mold and neglect. The scarves and scraps of cloth that had been so bright in Hailey's visions were faded from mildew and age and coated with cobwebs.

Nonetheless, Jacqueline shuddered and backed away until she was nearly at the bedroom door. "Monsieur . . ."

"No!" Hailey cried. "Don't say the name. His spirit comes when you say it."

". . . Henri," Jacqueline wailed as if she hadn't heard. Her hands shot out, making a sign against evil. She dropped to her knees and began to sway, mumbling some prayer.

As long as the altar existed, Henri de Noux was bound to do his son's bidding. Well, that would change. Hailey hoped the tyrant would go straight and permanently to hell. She pulled out the matches she'd brought, but the dangling shreds of fabric only smoldered. She lit one of the candles instead and held it up until a tattered piece of lace finally flared.

As the fire grew, Jacqueline became concerned. "What are you doing?" she asked, her voice shrill with disbelief.

"Ending something that should have ended years ago."

"Leanna would never disturb her brother's altar!" Jacqueline said.

"Strange how perspectives change after death." Hailey returned to the work, setting another scarf afire. As she did, she heard Jacqueline running up behind her and turned, nearly too late to avoid the attack.

Hailey's hands circled Jacqueline's wrists. Using all her weight, Hailey thrust her back. Jacqueline fell against the wall, all fight knocked out of her for the moment. "Do you know what he did? He stole Papa's body from the graveyard and used it to take control of Papa's soul. Louis sent his spirit into Joe and killed me."

"Monsieur Louis would never dare . . ."

"Louis would dare anything," Hailey retorted. She sensed

rather than heard steps in the hall, and added, "I will not be bullied into making my decision. If I choose to stay in this body or leave, it will be of my own free will. You loved Henri once, if you love him still, let this altar burn."

"A fine speech, Hailey Martin," Louis said. "The accent is almost perfect but Mama Jacqueline is right. Leanna would never have the guts to profane my work."

Louis stood in the doorway. His face seemed almost as pale as his white turtleneck, slacks and shoes. His arms were crossed; the stance and his expression held the insolence of someone completely in control. But what astonished Hailey most was how little fear his sudden arrival evoked in her or in the spirit sharing her body.

"Put the fire out," Louis ordered Jacqueline. Without waiting to see if she would obey his order, he gripped Hailey's arm and pulled her out of the smoky room. Hailey looked over his shoulder and saw Jacqueline crawling toward the altar, her eyes tearing—from smoke? From horror at what Louis had done? Hailey wondered if she'd ever know.

She stopped fighting Louis's grip, following him almost willingly down the stairs. She had brought Leanna here so they could face him together. She saw no use in putting off the inevitable. Besides, the dark presence she had sensed in the house seemed to be fading. She took this as a hopeful sign.

He took her into the solarium, pushed her gently down into one of the wicker chairs as if reluctant to harm the body his sister shared. "Do you like the room?" he asked. "I designed it for you."

He spoke to Leanna. Was her presence so clear to him or had he finally gone completely mad?

He sat beside her, brushing a hand over the dark curls as if Leanna had already returned and they were lovers once more. "And you've done her hair. How marvelous!" he went on. Hailey fought the urge to pull away as his fingers traced patterns on the back of her neck. "Come back to me, sister

Marie Kiraly

dearest. Come back to the one who has always cherished
you."

A good word choice, Hailey thought, hoping Leanna
would hear it. One cherishes possessions.

Hailey felt Leanna's struggle—to hide, or perhaps, hopefully, to find the courage she needed to face her brother.
Louis whispered a few Creole words. Hailey had heard them
before but could not recall the time. Perhaps Celeste had
used similar phrases when she'd tried to contact Leanna.

So far, at least, the incantation had had no effect save that
Leanna was fighting his summons. Hailey could feel her
struggles as waves of heat beating against her body, as
tremors in the center of her stomach.

*The night you faced your father you were as frightened as
this,* Hailey reminded Leanna. *Yet your power gave you
years of peace. Dare to use it again.*

"Don't look so smug, Hailey Martin. I can still call her
out, no matter how hard you struggle. There are many ways,
not all of them painless."

"It's over," Hailey said calmly, as much to Leanna as to
Louis. She looked past him at the smoke falling into the
dark foyer from the stairs.

He repeated the phrase, added another, *"Sorte Cimiterre,
toute corps moin senti malinque . . ."* Hailey felt weak,
sleepy, unable to resist when he pulled her to her feet and
kissed her.

Mute, blind save for what Leanna would let her see, she
watched Louis push her out to arm's length and study her
face with triumph. Then, for a time, nothing. . . .

In life Leanna had been an expert at hiding her terror. The
gift had not abandoned her in death. She moved away from
him and slowly turned full circle, letting him see the full
effect of her transformation. She laughed, all the beautiful
timbre of it as clear to her as to him. "It's not a bad body, is
it, Louis dear? Now I'm actually a few years younger than
I would be if I had never died." Her hands shook as she
brushed them over his face. She hoped he wouldn't notice,

or that if he did, he would assume that her new body needed
to learn to accept her commands. "Did you ever doubt that
I'd come back?" she asked.

Louis shook his head, and continued to stare into her
eyes. "Believe me, I never meant for you to be killed," he
said. "I love you so much. I'd rather be dead than without
you."

"I know," she replied, in her tone a hint of regret that she
hoped he would catch. "I waited for you. Why didn't you
follow me?"

"I tried. After you died, I went home and thought of so
many ways to end it." He smiled ruefully. "But you know
me, I've always been such a coward about pain."

"None of it is necessary now," she said, kissed his cheek
and ran her fingers through his hair. As she did, the smoke
stole through the hallway, the kitchen and into the room
where they stood, curling like a snake around their ankles.

Louis pulled away and stared at it. His hands clenched
into tight fists. His body shook with rage as he turned
toward the stairs. "That fool!" he said. "That damned fool."

"Jacqueline loved him." Leanna said. She gripped his
arm. "Let him go."

He pulled away from her. "Did death make you forget
everything you've learned? She hasn't sent him to hell.
She's freed him!" He rushed through the smoke and up the
stairs, screaming for Jacqueline to put out the fire. Leanna,
more frightened by the results of Jacqueline's loyalty than
of the fire, followed.

The smoker was thicker on the stairs. As they reached the
landing, a door slammed down the hall. "Get some wet
towels," Louis ordered.

Leanna went into the bathroom and did as he asked.
Though she worked quickly, she could not help but marvel
at the feel of the cool water on her hands, the way the heavy
soaked cloth made her arm muscles work.

Life! How precious. How beautiful.

Jacqueline had locked the bedroom door from the inside.

By the time they kicked it in, the fire, though still confined
to the closet, was devouring the cross, the bones. Jacqueline
stood in front of it, throwing in pieces of the rotting
bedspread to feed the flames.

The rush of new air made the flames grow. Leanna
noticed that the hem of Jacqueline's robe had begun to
smolder.

"Jacqueline, you're on fire. Get away!" Leanna called.
Jacqueline ignored her.

"Jacqueline, don't you understand, Henri is taking you
with him. Don't let him win," Louis called in his usual
soothing tone.

He held out his hand. Jacqueline stood and took an
unsteady step toward him, then stiffened, staring into the
space between her and Louis.

The smoke was denser there, turning into itself, coalesc-
ing into a human shape, a shadow creature with hands and
arms, and a face, leering and malicious in its triumph.

But the horror of that presence was lost on Jacqueline.
"Monsieur Henri!" she cried and stepped forward with her
arms outstretched and a giddy smile on her face.

Henri rejected her now as he had so many years before.
The shadow form thickened and flung itself against her.
Jacqueline screamed as she was thrown backward into the
rising, hungry blaze. Louis would have rushed forward and
pulled her out, but the form blocked his way, growing more
distinct by the moment, drawing power from Jacqueline's
approaching death.

"Leanna, she cannot die because of him," Louis whispered. He began an incantation.

Understanding, Leanna rushed past her brother and through
the ghost of her father, shuddering at the coldness of him, the
coldness of death.

She used the wet towel to beat at the flames then pulled
Jacqueline out of the fire and toward the door.

As Leanna rested the old woman on her knees, she could
feel the life leaving her body. Glancing up, she saw that the

shadow form of her father had taken on more of a human shape. Its eyes glowed with some terrible inner fire. Her brother's incantation seemed to have little effect. Henri's form was slowly growing, coming even closer to Louis.

And when it touched her brother, would it destroy him or take his body for its own use?

Leanna had faced Henri before with mixed results. She could face him as well as Louis, and this time she would win. The means were lying here before her.

She ran a damp hand over Jacqueline's singled hair, traced a pattern on Jacqueline's forehead, then bent forward, mumbled a quick prayer and inhaled the woman's soul.

Hailey's body gave her life. Jacqueline's soul gave her power. Leanna stood, for the first time confident that she would win this final struggle. Ignoring her father's presence, she faced the flames creeping slowly toward her across the floor, stared into them and spoke, "I call upon Almighty God, the divine good force, and upon Yemaya, my guardian spirit, to give me strength." She paused to catch her breath. Though her eyes teared, her voice was strong as she went on, beseeching the darker aspects of the gods she worshipped. "I call upon Damballa Ge-rouge and Legba Ge-rouge to open the doors to the netherworld and take this spirit of Henri de Noux on its final journey."

The fire crackled, hissed, the sounds becoming words, spoken, it seemed, by more than one being. "What sacrifice will you make for his banishment?" they asked.

Never before had the *loas* spoken to her directly! Leanna felt the ecstasy of her power, the humility of being in the presence of her gods.

"What sacrifice?" the gods bellowed, the volume of their combined voices shaking the walls and floor. The lamp on her brother's old desk crashed to the floor. The window glass shattered and downstairs something fell over with a loud crash.

Holding out her arms for balance, Leanna took a tentative step toward the blaze. Another. "I gave you my—"

"No!" Louis cried and ran toward her.

She stepped aside. Unable to stop his forward rush, Louis stumbled into the burning closet. The flaming cross shuddered then fell in pieces on top of him. The shelf broke, the bones scattering across the floor, the skull of her father coming to rest at Leanna's feet.

Louis rolled onto his side, beating at the flames as he screamed her name. She had always been there for him, ready to sacrifice for his sake. Instinctively she reached for him, then forced her hand back. He had brought damnation to himself; a quick end was far more merciful than years alone with his memories. With her eyes fixed on the fire, tears rolling down her cheeks, she whispered, "I give you my brother. Do what you will with him."

The final words had all the effect she'd hoped. Henri's presence slowly faded. The flames rolled back toward the closet and flared then, satiated by the lives and souls they had claimed, diminished to an ordinary blaze that spread slowly across the ceiling and hardwood floor.

Leanna looked at her reflection in the little wood mirror on the dresser. How many years of life had her brother stolen from her? How many years could she take back? She ran the hands over the arms, the breasts. Life called to her, its temptation insistent.

She shook her head. Even if this body had belonged to a stranger, she could never claim a life. "Thank you, sister," she whispered, looked into the blue eyes so much like her own eyes, then turned to face the flames once more.

"Joe," she whispered, speaking expectantly and with sudden deep longing. She needed him here to give her the strength she would have to have to abandon yet another chance at life.

In the center of the flames, his form swiftly took shape, drawn by her dwindling powers. "Beloved," she said. She stepped out of Hailey's body and moved to his side. . . .

Hailey returned to consciousness with a sudden snap. For

a moment only, through eyes tearing from the smoke and
hazy with confusion, she saw Leanna and Joe together in
death as they had been in life. Their faces, white and
glowing, were fixed on each other's as they thinned and
disappeared into the thickening smoke. Their story was
finished, her own work done.

She tried to take a deep breath and coughed.

Get out! Leanna's thought? Her own? No matter, the
warning was right. Nothing could survive here; even the
dead had abandoned her.

Coughing, Hailey stumbled weakly toward the door but
collapsed before she reached it.

Somewhere downstairs a smoke alarm went off, then
another. Wondering why the alarms had taken so long,
Hailey took in one deep breath of the purer air near the floor
and closed her eyes.

A voice came to her—male, unfamiliar, concerned.
"Lady? Lady, are you all right?"

She was still alive, or at least this was certainly a step in
that direction. She nodded and looked up at an old man in
a dark suede coat, at the little terrier dog he was walking.
The tiny beast growled softly, the hair on the back of its
neck rising with fear. She turned her head toward the house.
Smoke was pouring from the open door, and from the
broken windows on the second floor.

"The fire department's on their way," the man said. "Are
you all right?"

The lawn was cool and damp against her back, the fresh
night air reviving. She nodded.

"Were you inside?"

Hailey sat up and coughed, trying to recall what must
have happened in the last few minutes. Had she found some
strength to run? More likely Joe and Leanna had found it for
her. "The door was open," she finally answered. "I thought
I heard someone screaming inside but I couldn't get in. Too
much smoke. It must have knocked me out."

"You did what you could. That's all anyone can expect."
The man stopped, listened. "I don't think I got the address
just right. I better go out to the curb and wave them over,"
he said, as if the smoke itself wouldn't make it clear which
house needed their services.

As soon as he was gone, Hailey scrambled backward into
the bushes, then through to the side gate by the garage.
There she mingled with the crowd of neighbors wrapped in
blankets and bathrobes, congregating curiously on the
sidewalk.

The fire trucks were connecting their hoses as an unmarked New Orleans police car pulled up. Hailey watched
Craig Linden get out and stare up at the smoke pouring out
of second-floor windows.

Sensing someone watching him, he looked in her direction. Her features must have seemed familiar but apparently
he didn't associate the dark-haired woman in the tight-
fitting jeans with the prim blond Northerner he'd interviewed after Celeste's death.

The old man who'd found her on the ground outside the
house came up beside Linden. "I was walking my dog when
I saw the smoke and called you. There was a woman here a
minute ago. She said she heard somebody inside," he yelled
above the noise of the firemen unraveling their hoses, the
captain shouting orders to the pair getting ready to go in.

As the water roared down on the house, Hailey retreated
through the park.

The fire department would undoubtedly save the house.
She wondered what the officials would think of the remains
they discovered upstairs.

Within a week the bones would certainly be identified.
Hours after that, some anonymous official would leak what
was known of the story to the news. The reporters would
play with conjectures for days, maybe weeks. They always
did.

"Should I tell them everything I know, Leanna?" she
whispered, and for the first time in months, felt not even the

hint of a reply. The choice was hers, but not yet. There was time.

She looked up at the trees, at the slivered moon shining through them, at the few stars the city lights allowed her to see, and said a prayer for Joe and Leanna, for Jacqueline, for Frank, for Louis.

She thought of Ed, spending his first night with Willie, and how much she wanted to be with them.

There was time enough for that tomorrow.

Tonight she would sleep with only her own dreams for company.

She wondered if she would be lonely.